BREAKING
ALL THE
RULES

BREAKING
ALL THE
RULES

USA TODAY BESTSELLING AUTHOR
AMY ANDREWS

Entangled Publishing, LLC
644 Shrewsbury Commons Ave., STE 181
Shrewsbury, PA 17361
rights@entangledpublishing.com

Amara is an imprint of Entangled Publishing, LLC.

Visit our website at www.entangledpublishing.com.

Edited by Liz Pelletier and Lydia Sharp
Cover design and illustration by Elizabeth Turner Stokes
Interior design by Toni Kerr

ISBN 978-1-68281-563-2
Ebook ISBN 978-1-68281-586-1

Manufactured in the United States of America

First Edition January 2023

10 9 8 7 6 5 4 3 2 1

ALSO BY AMY ANDREWS

CREDENCE, COLORADO SERIES

Nothing but Trouble
The Trouble with Christmas
Asking For Trouble

To bunny slippers and breakfast pie.

At Entangled, we want our readers to be well-informed. If you would like to know if this book contains any elements that might be of concern for you, please check the back of the book for details.

CHAPTER ONE

Beatrice Archer needed sugar.

She didn't know what time it was, what day it was, or what season of *Supernatural* she was up to, but she knew she needed sugar.

Now. In the worst kind of way.

Bea didn't care in what form it was delivered—soda, cookies, cake, candy. Hell, she'd eat it granulated straight from the packet. When it came to getting sugar *right now*, she wasn't fussy. And if there'd been a single grain of it left in her apartment, anywhere, she'd have sniffed it out.

But there was none to be found.

Which meant she'd have to venture outside, because there was no such thing as Uber Eats in this little rural pocket of far, *far* eastern Colorado that she was temporarily calling home. Nope, in Credence, population 2,134, there wasn't even a taxi service. No way could she do something as fancy as pick up her phone, tap on an app, and have sugar delivered to her in whatever form she wanted.

Doughnuts. Ice cream. Waffles...

Bea's salivary glands and her stomach both made themselves known simultaneously. God, she'd kill for some waffles right now. With maple syrup and sprinkles. And sliced banana. Because she should probably eat some kind of fruit already.

Right, so...she needed to get her ass out of bed and go outside. Finally. After two weeks holed away in her new apartment—if one could call a cramped studio over a coffee shop with a Murphy bed and a shower the size of a test tube an apartment—it was time to explore. At least to Annie's and back, anyway. She'd noticed the diner on the way in, and if the sign on top boasting of the best pies in the county was anywhere near accurate, then the route between her apartment and the diner could become well-worn.

But would it be open? Diners usually opened early, right? *What time is it, anyway?*

Bea peered at the blinds on the opposite wall, which covered the small window just above the sink that overlooked the main street of Credence. She'd pulled the blinds down the second she'd moved in, and there they'd stayed, keeping everything inside nice and secluded and dark except for the bleed of sunshine around the edges.

If the sun was up, then Annie's was open. Now, where the hell was her phone?

She set aside her laptop and searched, lifting up pillows and looking under her duvet. All she found were a scrunched-up paper towel, an empty soda can, an almost-empty-except-for-a-few-burned-ones-on-the-bottom bag of microwave popcorn, and a couple of gossip magazines.

Damn. She really needed to clean some of this up.

Glancing over the side of the bed, she spied her phone on the floor next to an empty bottle of wine and an empty Cheetos packet. When she snatched it up, the screen came to life—nine thirty a.m. And only 3 percent battery left. *Great.* The charger was only two inches from where the phone had been all night. When had she ever forgotten to charge her phone?

Bea swung her legs out of bed and slid her feet into a pair of fuzzy bunny slippers. Why was it still so tits-freezingly cold in Eastern Colorado at the end of March? It was practically bikini weather in Southern California. She swayed a little as she stood, probably from how infrequently she'd actually been upright recently.

Maybe from the can of beer she'd consumed when she'd woken earlier.

Stretching, she groaned a little at the niggles in her neck and back. All this lying around on a mattress with several springs missing was screwing with her lumbar spine. Then she headed for the kitchen, stepping around the coffee table situated in front of the two-seater couch pushed up against the wall, and dodged multiple articles of clothing strewn about as she made her way to the sink.

She squinted against the light as she got closer, then located the bottle of Tylenol next to the sink full of dirty dishes, cracked the lid open, and shook two into her hand. Grabbing the closest drinking implement—an empty wineglass that must have had some red it in at one point, given the residue in the bottom and the purple ring on the laminate—she shoved it under the faucet, filled it, and swallowed the pills down with the resultant pink water.

Bea glanced at the sink as she tried to find a place for it, then shoved it back down on the purple ring when she realized there was nowhere to put it. Adding a glass might upset the delicate balance to the tower of dirty dishes. She really needed to do something about that tower. Because she was pretty sure she'd used the last clean fork last night.

Well, she'd put that on her cleaning to-do list. Or maybe she'd just buy more forks.

But first—*sugar.*

Turning away from the window, she headed back in the direction of the bed, dodging the clothing again. She needed to do some laundry after she'd taken care of the sugar craving, because she only bought fourteen pairs of underwear. And no, she didn't know that because she was one of those people who kept mental inventories of their underwear, but because she'd bought two packs of day-of-the-week underwear specifically for hiding away.

She'd left all that pretty, frilly, sexy—aka scratchy, prickly, constrictive—crap behind in her LA apartment, with all her stilettos and pencil skirts that *men* went gaga for, because she wanted to be comfy for once in her damn life and not subject her butt to more flossing than her teeth.

Bea hadn't been a total heathen—she *had* purchased the underwear from Peter Alexander—but for once, she had been prepared to sacrifice exquisite luxury fabrics for soft cotton comfort, even if it did mean walking around with the day of the week stamped across her ass. The added bonus was actually knowing which day of the week it was, given she no longer lived by a strict daily routine.

Not that she'd been particularly diligent about wearing them in order.

Looking over her shoulder now, she pulled on the band of her sweats to discover *Tuesday* emblazoned across her ass. But it could be Thursday for all she knew. Hell...it *felt* like Wednesday. It probably should be Friday, though, if she'd been here for—

Bea's stomach growled loudly.

Sugar, Bea. *Sugar.*

She reached for her dove-gray fleece-lined hoodie that had been discarded in a heap at the end of the bed and shoved her arms into the sleeves. It matched her sweats, which used to matter last month, but not so much now. Glancing down at her white T-shirt with its designer black-paint-splatter pattern, she noticed a stain down the front. Was that coffee, soy sauce, or beer? She pulled it out and gave it a sniff.

Beer.

She tried to remember when she'd put it on. Her sweatpants were clean yesterday, but the shirt...? Lifting her right arm, she sniffed at her pit. It seemed odor-free, but she should probably still change it. And also put on a bra. She wasn't that well-endowed, but her boobs had been roaming free for a couple of weeks, and she was sure they'd already dropped a little.

Screw being thirty-five.

No…she took that back. Screw bras, keeping women all constrained and strapped in and…*imprisoned*. She was never wearing a bra ever again. She'd just let the girls do their thing. From now on, she was going to wear what she wanted, eat what she wanted, and say what she wanted.

She'd spent fifteen years working hard, dressing the part, keeping her head down, following the *rules* set by her father and her grandmother—lest she turn out like her mother—then more rules set by various men who sat at the upper echelons of corporate power, and where had that gotten her?

Well…no more. And *screw* what anyone else thought.

She made a mental note to throw her shirt in the wash with the underwear, after she'd eaten *all* the sugar, and zipped up the hoodie with a vicious yank. Squatting, she delved through her handbag, which was lying discarded on the floor at the foot of the bed, and located her wallet, grabbed a fifty, and stuffed it into the pocket of her sweats. There was a hair band in the same pocket, so she pulled it out. Considering she couldn't remember the last time she brushed, let alone *washed*, her hair, putting it up was probably best.

Bea stood, scraping the layers of brown—like, a *truly unremarkable* mousy kind of brown—on top of her head and gave them a quick twist before tying the band around. Some of the layers made an immediate escape, which, given how fine Bea's hair was at the best of times, was unsurprising despite their current state of lankness.

God…all those useless, wasted *years* of product and messing around with it to give it body and *pizzazz*. She'd been *such* a sap!

Well, screw hair product, too.

Her gaze fell on her paused laptop screen and the frozen image of Sam and Dean Winchester deep in conversation, in all their Hottie McTottie hotness.

"Catch you later, guys," she said. "Mama's going to be right back."

She sighed. It was a pity to have to leave them even for a short foray, especially when she'd honestly thought she'd brought in enough supplies to last her the entire fifteen seasons. But obviously she'd miscalculated, considering she was only midway through season fourteen.

"Don't do anything I wouldn't do." Then she laughed hysterically, which might have been from the lack of sugar or, more likely, the yawning gulf between what Dean Winchester, Demon Hunter *wouldn't* do compared to her, Beatrice Archer, Advertising Executive.

Former Advertising Executive.

Or it could be the ridiculousness of talking to somebody *not* real living in a *not* real universe… Still—Team Dean forever. And screw the corporate world for depriving her of the delight that was the Winchester brothers for so long.

Bea wasn't sure she'd ever forgive Jing-A-Ling (or herself) for that.

She grabbed the apartment keys out from under more discarded paper towels she'd been using as napkins and several empty boxes of animal crackers littering the coffee table, then tromped down the narrow staircase to the door at the bottom, which opened to the small parking lot behind Déjà Brew. Sunlight flooded all around her, burning her eyes, and she shut them tight and almost hissed like one of those vampires the Winchester boys hunted.

Keeping her head down and shading her forehead with her hand, she waited for her frying retinas to recover before allowing her eyelids to drift slowly open. The sight that greeted her—two fuzzy bunny slippers—was alarming. Or at least it would have been prior to ditching LA. She wriggled her toes in them, and the bunny ears flopped, and she...laughed.

She *actually* laughed.

Clearly *not* alarmed at all. In fact, she tried valiantly to summon one single fuck but came up empty.

There was a certain liberation in being new to town. Apart from Jenny and Wyatt Carter—Jenny had handed her the keys to the apartment, and Wyatt had helped her move her stuff up the stairs—Bea didn't know another soul in Credence. Which meant she could strip naked and parade down the main street in total anonymity.

If she wanted to.

She could certainly walk to the diner and back in her sweats and slippers. It would take her thirty minutes *max*, and there was still quite a nip in the air despite the bright sunshine, so who cared if she looked like she'd just rolled out of bed? She *had* just rolled out of bed. And she was done with expensive hair volumizer treatments and bras and egg-white omelets for breakfast. She was over midnight deadlines and getting up at the crack of dawn to work out on the elliptical to stop her ass from sagging. Over the pressure to get Botox and lip fillers.

She was done trying to conform to seriously screwed-up societal expectations of women in corporate-landia and the insane pressure to be on top of everything *all the damn time* and never, ever complain lest she came across as a shrill bitch who couldn't cut it with the big boys.

Her stomach growled, and Bea swore it actually roared, *Sugar!!!*

Obeying as if her life depended on it, Bea and her bunny slippers hurried around to the main street and across the way to Annie's. A couple of cars passed her, but other than that, the sleepy little town was pretty much dead. Hmm...maybe it was Sunday? But Annie's was definitely open, and that was all that mattered.

Bea was inside within a second. A blast of warmth and the aroma of baked carbohydrates hit her at once, making her forget all about her appearance as saliva flooded her mouth, and she practically sleepwalked to the display cases brimming with pie. She pushed her hood back and unzipped the hoodie as her eyes found the selection of flavored ice cream beside the pie cabinet.

And *waffle* cones.

She barely noticed the way everyone in the half-full diner stopped what they were doing to stare or the sudden cessation of all chatter. She didn't care about the eyes on her slippers or her hair—Bea only had eyes for the array of sweet, sugary goodness at her disposal.

"Can I help you, doll?"

Bea dragged her gaze off the impressive selection of plump-looking pies to an older woman with a lined face; graying hair; gnarled, arthritic fingers; and a crackly, sandpaper voice.

"You're Annie," Bea said.

Prior to this moment, Bea hadn't had a clue whether there was an actual, *real* Annie or not, but one look at this woman and it was obvious from her sheer *presence* that Bea was standing before the foremost authority on pies in the county.

Annie beamed. "Yep, that's me."

There was pride in those words. And a whole lot of care, too, and Bea felt ridiculously like bursting into tears. "I need sugar."

Those old eyes smiled at her, flashing both understanding and delight. "Well, you've come to the right place, hon. Why don't you take a menu and a seat over there?" She tipped her chin at the tables over Bea's shoulder. "I'll come serve you."

Bea shook her head, aware suddenly of the silence all around her and the attention of who knew how many pairs of eyes. She wasn't ready for that kind of scrutiny just yet. Not until after season fifteen, episode twenty, anyway.

"I'd like to take it to-go, please." She shoved her hands in the front pockets of her hoodie. "If that's okay?"

"Sure is," Annie said. "Tastes the same at home as it does here. Now"—she picked up an old-fashioned china cake spade—"what's your poison?"

CHAPTER TWO

Austin Cooper was in the middle of a vehicle check that the chief had asked him to run when the phone at the front desk rang.

Despite having grown up in Credence, Austin was the newest and youngest member of the town's police department. He'd been back home for six months now, after five years in the city, and he fucking loved it. Even though everyone *still* treated him like he was wet behind the ears. He might be the youngest cop here, but at twenty-five, he was no kid.

Austin was vaguely aware of the continued ringing of the phone as he copied down more information from the monitor.

"Answer the goddamn phone, Cooper," Arlo grouched through the open door of his office.

The chief was in a bad mood. Full moons always put Arlo Pike in a bad mood and his spidey senses on high alert, owing to the uptick in idiotic deeds around town. A full moon affecting people's behavior might not be sound scientific fact, but Austin had witnessed it too often to doubt it.

One day, no matter how long it took, Austin was going to become chief. He liked small-town life and community policing, and he loved the people of Credence despite their quirks, which drove him up the wall half the time but ensured there was never a dull moment.

In the meantime, however, it was his job to answer the *goddamn phone.*

Austin picked it up, still jotting down information from the screen as he said, "Good morning, Credence Police Department. Officer Cooper speaking."

"Yes...good morning, young man. I'd like to make an anonymous report, please."

Austin grinned as Eadie Hutchens's firm, no-nonsense tone came down the line. Even if he hadn't recognized her voice, he'd know it was her. She was the only person who regularly reported everything from a car she didn't recognize to strange lights in the sky.

Always anonymously.

"Yes, ma'am," he said. "Everything okay?"

"Well, I don't rightly know. I just thought you should know that there's a...suspicious woman loitering outside Annie's diner."

Biting his lip not to laugh, Austin nodded seriously. "Suspicious, you say?"

Just last week, Eadie had called—anonymously, of course— requesting a welfare check on the woman who had moved in above Déjà Brew. There had been intense speculation about the newcomer who had drawn the blinds on arrival, and nobody had seen hide nor hair of her since. Some said she was disfigured, others said she was in the Witness Protection Program, and there'd even been speculation she was some kind of witch.

Eadie had been worried that the poor woman had actually passed away and was currently being eaten by her cats. Because apparently all women living by themselves and hiding away were "crazy cat ladies." A quick check with Jenny Carter had confirmed that the woman was, in fact, alive. Jenny said she'd been hearing regular movement overhead, and the mysterious woman had arrived with no cats.

"Well," Eadie continued, "she's definitely a stranger. And I'm pretty sure she's in her"—Eadie's voice lowered to a whisper—"*pajamas.*"

Austin blinked. That wasn't exactly an offense. "When you say loitering, what exactly do you mean?"

"What do you mean, what do I mean?" Eadie demanded. "She's standing outside Annie's, eating *two* ice-cream cones. At once. In *fifty degrees.*"

He stifled a smile at Eadie's scandalized tone. "Okay?"

"She's not just eating them, Officer...she's *savoring* them. Making a total spectacle of herself. It's practically... *pornographic.*"

A stranger—a woman, at that—eating ice cream in a *pornographic* manner? Austin stood. Never could it be said that he let down a Credence citizen of good standing in her hour of need. "Okay, ma'am, I'll go and check it out now."

"Thank you, young man. You can never be too careful about public safety."

"No, ma'am," Austin agreed with a smile. Who knew the kind of public disorder this could incite? One day pornographic ice cream consumption, the next mass street orgies.

Yep...never a dull moment.

• • •

Austin pulled up outside Annie's to find a woman, just as Eadie had indicated, with an ice-cream cone in each hand, licking from one to the other in the most hedonistic display of ice-cream consumption he'd ever witnessed. Her square face was turned to the sun, her eyes shut as she licked with the kind of long, slow licks that made him hear *bow chicka bow wow* music in his head—and in other parts of his anatomy.

So this was the woman who'd been holed up in the

apartment above Déjà Brew. Given he knew everybody in town except her, it couldn't be anyone else.

Ice cream was smeared on her lips as she got down to the cones, and he watched her devour them in great, crunchy mouthfuls, sighing as she fed the tip of the last one into her mouth before licking her fingers.

Austin actually went a little dizzy.

It was probably wrong to be salivating—not ice-cream related—and staring, right?

Say something, dumbass. Don't just sit there and watch her...fellate two ice-cream cones in public.

But he was momentarily struck speechless by her level of enjoyment, despite the wild hair, the baggy sweats, the stained T-shirt, and the...bunny slippers?

Maybe Eadie had been right about the scandalous pajama thing.

Austin jumped into action, getting out of his vehicle and stepping up onto the sidewalk. "Morning, ma'am," he said, touching the brim of his hat.

Her fingers slid from her mouth as she gradually lowered her head, until she was looking straight at him, pinning him with startling green eyes that reminded him of fancy glass and even fancier opals. A flare of annoyance ignited a rich vein of sparks in her eyes and puckered the space between her brows.

It was not the look he'd been expecting.

From the way she'd demolished her ice cream, he'd expected a slumberous kind of ecstasy. The sort he enjoyed seeing on a woman's face, especially if he'd put it there. Not a frown and a glare. And then, as her gaze traveled over his uniform, her eyes widened slightly. "Is there a problem, Officer?"

Her tone was somewhere between irritated and wary, but there was also a directness to it that told him, while the uniform had surprised her, she wasn't intimidated by it. Her pointy chin jutted defensively.

He cut to the chase. "Everything okay, ma'am?"

Sexy eating of ice cream aside, maybe this woman with the wild hair and the bunny slippers had deeper issues. Maybe she'd fallen and hit her head and was wandering around in an altered neurological state due to pressure or bleeding on her brain?

She blinked, her frown of annoyance turning to one of genuine puzzlement. "Why wouldn't I be okay? I was eating ice cream."

"Two, to be precise."

"I couldn't decide on a flavor." There was a definite note of *duh* in her voice. "Also"—she held up the brown paper bag that had been stashed under her arm—"I have pie."

Austin hadn't noticed the bag until now, although he knew Annie's brown paper bags quite well. The diner had been here since before he was born. "Are you hurt? Or...lost?"

She dropped her arm back to her side. "No."

So she always left her place looking like she'd been pulled through a hedge backward? "Do you know you're wearing... pajamas?"

Another frown. "These aren't my pajamas. Well..."

She gave a half shrug as she looked down at her clothes, then back up at him, pursing her lips, which drew attention to her lusciously full mouth. Austin—God help him—would bet his last penny that mouth tasted deliciously sweet right now.

"I guess, technically, I *did* wear them to bed last night," she said. "But that's only because I couldn't be bothered getting out of them and it was too cold to sleep naked."

Okay... "And the"—he glanced down at the two bunny heads with floppy ears on her feet—"slippers?"

This time she shoved her hand onto her hip. "Is wearing slippers outside illegal in your quaint little corner of Eastern Colorado?"

Amused, despite her inference that they were some backwater town, Austin shook his head. "No."

She dropped her hand. "It's cold."

It had been said like it was a perfectly reasonable explanation for wearing *bunny slippers* out in public. "Yes," he affirmed. "It's cold." But surely she had boots? Wear-outside-in-public boots? "What's your name?"

She stiffened, and her eyebrow kicked up. "I don't have to tell you my name."

"Well actually, ma'am, you do. Under town ordinance five eight three, section one, all persons must furnish ID if requested by an officer of the law." Austin knew few town ordinances by heart, but that one was his bread and butter. Policing 101.

"Oh, right, you're a *rules* guy. Of course." She folded her arms. "Just like Charlie goddamn Hammersmith."

Austin sighed. "All right, I'll bite. Who is this Charlie Hammersmith?"

"My asshole ex-boss."

"Okay." He wasn't sure that made it any clearer but whatevs.

"I'm not telling you my name." She glared at him mutinously. "I'm claiming my constitutional right to silence."

Oh...Jesus. *Give me patience.* "You're not under arrest, ma'am."

"So arrest me." She held out her wrists. "Cuff me."

In a different set of circumstances, Austin would have taken the greatest of pleasure in cuffing Credence's mystery woman, but that wasn't what she'd meant. "I'm not arresting you."

"Why not?" she demanded.

"Because there isn't a town ordinance against being a pain in the ass." He'd have committed that one to memory for sure. "Nor is it an arrestable offense."

Unfortunately.

"Fine." She dropped her arms and stuck out her chin. "What about jaywalking?" She brushed past him, stepping onto the road near the hood of his vehicle. "Is that against the law?"

Austin sighed and turned to face her. "Yes. Town ordinance four six seven, section two A." He was just making this shit up now, but she didn't have to know that.

"All right, then." And she walked into the middle of the road.

"Ma'am...what are you doing?" Given there wasn't a car to be seen anywhere up or down the street, Austin wasn't particularly worried about her being run down.

"I'm jaywalking. Arrest me."

"Ma'am."

She held out her hands again. "Take me to the pokey."

Austin couldn't help himself—he threw back his head and laughed. *The pokey?* She'd been watching too much television. "Ma'am, most people I know try to avoid going to *the pokey* at all costs. What's your story?"

"I'm a rule breaker," she said, frowning at first, as if she wasn't sure about the label, then nodding as if deciding she was okay with it. "That's right. I'm a rule breaker now."

Now?

She walked back to him, mounting the curb and stepping into his space—just a little—then she poked him in the chest. "And I'm going to be your worst nightmare, buddy."

Ordinarily, a member of the public getting up in his face—even here in Credence, where he knew everyone—would ring all kinds of alarm bells. He'd been trained to always be alert and to keep members of the public out of his personal space, but this woman didn't feel like a threat.

In fact, he felt absurdly like laughing his ass off.

"Officer Cooper," he supplied instead, pointing to the badge on his chest.

She nodded and said, "Officer"—*poke*—"Cooper." *Poke.*

Up this close, he could see those remarkable green eyes and those luscious lips and also the fine lines around her eyes. She was a bit older than him, he realized, before another realization hit—could he smell...beer?

He eased back from her a little. "Ma'am, are you drunk?"

"What?" She glared at him crankily. "No." And then her expression changed again. "Oh, wait...I did have a beer for breakfast. But I'm not drunk."

"You had beer for breakfast?" Now there were some life goals.

She nodded, suddenly all combative again. "Yeah. And you know why? Because I'm a rule breaker." And then he watched her face as it changed again. "Wait..." She narrowed her eyes a little. "Public drunkenness is against the law, right?"

Austin nodded and plucked some random numbers from his head. "Town ordinance one eight two dash nine."

"In that case, I am drunk. I am very drunk, *Ossifer*. I refused to give you my name, I jaywalked, and I'm drunk in public."

As if to emphasize her point, she burped—loudly.

Good lord, with her impressive belching ability, flyaway hair, lived-in clothes, questionable footwear, and her beer for breakfast, she was a frat boy wet dream. Austin had never been part of a fraternity, but he'd be lying if he said he wasn't just a little bit turned on.

"I'm a rule breaker," she continued. "It's your duty to arrest me." She thrust her hands out to him again.

Austin sighed. He'd never met anyone—man *or* woman— who wanted to be tossed in a cell so badly. Who was he to disappoint? "All right, then." He gestured at his car. "Get in."

She frowned and didn't move. "Don't you need to cuff me?"

"If you want me to cuff you, we can talk about doing that late one night after maybe some dinner and dancing, but I only ever cuff someone who's dangerous or a flight risk."

She quirked an eyebrow. "What makes you think I'm not either of those things?"

"Superior policing skills."

She rolled her eyes and said, "I could take you."

Austin suppressed a smile, admiring her bravado. "You're welcome to try, ma'am."

She eyed him up and down for a moment, like she was seriously contemplating it, before coming to the inevitable realization. "Fine," she huffed. "No cuffs. But forget the dinner and dancing; this was your one and only chance."

He grinned as she yanked the car door open. He never could resist a challenge.

CHAPTER THREE

Bea had never been in a police station in her life, so she hadn't really known what to expect, but it didn't seem that different from a lot of cop shows she'd snatched glimpses of throughout the years. Kinda old and worn around the edges, the color scheme something drab from who knew how many decades ago.

This place needed some serious help with branding.

A long desk—the top of which appeared to be made out of a thick slab of wood—was the first thing Bea saw. A middle-aged man in uniform and glasses stood behind it. He looked up curiously as they entered but didn't say anything as Officer Cooper ushered her beyond the desk to a central area, where four desks, each with their own computer monitor, had all been pushed together in a square formation.

Like kindergarten, minus the pots of paint and the Play-Doh.

One of them was occupied by another middle-aged uniformed man—there was a lot of testosterone around here—who took in Bea and her bunny slippers with a grin before saying, "Arlo's just going to love this," and turning back to his computer.

Bea wondered who this Arlo might be for about two seconds before Officer Cooper said, "Bite me, Reynolds."

Beyond the central desks were two offices. One had a large window with the blinds open but the door shut. The other office was open, a smaller glass panel in its door displaying the word *Chief* in some kind of hackneyed Wild West font. Her graphic-artist brain winced at its inelegance.

On the far wall to her left was a bank of filing cabinets— two on each side of a central open doorway. They looked a little dinged up, with various objects from flashlights to handheld radios to a yo-yo sitting on top. She could make out a corridor beyond the doorway, but where it led or what was behind it was hidden from her view.

A cell? Probably.

Removing his hat, Officer Cooper said, "Sit down."

Bea looked at the chair he was indicating and shot him a mutinous look. "This isn't the pokey."

The officer called Reynolds sniggered as the guy who had *brought her in* shoved his hands on his hips and shook his head at her before hooking his thumb over his shoulder. "It's that way." He opened the drawer at what she presumed was his desk—his very neat desk, of course, because he was a *rules* guy—and took out a set of keys. "Follow me."

He headed in the direction of the doorway, and Bea, still clutching her brown paper bag, followed, noticing for the first time that Officer Cooper had a very fine ass. It wasn't what she should be thinking, because he was literally about to lock her in a cell and was also *a man* and she wasn't fond of any of his sex right now.

Also, he had to be about ten years younger than her.

But it wasn't like she was going to jump him—that had been more her mom's thing—and she wasn't *that* mad at men that she failed to recognize the magnificence of his tush. And, while she was at it, the truly fabulous way his broad shoulders filled out his shirt and the seriously effortless length of his stride. Also, the way his sandy-blond hair just brushed the collar of said shirt at the back.

Following him to the left as they walked through the doorway, he took three paces—five for her—and they were at a cell. The first of two. A bona fide cell with *bars* and everything.

"In you go," he said, pulling the door open. "The *pokey* awaits."

Bea, her pulse speeding up, took two paces into the cell. It was small, spare, cold, and ruthlessly neat with only two pieces of furniture. A bench that was attached to the wall and a bare, metallic toilet bowl—no seat—in the corner, tucked in behind the bench. She figured it was supposed to afford some privacy but *ugh.*

Suddenly she regretted that breakfast beer...

But as the door clanged shut behind her and the key turned in the lock, she realized that, for most people, being put in here wasn't a choice, and how freaking awful would that be in this Spartan, dehumanizing, freezing box? With a toilet that was giving her hemorrhoids just looking at it and a camera, she noticed, up high in the opposite corner, watching her.

A long-buried memory hit then, of her mother being arrested at some protest march and her father bringing her home from the police precinct, absolutely furious. Bea had been sitting on the top step in her pajamas, hugging her knees, listening to their argument filter through the shut living room door and up the stairwell through the gaps in the banister. Her grandmother had found her and ordered her to bed.

"You want out?" Officer Cooper said.

Bea heard the not-so-ballsy-now-are-you note in his voice and shook the memory off. Voluntarily walking into a cell was not the same thing as being *in*voluntarily shoved into one. She wasn't about to go full *mom* no matter her father's dire predictions after he'd heard she'd quit her job.

Squaring her shoulders, she crossed to the bench and sat her ass on it, placed her bag of Annie's pie beside her, and moved around a little. The seat was hard as a rock.

"How do you feel?"

She folded her arms and jutted her chin as she looked at him with what she hoped was an air of defiance. "Like a rule breaker." Bea hadn't been sure about it when she'd first blurted out the words. It felt a little too close to something her mom might have said. But then she'd realized her mom hadn't ever *followed* rules to start with, which was a very different thing.

"Okay..."

He leaned a shoulder against one of the bars, obviously resigned to this playing out as he hooked his thumb in his belt near his hip. It was casual and relaxed—he really *didn't* see her as any kind of threat—and she dragged her gaze down to the way his police-issue pants molded to his narrow hips and long legs. They weren't tight but hugged and *cupped* everything just right. "Let's take this from the top," he said. "Your name?"

One of the things Bea had enjoyed most about the last two weeks was her total anonymity. She wasn't sure she was willing to give that up just yet. "Why do you need to know my name?"

"Because, if I'm going to write you up for all those offenses you just committed, I'm going to need a name. And an address and a social security number."

That seemed reasonable enough, but Bea was done being *reasonable*. "Yeah..." She shook her head. "Still pleading the fifth."

His mouth curved into a smile, which drew her attention to his face. Without the brim of his hat throwing a shadow over his features, he was really something. A very nice mouth, spare cheekbones, square jaw. The scruff covering his jaw seemed more lazy than designer. And those shoulders were just as good from the front, too.

"Ma'am, I know you're the woman who's rented out the apartment above Déjà Brew."

Bea was beginning to like the way he ma'amed her, which

was all kinds of screwy. "Oh?" She arched an eyebrow. "And how do you know that?"

"It's a small town. I know everyone in Credence and the surrounding areas, and I don't know *you* at all."

He said it like he'd remember if he'd ever met her, and Bea couldn't decide if that was a compliment or even why in the hell it mattered. "And what else do you know?"

"You drive a BMW."

"Oh, really? And how exactly do you know *that*?" Putting two and two together over her identity seemed fair enough, but this seemed kinda specific.

"Because a brand-new M3 has been in the parking lot at the back of Déjà Brew for two weeks. Nobody aside from Wade Carter can afford to drive a Beamer around here, and A) he's not in town right now and B) he drives a Tesla since CC came on the scene."

Bea had discovered after that dart had landed on the Credence dot on the map that it was also the home town of the famed ex-QB of the Denver Broncos. She'd never had time to watch football, but even she knew who he was. "I refuse to confirm or deny."

"Suit yourself." He shifted, bending forward at the hips a little, his arms sliding between the uprights, his elbows resting on the middle crossbar, his fingers interlocking on her side of the cell. "I can just go ask Jenny Carter."

"Okay, then." Bea shrugged. "You do you." She reached for the brown packet and opened it, her nostrils flaring instantly at the waft of pure sugar. Salivating like a St. Bernard after a Lidocaine tooth extraction, she buried half her face inside the packet and inhaled the essence deep into her lungs. "I'll just be here, eating my pie."

But which one? She'd bought three different slices. A piece of cherry, a piece of apple, and a super-size piece of key lime.

"Ma'am...are you sure you're okay?"

The note of genuine concern in his voice drew Bea's attention away from the pie, and she sat back, the crown of her head bumping against the cinder-block wall behind. "Do I seem a little unhinged to you?"

She probably did. Or erratic, at least, with the sweats and the bunny slippers and her face practically shoved inside a paper bag, breathing in carbohydrate essence like she was chroming paint fumes.

Well...*good*. Bea was tired of being so damn predictable and centered and *sensible*. She was on a break.

"No," he admitted. "But maybe you...tripped and hit your head on something?"

Bea put the pie aside. "You think I'm having some kind of...neurological event?" To be fair, she was pretty sure that's what Charlie Hammersmith, the CEO of Jing-A-Ling, and the five other male executives had thought when she'd told them to shove their job up their asses.

"Do you know where you are? Or what year it is? What about the day of the week?"

"I don't know. But my underwear says Tuesday, so..."

He laughed again, and this time she noticed that the skin crinkled at the corners of his eyes, which made him look older, and that made her feel a little better about her salacious thoughts. "Your panties have the day of the week on them?"

Oh, dear lord, the way the man said *panties* did strange, tingly things to her body. Not the way she was probably supposed to be reacting in a cell in a police station in Buttfuck, Colorado, with a cop who was about to write her up for several infractions of town bylaws.

There was something low and *male* about how the word rolled off his tongue.

"What? You've never worn day-of-the-week underwear?" she asked.

"Of course. When I was five."

"Yes, but this is *designer*."

"Oh, well then." He grinned, and it was just a little bit wicked. Kinda like Dean Winchester. "That makes all the difference."

And damn if that grin didn't make Bea's heart do a funny little giddyap and her mouth curve into an answering smile, and before she could check herself, she was asking, "What's your name?"

He pointed to his badge. "Officer Cooper, remember?"

Bea bugged her eyes at him. "I mean your first name."

"Excuse me?" He feigned insult, but he didn't look that insulted. In fact, Bea thought the man was probably too laid-back to take insult at very much at all. "So I have to tell you my name, but you get to plead the fifth?"

"Yeah, it *sucks* to be you, right?"

He chuckled then—actually freaking chuckled—and that was more lethal than his grin. God, he was so damn...cute.

"You're quite good-looking, aren't you?"

Shaking his head, he laughed some more. "Do you always say whatever's on your mind?"

"No." Bea sighed, the thought horribly sobering. "I *never* say what's on my mind." She just kept everything crammed inside until she was ready to explode in a fit of *shrill female hormonosity*.

Yeah, *not* a word, but that hadn't mattered to that asshole Charlie Hammersmith.

"That's not the impression you've given me so far."

She drew her knees up, wrapping her arms around them and tucking them under her chin. "I'm turning over a new leaf. From now on, I'm just going to say whatever crosses my mind."

"Lucky me." They smiled at each other, and his lack of foreboding was charming as all heck. "It's Wednesday."

Bea, a little more befuddled by that smile than a woman of her age and experience should be, scrunched her brow. "Your name is Wednesday?"

"No." He grinned. "The day of the week. My name is Austin."

"Of course it is." God...even his name sounded *young.*

"Oh yeah?" He turned his head to the side—his smile deadly even in profile—then back again. "I look like an Austin to you?"

Bea wondered if there was a city ordinance she was breaking right now by imagining how scruffy whiskers belonging to an officer of the law would feel rubbing in unmentionable places. Unauthorized fantasizing over a county official, maybe?

Or mental undressing of a police officer on duty?

"More than you look like a Wednesday," she quipped.

He hooted out another laugh, and the fact that he seemed to be enjoying himself during this verbal ping-pong was a curious delight to Bea.

"I have a suggestion, if I may," he said after he'd sobered, "to do with keeping track of what day it is. It's probably highly"—he glanced up at the camera in the corner—"inappropriate. But...why not, especially given your possession of *designer* day-of-the-week panties?"

Oh lordy... She could listen to him say *panties* all day long.

"Just correlate the days with the underwear. Like, tomorrow is Thursday, right? So...if you wear your Thursday panties tomorrow, then hey, presto. You're back on track."

Thursday panties.

God, she loved her Thursday panties more than all the others already. Hell, she might even go home and get into them immediately. Or after she'd washed them, anyway. Bea mentally apologized to the other six days of the week, then wondered if it was possible to orgasm from a man rolling the word *panties* off his tongue with such dedication and frequency.

Oh...for heaven's sake. *Pull your shit together, Bea!*

She dropped her legs, returning her feet to the floor as she sat a little straighter. "I'm afraid that's just not possible," she said, trying to channel Cranky Bea from outside Annie's.

He eyed her speculatively for a beat or two. "Let me guess. Because you're a rule breaker now?"

Bea tucked in her chin. "Damn straight I am."

"Okay...I'll bite. *Why* are you a rule breaker?"

Even the question got Bea's motor running. The rage and impotence from a month ago, when she'd walked out of her cushy advertising role in LA after being screwed over for a promotion yet again by a boardroom full of men, returned. As did the injustice of her father's scathing condemnation. A corporate ad man himself, he'd called her actions harebrained and impulsive—*just like your mom.*

When she'd tried so damn hard all her life to be the exact opposite.

Officer Austin Cooper McCutie and his *panties* were temporarily forgotten as the visceral double gut punch of that day was revisited. She pushed off the bench and started to prowl back and forth across the width of the cell. Six paces to the wall opposite and six paces back.

"What good did following the rules get me?" she asked finally, whipping around to face him from the middle of the cell.

Being a *good girl* as per her grandmother's constant refrain.

"What have I gotten for it?" she demanded. "Nothing, that's what." She started to pace again. "More than fifteen years at the same agency and passed over for promotion time and again. That corner office I've been coveting ever since I was a junior copy editor, the one that has been promised to me every year for the last *five* years going to yet another less experienced, better connected *man.*"

She kinda yelled the last word as she stopped and glared at him, and Austin Cooper, the *police officer,* held up his hands—still clasped together through the bars—in some kind of surrender.

It would probably be funny if she was viewing this from the outside.

"I haven't had more than six hours of sleep a night in the last decade. I haven't had a pet. I haven't had…a girls' night." She gave a laugh that tasted bitter. "Who am I kidding, I don't *have* any girlfriends anymore, since all I do is work."

She paced again, the rage complementing the air of hopelessness in the cold cell to perfection. Reaching the middle, she turned to him again. "I haven't eaten a carb." She held up her thumb to count off all her woes. "I haven't been on a date in forever." She raised her index finger to indicate woe number two. "I think my boobs are dropping."

She went to stick up her middle finger but changed her mind, looking down at her chest as she clasped both hands over her breasts, weighing them up for evidence.

Definitely dropping.

"Hell—" Removing her hands, she glared at him again. "I haven't had sex in more than a year." A thought hit her. "God…I haven't had an orgasm delivered by a human being for *longer* than that."

"Oh-kay."

If Bea had been less sad about that sudden realization, she might have been embarrassed to have groped her own breasts and admitted something so deeply personal to not only a virtual stranger but a police officer who'd put her in a cell and turned her to mush with his frequent use of the word *panties*. But, as with everything since quitting her job, there were no fucks to give.

He didn't seem to be too perturbed by her frankness, at least. Not that a young, sexy guy could understand the tragedy of going without sexual gratification. She doubted he went a week without seducing some young, perky-boobed woman out of her *panties.*

Momentarily exhausted of rage and words, Bea headed back to the bench, her eyes landing on the brown paper packet. Oh God yes, *shhhugar!* She snatched it up, reached in, and pulled out the first piece of pie her fingers touched.

Pie would make it better.

Barely stopping to check out the type, she took a huge bite. *Mmmm.* Cherry. Plump and gooey. Tart and sweet all at once. With a hint of vanilla and something else she just couldn't place. Bea moaned as she took another bite, her blood sugar rocketing straight into the danger zone as her eyes practically rolled back in her head.

So. Freaking. Good.

So good, in fact, she turned back to face Austin just so she could share in the marvel. "Oh my God," she said around her second mouthful, "this pie is *ah*-mazing."

He grinned. "I know, right? Annie is a goddess."

Bea nodded, crossing over to him, because she couldn't believe that *anything* could taste this good, and she needed to make sure Austin *understood* that this pie was a total party for the mouth. Stopping about a foot from where his hands were still clasped together through the bars, she took another mouthful, her eyes shutting involuntarily on a wave of bliss.

Hell, her left *nipple* hardened.

Swallowing her mouthful down, her eyes blinked open to find him watching her intently. Up this close she noticed his eyes were blue. Not the kind of intense blue of a sapphire or the hot blue of a gas flame, but the temperate kind of blue that said, *Come on in, the water's warm and there are margaritas here. And pie.*

Her right nipple hardened.

And a very pleasant sensation twinged between her legs. Any more of this and she could reset the clock on the orgasm thing.

"You should eat pie more often," he said, his voice a low kind of rumble that wrapped around her waist and urged her closer. "It looks good on you."

She resisted the pull but let the compliment go to her head, where it mixed with the heady aroma and sweet decadence of cherries, sugar, and pastry. "I intend to." She took another bite. "They don't have pies like this in LA," she said around the mouthful.

He grinned then, his intensity evaporating like a mirage. Perhaps that's all it had been—one her pie-addled brain had conjured up. "LA, huh?"

Bea ignored him, continuing to devour the pie.

"You're a long way from home," he said. "Why Credence?"

Swallowing the last mouthful down, she decided to throw Officer Blue Eyes a bone. "I wanted out of the rat race for a while. I wanted to spend some time in a cute, small, friendly town where nobody knows my name, but they welcome me with open arms anyway."

"And yet you haven't come out of your apartment for two weeks."

"You noticed?" Bea asked, intrigued by Austin's ninja-level observance.

"Ma'am, this is a small town. *Everyone's* noticed."

Hmm, okay, not quite as thrilling as the notion that McSexy had been keeping tabs on her for the last two weeks, but still kinda sweet that the town she'd chosen to call home for the moment was already looking out for her.

Or maybe everything was looking better now she had pie on board. Not that she didn't have room for a second piece. Returning to the bench, she grabbed the slice of key lime out of the bag, then bit into it as she returned to where she'd been standing. Citrus—light and tangy—exploded across her tongue, and everything below her belly button went a little weak.

Annie's pies had gotten her closer to orgasm in a few

minutes than she'd been for a long time. They should come with a warning. Or a red light.

Conscious of Austin just there, watching her, Bea cleaned up her pie-eating act, nibbling and quietly savoring instead of moaning and fitting as much in her mouth as possible.

"Apologies for my absence," she said around bites. "I haven't been able to drag myself away from Dean and Sam."

He quirked an eyebrow, but his eyes were laughing. "You've been having a threesome up there for the last two weeks?"

Bea's eyes laughed back. Well, she was pretty sure they did, anyway. "I'm sorry." She batted her lashes at him in an exaggerated fashion. "You going to write me up for that, too? There must be some kind of indecency bylaw I've broken?"

A Winchester sandwich seemed deliciously indecent.

"No, ma'am. What you do in the privacy of your own home with fictitious television brothers is entirely up to you." He grinned, and Bea couldn't help but laugh. Clearly Austin was up on his pop culture. "And if you ever want to switch them out for, say, Sansa and Arya, then let me know so I can come watch."

Bea had no idea who he was talking about, but she was pretty damn sure Austin Cooper was flirting with her now. And it wasn't entirely unpleasant. Preposterous, of course, and possibly breaking some fraternization rule, but *not* unpleasant.

"Cooper?"

Bea startled at the intrusion of a male voice echoing down the corridor. She'd forgotten for a moment they were in a police station, and she blinked as a guy an inch or so taller than Austin appeared at his side. He filled out his uniform very well, too, but with his unquestionable air of authority and dark military-style buzz cut, she put him closer to her age—maybe late thirties?

Something told her this was Arlo. It seemed like Credence

was punching above its weight in the hot-cops division.

Even if it was a true dick fest.

"Yeah, Chief?" Austin, clearly unconcerned by the irritation in the other man's voice, glanced at him casually as he straightened, removing his arms from between the bars.

The chief gave her a polite nod and said, "Ma'am," before turning his attention back to Austin. It was brisk and polite, nowhere near as lethal as Austin's *ma'am*s. "Is there a reason why this woman is in a cell?" He glanced at Bea again, his gaze falling on the piece of pie she was trying to eke out and not stuff into her mouth like Cookie Monster. "Are we opening a diner I don't know about?"

Austin shrugged. "She was insistent about being put in the *pokey*."

Arlo studied her again for a moment before continuing his conversation with Austin. "Because she's done something wrong, or does she have a...fetish?"

Bea frowned. *Fetish?* "I'm a rule breaker," she announced.

Arlo looked at her, then back at Austin, who nodded. "She's a rule breaker. Although I think she might also have a bit of a fetish going on."

"Hey!" Bea protested around a mouthful of pie.

The chief shrugged. "She wouldn't be the first."

"It's definitely a thing," Austin said, although it sounded like he had no idea why, and given that she was on the locked side of these bars, Bea had to agree.

Arlo raised one shoulder. "Not up to me to yuck on someone else's yum."

Bea blinked. So did Austin. Was he also wondering why his no-nonsense boss, the chief of police in Tiny Town, Colorado, sounded like a Gen Z TikToker?

"She's refusing to give me her name," Austin said, obviously deciding not to do a deep dive into Arlo's surprising turn of phrase.

"Because she's a rule breaker?" Arlo asked.

"Uh-huh."

Arlo turned his head and locked his gaze on Bea's. "Ma'am, this cell is for *actual* criminals." Then he turned to Austin and said, "Fix this, Cooper."

Bea swore he muttered something about the full moon under his breath as he departed, but she was down to the last two bites of her pie, and that, frankly, seemed more important right now. Thank God for her sweatpants and their stretchy waist.

"Okay." Austin leaned in again, sliding his arms between the bars. "How about I *guess* your name?"

"This a slow crime day, Officer Cooper?"

"Humor me."

"Okay, sure." This ought to be good...

He regarded her for a moment or two, his eyes roving over her with a thoroughness that led her to believe he was probably very good at taking down descriptions. A good trait for a cop, but it didn't feel professional. It felt like something just between him and her. Hot, wild, thrilling. And damn if she wasn't just a little bit out of breath by the time he finished.

That's what happened after two weeks away from her nemesis—the elliptical.

"I think," he said, pausing a little, obviously enjoying prolonging the suspense, "you look like a—"

"Beatrice?"

The incredulous female voice coming from somewhere off to the left had Austin grinning big. "Beatrice," he said triumphantly.

Just then, Jenny Carter appeared by Austin's elbow. A lot smaller than the last person who had stood there, although no less a presence as she practically vibrated with incredulity and shock. "There you are. Arlo told me you were back here. I couldn't believe it when Annie called to say you'd been taken away in a police car. What are you doing in a cell?" She turned to Austin, indignant eyes blazing. "What's she doing in a cell, Austin? Did you arrest her?"

"Nope." He shook his head, thoroughly bemused now. "She's not under arrest."

"Then what are you doing? Let her out," Jenny demanded. "Since when is this the way we treat a guest to our town? I thought we were trying to attract people to Credence, not drive them away."

Austin cocked his eyebrow at her, and Bea sighed a little and nodded. This had been a fun, if slightly strange, morning, and she didn't think Jenny would understand why or how she'd ended up in the town clink.

How could she, when Bea didn't even understand herself? When the wild impulse that had seen her goad Austin into locking her up still beat its wings inside her chest.

God...maybe she *did* have a fetish.

Austin reached into his pocket for the key, undid the lock, and pulled the door open. "She's free to go?" Jenny asked, oblivious to the strange vibe that hummed between Bea and Austin as she brushed by him on her way out of the cell.

Bea felt *alive*, and she hadn't realized she *wasn't* until just now. A small-town cop who'd taken her ranting in stride and flirted with her had bucked her right up—even her boobs felt perkier. Between Austin Cooper and the Winchester boys— now *there* was a sandwich—she was riding high.

All younger men, she noted. But that was fine—two weren't even real people and the other was just a...fleeting distraction.

"You're not fining her?" Jenny continued. "There won't be any record?"

"Nope. She's free as a bird."

For some strange reason, Bea remembered that totally sappy thing she'd heard once about letting go of something you loved, and if it returned, that's how you knew it was reciprocated.

Or some such garbage.

Why that was on her mind now, she had no idea, but as she walked out of the station with Jenny apologizing profusely at her side, Bea wasn't thinking about Dean Winchester anymore. She was thinking about small-town cops, fetishes, and Thursday panties.

CHAPTER FOUR

Pie drove Bea out of the apartment again the next day. She'd pretty much mainlined *Supernatural* since returning to her apartment after her time in the pokey and had only slept for four hours after being woken by a completely inappropriate dream about a certain Credence police officer. But she was halfway through season fifteen now—the final ever season, *sob!*—so the end was in sight. And she planned on being totally unsociable until then.

But a girl had to eat, right?

Tomorrow she'd stick her head out of the apartment and do a shopping run, maybe even try meeting a few folks. But for now, it was a pie run, then *Supernatural* until Dean and Sam drove off into the sunset in their Chevrolet Impala. And if they didn't? If one of them so much as had a cold at the end, she was going to be seriously pissed!

But when she got to Annie's—her wardrobe of choice still sweats and a hoodie, with her hair twisted up into another haphazard knot, but no bunny slippers this time—the older woman convinced her she really needed to try the pancakes, as well as taking some pie to go, and, well...who was Bea to rebuff someone who clearly knew quality food?

She was scarfing down a stack of blueberry pancakes with maple syrup, ignoring the probing looks she knew were sailing her way, when Austin Cooper sat his very nice ass down on the other chair at her table.

"Hey," he said.

It was so friendly and casual, and he looked so freaking hot in his uniform, ruffling his hair as he removed his hat, that Bea was suddenly very aware of her Thursday panties. She was sure as hell pleased she was doing something else with her mouth, lest it decide that licking a police officer was a better use of its time.

So much for a fleeting distraction.

"Officer Cooper," she acknowledged as she swallowed her mouthful of pancake.

"You can call me Austin."

Yeah...but *Officer Cooper* sounded older. She sighed. "How old are you?"

He grinned. "Twenty-five."

Oh God...he was barely out of the academy. So that dream she'd had about him last night with the handcuffs? She was going to hell. Probably also giving her grandmother apoplexy.

Annie shuffled up to the table. "Coffee, hon?" she asked Austin, tipping her chin at the cup upside down on the saucer.

"Yes please, Annie." He turned the cup over. "And can I get a serving of those pancakes, too?"

"Sure can," she said as she filled up the cup from her ancient pot. "I'll send them right over." And she shuffled off.

"No bunny slippers today, I see?"

Bea ignored his observation. "Aren't you supposed to be working?"

"I am working."

Bea snorted. This was some life he had. She'd never stopped for pancakes anywhere when she'd been toiling away at the agency unless she was at a breakfast meeting with a client. But even then, she'd have eaten an egg-white omelet or granola. "So, the whole doughnut-eating cop thing is true, then? Not just some giant cliché?"

He patted his stomach, and Bea's eyes were drawn to the flatness of it, to the snug fit of fabric, the fascinating line of buttons. Was his skin smooth underneath all that or was there one of those endlessly fascinating trails that led all the way down to his boxers? And beyond...

"A man's gotta eat."

Determinedly pulling her mind out of Austin's boxers, she said, "You wanna watch it. You won't be so young one day, and those pounds will creep on before you know it." It was a kinda mean thing to say, but the fact she was now *day*dreaming about him in full view of an entire café *and* the man himself was flustering. And that made her cranky.

Also, it was true—pounds were sneaky little suckers.

Clearly completely unperturbed by her dire predictions, he shrugged. "I'm not so worried about that. I have a pretty good metabolism."

Yeah, that was the problem with Austin Cooper. He had a pretty good *everything.*

"So, Beatrice, huh? As in Potter?"

She sighed. "That's Beatrix. Bea-*trix* Potter, the English author of cute animal stories. I'm Bea-*triss*. As in Beatrice of York, the English princess."

"Ahhh," he said, but he was smiling, and Bea wasn't entirely sure he hadn't known that already and was just being deliberately obtuse. "So, you're Beatrice, formerly of LA, now of Credence?"

"For now, yes. At least until I've decided what to do with the rest of my life."

"Do you have a time frame for that?"

"Nope." Screw deadlines. Bea was over deadlines.

"Are you feeling better today?" he asked.

"I was feeling fine yesterday," she said with a glare, a chunk of pancake speared on the end of her fork. "I just needed some sugar."

"And to break some rules."

"Yes." Bea lowered her eyes as she shoveled the fork into her mouth. She was a little embarrassed about her behavior yesterday. Everything she'd said she'd meant, but she barely knew this guy, and she must have come across as slightly nutty.

Annie interrupted with Austin's food, placing the plate in front of him. "You want more, doll?" she asked, assessing Bea's almost empty plate.

Bea wanted more pancakes with a craving that was entirely foreign—this was the peril of succumbing to simple carbohydrates. But she was almost full, and she was taking pie to go, so… "Thanks, but no. I'll be over for my pie soon."

"Already boxed up for you." Bea had decided to go with a whole pie this time because it should see her all the way through to episode twenty.

Annie departed, and Bea returned her attention to what was left of her food and the hole that Austin had already made in his—he clearly liked his pancakes. "So," he said around a mouthful of food, "you're determined to break some rules, huh? Any thoughts on which ones?"

Bea wondered what ordinance she was breaking now, thinking about drizzling maple syrup all over Austin's abs. In public. "Well, that depends," Bea said, eyeing him speculatively. "Is this Austin asking, or is it Officer Cooper?"

"Well, that depends." He smiled at his repetition. "If you want to know the number of each law you intend to break, then it's Officer Cooper. If you just want to shoot the breeze about it, then it's Austin."

"Can I take a little bit of A and the rest B?"

"Beatrice," he said, his loaded fork poised between the plate and his mouth, "you can take whatever you like."

Beatrice.

Only her grandmother called her Beatrice. It had seemed

drearily old-fashioned as a kid, when all the other girls had been called Kimberly and Crystal. So she'd grabbed hold of the shortened version, Bea, and run with it. But *this* guy using her full name? That was something else. It rolled off his tongue soft as a caress and made it sound contemporary.

And...swoony.

Austin Cooper seemed to know all her swoon buttons, and she hadn't even known she possessed any. Hell, she hadn't even known swoon buttons were a *thing*.

And then he grinned, his face so arrestingly sexy and his damn...*teeth* so straight and white and even and...*young*. Popping the food into his mouth, he ate with relish, forcing Bea to look out the window to stop herself from wondering if he was a fan of eating *things other than food*, and she didn't want to take *that* into her dream world tonight.

Younger men were a *hard* limit. Even in her sleep.

"So, come on," he said, after he'd swallowed and before his next pornographic swipe of his tongue across sticky maple-syrup lips. "Spill. What's on your rule-breaking list?"

"I don't have a list."

"That's a pity." He shook his head, his expression faux crestfallen before his gaze locked on hers. "You said you were going to be my worst nightmare. I was looking forward to that."

Bea's breath hitched at the low note in his voice. "I was suffering from a sugar rush. I may have exaggerated."

He grinned. "I would never have guessed."

She shot him a quelling look. "I'm just not sure I want to be on that corporate treadmill anymore. Working all hours of the day and night and being the same boring, predictable Beatrice with no life."

"Okay, so that's what you *don't* want. What *do* you want?"

There was a challenge in his voice that needled at Bea. How could a twenty-five-year-old dude have his shit together more than she did? To be fair, she'd had her shit together *waaay* back in her twenties, too. Why hadn't anyone told her she was going to regret the hell out of that?

"I just want to be…" She shied away from the word *impulsive* because that was synonymous with her mom. "I want to live a little. For a change."

Not forever. Just for now. She'd held back from doing things other people had told her not to do her entire life. Maybe it was time, while she was taking a break from the rat race, to do *exactly* the opposite. To do everything she'd been told *not* to do.

He nodded encouragingly. "Like?"

"I don't know." Bea cast a net for something impulsive and outrageous. "Flash somebody. Or maybe moon them. Or…go skinny-dipping." Her grandmother, who had practically raised her, was very *specific* about the perils associated with a lack of feminine modesty.

"Ooh, now…that's badass. They all fall under ordinance seven four two, subsection three of the public nudity act."

Bea blinked. She was badass? And there was a public nudity act? "You're just making this shit up now."

"God's truth," he said, placing his hand over his heart, but he was smiling in such a way that Bea still didn't believe him. "What else?"

"Um…" She tried really hard to think of something outrageous. "I'd like to do something reckless in my car, like burn rubber or compete in a drag race?" Her father considered it the height of irresponsibility to drive recklessly. Which, for him, meant going any more than five miles over the speed limit.

"Yup." He ate more pancake, then chewed and swallowed it before he continued. "There's a couple there. Reckless driving. Number two sixty-two. And public nuisance, number four one nine slash ten." His tongue flicked out to remove the shine of maple syrup from his lips. "What else? Feel free to really test my knowledge of local and county statutes here."

Bea toyed with the idea of saying *rob a bank* just to see what Officer Syrup Lips would say to that. But essentially, she was coming up blank, because she'd spent thirty-five years being a law-abiding citizen—and less than twenty-four hours as the opposite. "It's not necessarily about breaking the law," she clarified. "It's about breaking the…strictures of my life."

Put on her by her father and her grandmother and every damn boss she'd ever had.

"Okay…like?"

"Like…" Bea flailed around mentally for a moment or two. "Sleep in. Drink beer for breakfast." She realized those probably sounded pathetic. Plus, she'd already done that quite a lot these past two weeks. "Ride a horse." They had to have horses around here somewhere, right?

Her best friend in high school had a horse, but Bea had been expressly forbidden to ride it because apparently smelling horsey wasn't ladylike.

"Dye my hair." Charlie Hammersmith had intimated that women in advertising were far too *distracting* to the men in the room, so it was important to be inconspicuous.

Attractive, *of course*, but not flashy or showy.

She rooted around inside her head for something else. "Shoot a three-pointer." That was better, considering Bea had never played basketball in her life. "And…line dance."

God, her grandmother would be horrified by a line-dancing Beatrice. The only form of dance she rated was the ballet. And only if it was at Carnegie Hall.

"Line dance?"

He'd said it exactly the way her grandmother would have, like it was some kind of abomination that should be outlawed.

"Yes."

She sat a little taller in her chair. Why not? She was far too old to learn ballet, and if beer for breakfast and Annie's pie became a regular thing—from her brain to God's ears—she'd need to do some form of exercise. It was probably a hell of a lot easier than a three-pointer, too. "Also, sleep under the stars." Camping had been considered low-class by her grandmother. Another thought popped into her head. "Get a fondue set."

God, *cheese*. Gooey, melty cheese. Her mouth watered just thinking about it. But she'd denied herself the pleasure of cheese since Charlie freaking Hammersmith had informed her at a work function, just after she'd been promoted to junior executive, that the firm had a certain image to project, as he looked pointedly at the third portion of deep-fried Camembert she'd snagged from a circulating platter.

So she had to be attractive—but not distracting. And God forbid she even be the teeniest bit fat.

Austin, who clearly thought she was getting significantly less badass, shot her a pitying look. "What else?"

Bea thought hard. "Get a cat. Something cute and sweet and adorable."

"You had a rule against getting a *cat*?"

Stabbing a glare in his direction, she said, "I was never home to either look after or give proper attention to an animal."

"Okay."

His tone suggested this item was probably the most pitiable of them all and, goaded by that and by the way he licked his lips—*again*—she blurted out what was really on her mind. "Have a lot of orgasms."

It occurred to Bea that this might not come across as cool and edgy but, rather, a little TMI. And, well…sad. It shouldn't be a surprise, given she'd told him about her lack of satisfaction yesterday, and reiterating it today was probably bordering on desperate, but hell, she *was* desperate. Not that he seemed to be judging. In fact, he seemed to be very much enjoying it, a smile quirking his lips to one side.

"Lucky you. No town ordinances against that."

Ha! There was the way she was planning on having them.

"They'll be very loud." And because she felt it needed further clarification, she added, "And with outrageously unsuitable men."

"What does outrageously unsuitable mean, exactly?"

Someone like you.

Except, yeah, she wasn't going to say that. "Someone who doesn't know the meaning of *brand awareness*."

He laughed. "*That's* who you deem as unsuitable?"

"What'd you think I'd say?"

"I don't know." His laughter dropped away. "An ex-con or a…circus clown?"

Bea could probably give the ex-con a chance, depending on what he'd done, but she wasn't sure how desperate she'd have to become to let a circus clown get her off. Although she supposed there was no reason why they weren't just as good at delivering orgasms as everyone else in the general population. It seemed discriminatory to exclude them, after all.

And now she was thinking about clowns in an entirely inappropriate manner…

Bea's brow wrinkled in irritation. "I just meant someone who isn't an ad executive. Who isn't *suitable*." Her grandmother loved that word. "Someone who doesn't have a good job and a flashy suit and an expensive car."

Like they were the holy grail of the male species.

He made a face. "They sound boring."

"No." Bea sighed. "They're not. They're perfectly fine. They're just not…" A hot young cop from Hicksville who says *panties* and licks his lips like he's in an ad for blueberry pancake–flavored ChapStick. He was definitely *un*suitable. "Dean Winchester, you know?"

"To be fair…there is only one Dean."

He grinned then, and Bea grinned back—the man was impossible to dislike. "This is true."

Pushing his plate away, Austin picked up his cup of coffee.

"Well, now you got yourself some ideas, what are you going to do first?"

Bea stared at him. Just coming up with those things had been hard enough for one day. He couldn't seriously expect her to pick one and do it as well? He quirked an eyebrow and murmured, *"Bok, bok, bok."*

Chicken noises? He was making *chicken noises*. "Aren't you supposed to be maintaining law and order around here? How would your chief like it if he knew you were encouraging anarchy?"

"Oh yeah, let me know when you buy the fondue set so Arlo can call in the SWAT team."

Goaded by the implication she was no threat to civilian order, she sorted through the ideas she'd put forward and picked one. "Burn rubber." Why not start at the beginning? Especially given how pissed she was at her father for his suck-it-up-and-go-apologize response to her quitting.

"Great choice." He nodded appreciatively. "You do know how to *burn rubber*, right?"

"Nope." *Not the first clue.* "That's why God invented YouTube."

"Would you like me to show you?"

Bea blinked at the suggestion. Not just because a member of the police force offering to help (wasn't that aiding and abetting?) her break the laws he was sworn to upheld didn't seem right but by how swiftly it had been delivered. "Wouldn't that be wrong? You showing me how to commit an offense? What number was it again?"

"Number two three nine."

Bea was pretty sure that hadn't been the number and Austin was just pulling these statutes out of his ass, but she honestly didn't care.

"If I'm on duty, in my uniform, not a good look, but when I'm off duty and I'm just Joe Citizen? Then Arlo's gotta catch me first."

He broke into a broad grin, and Bea laughed despite herself. But, hell, there was no denying doing something like that made her nervous. "I don't know, maybe I have to work up to that one?" She should choose something less risky as her opening salvo.

"Bok, bok, bok."

"Really?"

"Come on, Bea*trice*. Ask yourself, WWDD?"

Trying not to get sidetracked by how good her name sounded on his lips, Bea tried to figure out what WWDD meant. She came up empty. "Okay. I give up. What the hell is WWDD?"

He smiled a smile then of such supreme confidence and sex appeal, Bea didn't just feel it between her legs—it reverberated through her entire reproductive tract.

"What Would Dean Do," he said, then waggled his eyebrows.

Bea laughed. What would Dean do? Well hell...what *wouldn't* Dean do? Burning a bit of rubber was very low on the hazard scale compared to, say, *demon slaying*. Bea had to admit, WWDD might be a very good catchphrase going forward. Why not use him for bravado as well as eye candy?

"Okay." She nodded. "Let's do it."

"Great," Austin said, and Bea noticed how he was very careful not to seem too triumphant, but he was clearly pleased by her agreement. "I know the perfect spot. Why don't I pick you up just after four out front of Déjà Brew?"

"Oh, sorry." Bea remembered she had a prior commitment. "Can't."

"You have someplace else better to be?" One eyebrow kicked up. "Got a hot date?"

"As it happens, I do." Dean and Sam were calling. "The Winchester brothers wait for no one." She picked up her napkin and dabbed at her mouth to wipe away any pancake crumbs.

"How about same time tomorrow afternoon?"

She'd have finished the season by then, and it was time she stopped hiding out in her apartment. Credence might just be a stopgap for her while she figured out what she wanted to do with the rest of her life, but she had every intention of getting fully involved, so it was time she stuck her head outside.

Might as well start with Officer Syrup Lips by her side.

"Yep," he confirmed. "Sounds like a date."

"Nope." Bea eyed him seriously. She might want orgasms and Austin Cooper *was* outrageously unsuitable, but younger men cut a little too close to home for her and was a line she would not cross.

And, in the meantime, she'd brought her vibrator. Sure, it had been a long time since she'd used it, but it had three speed settings and it never snored, ate soup too loudly, or stared at other women's boobs.

"Definitely not a date," she said. "A purely instructional joint outing."

"Okay." He shrugged. "Whatever."

Bea was so used to men always trying to push their own agendas or take an inch, she didn't know what to do with one who wasn't.

"See you tomorrow," she said before heading to the counter for her pie, excruciatingly conscious of every eye in the diner following her progress but of one pair in particular staring at her like twin X-ray beams, trying to discern the word Thursday stamped across her ass.

CHAPTER FIVE

Austin nodded to Jenny the next afternoon as he leaned his shoulder into the frame of the open door of her café.

"Hey," she greeted. "Sorry, I've just cleaned the machine. I can still do a mocha frappe or something, though, if you want? Or there's soda in the fridge."

"I'm good, thanks, Jenny." He touched the brim of his hat. "Just waiting for Beatrice."

"Oh." She blinked at him, clearly surprised. "I hope you're not harassing her, Austin Cooper."

Austin smiled at the thought. Harassing women wasn't his thing—professionally or privately. Credence wasn't exactly flush with women his age, but Denver wasn't that far away, and it *was* flush with women who loved a man in uniform.

"No, ma'am." He might have gone home, showered, and traded his uniform for jeans, boots, and a T-shirt, but some habits were ingrained, and sometimes a *ma'am* was required. "I've just offered to…show her around."

There wasn't any point in divulging the exact nature of their afternoon mission. He might be okay pushing the limits of the law, but Arlo was a stickler for it, and there was no doubt in Austin's mind that Arlo *would* write him up without thinking twice. There was no need to advertise.

"Oh." She cocked an eyebrow. "I see. That's right neighborly of you."

Austin grinned at the I-call-bullshit tone in Jenny's voice. He shrugged. "What can I say? My mama raised me right."

She grinned back. "Yes, she did."

"Hey."

Austin turned at the soft voice behind him to find Beatrice. She was clearly not dressing to impress him, with yet another pair of baggy sweats teamed with a plaid shirt that sat loose around her hips, the sleeves rolled up to her elbows. But it was unstained as far as he could tell, and her hair was soft around her face and shoulders, fluffy like feathers, and appeared not only brushed but like she might have actually washed it.

From what he'd seen so far of her clothing style, this was practically formal.

There was probably something really wrong with him that he found her don't-give-a-fuck and show-as-little-skin-as-possible fashion choices such a turn-on. Yeah, they were still having some cold snaps in these parts, but until this point in his life, Austin had been much in favor of the show-all-the-skin school of fashion. He was a twenty-five-year-old male in his prime who loved how women put themselves together, and while ogling was a dick move, respectful appreciation was not.

And hell if he wasn't appreciating Beatrice right now.

There was just something about her all covered up that made him want to *unwrap* her. Made him wonder if she'd taken his underwear advice and was wearing her Friday panties. And that plaid shirt...*fuck yeah*. It was a make and a style he'd always considered overwhelmingly masculine—he had about a zillion of them at home—but the way the V-neck sat in her cleavage and formed the most intriguing little shadow made it sexy and seductive and utterly female.

"Hey," he said, pushing out of his lean, hoping he sounded cool and laid-back, when in actuality, his tongue felt like it was glued to the roof of his mouth.

"Hi, Bea," Jenny said.

Bea… Austin rolled that around in his head. He liked Bea. It suited her.

She looked past him to Jenny behind the counter. "Hey."

"I see you're finally getting out and about?" she said.

"It's time."

Jenny laughed. "You're in safe hands there."

Austin wasn't sure he could guarantee that—at the moment his hands were up for a whole lotta *un*safe behavior. Unfortunately, Beatrice had made it very clear she wanted to keep a boundary between them. Which was fine. Particularly when she was vague about how long she was sticking around.

"Shall we go?" he asked, gesturing to his truck, which was angle-parked at the curb.

Bea frowned at the vehicle. "That's your car?"

"Yup." Austin had to admit his silver two-door Ford pickup wasn't the most elegant automobile specimen in the world. It was a work vehicle and had been ten years old when he'd bought it last year, because he knew he was returning to Credence. There was a ding in the tail gate and the odd pockmark in the panels, and he hadn't washed it in a while. "It's perfect for what we're about to do."

It was big and sturdy. Heavy. Not made to be light and responsive and fancy. Something that'd grip the road and keep them steady and stable.

"You wanna take the Beamer for a spin instead?"

Austin blinked. Ah…*hell yes*. He might be a pickup kinda guy, but he'd be more likely to see aliens in his lifetime than ever sit in, never mind *own*, a BMW.

It was like asking him if he wanted a hand job or a blow job. They had the same end result, and really any touching of the penis was pretty damn fine, but one was a more superior experience.

Jesus, dude, do not *think about BJs right now.* "Hell yes."

She grinned. "Come on, then. It's parked around back."

"Just gotta grab something. I'll be right behind you."

"Okay."

Austin watched her go. That shirt… He was seriously hot for how well she wore that shirt.

"You playing statues out there, Austin?"

He glanced over to find Jenny beaming at him from inside the café. He smiled sheepishly, touching the brim of his hat as he said, "No, ma'am," then quickly covered the distance to his pickup, grabbed the brown paper bag from the seat, clicked the locks—a habit he hadn't kicked from Denver—and followed after Beatrice.

She was sitting in the passenger seat, waiting for him as he crossed the parking lot, which did funny things to Austin's gut. But that was temporarily forgotten as the sleek quality of her vehicle took precedence. When he'd first seen the M3, he'd thought it was black, but with the afternoon sun bathing it in gentle light, he could see it was a deep midnight blue with the magnificent attention to design and detail for which the German car maker was known.

Austin didn't hesitate to open the driver's door and slide into the softness and comfort of the leather seats. *Achtung, baby.*

"Electronic seat adjust at the side," Beatrice said.

Of course there was. Austin fiddled with it to accommodate the length of his legs, then he tossed his hat and the packet containing Annie's pie on the back seat and buckled up. Before starting the engine, he took a second to just absorb the moment, one hand resting on the wheel, the other on the rounded knob of the stick shift. Rolling his head along the padded headrest, he faced Bea with a smile and said, *"Nice."*

And he wasn't just talking about the car.

She started to smile but then faltered. "Do I smell pie?"

Austin laughed. The woman was some kind of bloodhound

when it came to pie. All he could smell was leather and that unique blend of plastics and chemicals that made up the quintessential aroma known universally as *new car smell*.

Grabbing the brown packet from the back seat, he handed it over. "I stopped at Annie's. I don't know if you've tried any of her cream pie yet, but I swear, it's almost a religious experience."

Bea didn't take the packet. "Thanks, but I think I'll pass, thank you. I've eaten so much pie these past couple of weeks, I swear I can hear my pancreas sobbing late at night. I'm going to have an ass as wide as the Grand Canyon if I keep this up."

Austin thought how very, very sad it was that Bea would deprive herself of one of the nicest things a person could put in their mouth because society judged women on the size of their asses. She'd told him two days ago she was going to eat pies more often, and here she was already tempering her appetites. Screw that. If he did nothing else for Bea, he could feed her pie.

Personally, if that's what she wanted.

The woman looked good in this BMW but nowhere near as good as she looked when she was eating pie and making those appreciative little noises that went straight to his groin. Austin opened the packet to allow the smell to waft out, and he swore she leaned in a little more.

"Are you sure? It sounds like you've spent a lot of time *not* eating pie or any kind of carbs. Why not make up for lost time?"

She sighed. "Because I'm thirty-five and I don't"—her eyes traveled over him, up and down, in a way that probably should have made Austin feel objectified. It did not—"look like you."

"Hell, Bea." He stopped abruptly when he realized what he'd said. "Sorry, can I call you Bea?"

"Oh…" She paused for the briefest of moments, but Austin noticed. "Sure."

And wasn't that a ringing endorsement? "But...you don't want me to?"

"No, it's fine." She gave a quick shake of her head. "Everyone calls me Bea."

Yeah. Except Austin didn't want to be lumped in with *everyone*. "Beatri*ss*," he said, dragging out the end syllable a little as he ran with his gut feeling. "Life's too short not to eat pie. Eat the damn thing. If you want"—he waggled his eyebrows—"I'll keep an eye on your ass for you."

Her lips twitched. "You're an ass man, huh?"

"No, ma'am. I don't play favorites. I like *all* the bits."

It was gratifying to hear the hitch in her breath and watch her throat undulate like it was a little hard to swallow. "Well," she said, her voice thick, "are we doing this or not?"

"Are you eating that or not?" Austin parried.

Glancing at the packet in his hand like she'd temporarily forgotten it existed, she opened the glove box, took the packet off him, and stashed it inside. "Maybe later."

It wasn't quite the same as watching her eat pie, but it wasn't a no, either, so Austin shelved his disappointment. "Okay," he said, his finger hovering over the ignition button, hesitating for a beat or two. "Are you sure you want to do this in your *very* nice car?"

She nodded firmly. "Yup."

"Beatrice, it's an eighty-thousand-dollar car. You sure you want to take some rubber off the tires?"

She stared at him for a moment as if trying to compute what he'd said, and then she barked out a laugh. "Oh, Austin. It's a *hundred-thousand-dollar* car, and the answer is still yes."

Christ. Austin whistled. "One hundred big ones? And you...lease it...or...?"

His mama always told him it was impolite to ask about someone's financial status, but his ass was sitting in some serious money right now.

"I own it." She grinned. "Outright."

"Man...so you're, like...loaded or something?"

Apart from Wade Carter, the only other person he knew with serious money was some guy he'd gone to high school with whose old man had paid seventy-five thousand for some stud Wagyu semen for his herd cows.

But for damn sure, a BMW trumped bull spunk any day.

She grinned. "I do all right. I've worked in advertising for fifteen years at a prestigious LA firm. The last seven years I've been a junior executive. The salary package was generous, the bonuses even more so, and I'm still making rent on my apartment in California. Suffice to say, I don't have to run out and get a job anytime soon."

"So you're just going to...swan around in your Beamer, being a lady of leisure, huh?"

"For a while." She quirked an eyebrow. "Intimidated?"

Austin shook his head slowly. "A little turned on, to be honest." He liked that she wasn't being coy about her achievements. She sounded pretty kick-ass to him.

She laughed. "Not happening, Officer Cooper."

He didn't answer, just pushed the button and revved the engine as it gunned to life. "Let's go burn some rubber."

CHAPTER SIX

"So? Why Credence?"

Beatrice glanced away from the Farewell from Credence sign they'd just passed to take in Austin. She'd been trying to pretend he and his flirty eyes and his flirty tongue and his flirty pie and his very flirty *a little turned on, to be honest* weren't sitting so damn close. Even staring out her window, though, he was still a tempting hunk of man in her peripheral vision. The temptation level increased a hundredfold when she was looking right at him.

"Would you believe the throw of a dart?" she replied.

He laughed, and it was rich and deep and also flirty. Okay, maybe it wasn't. That was probably just her reading too much into everything.

"No way."

"Yes way." Beatrice nodded. "I threw a dart at a map, and it landed on Credence."

"So you're telling me that of all the places in the continental United States, the dart hit Credence?"

"Well...eventually, yes."

He quirked an eyebrow in her direction. "Eventually?"

"The process was a little more convoluted than that."

"Oh, this sounds good." He laughed. "Convoluted how?"

"Well, see, I drew a big red ring around all the central states because I wanted to go to a small town and get away from as many people as possible because, frankly, people *suck*."

He nodded. "They really do."

Bea supposed she was preaching to the choir with an officer of the law. "Then I enlarged that part of the map up until it was about three feet by three feet and stuck it to my wall and threw a dart at it."

"And the dart *eventually* landed on Credence? So, what… You kept throwing until you hit something that sounded okay?"

"No." She shot him a withering look. "First, it took me several throws to actually hit the map." The first one hadn't even made the wall, and the second one hit the wall sideways. It took a few more after that to get the dart *on* the map, as several small holes in her wall could attest.

He laughed again. "What?"

"It was late," she huffed. "I'm not exactly the most coordinated person in the world, and there may have been alcohol involved."

"Sounds like you'll be perfect for the Credence darts team."

Credence has a darts team? "Credence has a darts team?"

Austin laughed harder. "I'm just messing with you."

"Oh, I see, baiting the city girl, huh?" Feigning insult, Bea returned her attention to the window. "For that, you don't get the rest of the story."

"Okay, okay. No more city-girl baiting, I promise."

Bea pressed her lips together so she wouldn't smile as she kept her gaze firmly trained on the flat landscape whizzing by.

"Come on, Beatrice, spill. You know you want to."

And hell if she wouldn't have told him she'd seen aliens at Roswell if he'd asked. "Fine." She rolled her head to look at him again. "When I did start hitting the map, many of my throws landed in areas where there wasn't a town, while others landed between two towns or just outside a town."

"Who knew it'd be so complicated, right?"

He was clearly having some fun at her expense, but it was good-natured and Bea, just as good-naturedly, ignored him and continued. "And I'd made a pact with myself to only go with a place where the dart hit the town dot square in the middle. It needed to be definitive."

"And how many throws did it take to land on Credence?"

Bea sniffed. "Eleven. Or maybe it was twelve." She held up a finger. "Don't you dare laugh."

Pressing his lips together, Austin said, "No, ma'am."

Oh, sweet baby Jesus. This man could *yes ma'am, no ma'am* her all day. Throw in a *Beatrice* or two and she'd be happy as a clam here in Credence.

"So," he said, valiantly trying to keep a straight face as the BMW efficiently ate up the miles, "the dart landed on Credence *eventually* and you just moved here. On a whim?"

"Pretty much."

"That's…" He shook his head as if searching for the right word. "Brave."

"What?" Bea's face screwed up. "No." He was joking, right? "Brave is what *you* do. It's what our soldiers do and our firemen and everyone else out there who puts their life on the line every day in their job or for a cause they believe in. I was just…*done* with my old life, and I'm lucky enough, *privileged* enough to be able to pick up and take off and land somewhere completely random without a second thought. Not everyone can do that."

"Yeah." He nodded slowly. "That's very true." And he lapsed into apparent contemplation for long moments. "So," he said, finally breaking the silence, "where did you *almost* end up? Which dart throws got close?"

Bea remembered that night, three days after quitting. Three days of stewing, which had led to her decision to get the hell out of Dodge. She might have had a little too much wine affecting her thought processes *and* her throwing arm, but she remembered at least some of the contenders. "Colby in Kansas. Douglas in Wyoming. Farmington in Missouri."

He flicked a glance at her. "Well, may I say, Kansas's, Wyoming's, and Missouri's loss is our gain."

Well, hell yes, Officer Smooth Talker, you may.

His low compliment slid into all the places that still felt raw and angry and *pissed* about how all her ambitions had come crashing down, soothing them like a cool cloth on feverish skin. It should be illegal for this man to flirt. Or just...be nice, really. To women who were thirty-five and going through a major identity crisis.

Bea wasn't sure what she was supposed to say to that other than something unintelligible like, *"Hunhmmph,"* but Austin's attention switched back as he slowed the car and flicked on the turn signal. She glanced at the approaching intersection: a big, old red barn that looked like it had seen better days sat on the corner, and a sign indicated the lake was thirty miles down the road.

It took another few minutes after turning right to reach their destination, during which Austin was silent again. *Thank you, God.* It was bad enough that the bulk of his thigh sitting snug within the confines of his blue jeans was like a flashing light in her peripheral vision. She didn't need him *ma'am*ing her and *Beatrice*ing her and encouraging her to eat pie on top of all that.

He turned the car into what looked like an abandoned industrial estate on the left. It was dominated by deserted concrete shells that might have once housed businesses. There was a general air of decay. Peeling paint, broken windows, pockmarked exteriors. Even the graffiti was faded. Aged tire tracks stained streets that nature had taken back. Weeds thrived in the cracks of the road and the pavements and even the walls of buildings. Bea absently thought it'd be the perfect place to film a zombie movie. Or murder someone.

He hooked some lefts and rights until he was driving into a

large abandoned parking lot with plenty of space to do illegal things with a motor vehicle in relative safety. Which led her to thoughts of other illegal things they could do with a motor vehicle that involved the back seat, not the back tires. Which really wasn't helpful.

Stopping in the center of the lot, he turned off the engine, and the low rumble cut out, the silence suddenly charged. He half turned in his seat to face her. "You sure about this?"

Bea appreciated that he kept checking on her, but she really didn't need such propriety. Yes, this was the first time she'd ever done anything remotely reckless, but she'd never felt so damn *alive*. The echo of her own heartbeat was already growing louder in her ears and pulsing through her temples and her fingertips. And they hadn't done a damn thing yet.

Just the thought of what they were about to do and the endless list of possibilities of what they *could* do out here was making her breathy and squirmy. A potent mix of anticipation and danger brewed in her veins, and the sudden need to do *something* with it rode her hard. It made her edgy and...*horny*. It was burn rubber or reach over and yank down Austin's fly.

"I am."

"Okay." He pushed the start button again. "Watch and learn."

Bea listened intently as Austin went through the process of how to perform a perfect burnout while the car was stationary. She watched his feet movements on the brake and clutch and accelerator and how he held the wheel. His instructions were clear and easy to follow, his teaching style impressing her probably way more than it should. And her gaze didn't wander once to his mouth or the way his throat moved as he spoke because she wanted to get this thing right the first time and impress *him*.

With the theory part of the lesson over, he said, "And now for the demo. Hang on to your seat."

A thrill the size of a tsunami zipped up Bea's spine as she slid a hand to each side of her seat and curled her fingers into the leather. Austin revved the engine just as he'd talked about, and it *roared* responsively. Everything inside the car vibrated with the throaty noise, including her seat, which was kinda dangerous given her current rather excitable state.

Next, with one hand on the wheel and the other on the gear knob, his feet worked the pedals. The tires squealed loudly, and the back of the car started to slip and slide a little as the wheels spun, but the vehicle held its ground. Bea could feel the urgent prowl of the car chomping at the bit to be set free, and her heart rate spiked. A plume of white smoke enveloped the car, shrouding the way ahead in a toxic cloud as the squealing seemed to get louder and her pulse roared in frantic syncopation.

And then, despite hardly anything being visible through the windshield, they were moving forward in a straight line. Or as far as Bea could tell, anyway. They weren't speeding but definitely accelerating, the engine revving, the back wheels squealing, the smoke getting thicker. Her breath hitched in her throat, her heart rate catapulting into the stroke range. It felt like they were going to either rocket into space or her tires were about to burst into balls of flame, and who knew that could be so damn exciting?

If this was foreplay in the drag-race world, then sign her up.

They'd barely gone any distance at all when Austin braked and the revs cut out, and they were just sitting in the unused parking lot, smoke gradually dissipating with nothing but the low rumble of the engine and the sound of her ragged breathing.

Holy freaking moly—who needed drugs when there was burning rubber?

"Okay, Beatrice," he said. "Your turn."

CHAPTER SEVEN

Putting the car in neutral, Austin undid his seat belt, opened his door, and exited. Bea stared after him, not moving for a beat or two, her hands and her legs shaking so hard from adrenaline and anticipation. Then he was at her door, opening it, blue denim filling her vision. "You don't have to do this."

Oh *yes*, she did. She really, *really* needed to do this. If it had felt this good as a passenger, how good must it feel to be the one in the driver's seat? Bea had been kicked out of the driver's seat of her life, and she wanted it back.

And really, the only true question was: WWDD?

Unclipping her seat belt with fingers that refused to cooperate took longer than Bea would have liked, but she finally managed, climbing out of the car on unsteady legs, her gaze locking with his for the briefest moment. And in that nanosecond, with the acrid stench of burned rubber making her dizzy, she saw the same reckless kind of craving lurking in his eyes she knew lurked in her own. She wondered if he could feel it in every cell of his body like she could?

Feel it in every atom of oxygen in his lungs?

Passing by him, she scuttled around the idling car on her still-trembling legs to the driver's side, praying like hell she didn't trip over her feet and fall on her face. She didn't.

After sliding into the driver's seat, Bea shut the door with a reassuring *thunk* and buckled up.

"Okay, remember what I said?"

Yes. *No.* Yes. Bea nodded. "Sure." She could do this.

"Good. Turn the car around so it's facing back the other way, so you have plenty of road ahead."

Bea's hands slid onto the wheel. It was thick and solid as she wrapped her fingers around the circumference, the soft leather cover giving it an almost silky feel. She'd never noticed until right now with every cell in her body in a state of frisson and Officer Sexy Mouth beside her generating pheromones by the bucketload, just how phallic a steering wheel could feel as it slid between her curled fingers.

Thankfully the smoke had cleared, and Bea was able to put the car into first and follow his instructions. In less than a minute, they were stationary in the parking lot, facing the opposite direction. She revved the engine just for the hell of it, and her inner thigh muscles contracted deliciously at the corresponding roar.

Her nipples went hard as nickels.

"You ready for this?" His voice was low and loaded, and Bea was pretty sure he wasn't just asking about the burnout. But that was all she had eyes for right now. The asphalt ahead, the mad skip of her pulse, and the drag of her lungs as she revved the engine several more times.

With her foot planted squarely on the brake, the car roared like a 737, and lust and sex and anticipation swelled in Bea so hard and so fast every fiber in her belly pulled taut.

"That's it," he said, "good hold."

His compliment was low in her ear. Or maybe it wasn't, but she could barely hear him over the thrum of her pulse through her head. Bea's face heated and her breathing grew thicker as the wheels started to spin and the tires squealed on the asphalt and the smoke started to billow up in the rear window.

She was doing it. Holding this screeching, belching,

demanding animal in place, snarling and snapping to be let free, with just her feet and her hands and her freaking *mind*, and she'd never been more terrified or more turned on in her life.

"Good," Austin murmured, just audible over the jungle beat of her heart. "Ease her out now, but keep her close."

Bea did as she was told, the car slewing crazily to one side for a moment as it squealed to be let go, but she pulled it back in to its forward trajectory, her knuckles blanching as they tightened around the steering wheel and thick white smoke billowed around them. She drove the vehicle about thirty or forty feet, keeping the beast well and truly leashed, before bringing it to a screeching halt.

Silence filled the car, and Bea finally let out her breath as she put it into neutral, the taut bow of her body slumping against the seat.

"Holy shit," she whispered, raising her trembling hands and staring at them, her body one giant reverberating *thrum*.

He laughed a great honking laugh. "You did it."

Bea turned her head and stared at him. "I did, didn't I?" And she laughed, too. Pressing her hands to her chest, she laughed in a way she hadn't laughed in years.

"You did that like a pro," he said when their laughter finally faded.

"That's because I had a good teacher."

"Well…" He shrugged, feigning an aww-shucks expression. "I don't like to brag."

Bea raised eyebrows that hadn't had any kind of sculpting in well over a month and probably looked like twin giant pornstaches high on her forehead. "But you will."

"I think someone who can get you all flushed with excitement like that deserves a moment to shine."

She didn't need a mirror to know she was pink-cheeked; she could feel the heat radiating off her face. She felt—and no doubt looked—like a *wildling*. "This isn't excitement. This is terror." It was amazing how closely the two were related.

Laughing again, he said, "Feels good, doesn't it?"

It felt freaking amazing. Best thing she'd ever done with her clothes on. This whole being-reckless, living-on-the-edge thing was utterly titillating. Every cell in her body *buzzed* with accomplishment. Was this how her mom felt when she'd been in the middle of one of her impromptu painting frenzies and she wouldn't sleep or eat or bathe, yet she seemed to glow from the inside out?

And why in the hell wasn't the mere thought of that scaring the crap out of her?

God…who even *was* she right now? Sitting here burning rubber in a hideously expensive car with a guy—a police officer—ten years younger than her, in a town literally in the middle of nowhere.

Maybe she *was* like her mother. As her grandmother so often said.

She'd never meant it as a compliment, though, and those words had always made her father tense, but whatever was happening right now wasn't *her*. Bea couldn't remember the last time anything less than scoring a major account was able to get her this jazzed.

But she was damned if she was going to give Officer Sexy Teacher any heads-up as to the internal fireworks going off inside her at the moment. She had the feeling he'd know exactly what to do with them. "Like I said," Bea replied noncommittally, trying to rein in the flood of exhilaration, "you're a good teacher. Some people suck at it."

"I bet you're a good teacher, too. I bet there are things you could teach me."

He grinned at her, and his eyes were sparkling and the skin around the corners of his eyes crinkled and he was teasing her and so *in* to teasing her, it was causing a funny skip in her pulse.

She doubted very much that she could teach Austin Cooper what he was implying. She was no Mrs. Robinson. Whereas he, on the other hand, looked like he'd been born with *The Joy of Sex* chip already fully integrated with his *mainframe.*

He could probably teach *her* a thing or two...

But the engine was idling at just the right level of rumble, keeping everything on a kind of simmer, and Bea was finding it increasingly hard to take a deep breath, and she just wanted to lean in and kiss that smile right off his mouth.

Which wasn't going to happen.

She might be in the middle of a personal and career crisis that had knocked her on her ass and left her questioning every single thing she ever knew about *everything*, but she knew this—kissing Austin Cooper would be a bad move. Putting aside the fact that getting tangled up with a younger man hadn't ended well for her mother, Austin was a human being. Not a distraction. Not someone to play with to make herself feel better or forget.

Credence was her home—for the time being. It was a... circuit breaker. A place to hide away and regroup. When she figured out what she wanted to do next, she'd be moving on, and she didn't want to leave with any ill will surrounding her stay.

"Unless you're into brand analysis and what age demographics are more or less likely to buy perfume, halogen lamps, or canned salmon, *and* where these demographics intersect, probably not."

He nodded and deadpanned, "That sounds totally hot."

Bea laughed. "Uh-huh. Sure it is."

"Sounds like you have a lot of..." For a moment, Bea thought he was going to say *useless crap*, but he didn't. "Data inside that head."

Oh yeah. Bea had critical levels of data, aka *useless crap*, taking up space in her head. Hell, she could be on an episode of *Hoarders*, it was that cluttered up there.

At least here in Credence, she could Marie Kondo the hell out of her brain.

"I do." And she was done thinking about it. "But I'm on a high here—don't spoil it."

"Fine by me." He shrugged. "So...what *do* you want to do now?"

The question was about as loaded as was possible and, because she was *amped up* and *kiss Austin* was whispering through her head, she grabbed the next sweetest option. "Pie."

His left eyebrow kicked up. "I thought you were worried about your ass?"

Not as worried as she was about what she might do with her mouth if it wasn't busy doing something else. "What can I say? Recklessness makes me hungry."

He grinned. "Lucky me." Then, turning his attention to the glove box—thank you, sweet Jesus—he pulled out the brown paper packet and handed it over.

Bea was salivating even before the waft of sugar filled her nostrils. She pulled out the very generous slice of coconut cream pie and, while it wasn't an orgasm, it was the next best thing she'd allow herself inside the BMW. She stared at it longingly before glancing at Austin, who was looking at it like it was the answer to world peace. "You want half?"

He raised his eyes to meet hers. "I couldn't possibly deprive you." And the way he said *deprive* left Bea in little doubt he wasn't just talking about pie. His eyes seemed to be saying that deprivation was wholly unnatural. Wholly unnecessary. He tipped his chin at the airy concoction of cream and sugar. "You go ahead."

Bea smiled. "That was *so* the right answer."

"I'll watch."

Bea rolled her eyes. "You, Officer, are a pervert."

She didn't know if he responded, he may well have made

some reply, but Bea didn't hear anything from the second she bit into the pie. Sweetness infused her taste buds; the lightness of cream and the buttery flakiness of pastry followed in rapid succession. The crunch of toasted coconut brought up the rear. The heady essence of vanilla filled her nostrils. A choir of freaking angels sang the "Hallelujah" chorus.

"Oh...my...God," she muttered, barely chewing and swallowing the first mouthful before she went in for the second. She'd already known that Annie was a pie goddess, but this pie was something else. Something...otherworldly. She glanced at Austin. "Seriously," she said around her mouthful. "Annie's the devil, isn't she?"

He chuckled. "Didn't I tell you it was a religious experience?"

Bea shook her head. "I think the word you're searching for is *cult*."

Indulging like this was a hedonism that bordered on sexual. Completely selfish, utterly thrilling. And between the adrenaline charge of burning rubber in her BMW and the sheer oral indulgence of Annie's coconut cream pie, Bea had a new insight into the pull of the risqué. Of just surrendering to the decadence of pleasure and to hell with the consequences.

A new insight to her mother.

On the third bite, she actually moaned while plotting where they could build their pie-cult compound, and she knew she was putting on a spectacle by the intensity of Austin's gaze on her mouth, but she couldn't help it. How anyone could eat this piece of pie and not be vocal with their appreciation, she had no idea. That would be like watching Dean Winchester strip naked and *not* sigh/whimper/drool.

Or all three at once.

But she was not Austin's personal live-feed food (or other) porn channel, and this wasn't the way to set boundaries.

"Here," she said, pushing the pie in his direction, because

even though he'd already declined, there was little else to do in the stationary, idling car except eat, and the thought of smearing it on his neck and licking it off was presenting itself as a perfectly acceptable way to eat right now. Inviting him to take his own bite seemed safer. "I'm not giving you half, but for introducing me to this wonder, you get a bite."

He glanced at the offering. "It's fine. I know what it tastes like, and watching you is much more satisfying."

Oh, hell…he really shouldn't be talking now. She nudged the pie closer about an inch from his mouth. "I insist."

After a beat or two of heated looks, Austin leaned in, opened his mouth, and bit into the soft center of the pie before pulling away, licking cream off his lips as he went. And now he was *her* food porn channel.

Holy shit. Stop it, Beatrice. Pull yourself together.

"Did the police academy teach you how to do that?" she asked, leaping on the first thing that came into her head. Conversation was a good distraction, right?

"Eat pie?"

Bea rolled her eyes but was pleased to be steering away from the teetering edge of their attraction. "Burnouts."

"Ah." He chuckled. "No. I grew up on a ranch just outside Credence. As soon as I could reach the pedals, I was driving. My older brother taught me how to spin the wheels, and there were a lot of bonfire nights with buddies where we burned a helluva lot of rubber."

He laughed, the kind of laugh that was soft with good times. She could picture him as a teenager, the glow of a roaring fire lighting his face as he climbed into his pickup, all legs and hormones—ten feet tall and bulletproof. She wondered if he'd known then that one day he was going to turn a woman on with sheer horse—and pie—power alone.

Without even touching her.

His hand splayed on his chest as he laughed, and the

relaxed, un-self-conscious gesture was somehow endearing as all get-out. He wasn't censoring himself around her—this wasn't Austin the cop in the car with her.

This was Austin the man.

He shook his head absently, his hand falling to his lap. "It's a wonder we didn't kill ourselves. My mother would have whooped our asses if she'd known what we were getting up to half the time."

Bea felt the obvious affection for the place he grew up and for his family like a tangible force. He wore it like a halo. And a pang of what felt very much like envy cramped through her chest. It wasn't the first time she'd ever wished she'd had a different upbringing in a house full of love and family, but it had been a very long time since she had.

"You have just the one older brother?"

"And four older sisters."

Bea blinked. *Four* older sisters? No wonder the guy had taken her...*quirks* in stride. He was clearly used to being around women.

"Two live in Wyoming now. One in Delaware. The other lives three counties over."

There was that soft affection again.

"You miss the ranch?" she asked as she nibbled more sedately at the pie, trying to make it last.

"Hardly." He grinned. "I still live there. Moved back home when I left Denver last year."

Bea stopped chewing for a split second. *What?* Oh no. Oh *dear God*, no. "You live with your parents?"

"Yes."

If that didn't scream younger man, Bea had no idea what did. God...she was lusting over a guy who still lived at home with *Mom and Dad*.

What was wrong with her?

"So does my brother and his wife, Jill. The ranch is big

enough for all of us, and I'm able to lend a hand around the place."

Clearly it sounded like the most natural thing in the world for Austin, but it was just the bucket of cold water she needed. "I see."

She bit into the pie again, not really tasting it anymore. Well, she had started this conversation to distract her from Austin Cooper eating pie, and it had certainly achieved its goal.

"I especially like the laundry detergent Mom uses and the way she irons my work pants and still cuts the crusts off my sandwiches when she fixes my lunch."

Bea blinked. "Right." His *mother* still ironed his clothes and made his lunch?

Suddenly he burst into laughter, slapping his thigh and doing that hand-splayed-across-his-chest thing again. "Oh my God, you should see your expression." He laughed some more and pointed at her face. "You look like you don't know whether to be outraged or disgusted."

Right now, as a cooling surge of relief hit her system, Bea was just grateful. More than she wanted to admit for a woman who wasn't supposed to be invested in Austin Cooper and what he did and didn't do. His mother could still tuck him in at night and kiss his boo-boos better for all she cared.

She narrowed her eyes at him. "Very funny. So you don't live at home?"

"Oh, no, I do live on the ranch. But I have my own cabin and wash and iron my own clothes. And fix my own lunch. In fact, I'm quite handy in the kitchen."

He was looking at her as if waiting for praise for his stunning example of modern masculinity. Which made him shit out of luck. "What? You want me to throw you a parade because you know how not to starve to death?"

"Hell no." He laughed. "I was just thinking you might like to come to dinner one night so I can impress you with my prowess."

Aaaand they were back to the flirting and the innuendo.

Because for damn sure, he wasn't just talking about his cooking prowess. She didn't need a crystal ball to know how that would go down, holed up in a rustic cabin with Austin at his most flirty and charming, seducing her with food and the way he said *Beatrice* like it finished with an *S*. Or several of them.

Bea*trisss*.

"And ruin my reputation as the town hermit?" she quipped.

He laughed, and the way it brushed against all Bea's erogenous zones was decidedly wicked. The man had a very *busy* laugh. Glancing at the last couple of mouthfuls of pie balancing on her fingertips, she pushed it in his direction again. "Here. Last bit for you."

"Nah." He waved it away. "All yours."

"Can't, I'm stuffed full." Which was true—it had been an enormous slice, and he looked like the kinda guy who was a bottomless pit with all that muscle mass and his twenty-five-year-young metabolism. "And it would be a crime to waste it."

He shook his head. "Bea*triss*, that would be a *sin*."

And then, instead of reaching for the remaining pie with his hand, like she'd expected, he leaned in again, opened his lips, and took it with his mouth. Bea's breath caught in her throat as the tip of his tongue swept over the pads of her fingers, followed by hot, wet suction as he slowly pulled away and her fingers slid from his mouth.

It was an utterly filthy, low-down move.

"Thank you," he said around the mouthful as he sat back a little, clearly savoring the taste.

Bea barely moved; in fact, her fingers were still kind of hovering halfway between them, mesmerized by the heat in his gaze, the moist sheen of his lips, and the slick of cream at the corner of his mouth.

"You have…"

She pointed at the small white dollop, but the sentence

kinda drifted away as she stared at it. Bea had never been gripped with the urge to lick food off another person's mouth. Which, to be fair to herself, was a reasonable standard of hygiene, but maybe it was just another indicator of how lacking her life had been.

Nevertheless, here she was, *needing* to lick the cream off Austin's mouth. God...her life really *was* spiraling out of control.

"What?" His voice was low, his gaze finding and locking with hers, his eyes hot and probing and...daring. "What do I have?" he asked as he leaned in ever so slightly.

Bea couldn't tell if the noise bubbling around them was the rumble of the engine or the staccato beat of her heart. All she was conscious of was his heat and his intensity and the way his eyes had dropped to focus on *her* mouth.

God. Oh God, oh God, oh God.

And then, the sweet smell of pie and the heady effects of adrenaline still sizzling through her system joined forces, goading her to do *it*. To forget the past and live in the moment, just this one moment.

Kiss that cream off his mouth. Enjoy every sweet second.

And for once in her life, she forgot about being the daughter of a woman who had run away with a younger man— abandoning her kid and ruining her marriage in the process— and just did it.

Leaning swiftly in, she closed the gap between their mouths as if she'd been doing it forever instead of for the first time. Her hand slid into the back of his hair as her mouth landed on the corner of his and settled there, her tongue automatically lapping at the seal of his lips.

She heard herself sigh and a noise from the back of his throat that may have been a strangled kind of groan. But neither of them pushed to deepen the kiss. Frankly, Bea's pulse was hammering so hard, her cardiovascular system couldn't have taken the extra stimulation. She just sat there, holding his head in place, enjoying the soft yield of his mouth and the taste of his lips and the utter thrill of being in the moment.

She'd met Austin three days ago, and now here she was, breaking all the rules with him.

Pushing all her limits, tangling herself up with a younger man.

It was just the thought she needed to bring her back to reality, and she withdrew, sitting back in her seat. "I'm sorry." She grimaced even as she fought the urge to go back for more. "I should *not* have done that."

"Because you're going to want to keep doing it?"

Bea laughed despite her inner turmoil. "You have a very healthy ego—anyone ever tell you that?"

"I have been told, yes."

He grinned, completely unconcerned by the character assessment. Officer Hot 'n Tot, Bea decided, was what her grandmother called *incorrigible*.

"Also, and this is just a thought, I'm...putting it out there while my ego is still all puffed up. *I* could be that outrageously unsuitable guy you were talking about."

Oh yeah. That he could. He was the very definition of *outrageously unsuitable* in ways he couldn't even begin to fathom. Bea's pulse fluttered, despite her brain shutting down the idea. "You want to be a check mark on someone's shitty list?"

"Yeah. Why not?" He grinned. "Besides, maybe I have a list, too? And on my list is to be someone's outrageously unsuitable guy?"

Good lord, he was so damn cute, she wanted to take him home and pet him. Among other things. But Bea *wasn't* going to go there. "Austin...I'm very flattered that you're flirting with me, but I don't want to take advantage of you—"

"You should totally take advantage of me."

Bea rolled her eyes. "Or objectify you."

"Objectify me. I'm up for that."

"Austin." She shot him an impatient look even as a million ways she could objectify him battered against her brain like a ram. "I like you. But—" There was no way Bea was unloading the reasons why she wouldn't get involved with a younger man. She'd known him three days and already told him too damn much. "I'm not here forever, you know? It'll just make things weird between us."

"Why would they be weird?"

She gave a half laugh. *Oh, the innocence.* "Trust me, they would."

Bea had always marveled at people who could have normal interactions after a sexual interlude. She'd never quite mastered that trick. Advertising was a small world, and it always felt awkward knowing that someone sitting across the table or at an industry party knew intimate things about her. That she knew intimate things about them.

And Credence was *waaaay* smaller.

His jaw tightened. "Beatrice, I might be twenty-five, but I'm a big boy. I can deal." Then he sighed, a slow smile ironing out the tension. "However...your wish is my command. Just know that the offer is always open."

Bea laughed. "Thank you. I'll keep it up my sleeve."

Like she was going to think about anything else.

CHAPTER EIGHT

The next morning, after getting up late, Bea ventured out properly into Credence for the first time—not as a means to go to Annie's, although she was certainly going to finish up there, but as a getting-to-know-you walking tour. She actually made an effort to get dressed this time, too. If donning a bra and brushing her hair for the second day in a row could be counted as effort. She wasn't up to surrendering her sweats yet, but they were clean and she was wearing a clean shirt and a pair of Skechers on her feet.

First stop was downstairs at Déjà Brew. "Hey, Bea," Jenny greeted, and if she looked surprised to see the Credence newcomer out and about and not looking like a hobo, she was too polite to say so.

"Morning." Bea smiled at the only other female she knew in Credence besides Annie. "Could I get a cappuccino to-go, please?" Bea wasn't much for fancy coffee—she was more an herbal-tea drinker—but given Jenny had pretty much bailed her out of the pokey, it felt incumbent upon her to support Jenny's business.

There were no other customers in the café, so they chatted while Jenny fixed the cappuccino. "You off somewhere?"

"Thought it was about time I showed my face around here."

"Ah." Jenny nodded and shot her a twinkly smile. "To deny

reports of your disfigurement and premature death?"

"And subsequent mauling by my cats? Yes."

Jenny laughed. "People will be relieved to see you're alive and intact."

"I'll consider it an act of public service, then." Jenny handed over the coffee and she took it. "But seriously, I just thought I'd have a look around and introduce myself to a few locals."

She nodded approvingly. "They'd like that."

Handing over the money, Bea smiled her thanks. "Wish me luck."

"You won't need it. Folks around here can be pretty nosy and in your business, but they love a new face and will be thrilled to finally meet the mystery woman. Even more so given you'll be sticking around for a while."

On that note, Bea took herself down the main street. It wasn't exactly bustling. A lot of business premises were unused—either boarded up or displaying faded to-lease signs in their empty windows. But she did meet a few local people along the way, making a point of stopping to introduce herself. Jenny was right: she was greeted warmly, asked if she was okay after her public *incident* at Annie's, and what her plans were.

Considering she didn't even know the answer to that, Bea kept things suitably vague.

The health of her nonexistent cats was also a topic of much discussion. As well as advice about everything from the best spots by the lake to catch a fish to the best bench in the park to the best place to buy Halloween pumpkins. Although she wasn't sure she was going to be here *that* long.

She was even invited to Wednesday night line-dancing classes at a bar called The Lumberjack. Seriously—line dancing?

It was a *sign*.

She'd just plucked that option out of the air when she'd been speaking to Austin, but clearly it was meant to be. She had a very good feeling about Credence. Like she and this town would go together like peanut butter and jelly.

Like perhaps she'd always been destined to spend some time here.

The best part of the morning, though, was stumbling upon Mirror Mirror. The very modern beauty salon with its feature wall of colorful mosaic tiles, Hollywood lights, and an actual glitter ball hanging from the ceiling looked out of place amid the faded desperation of the rest of the Credence main street.

The small swinging plaque on the inside of the door was just being flipped to closed when Bea decided Mirror Mirror was another sign. Her hair needed some serious work, and this place looked like just the ticket. A smiling woman with choppy dark hair, large chunks of which were dyed cotton-candy blue, opened the door.

Bea entered. "I'm sorry," she apologized. "I can come back on Monday. Are you open then? Could I grab a card or maybe I could make an appointment now? As you can see, my hair is in dire need of service."

The woman glanced at Bea's hair and winced, leaving her in no doubt her hair had surpassed the need for service and required nothing less than a major overhaul. "I can do it for you now," she offered in a strong Brooklyn accent.

Wow. It *must* be bad if it couldn't wait two days. "Oh...but weren't you closing?"

"It's fine," she said with a smile, ushering Bea over to a black swivel chair in front of a mirror. "Business isn't exactly brisk around here, so we always value walk-ins."

We? Just then, from a doorway behind that was covered with a heavy bead curtain, another woman appeared. They were strikingly similar—twins, Bea realized. Maybe in their late twenties? They both had long, lean builds with cute chipmunk cheeks. The only hope of telling them instantly apart was their hair. The woman who'd just appeared had a more conservative cut, all one length that brushed her shoulders, the ends kicking up in a cute little flick.

They both had truly magnificent eyebrows, thick and perfectly arched.

"Hey, welcome to the disco," the other women greeted, also in a Brooklyn accent.

"Hi."

"I'm Marley," the twin who had seated her said. "That's my sister"—she jerked her head to the side—"Molly."

Bea smiled at them both in the mirror. "I'm Bea."

"You're the woman in the Witness Protection Program, right? With the cats?"

Bea laughed. Okay, the thing with the cats had to stop. "No. I can assure you stories of my past are greatly exaggerated. I'm a recovering advertising executive running away from the circus that is LA, not a criminal past, I promise. And there are no cats."

"As recent New York escapees, we can relate," Marley said warmly.

Bea glanced above her. "It feels very New York in here."

"Oh yes." Marley smiled. "The glitter ball caused quite the sensation. Now..." Turning her attention to Bea's hair, she ploughed her fingers through it, inspecting it all over like she was searching for lice. Glancing into the mirror, she asked, "What were you thinking?"

Bea laughed at the inquiry. Was Marley asking Bea her thoughts on the cut and style she was wanting, or was she asking Bea why she'd let her hair get into such a state in the first place? She assumed it was the former, because Marley's tone was neither incredulous nor unkind.

"Surprise me."

Bea gulped as the words slipped from her lips and wondered if she'd been abducted by aliens and had her brain snatched. She'd never just handed herself over to a stylist before—she'd *always* been very particular about her hair. The fineness of it had been the bane of her grandmother's existence, but with her guidance, Bea had figured out a style that worked. Long enough to pull back into a loose chignon at her nape for volume and counteract any flyaways. No bangs to betray just how impossibly fine and straight it was. And a light chestnut tint to give the mousy color some depth.

But when she'd quit, she'd been due for another cut and color, and since then, she'd been a hermit letting everything grow wild, and it was longer and scrappier and duller than it had ever been. She winced at herself in the mirror.

God…she was a hobbit.

Definitely time for a change. And if this was her time for being reckless, that had to include her hair as well—her grandmother be damned. "I desperately need a style and some color. My hair is ridiculously fine with a mind of its own, but I'm ready for a change." Her gaze flicked to the blue in Marley's hair. "Nothing too…outrageous." Reckless could come in baby steps, right? "Just different."

Both the women nodded, and then a conversation followed between them as they both sifted through her hair, flipping it back and forth, lifting it up and letting it fall, peering at the roots, prodding at the scalp. After about a minute without what Bea could see as any kind of plan or consensus forthcoming between them, Marley nodded a few times, then glanced at Bea's reflection in the mirror. "Do you trust me?"

Lordy. Bea had no earthly reason to trust someone she'd just met, especially when it came to her hair, but hell, her father, who had never understood his mother's constant wrangle with Bea's hair, always said the only difference between a good haircut and a bad haircut was a couple of weeks. And she had enough hoodies to hide a disaster for a while. She wasn't sure if it was the solidarity of three Credence outsiders united in their makeover quest or just that buzz of excitement glowing in the other woman's eyes, but Bea actually did trust Marley, blue hair and all.

"Yes."

Charlie don't-be-too-distracting Hammersmith could go take a hike.

Marley pumped her fist and grinned. "Okay." She whipped out a cape, and Bea was wrapped up in the blink of an eye.

"Would you like Molly to do your nails? A pedicure, maybe?" She gestured to the other chair in the salon, complete with a foot bath. "She can do that while the color takes? We also," she said as both twins looked rather pointedly at Bea's shaggy, unruly eyebrows, "offer a full waxing service."

Molly nodded. "Eyebrows, underarms, legs, bikini line." She lowered her voice a little. "Brazilians."

Bea blinked. If a glitter ball had caused a sensation, she could only imagine what kind of stir the waxing of hoo-has had created.

"Thanks. Eyebrows and a mani-pedi will be fine."

No way in hell she was letting Molly anywhere near her bikini area. If the twins thought her eyebrows were concerning, Bea did not want to expose them to how wild things had gotten *down below*.

She doubted there was enough wax in all Eastern Colorado for that job.

• • •

"What on earth are you looking for, Junior? You've been clattering around for ages."

Austin, on his hands and knees, his head stuck inside the corner cupboard in the kitchen, grimaced at the nickname he'd had since forever. *Junior.* It felt particularly sharp and pointy right now. He'd gone to Denver, struck out on his own for five years to prove to everyone he wasn't *Junior* anymore, but old habits died hard.

"Didn't you used to have a fondue set?" His mother's love for/obsession with kitchen gadgets had resulted in much clutter over the years.

"A fondue set?" The puzzlement in his mother's voice reached right inside the cupboard.

"Yeah," he confirmed as he eased out and rested back on his haunches.

She placed a basket full of vegetables she'd obviously just picked from the garden on the drainer of the sink. His mother had an amazing green thumb, her garden bursting with seasonal goodness all year round. As far as Margaret Cooper was concerned, there was nothing as nice as freshly picked produce.

She frowned as she proceeded to rinse away the dirt from her harvest. "The one we got as a wedding present from my cousin Avery and his wife?"

"Um…yes?" Austin didn't really care about its provenance.

"Why do you want that old thing?"

Because he couldn't stop thinking about Beatrice. Ever since she'd kissed him yesterday, Austin had thought of little else. Of how nice it had been. Of how he'd like to do it again. Of how much he *liked* her.

Of her skittishness…

"I hear they're making a comeback," he said.

She glanced over her shoulder at him. "Oh, okay…"

This morning, as he'd been helping out in the yards, he'd randomly remembered the old electric fondue set his mom would bring out on occasion for a birthday party or a sleepover and figured he could give it to Beatrice. But he didn't want his mom to know that. Just because he was living back home again didn't mean she got to know everything going on in his life.

The fact that he still lived at home had seemed to freak

Beatrice out enough without seeking his mom's approval or counsel.

Returning her attention to the vegetables, she said, "Have you looked in the big old chest in the barn?"

Austin blinked. "No." Why in the hell would it be in the barn?

"Last year we decided to try and declutter in here a bit."

Austin almost smiled at that. *We* meant only his father. Decluttering wasn't something his mother usually embraced. She wasn't a hoarder exactly, but everything had a story attached to it, which made her stuff feel like friends rather than objects—the cousin-Avery anecdote being a classic example.

"We put a bunch of disused things in the chest to donate to Goodwill."

"Okay." Austin rose. "Thanks."

"Lunch is in fifteen minutes," his mother called after him as Austin strode out the door.

• • •

It took him ten minutes to unearth the item buried under a veritable treasure trove of gadgets that belonged in the previous century. He had no idea if the set still worked or not—he might have to do some rewiring. He could have sourced one online, but this would be quicker.

Plus, this was more personal. And *everything* about Beatrice felt personal.

By the time he was tromping back into the big central farmhouse kitchen via the mudroom, his father and brother and sister-in-law were already there, laughing and chatting as they set the table.

"Oh, you found it!" his mom exclaimed, obvious delight coloring her voice as Austin crossed to the bench near the sink and plugged it into the socket.

"I did," he said as the red light glowed instantly. *Yes.* The pot could benefit from a bit of spit and polish, but it would do.

"And it still works, too."

He grinned at his mother. "It does."

"Umm, the seventies are calling, Junior, and they want their heart attack in a bowl back."

Austin turned to face his brother, leaning his ass against the bench top. Clayton was older than him by five years. They were similar in looks, but Clay's build took more after their mother—shorter and stockier. Austin was more his father—longer, taller, leaner.

They were close in that hard work, beer, and smack talk kinda way.

"This is true," Jill, his sister-in-law, agreed. "Plaque forms in *all* vessels, if you know what I mean." She waggled her eyebrows suggestively, grinning at him as she lost the battle with being serious. She and Clay had been together forever, and Jill enjoyed smack talk almost as much as they did.

"Look, Brian, I can't believe it still works." Margaret pressed her hand to her chest, which was a surefire sign there were tears brewing. That was his mom—ridiculously, wonderfully sentimental. "It's forty years old."

Brian sidled up to his wife. "So it does." They both looked at the glowing light like it was the second coming. He pecked his wife on the forehead, then clapped Austin on the shoulder. "Ah, son, have I mentioned lately that I'm fondue you?"

Austin rolled his eyes as both Clay and Jill groaned behind them. His father loved a good pun as much as his mom loved a good cry. But she was laughing now as she snuggled into her husband's neck. "The cheese is strong with this one."

"Great. Thanks, *Junior.*" Clay sighed. "You know it's going to be nothing but cheese over lunch."

Their father snorted. "Nonsense. I can get through lunch without a cheese pun. Set your minds at cheese, boys." He cracked up, followed closely by their mother. For a man who wrangled cows and ran the ranch with a firm hand, he was the ultimate dad joker.

"We should run now," Clay said to Jill. "While we still have the will to live."

"Do you mind if I give this away?" Austin asked when his mom's laughter settled. He had contemplated just asking to keep it, but knowing his mother, she'd probably end up at his doorstep one day with several packets of cheese, insisting they have fondue, and then he'd have to lie to her and tell her it stopped working or something.

Given how the presence of a light alone had almost made her cry, he didn't want to break her heart. Plus, he'd never once managed to lie to his mother and get away with it. Nobody who knew Margaret Cooper was foolish enough to take her soft, sentimental heart as the measure of her. His mom could sniff out a lie, a stashed bottle of Jack, or a girl in the barn quicker than he could blink. *She* should have been a cop.

"Sure," she agreed readily, then she frowned. "To who?"

"Someone mentioned wanting one a few days ago," he said with as much casualness as he could muster while he pushed off the bench and walked over to the bubbling pot of chili on the stovetop.

"And is this a he someone or a she someone?"

Austin's spidey senses went on full alert—his mom's nose was in action. "Just a work thing," he dismissed as he inhaled the aroma of lunch.

Which was not technically a lie. He *did* meet Beatrice because of work. But that didn't mean his neck wasn't sweating as four sets of eyes bored into his back.

"Arlo doesn't strike me as the fondue type," she fished.

Austin almost laughed out loud at that image. The only part of a fondue set he could imagine Arlo being interested in were the potential of the skewers to be used as weapons.

"Nothing to do with Arlo."

"Someone in…Denver?"

"Nope."

His mom had always been worried he'd take up with a *city girl* and she'd never see him again. Which was utterly ridiculous. Austin was home now, and that's where he was staying. Although, technically, Beatrice was a city girl. Not that he'd *taken up* with her, and she was living here now—for the foreseeable future, anyway.

His mother narrowed her eyes. "Who is she, Austin Cooper?"

Well, at least she hadn't called him Junior. "Mom."

"Is she cheesy on the eyes?" Brian added, clearly amused.

Clay winced and Austin grimaced as they both said, "Dad," in unison.

Jill laughed, because she'd always dug Brian's puns. Clay, however, turned pleading eyes in Austin's direction. "Seriously, bro. You're a cop. Can't you arrest him or something?"

Unconcerned at the possibility of being clapped in handcuffs, his father crossed to where Austin stood. "While it is fun watching you get grilled"—he stopped and smiled, savoring the more subtle pun for a second or two like a true craftsman—"in front of us all, you might as well spill, son. You ought to know by now that resistance is futile."

Austin sighed and glanced at his mom. "It's not a…thing. I'm just being…neighborly. Like you taught me."

"Uh-huh." She crossed her arms. "And does this neighbor have a name? Is it one of those nice girls who own the salon? Or that lovely young woman who came out and fixed my laptop?" She glanced at Brian. "We should have tipped her more."

"No," Austin hastily assured. The last thing the only computer fix-it person in town needed was a dozen bogus calls out to the ranch just so his mother could ingratiate herself. "She's new to town."

Of course, there was only *one* person new to town, and it took his mother about 2.5 seconds to connect the dots. "Oh." Her eyes lit up. "The mystery woman? The one living above Déjà Brew?"

Austin sighed, resigned to his fate. What the hell, if he ever did convince Beatrice to go on a date with him, it'd be around town fast enough anyway. "Yes."

"The one with the cats?"

He laughed. "No cats."

"I heard she was a spy," Jill said.

"It doesn't really matter as long as she's fondue you."

Clay groaned. "Jeez, Dad, enough already."

"What's her name?" Margaret asked.

"Beatrice." Even saying her name caused a little hitch in Austin's breath.

"Like the princess?"

"Well, yes." Austin blinked at his mother's choice of words. "Like the princess."

She took a few excited steps toward him. "What else? Where's she from? What does she do? What does she look like?"

Apart from not being any of his mother's business, Austin didn't think telling her Beatrice was fond of sweats, day-of-the-week underpants, beer for breakfast, and not brushing her hair would endear the woman he couldn't stop thinking about. And as the only other woman in his life who mattered, he really wanted his mom to like Beatrice.

Because he really, *really* liked Beatrice.

Maybe it would go somewhere, maybe it wouldn't. All he knew was he couldn't wait to see her again and give her this old fondue set. One step at a time. They had time, after all. She was sticking around for a while.

"Mom…it's a fondue set."

"Okay, okay." His mother held up her hands. "I get it.

You've only just met and you're taking it easy—"

Brian snorted out a laugh, interrupting. "Taking it cheesy," he uttered delightfully under his breath.

Unfazed by the continued puns, his mom plowed on. "We'll speak of it no more. But if it becomes more than a fondue set, I hope you'll bring her out here to meet us."

"It's a fondue set," he repeated.

His mother nodded, but her eyes sparkled mischievously, and Austin could tell she was tickled pink by the news. "Of course." She tapped her nose twice and winked. "Now"—she undid her apron—"let's eat lunch, shall we?"

"Hallelujah," his dad said. "Praise Cheeses."

CHAPTER NINE

Bea was old enough to know that big changes could be achieved in a few hours. A baby could be born, a new advertising account could be won or lost, a friendship could start. But she'd never thought a few hours alone could bring about such change in *her*.

Sure. She was still the same person. Still the same height, still the same square-shaped face, green eyes, and pointy chin. Still bigger in the hips than she was in the boobs. The almost permanent little *V* etched between her brows was still in situ. But when she looked in the mirror—which she couldn't stop doing—she was *transformed*.

A vibrant corona of fire-engine-red hair floated around her head, taking her face from pleasant-but-nothing-to-write-home-about to, well… If she'd been looking at someone else, Bea would have said *stylishly attractive*.

The way Marley had kept the length but cut choppy layers in around her head so it was able to swing on multiple levels and gave the impression of fullness was genius. Bea had always feared layers getting away from her, but she could see how they created an optical illusion of volume. And the color…well. The color was spectacular, highlighting her green eyes and giving her a vibe that was both sassy and ass-kicky.

She might not feel either of those things, but this color

reminded her she *could* be.

Marley had told her to pop in every day if she wanted to have a quick wash and a blowout. It seemed like a preposterous thing to do. She'd never had the time to go to a hair salon *every* day to have a blowout. But she did now, and she certainly had the means, and if this was the result, then Bea was totally on board with the idea.

Bea lifted her hand to push back her long bangs that fell full and sexily across her face, tucking them behind her ear, increasing the sass. Her fingernails flashed a pearly pink in the mirror—the same color as her toenails—as she ran a finger along first one and then the other eyebrow. They were both now twin arches of perfection and joy.

They were the McDonald's of eyebrows.

She had to wonder, if this was the magic Molly could weave on eyebrows, what sort of miracle could she perform on more... delicate areas of Bea's body? Maybe next time she'd put herself in Molly's hands and let her create a garden of wonder from the bracken down under.

A sudden and unexpected knock at the door interrupted Bea's musings, and she blinked. She'd been here for almost three weeks and nobody had knocked on her door. Dragging herself reluctantly away from her narcissistic staring in the mirror, Bea took the two steps out of the bathroom and another dozen to the front door.

She knew it could only be one person. Well, actually, theoretically it could be *anyone*, but in her bones, Bea knew who was knocking. *Austin Cooper.* A bolt of nervousness knotted her belly as she reached for the doorknob. What would he think of her new look?

Pulling the door open, her suspicions were immediately confirmed. Austin was on her doorstep in jeans and a navy-and-red-checkered button-down and a bulky fleece-lined jacket. He looked seriously hot, especially in comparison to her usual baggy sweats, tee without a bra, and bunny slippers.

He opened his mouth to say something, then stopped and stared at her, his gaze roving over her hair. *"Wow."* He whistled. "You look…ah-*mazing.*"

Given what she was wearing, Bea told herself not to get too carried away at his genuine compliment and the unbridled interest in his gaze. It was obviously just about the hair. Considering her hair had barely been brushed the few other times they'd seen each other, she was coming off a fairly low bar. Seeing it all newly washed and colored and bouncy was bound to cause a double take.

Still, she touched her hair self-consciously. "You like it?"

"Hell yeah I do." He grinned. "When you said you wanted to dye your hair, I figured you'd probably go blond. But red…" His gaze roved over her head again. "That's a bold statement. I like it."

Bea laughed. "I don't know about *bold statement.* I just put myself in Marley's hands and, hey presto, she went all fairy godmother on my ass."

"They've been making a lot of Credence customers happy since they set up shop."

"There are worse things you can do in life." Like sell age serum to twenty-year-olds. Or useless gadgets to people who couldn't afford them. Or expensive water in plastic bottles when the planet was dying.

"I brought you something."

Bea gave herself a mental shake as the realization Austin was carrying something filtered through. "Is that a—"

"Yup." He lifted it so she could inspect his prize. "It's an electric fondue pot belonging to my parents, but they don't use it anymore. It's forty years old but still works like a charm."

The pot was a decent size, with a very retro feel to its design. A squat bowl with squat black legs. "It's…"

"I hope you're not going to go with a cheese pun, because

I've suffered through more than my fair share over lunch, thanks to my father."

"Your father is a pun man?"

"My father is a pun tragic."

Given advertising often exploited puns, Bea was quite fond of them. But they weren't everyone's cup of tea. "No puns, I promise. I was going to say, it's gorgeous." She could almost taste the hot, melted goodness of cheese dripping from a fat crouton.

"And it's red," he pointed out. "You're making bold statements everywhere."

The teasing in his voice caused a hitch in Bea's breath and a lurch in her belly. "Oh yes, that's me. A dye job and a fondue set. Is there no end to my subversiveness?"

He laughed. "May I bring it in for you and set it down somewhere?"

Bea was perfectly capable of taking the damn pot, and being alone in her apartment with him probably wasn't the wisest move, but it'd been a whole twenty-four hours plus since she'd seen him, and she'd been having trouble saying no from the second she'd met this man.

And besides, Austin was good for her ego.

She stood aside. *"Entrez-vous."*

"Mmm. French," he murmured as he brushed by her. "Ooh la-la."

With a second tummy lurch, Bea gripped the knob for a moment before closing the door, his cologne adding to the dizzying effect of his presence. She wasn't sure what he was wearing—she'd known some advertising people with better noses than a perfumer—but it was rich and earthy. Hay and leather. Rain and dust. Sunshine and sweat.

Cowboy in a bottle.

Her brain took a moment to think about the kind of campaign she could create for such a product, which was, unfortunately, an occupational hazard for her—or at least it had been, anyway. She hadn't realized that shit would be so hard to switch off, but here she was picturing Austin naked—except for his hat—in a half-full bathtub with a few appropriately placed bubbles, in the middle of a field, surveying his land as the sun went down, golden rays falling softly against his body. The caption at the bottom would read...

Bea thought for a moment.

For real men only.

"Where would you like it?"

Oh, *lordy.* Where wouldn't she like it?

"Bea*triss*?"

His soft inquiry yanked her out of her libido spin, and she turned to find him in the middle of the open area that was her living room, looking around for a spare inch of clear space.

"Oh, sorry..." She gave a mental shake to clear her head of hot steam rising off bubbly water as she strode to the coffee table, then cleared away her laptop, hoodie, several used glasses, and two empty beer cans. "Put it down here."

Austin did as he was told, then stood looking around some more at the apartment, his eyes skimming over the unmade bed and the couch currently being used as a clotheshorse and the kitchen bench cluttered with dishes and the groceries she'd picked up yesterday morning and only half put away. A box of Lucky Charms, a giant jar of peanut butter, several bags of corn chips, packets of microwave popcorn, two six-packs of beer, a supply of Oreos, and three rolls of paper towel.

To be fair, the kitchen bench was quite small, so it didn't take much to look cluttered.

"Sorry, it's a bit of a mess." But it was an improvement from a couple of days ago. She'd washed the dishes yesterday, even if she hadn't put them away yet. And she had picked up half of the discarded clothes on the floor. Bea called that progress.

"This is an...interesting choice of interior decoration. Were you going for a particular style?"

Style? He was such a smart-ass. "Frat-house chic?"

He laughed. "Yeah, I've been in a couple of those since being on the job. I think you nailed it."

"You don't approve?"

He held up his hands in a surrender motion. "Bea*triss,* honey, I can honestly say I couldn't give a good goddamn."

Bea had never been called *honey* by a guy under about the age of eighty in her life. Frankly, it could be kinda condescending, and she'd have thought that would go a hundred times over for a guy ten years her junior. But…apparently not. The way Austin said *honey*—all sweet and gentle and silky and clearly a term of affection and endearment—practically had her purring.

"Unless, of course, you're in violation of some fire code, in which case I'll have to take you back to the pokey."

Bea laughed a little too loud at his joke, her body still recovering from the shock of being called *honey* by a cocky twenty-five-year-old.

"Well, I like it," she said. "My apartment in LA was always spotlessly clean—nothing was out of place. I had a cleaning service come in once a week for what must have been the easiest job in the world. It always looked like a display home. It never looked lived in because I was hardly ever there to *live* in it. This"—she threw her arm out—"looks lived in."

Just articulating her feelings out loud helped crystalize why this level of mess wasn't bothering Bea. Why she was suddenly craving clutter and disarray when once she'd shunned it. She was turning over a new leaf, learning to live in the moment, and that included the space in which she'd chosen to live.

"Well…" Austin looked around again. "It definitely looks lived in."

Bea smiled. Yeah, she might have gone too far the other way, but she was confident she'd find a happy medium over the next little while. "Thanks for the fondue pot. I love it."

"Consider it a welcome-to-Credence gift."

"You already put me in jail; you didn't need to get me anything else."

He laughed, shaking his head. "You are such a weirdo."

Bea grinned, taking it as the compliment Austin had clearly meant it as. She'd take eccentricity over her old status of conformity any day. "Thank you."

"Maybe you'll invite me over one night for fondue?"

Gah! The man was impossible to resist. "Maybe I will."

"In the meantime," he said, "I thought you might like to come and hang out at Jack's with me. Meet some people?"

"That's The Lumberjack? Where they do the line dancing?"

He grimaced the same way he had at Annie's that morning when she'd mentioned the L-word. Clearly the thought of line dancing gave him heartburn. "Yep," he said. "The finest bar in all of Eastern Colorado."

Bea didn't need to be asked twice. She suspected the people she'd met around town today were probably different from the people who went out to a bar on a Saturday night. "Sure. I'll just..." She glanced down at her clothes. "Change my outfit."

He shrugged. "Don't do it on my behalf. You look great."

Bea blinked. Well...*bless his heart.* But with all the rose-colored glasses in the world, *great* was stretching it. Sure, her hair was *ah*-mazing, but the rest was a catastrophic mix of laissez-faire and what-the-hell. Austin was good for her ego, but she was starting to doubt his powers of observation...

"Thanks, but I think, like my hair, it's time for a change. Bars are not the place for sweatpants." It could, of course, be argued that sweats should be worn *nowhere* in public other than on people who were competing in some kind of sporting event or physical fitness activity, but Bea was having a good time making up her own rules as she went along.

"Okay." He pointed to the door. "I'll wait downstairs for you."

She nodded. "I'll be ready in ten."

He cocked an eyebrow, his face indulgently amused. "Okay."

Bea just smiled as he walked out the door, then made it downstairs with a minute to spare.

CHAPTER TEN

Even though the days were getting warmer, it was still nippy at six on a Saturday evening in Eastern Colorado. Bea's breath fogged into the cool air as she and Austin walked briskly down the main street to Jack's. She felt good about herself even if her jeans were a little tight in the waist. But it was amazing how confident a pair of red boots could make a woman feel, and the way her khaki fleece complemented her new swishy hair had been the cherry on top.

With a bra *and* her Saturday panties, she felt like she was walking down the red carpet at Cannes.

"Entrez-vous," Austin mimicked as he opened the heavy wooden door to the bar, and Bea smiled at him. His answering flirty grin caused her heart to skip a beat.

The low notes of a Waylon Jennings song and a cloud of warmth engulfed Bea as she stepped inside, and she sighed at the instant relief. Heat seeped into her bones and melted her cold face and tingled in the tips of her ears and fingers. She waited for him to shrug out of his jacket and hang it on one of the many hooks near the door while she unzipped her polar fleece but kept it on. With Austin indicating she should precede him again, she walked toward the bar.

She wouldn't say the place was jumping exactly. Not in an LA way, anyway. But about half the booths were full and half the stools along the long bar were occupied. There was a group of people milling around the jukebox, and some were dancing on the small square of floor to the side of the jukebox obviously provided for the activity. Beyond that, through an open door, she could see more people playing pool.

"Junior!"

Bea's gaze landed on a good-looking guy standing behind the bar who was smiling at them with a wide grin. Like the rest of him, the man's smile was *very* nice. "Hey, Tucker," Austin said with a sigh as Bea's gaze wandered to the bartender's biceps. That was some major arm candy right there.

Two other guys on the stools closest to the best-looking bartender Bea had ever seen—and *hello*, she'd lived in LA for fifteen years, where almost every bar dude was an impossibly handsome, out-of-work actor—half turned in their seats and also greeted Austin.

"Hey, Drew." Austin nodded. "Hey, boss."

Boss? Bea realized Arlo was one of the guys sitting at the bar.

"Isn't this past your bedtime, Junior?" Arlo asked.

"Quit it, dude," the guy called Drew said. "I bet he's got a written note from his mommy to be out past curfew."

Bea blinked at the easy back-and-forth. These guys were obviously used to this kind of communication, but a part of her—the bit that felt uneasy about their age difference—wanted to leap to Austin's defense. But, apart from the initial sigh, he took it all in stride, grinning good-naturedly and saying, "Bite me, assholes," and Bea relaxed.

Okay, this was...smack talk. And Austin could obviously hold his own.

With their banter done, three sets of eyes turned to Bea. "Austin," Drew said, "I think you need to introduce us to your friend."

Austin smiled at her as he said, "This is Bea*triss*." Even in front of these guys and a half-full bar, he put that sexy little inflection on the last syllable of her name that had Bea melting into a puddle on the floor.

"Hey, Beatrice," Tucker said, holding out his hand.

"Bea," she said quickly, accepting a shake from both Tucker and Drew. The latter was also a hottie—tall, broad, and waaaay closer to her age. They all were.

"Arlo. You remember Beatrice. From the other day."

Arlo frowned for a beat or two, then Bea watched as realization slowly dawned. He looked taken aback for a moment but recovered gallantly to smile and reach out his hand. "Of course, apologies, ma'am. It's the lighting in here."

Bea almost laughed out loud as they shook hands. He was being very polite, but she didn't blame him for not recognizing her. There were better put-together bag ladies in LA than she'd been the day they'd met.

"I keep telling this dipshit"—Arlo tipped his head at Tucker as he continued—"that people need to be able to see where they're going in here, but apparently, subdued light flatters his tan."

Unfazed by the dig, Tucker fluttered his lashes and said, "I think you mean my eyes."

Arlo sighed dramatically, ignoring Drew's and Austin's laughter. "He's in contravention of about a dozen city bylaws. Someone's going to sue him one day."

At the mention of breaking bylaws, Bea slid her gaze to Austin to find his already on her, and her nipples, which had only just decided to thaw in the tropical heat of the bar, suddenly tightened again.

"So arrest me, dickhead, or quit whining about it."

"You see the respect I get around here?" Arlo asked, turning questioning eyes on Bea, a smile hovering on his mouth.

She hadn't really gotten a good look at Arlo the other day,

but he cut quite the figure. He was more RoboCop with his black buzz cut and spare, angular face than Austin's laid-back you-catch-more-flies-with-honey charm, but she supposed, as chief of police, the safety of the town rested on his shoulders. Luckily, his shoulders appeared to be up to the job.

If this—Tucker, Arlo, Drew, and Austin—was a typical sample of the Credence men, then maybe she should have put her faith in the throw of a dart a lot earlier.

"What can I get you to drink?" Austin asked, interrupting the smack talk.

"I'll have a Bud, please."

"Two," he said, motioning to Tucker.

The bartender nodded. "Coming right up."

"So," Drew said as Bea settled on the empty stool beside him and Austin settled on the stool on her other side. She was hyperaware of Austin's scent and the warmth of his thigh that was almost touching hers, and she shifted slightly so their legs touched because...well, just *because*. "Are you...passing through or...?"

"No, I've just moved here. From LA."

A frown flitted across Drew's brow, then his eyes slowly widened. *"Ohhh."* He pointed at her. "You're the cat lady."

Bea laughed. "Apparently, yes. Although I can assure you, I don't have any cats."

Tucker put the beer bottle down on the bar in front of her. "I heard you were a spy from the department of agriculture."

What the hell? "The department of agriculture has spies?"

Bea took a mouthful of her beer. She may be looking at and talking to the very dazzling Drew, but he was not who was overheating her system. She was only really aware of Austin, of the feel of their thighs pressed together. Things were running hot inside her right now, and a cold beer was just what she needed.

"According to Don, the mayor. Something about corn rebates."

"I wouldn't know one end of an ear of corn from the other. I'm an ex–advertising executive taking a break from LALA land."

"Really." Drew sat a little straighter in his chair and eyed her speculatively. "You might be just the person I need for my business."

Now, if Austin had said something like that, Bea would have slid right off her stool, but Drew saying it did nothing but pique her curiosity. Why, she had no idea. He was her age, he was her type—professional, obviously a business owner—he was very easy on the eyes, and he was flirting. Yet…nothing.

Austin, on the other hand, was revving her engines just from his nearness.

"Oh?" She took another sip of her beer. "Why's that?"

"I run a funeral home here in Credence and, well, as you can imagine…that's not a particularly sexy profession…"

Drew was in the *funeral* business? Honestly, if Drew had said he was a garbage man, she'd have been less surprised.

Arlo and Tucker groaned. "Not this again," Tucker complained.

Bea tried not to smile at the sidekicks who'd clearly been here before. "I guess it's kinda hard to get laid if you're a funeral director," she said sympathetically.

Even one who looked like Drew.

He turned to his friends. "Now see? Bea's been here for five minutes and she *already* understands my conundrum."

Bea shrugged. This was what she did. Or what she'd done anyway. It was what she'd been good at. Identifying what the client needed even if *they* didn't know what it was.

"We understand there's nothing sexy about the word mortician," Arlo said derisively. "We've just heard you talking about it a million times."

"Yeah." Bea winced. "*Mortician* is a hard sell. What you need is a rebrand."

A portal opened up in her brain just then as images for an advertising campaign she could run for this guy who should be able to sell just about anything—even coffins. But she quickly shut it down. She was at a bar in her town of choice, having a beer and meeting people. This was her world now, not the one she'd left behind, because it had *chewed her up and spat her out* without so much as a thank-you.

"*Yes.*" Drew took a swig of his beer. "I've been trying on alternative names for a while now, but nothing seems to pop."

"What have you come up with so far?"

"I was leaning toward bereavement agent," Drew said.

"Personally, I thought life celebrant was a winner," Tucker offered with heavy sarcasm.

"Nope." Arlo shook his head. "Afterlife liaison has been the best yet."

Bea blinked at the suggestions and the banter. It was clear these three guys knew one another well. "Right…well, they're a good starting point."

Arlo and Tucker laughed as Drew sighed and took a big swig of his beer. "Wait," Tucker said, "I got one. How about"—he palmed the air as if he was reading a sign—"Drew Carmichael, your local *last* responder?"

There was more laughter, but Drew was clearly unamused. "Oh yeah. That's hysterical. You should totally give up your day job for stand-up comedy."

"Hey." Tucker feigned insult but ruined it with a huge grin. "Della thinks I'm hilarious."

Arlo snorted. "My sister thinks you poop sparkly unicorn glitter."

"Dude, I *do* poop sparkly unicorn glitter!"

Bea, waiting to get a word in edgewise, glanced at Austin. He rolled his eyes, then winked at her, and her pulse skipped. Why was it that, sitting in the midst of these truly remarkable-looking guys who were all about her age, it was twenty-five-year-old Austin who made her heart pump a little faster? He was looking at her like she was the best thing that had happened to him today, and Bea felt that right down to her toes.

She'd been in a few relationships over the years, but she'd never been with a guy who made her feel with one glance like she was the best part of his day, and that was *heady*.

Maybe it wouldn't be *that* crazy to just dive in to Austin and go for it?

"Who poops unicorn glitter?" asked a female voice from behind.

"Oh, Jesus," Arlo muttered under his breath as Bea turned in her chair to discover the owner of the voice.

"I do," Tucker said with a smile. "How you doing, Winona?"

Winona was a tall, imposing figure of a woman in that Xena: Warrior Princess way. Bea's grandmother would call her *big-boned*. She had a head full of bouncy caramel curls and a mischievous glint in her eyes and held herself like she was the queen of everything she surveyed. Bea liked her instantly.

"Fabulous, thank you, Tucker. Just fabulous. Hey, Drew. Hey, Austin." She nodded at them both. Her smile became cooler as she acknowledged Arlo. "Evening, Cap'n Nemo."

"Winona," Arlo acknowledged. "You've been quiet of late."

She shrugged. "On deadline."

Deadline? Hmm…interesting. Bea eyed the other woman speculatively. What did Winona do that had her on deadline?

"Have you missed me?" she asked Arlo with a small, wry smile on her lips.

"Nope." He shook his head. "Not even a little bit."

Winona clutched her chest in faux shock. "But…I'm such a delight."

"Yeah, you're a real treasure. You and him"—he tipped his chin at Tucker—"unicorn glitter everywhere."

She beamed. "I know, right?" Shifting her attention from

a beleaguered Arlo to Bea, Winona smiled and stuck out her hand. "Hi, I'm Winona."

"Bea," she said, and they shook.

"Are you here with one of these bozos, or do you want to come sit with us?" She hooked her thumb over her shoulder, and Bea spied Molly and Marley at a booth with another woman she didn't know. They all waved at Bea. "For conversation that doesn't involve unicorn poop?"

Bea laughed. "I came with Austin."

"Austin." She eyed him speculatively for a beat or two, her gaze dropping to the way Bea's thigh was pressed against Austin's before switching her attention back to Bea and nodding approvingly like she was totally on board with whatever was happening.

With Austin. Who was *twenty-five*. Bea shot her a *nothing-happening-here* look. Winona's gaze clearly called bullshit on that notion.

Glancing at Austin, Bea cocked an eyebrow in question. She was quite eager to make female friends and have a girlie chat, but it seemed rude to just abandon the one who brought her.

"It's fine—go," Austin assured. "Enjoy. I'll be here when you're ready to head back to the apartment."

"Excellent." Winona beamed. "Tucker, my book is done and my friends and I want to get boozy. Can we get a round of piña coladas to the booth and keep 'em coming?"

Book? So Winona was a writer?

"Yes, ma'am," Tucker said with a smile and a salute.

Bea waited for Tucker's *ma'am* to go to her ovaries. For his salute to do funny things to her heartbeat. But it didn't happen. She thought Tucker was cute, but she didn't want to dribble melted cheese all over his pecs and lick it off.

"Also, a couple of rounds of the house garlic bread."

"Can do."

"C'mon," Winona said. "Let's go. I'll introduce you."

Grabbing her beer, Bea nodded politely at the men at the bar before sliding from the stool and following Winona across the room. "I've not seen you around before?" she asked. "Are you visiting?"

"No. I moved here a couple of weeks ago." Bea braced herself for the inevitable.

"*Ohhh*. You're the cat woman."

Yeah, clearly she was going to need a not-the-cat-lady tattoo on her forehead if she wanted to avoid these conversations for the next little while. "No, I don't—"

But her protest got lost as they squeezed past some people and then arrived at the table, where she was greeted enthusiastically by Molly and Marley, who fawned over her hair a bit more, and introductions to the other woman in the group were made. "This is Mia," Winona said. "She's Credence's computer fix-it wiz." Mia had dark hair; dark, studious eyes; and a warm smile.

"Hey," Bea said as she slid into the booth, about to offer her name, but was beaten to it by Winona.

"This is Bea. The cat lady."

"She doesn't have any cats," Molly jumped in. "That's not true. It was just a rumor."

"Like the one about you being a runaway heiress?" Mia asked.

Bea almost choked on her mouthful of beer. "What?" She laughed. "Definitely not true. What other rumors were circulating about me?"

"That you were on the run from the law," Marley offered.

"Or in the Witness Protection Program," Molly added.

"That you'd been in some kind of accident and were disfigured and/or blind, depending on the day and the person telling the story," Mia said. "Keeping your windows covered seemed to popularize the whole disfigurement thing."

Winona sighed. "I liked the witch rumor the best."

Marley laughed. "That's only because you wanted to taunt Arlo with the prospect of a coven setting up home in Credence."

Winona grinned. "Serves him right for having a giant stick up his ass."

Tucker arriving with their cocktails interrupted the conversation, and Bea quickly downed the rest of her beer as she accepted her piña colada. She wasn't much of a fruity cocktail fan—she was a beer girl through and through—but she could suffer through one.

"Here's to new faces," Winona said, picking up her glass in salute. "Welcome, Bea."

The women all raised their glasses, too, and clinked them together. Bea sipped at her cocktail, given her palate wasn't exactly in the most receptive mood for something sweet after the beer. But it tasted light and fresh, and Bea knew from experience that she just needed to drink more to get her palate adjusted, and with great company, that wouldn't be a hardship.

"So, Bea. Tell us about yourself," Mia invited.

It took about ten minutes for Bea to tell the abridged version of her life and what had brought her to Credence. Not one of her new friends thought it was strange that she would just up and move on the throw of a dart, but then these women had all moved here off the back of a national Facebook campaign. If anybody understood impulses, it was them.

Bea had definitely found her people.

The garlic bread, along with another round of cocktails, arrived just as Bea was getting to the end of her tale, and the women swooped in. "Oh God…" Bea groaned as the buttery, cheesy, salty, garlicky goodness caused the kind of sensation in her mouth that Austin caused inside her day-of-the-week panties every time he said Bea*triss*. "Carbohydrates are the devil."

"Amen to that," Winona agreed.

They consumed the bread—two large triangles each—to

the background murmur of the Saturday night crowd and the crooning of Keith Urban. None of them spoke until the bread was gone, which was the kind of reverence that should be given to food that could make the earth move. But once they were done, the questioning resumed.

"So," Winona said, licking her fingers, "what are your plans while you're here?"

"Honestly?" Bea shook her head. "I don't know. I...didn't think that far ahead. I'm secure enough financially not to *have* to do anything for a time, so I guess I'll figure it out as I go along. I just needed to get far away from LA."

"Okay, but..." Mia quirked an eyebrow. "What *have* you been doing for the couple of weeks you were locked away while we were all speculating whether you were a Gryffindor or a Slytherin?"

Bea laughed. If only she'd known there'd been such interest, she might have played along. Hung a rubber bat in the window or put a cauldron there for everyone to see. "I binge-watched all fifteen seasons of *Supernatural*."

There was a moment of almost reverential silence as the women gaped at her. "Was that the first time you've seen them?" Mia asked.

"Yeah." Bea gave a self-deprecating smile. "Most of the TV I've watched in fifteen years was about the ads, not the actual shows. I basically didn't have a life."

"Oh...I remember being a *Supernatural* virgin." Marley's hand fluttered over her chest. "Popping that cherry was sweeter than my *actual* cherry being popped."

"I can't think of a better use of your time," Molly agreed sincerely.

Winona raised her almost-empty glass. "Respect."

"So, are you Team Sam or Team Dean?" Molly asked.

Bea frowned. Was that a trick question? "Is...Team Sam a thing?"

They all laughed. "Apparently," Mia replied.

"Oh, well...I mean, Sam's cute. For sure. And principled. There's a lot to be said for a bleeding-heart hot guy, right?" Everyone nodded. "I sure wouldn't kick him out of my bed for spilling crumbs. But he's impulsive and hotheaded and..."

"Whiny," Marley supplied.

"Yes." Bea laughed. "*So* whiny. And Dean...well..."

"Right." Winona nodded. "Dean wins."

"Dean all the way," Mia agreed.

Molly nodded. "He's hot."

"And he's obsessed with pie." Bea flicked her gaze around the group. "I mean, you gotta be into a guy who loves pie, right?"

"Hell yes." Marley raised her glass. "Eat pie, kill demons. Cheers to that."

Everyone clinked glasses and drank, then Marley said, "If you haven't seen a lot of TV in the last fifteen years and you're looking for some other television recs to while away the days, I can highly recommend *Friday Night Lights*."

Molly nodded. "God yes. Team Riggins for the win."

"*True Blood*," Winona suggested. "Team Eric."

"*The Walking Dead*," Mia added. "Team Daryl."

Bea laughed at the rapid-fire suggestions. "Hang on." She grabbed her phone and opened a new note. "I'd better write these down."

"If you're looking for something to do," Winona said as Bea's thumbs flew over the touch screen of her phone, "you can come visit me out at the lake. I'm building a house out there, which has taken a bit longer than I'd hoped. I've just moved into a caravan on-site this week now that the worst of the weather is over, but I'm happy to show you around. It's really nice out there. Peaceful and pretty."

With the recommendations duly noted in her phone, Bea placed it on the table. "You mentioned something to Tucker about finishing a book. Are you a writer?"

Molly grinned. "Winona writes *erotic* romance novels."

Bea blinked. She wasn't sure what she'd thought Winona might write, but this hadn't been it. Something deep and literary maybe. Or grisly—spy novels or murder and mayhem. Not love and sex. But there was a definite hedonistic bend to the way Winona spoke and ate and drank and laughed and flirted that Bea could imagine went well with writing in the erotic romance genre.

"Really?" Bea asked her. "Like...for a living? You're published?"

Winona nodded. "Yes, I write full-time and earn decent money. I've hit several big lists and won a couple of awards, and I've just finished book sixteen."

"That's..." Bea didn't know what to say. She'd occasionally met authors—big-name ones—when the firm had been handling national advertising for particular publishers, and she'd always been fascinated by the tenacity that must be required to finish a book. Her job was creative, too, but in a very different way. "That is *awesome*."

"I know, right?" Winona agreed with a grin and took another drink.

"Well, I guess reading one of your books just went to the top of my to-do list." Once upon a time, during her teen and college years, Bea had read a lot. Now, she was lucky to read a couple of books a year, and that was usually in dribs and drabs at airports and on planes.

"Here." Winona delved into her bag and handed over what appeared to be a bookmark with all her details on it, including a very interesting tagline. *No yucking on someone else's yum.*

Bea glanced over at Arlo, then back at Winona. Interesting...

"Check out my website," she continued. "If you want me to recommend something, let me know."

"Thanks." Bea took it and slipped it into her bag. "I will."

"Well, that's one thing sorted for your list," Mia said.

"What else can we hook you up with?"

Bea shrugged. "A cat, I guess. I might as well go ahead and get one, seeing as how everyone around me is under the impression I actually have a room full of them."

"But do you *want* one?" Mia frowned. "If you don't mind my saying, you don't sound that enthused."

"I *do* want one. I like cats. Well…actually, I don't have an opinion about cats or any other domestic animal, really, because I've never owned a pet—" There was a general gasp at the admission, but it was true. Her grandmother disliked animal hair getting everywhere. "But I would like to get a cat now that I have the time to look after one." She shrugged. "They're cute and fluffy and low-maintenance. It's not like I have to walk one or anything, and I quite like the idea of a warm, purring body to snuggle into at night."

Winona cocked an eyebrow. "I thought that was what Austin was for?"

The other women laughed, and Bea actually *blushed* as her gaze slid to the man in question, drinking a beer and listening to whatever Drew was saying. As if he knew she was watching, he looked over his shoulder and their eyes met, and Bea felt the same yank of connection she had from the first time she'd laid eyes on Austin Cooper.

She blushed some more as she returned her attention to what was going on in her booth. "It's not like that," she dismissed. "He's just being friendly."

"Uh-huh," Winona said drily, and they all laughed again.

Desperate to steer the conversation away from Austin and how friendly she was avoiding getting with him, Bea asked, "So how would I go about finding someone who might have a cat or kitten, even"—how much fun would a cute little fur ball be?—"they want to offload?"

"I got mine from a litter at one of the farms out of town," Mia said.

"Annie will know," Winona mused. "People tell her stuff like that."

"Oh, yes." The mention of Annie's made Bea's tummy grumble despite it being full of cheesy garlic bread, beer, and piña colada. "Good tip, thanks. I'll ask."

Bea sucked to the bottom of her second cocktail, making a loud slurping noise. It wasn't very ladylike, but it was as satisfying as the drink. Maybe she would become a cocktail convert in Credence? Then miraculously, Tucker appeared again, putting another round of five piña coladas in the middle and removing the empties.

"Tucker," Winona said, "Della is right—you are a god among men."

He laughed. "Well thank you, *ma'am*, but I don't think she's referring to my cocktail prowess."

Winona hooted out a laugh. "I don't think so, either."

With that, he left, and Bea felt so damn happy to be sitting here, far away from her old life with new friends and a new future ahead of her, she grabbed the third cocktail.

"You ever met a movie star?" Marley asked, leaning in.

Bea grinned, took a long drag of the pineapple-flavored rum through her straw, and said, "Who do you want to know about?"

CHAPTER ELEVEN

Austin was barely listening to the conversation among Tucker, Arlo, and Drew. He was too conscious of the five women in the booth behind him, laughing and drinking and having a good time. Well, just the one woman, really. Every time he glanced over, she was smiling and animated, and she'd taken off her fleece jacket, revealing a snug-fitting black top, and she was so relaxed and happy compared to the woman she'd been that first day he'd met her, he just wanted to be over there soaking up her aura.

Of course, had she suggested going back to her place so he could lick melted cheese off her body, he would have been up for that as well. Apparently, you could also melt chocolate in a fondue pot—he'd googled it. God…if his mother only knew the deviant thoughts he was having about that fondue pot, she might not have been so enthusiastic about giving it away.

"And then," Arlo said, "we heard reports over the radio that the perps were heading out to the Cooper ranch to steal all their bulls and burn down their barn."

Tucker *tsk*ed. "Did you try and stop them?"

"I said they should just go on ahead and do it, not my place. They're probably still out there now, ransacking things."

Drew shook his head as he surveyed Austin, then glanced at his friends. "Nuthin'."

"Earth to Cooper." Arlo snapped his fingers in front of Austin's face. "Come in, Cooper."

Austin blinked as he came back to the conversation to find all three men staring at him. With bemused expressions. "Sorry, I was miles away."

Tucker laughed. "Yeah…'bout point zero zero zero zero one of a mile." He tipped his head in Beatrice's direction.

"You think you got a chance with her, Junior?" Arlo asked.

Arlo had known Austin all his life and had taken great pleasure in calling him *junior* the second he'd walked through the door in his uniform. Not when they were on official police business—then it was usually just *Cooper*—but when they were socializing, absolutely. Until Beatrice had arrived, Austin had found it kind of amusing.

Now it was just plain irritating.

"No comment." He might not have Arlo's years of experience with women, but even he knew they didn't take guys speculating about them like this very kindly.

Tucker patted him on the shoulder. "Atta boy, good answer. But if you need some tips for your first time, you know you can talk to us, right?"

"I can even slip you some condoms," Drew offered.

Austin grinned at their good-natured teasing. "But, Mr. Carmichael, my momma told me I should save myself for my wedding night."

The guys laughed. "Seriously, though," Tucker said, "you don't think you're punching above your weight there?"

There wasn't one atom in Austin's body that *didn't* think he was punching above his weight. Beatrice was *wonderful*, and he'd thought that when she'd had scary hair and was dripping ice cream everywhere as she gave him a hard time. But she'd sat here holding her own with three other good-looking guys and hadn't shown the slightest interest in *any* of them.

Austin had been worried initially that she might. That

she'd be charmed by three men closer to her age than he was, being all *howdy ma'am*. Hell, Drew, that bastard, had even flirted with her. But it had been *him*—Austin—who she'd looked to and smiled at. It had been *his* thigh she'd pressed along. The movement had only been slight, but he was sure it had been deliberate.

"She's a little..." Tucker dropped his voice. "Older than you."

For a man, Tucker managed the statement with great sensitivity. Austin knew a lot of guys who would have just come straight out with the word *cougar*. And that would have been a shame, because he'd have had to object to it quite strenuously, and his days for bar brawls were long over.

"I'm just being neighborly," he repeated. "Introducing her around."

"She's okay now?" Arlo asked, growing serious. "She seemed a little...edgy the other day."

"Yeah." Austin sipped his beer. "She's good. She was just having one of those days, you know."

"Yeah. I know." Arlo nodded the kind of nod that left Austin in little doubt he *did* know. Between losing his leg on the job years before and rescuing his sister from her abusive ex, Arlo had probably had *a day* or two himself.

"Don't worry, boss, I'm looking out for her."

Arlo snorted. "Well, you've already fucked that up when you let her go with Winona."

Austin grinned. Arlo and Winona's long-standing friction was the kind of extended foreplay that was both icky and amusing to witness.

Why they didn't just get it on already, he had no idea.

"She looks like she's having a good time," Austin said, glancing over. Beatrice was laughing at something Marley was saying, and it made him so fucking *happy*.

"Pfft." Arlo squinted at the group, then turned back to the

bar. "They're probably plotting some kind of *Guinness World Record* mass live erotica reading or an orgy at the lake."

Drew almost choked on his mouthful of beer. "I see no problem with that."

Austin's phone buzzed in his back pocket, and he pulled it out. It was his father. "Load of hay arrived late," Brian said without greeting or preamble. "Clay and Jill have gone into Denver overnight for date night. How far away are you? I could use a hand."

This, Austin decided, was the downside of being unattached and living on a ranch—his time was expendable. Not that Austin minded. His father and brother had run the ranch for the years he was in Denver, and he didn't begrudge Clay a date night. But if he and Bea had been on a date? Or doing... nasty things with cheese, he'd have minded a lot.

"I'll be there in fifteen." He drained the beer he'd been sitting on for an hour and stood. "Gotta go."

"Everything okay?" Tucker asked.

"Yeah, fine. Load of hay just came in." They'd been buying in feed the last few weeks to get the stock through until the pastures recovered from winter.

"What about your guest?" Arlo tipped his head in Bea's direction.

Austin glanced over at the fun booth. "She looks like she's in good hands."

"Yup. Absolutely." Drew nodded. "You go on, Junior, don't worry. I'll take good care of her. I'm great with women," he said, barely keeping a straight face.

Austin knew from the shit-eating grin Drew was wearing that he was just yanking Austin's chain, but the *Junior* made it rankle more than usual. He shot Drew his best resting cop face. "You even look at her wrong and I'll throw your ass in jail."

Drew hooted out a laugh, clapping Austin on the shoulder. "That's abuse of power; you can't do that."

Austin pointed at Arlo. "He can."

It was Arlo's turn to grin. "And it would give me the greatest of pleasure."

"Thanks, boss."

Arlo grunted. "Go do hay now."

Austin didn't need to be told twice as he headed to Bea's table, dodging bar customers. "Hi," he said as he approached.

She looked up at him and smiled, her new red hair swishing like a shampoo commercial. Her eyes were sparkling, her cheeks pink. "Hey there, it's Officer Cutie Patootie."

Laughing, Austin said, "I don't know how many piña coladas you've had, but you should definitely drink more." She was clearly a little boozy, which was making her flirty, and Austin approved wholeheartedly.

"We should all definitely drink more," Winona chimed in.

He laughed again. "Here." He pulled out his wallet and threw a fifty on the table. "Have another round on me."

Bea did an exaggerated eyelid bat. "Why, Officer, are you trying to get us drunk?"

"No, ma'am." Her smile slipped a little then, and her nostrils flared, and things went from flirty tipsy to jungle steamy in one second flat. Heat surged to Austin's groin, and his breath was thick in his throat as he swallowed. "It's just a parting gesture."

"Parting?" She pouted, the flirt back again. "Where are you going?"

"Sorry, I've gotta head out to the ranch to help Dad offload some hay."

"Oh…"

The flirt slipped again to disappointment, and the fact that she seemed genuinely sad about his imminent departure totally went to Austin's head. *Both of them.* "I assume you want to hang here for a bit longer. Or do you want me to walk you back to the apartment before I head out?"

"Oh, no." She shook off her disappointment and smiled at him. "You go. I'll be fine here."

"Yep. Bea's been telling us all about the stars she's met at Hollywood fundraisers," Molly confirmed.

Winona, who didn't seem anywhere near as boozy as the others, said, "We'll see she gets home safely, Officer *Cutie Patootie*."

Austin groaned. He had a feeling that was going to stick. But he had no doubt that Bea was in safe hands. "Thanks." He glanced around the group, nodding collectively at the women. "Night, ladies." Then his gaze zeroed in on the one woman he hadn't been able to stop thinking about. "Sweet dreams."

She smiled at him, her eyes soft. "Sweet dreams are made of cheese," she said, and then she laughed at their little private joke, and Austin wanted to sweep her up in his arms and kiss the living hell out of her.

As soon as humanly possible.

CHAPTER TWELVE

Monday morning, just before lunch, Bea found herself pulling up in the main parking lot at the lake. It was a truly spectacular day. The sky was an endless dome of candy blue with not one cloud marring its perfection. The sun sparkled on the surface of the lake like a galaxy of tiny suns, and the trees that surrounded the lake on every shoreline were thick with new growth.

She grabbed the brown paper bag off the passenger seat and exited the car. The sun was warm on her face now despite the cool start to the day, and she shrugged out of her fleece. It was so quiet—not a soul to be seen—although there was another vehicle in the lot. Bea inhaled deeply, appreciating the pine needles scenting the air with their woodsy fragrance.

No wonder Winona wanted to live out here.

Bea had passed what she assumed was Winona's place a few minutes ago, if the bare A-framed bones of a house and the caravan to the side of the lot were any indication. She planned on dropping in and seeing her as per her invitation on Saturday on the way back, but for now she wanted to explore what the lake had to offer. Find a nice spot to really appreciate Annie's Monday morning offerings of peach cobbler and raspberry pie.

Leaving the parking lot, she followed the sign on the tree-lined path that said pier and playground and headed in that direction. Her boots—ankle height in brown leather this time—crunching on the loose gravel echoed in the loud hush of nature. By the time Bea had walked a minute, she swore she could actually hear the low beat of her heart.

She'd never done this in LA—gotten out in nature. Hell, she hadn't even gone to the beach much. There'd always been an excuse to keep her at her desk both at the office or at home and, with her trusty elliptical, she hadn't needed to go out to get exercise. But Bea wasn't doing this for the exercise. She was doing this for the sheer joy of doing nothing.

Which probably wouldn't make sense to a lot of people, but it did to her.

As she rounded a bend in the path, the trees fell away and the view opened up to the playground and a large, well-kept picnic area. There were several permanent table-and-chair sets scattered around and plenty of trees left standing to provide shade to those who hadn't been lucky enough to score a bench or who preferred to picnic on the ground. The grassy area gave way to a narrow, pebbly shoreline that curved off into the distance, the lake lapping it faithfully all the way around.

To the left a little, wooden jetty reached out into the lake, about thirty feet long and low across the surface. No handrail. On the end where the boards widened into some kind of large platform, no doubt used by kids and adults alike to launch themselves into the lake, sat a blond woman in a chair. She was facing the lake and appeared to be sitting in front of a... canvas?

Was this who belonged to the other car in the lot?

Curiosity piqued, Bea made her way across the picnic area and onto the beach, pleased for her sunglasses as the glittering water became more intense the closer she drew. There was only a couple of feet of gritty sand before it blended into pebbles and her boots scuffed and crunched. The sound must have carried in the stillness, causing the woman on the pier to turn.

If she was surprised, she didn't show it, just waved and turned back to her canvas.

Bea ambled to the wooden steps that led to the pier. There were only two and she mounted them unhurriedly, taking in the vista as the man-made lake opened up in front of her, revealing the vastness of the distant shoreline. It was strange not to see mountains nearby, but the woodland that ringed the lake was easy on the eye as well.

The thud of Bea's boots against the boards echoed around the cauldron of the lake, and the woman turned again as Bea drew closer.

"Hi," she said with a smile.

"Hey," Bea returned, her gaze falling on the canvas that seemed a melting pot of color right now more than anything discernible.

It was an achingly familiar sight. One that both resonated deeply and evoked anxiety at the same time. So many memories Bea had purged from her brain over the years as effectively as her grandmother had purged her mother's studio and the house of her art the day after the funeral.

Except they were still there. Not purged, just...buried. Waiting to be unearthed.

The other woman stood, her ponytail swishing. "I'm Suzanne," she said but pronounced it *Su-sahn*.

Bea dragged her attention from the canvas. "I'm..." She stalled for a moment before deciding to just cut to the chase. "I'm the cat woman everyone's talking about." She held out her hand. "But you can call me Bea."

Suzanne laughed as she shook, her fingers stained with paint. "So *you're* the famous...infamous"—her brow crinkled like she was trying to decide which one best suited—"cat woman."

Bea winced. "God, does everybody know about me?"

"Oh, yes." She nodded cheerfully. "I would think so. I live

at a ranch out of town and don't hear a lot of gossip, but I heard about *you*. Do you really have a dozen cats who are your minions of evil?"

It was Bea's turn to laugh. "Would you believe I have *no* cats?"

"I would, actually." Suzanne shook her head. "The good people of Credence do love a mystery *and* to gossip, and from what I hear, you've kept them guessing. If they can't find out the facts, they'll fill it with fiction until otherwise directed."

Bea had figured as much. Her eyes drawn back to the canvas, she asked, "You're an artist?"

"Yes."

The admission slipped so easily from Suzanne's lips, and Bea envied her that. "Would I have heard of you?"

"Ha! Goodness no. I mostly do reproduction work for private clients and art galleries for insurance purposes."

"That sounds..."

"Dull?"

"What? No..." Alarmed, Bea hastened to assure her. "I was going to say important."

"It is, I guess, but lately I've been doing my own stuff. Portraits mainly. I'm working on one for the mayor at the moment. Grady, my husband, said good luck trying to make him *not* look like a pompous windbag." She smiled and Bea smiled back. "Occasionally, I get inspired by a landscape or two."

Bea looked around at the dazzling display of nature. "Not hard to be inspired by this."

"No." Suzanne sighed. "It's not. This your first time out here?"

"Yep. I just came to check it out. Get back to nature for a while." She lifted the packet up. "Eat some pie with a view."

Suzanne laughed. "I see you've discovered the delights of Annie's already."

"Hell, yes, I'm only sorry it took me two weeks. Although my waistline is not."

"Yeah, diabetes never tasted so good, right?"

Bea grinned. She couldn't have put it better herself. "Well…" She took one last look at the painting waiting to emerge from the canvas. "I'll let you get back to your work."

"Don't be silly." Suzanne waved her hand dismissively through the air. "Stay. This pier's big enough for the two of us as long as you don't mind me working while I talk."

"Umm…" Bea was torn between *wanting* to stay and watch Suzanne do her thing and the familiar urge to quash the desire. "Are you sure?"

"Of course. I can't offer you a seat, but the boards are quite comfortable."

Bea sat down cross-legged, the warmth of the wood heating right through the denim of her blue jeans to her backside, and she shut her eyes and sighed at the bliss of it for a moment. Suzanne resumed her chair. Between them was a voluminous wicker basket stained with splashes of paint and stuffed full of supplies. Bea opened the brown paper bag.

"Which one would you like?" she asked Suzanne. "I have peach cobbler and raspberry pie."

Suzanne's eyes went a little rounded at the offering. "Oh my." She laughed. "I like your style, but I just finished a snack." Then she picked up her brush and resumed painting.

Neither of them said anything until after Bea, who was studiously not watching Suzanne paint, had finished the cobbler. "I can't get over this sky," Bea said. "You can actually see it. Like, all of it. *All* day. Even early in the morning."

It was usually midmorning in LA before the smog cleared enough to even tell what kind of a day was ahead.

"I know what you mean. I came from New York, and you could barely see the sky for buildings. The night sky is the best, though. I didn't realize how many stars I *wasn't* seeing till I moved here."

"New York, huh?" Suzanne's accent was far more subtle than Molly's and Marley's.

"Yep. Came for Christmas, stayed for love."

They wiled away half an hour chatting about life while the sun moved overhead and the water sloshed around the pier footings and the lake dazzled like sequins.

"So you don't know what you're going to do yet, but you don't want to keep doing what you've been doing?" Suzanne clarified.

"Pretty much."

"Like, what's an example? What wouldn't you have done in LA that you've done here?"

Lordy...*so much*. Where did she start? The burnout, the red hair, developing an obsession for Dean Winchester. Missing even one of her daily despised workouts with the elliptical. Made bras optional rather than mandatory. Flirted with a guy ten years younger who curled her toes with one look.

"Plenty." Bea laughed. It was impossible to choose just one.

"Okay then. What's your most recent transgression?"

Well, that was easy. "I had cheese fondue for breakfast."

Suzanne looked at her, startled, then she laughed. "*Wow*. That's a lot of cheese for breakfast. I salute you."

Bea smiled, very pleased with herself. "I'm not sure my doctor will be so forgiving during my annual triglyceride check, but thanks."

"Some foods are worth taking statins for."

Truth. Also, such a first-world problem. They lapsed into silence again and Bea, who had been ignoring the canvas until now, could ignore it no longer. Suzanne had taken the blobs of paint and brushed them across the canvas, shaping them into details—water, trees, sky. It was effortless and utterly mesmerizing.

She used to love watching her mother paint, almost as

absorbed as her in the strokes and the colors and the ethereal way she smiled when she was creating a work. Bea might have been young, but she understood in a way beyond her years that *art* was her mom's happy place. She'd spent a lot of time wishing that *she* could be that happy place instead, but also somehow aware that it wasn't a conscious choice for her mother.

Maybe because, before she'd ruthlessly suppressed it, Bea had also felt that innate tug to create.

Not consciously aware of what she was doing until it was too late, Bea gestured to the basket between them. "Do you mind?" she asked, her pulse a low, slow beat through her head as she pointed to one of several sketch pads.

Suzanne's brows rose. "You're an artist, too?"

"Oh, no." Bea blushed but, despite her denial, she remembered a time when she'd been good—not Suzanne good, not her mom good, but not bad. That had been a long time ago, though, back when her mother had been alive and her fledgling art hadn't been…discouraged. "I've dabbled over the years," she continued dismissively. "Sketching, really. Doodling. For work."

"What's your occupation?"

"Advertising. I did graphic design in college. Started in the art department as an intern."

And she'd kept up with all the tech as she'd advanced through the company over the years, so she understood the processes and the kinds of things she was asking of the art department. It was that attention to detail that always made her campaigns stand out from the others.

But graphic design wasn't *art*.

"Although…" A memory popped into her head. Something she hadn't thought about in a long time. "I used to make hand-painted birthday cards with funny cartoonish characters. For my college friends and work colleagues."

Not art, either.

"Sounds like fun."

"Yeah." Bea laughed as she thought about some of those creations. "It was."

"Well, be my guest," Suzanne said with a smile. "There are a couple of new sketch pads in there, as well as pencils and pastels and charcoal and all kinds of things. Have a dig around."

Bea's hands shook at the possibility, her heartbeat picking up tempo. It had been a long time since she'd free-sketched anything, and she had no idea why she was even trying, but suddenly it felt like the most important thing in the world to do *right now*.

Grabbing what she needed, she opened a medium-size pad and flipped to the first pristine white page. She closed it again, suddenly intimidated beyond belief. But something urged her on, something steely and stronger and bigger than her—maybe bigger than the whole lake. The same something that had urged her that night to throw a dart at a map, and she took a deep breath, flipped it open again, and stared out over the water.

How she sketched anything with her hands trembling so hard, Bea had no idea. But once she'd started, she couldn't stop, and there was nothing but the scratch of charcoal on paper and the soft *swoosh* of sable on canvas between her and Suzanne for an hour. The sun warmed them, birds turned lazy circles above them, an occasional fish jumped in the distance, but Bea wasn't conscious of any of it.

When she was done, she stared at it disbelievingly. She'd brought the lake to life in black and white, and a strange swell of pride and accomplishment mixed with the almost driving need to do it again. But that compulsion didn't fill her with joy and wonder. It filled her with foreboding. This was the *slippery slope* she heard her grandmother talking to her father about late one night when she'd been twelve and had asked if she could do art lessons after school.

Do you want her turning out like her mother?

Bea had recoiled at the prospect then, because although she'd loved her mom, living with her artistic temperament had been full of highs and lows. Often erratic and unsettled and sometimes scary. Like that time her mother had left her with someone she barely knew for two whole days so she could go off and paint the wildflower bloom on Carrizo Plain.

It had been fine, the woman had been kind and a good cook, but Bea had been frightened of her big dog and anxious her mom might forget her.

Bea hadn't wanted to be that person at twelve. Someone who made her father beside himself with worry as to their whereabouts. She didn't want to be that person now. And yet... this past hour, she'd felt that old connection with her mother stir again. The one she'd always felt whenever she'd watched her mom paint.

And that felt good.

"Damn," Suzanne said, looking over as Bea put the charcoal back in the basket and stared down at what she'd produced. "You're good."

Bea blinked back tears that had sprung from nowhere. She shrugged. "It's okay."

Suzanne laughed, then leaned in conspiratorially and whispered, "I hate to break it to you, Bea, but I think you might just be an artist after all."

Laughing nervously, because *no*...this was just doodling... not art—she was a scribbler, not an *artist*—Bea got to her feet. "Well, thanks for the company, but I've got get going." She had a busy day of nothing planned.

As she was about to tear off the sheet, Suzanne reached out and stilled Bea's hands. "Keep the sketch pad. Just in case the muse strikes again."

Muse. That's what her mother used to say—*I'm waiting for the muse to strike*—and the urge to toss the pad into the lake was almost overwhelming. But Bea...couldn't. So she nodded, said, "Thanks," then bade Suzanne goodbye before walking away on unsteady legs.

· · ·

On Wednesday afternoon, Austin pushed open a gate and strode along the path that led to the neat pale-yellow clapboard bungalow on Walnut Street. The grass was immaculately cut, the edges ruthlessly manicured so there wasn't a single blade of grass touching the bordering concrete edging. He walked up two steps to the porch and strode to the front door, which was a deep, glossy brown with a shiny brass knocker at nose height. The door was flanked by a half dozen potted plants of various sizes lined up against the outside wall of the house.

These had to be the reason he was here.

He'd been walking out the door to head home at the end of his shift when Arlo tasked him with this call. Something about a missing tiara and some plants being knocked over. It had all been very vague, but Arlo had wanted him to take care of it, so Austin had gritted his teeth and obliged.

Normally he'd have smiled and said, *On it, boss*, because policing in a small town was usually about petty things, and he *liked* that, but he hadn't seen Beatrice since the weekend, and all he'd been able to think about was stopping by her place after work, and anything that delayed this plan was an irritation.

It was his fault for staying away. And not to be all cool and flippant and *whatevs, baby*, but because he didn't want to come on too strong or appear too eager or desperate. She was finding her feet and making friends, which was a *good* thing. It was obvious she was still pretty pissed at what had happened to make her part ways with her old life, and he wanted to be a fun part of her new life, not some guy who was coming on all heavy from the get-go.

Yes, they'd flirted, and Austin was pretty sure what was happening between them was inevitable, if she felt this tug even half as much as he did. But he wanted Beatrice to want it, too, for it to be fun and natural and something *she* sought. Not something he pushed, not some agenda he was following.

Austin got the impression that she didn't really take him seriously as a boyfriend or a potential partner because of his age, and he got that. Which was why he was happy—well... resigned, anyway—to kick back and let it unfold at its own pace, because he'd never felt like this about a woman in his life and he didn't want to screw it up.

So he'd been playing it cool, but four days was enough. There'd be line dancing at Jack's tonight—maybe she'd like to go with him?

But first, he had a tiara problem to solve.

Austin gave two brisk taps, and Old Mrs. Jennings promptly answered the door. She wore glasses with wire frames, and her white hair was pulled back in the same clasp she used to wear when she worked at the post office when he was a kid. "Hello there, Junior," she said with a smile. "I'm so sorry to disturb you over this. It's silly, really."

"Not a bother, Mrs. Jennings." Austin smiled reassuringly, despite how much he was coming to despise his old nickname. "You can always contact us if something is concerning you; that's what we're here for."

Austin stepped back as she opened the door and said, "Come in, dear."

He gave his boots a good wipe on the mat before he entered the living room, the polished floorboards gleaming in a shaft of afternoon sunlight coming from the open door. "Have a seat down there," she said, indicating the couch to his left. "I'll be just a jiffy."

She scurried away then, and Austin assumed she'd left to fix him a plate of cookies or other home-baked goodies, and he couldn't object without it causing some kind of offense. Because that's the way things were done around here. If someone came knocking, you gave them the very best of Eastern Colorado hospitality, and he'd learned a long time ago that police work was secondary to Credence cordiality.

Even if it meant disrupting his plans to see Beatrice.

Austin sat while he waited, pulling out his notebook and pencil from his shirt pocket, ready to take down any details. The room was as clean and neat as the rest of the house, immaculately kept, and smelled like disinfectant and furniture polish. But it was all very modest. Nothing flashy or expensive. Not ostentatious. So where the hell a tiara came into this, he had no idea.

Mrs. Jennings didn't look the tiara type. No one in Credence did.

"I feel terrible about doing this," she said from somewhere in the kitchen, "but I just can't do it anymore."

Austin frowned. Couldn't do *what* anymore?

"I promised Cecil I'd look after his Princess, but the pots were the last straw."

"Cecil from next door?" Old Cecil Grainger had died a month ago.

"That's right," Mrs. Jennings confirmed. "I mean, the man was dying and fretting so much about what would happen to his Princess, I couldn't say no."

Princess? Was that something to do with the tiara?

"But since the tiara fiasco—"

Aha. They were finally cutting to the chase.

"Princess hasn't been happy," she continued from the other room, "and she knocked over all my potted plants this morning and it was just the last straw and I was at my wits' end when I called the police, and then Arlo said you'd be around to take care of it." She appeared again, her arms full of some kind of giant...creature. "And so here she is."

Mrs. Jennings crossed straight to him and dumped the... cat? in Austin's lap. The animal landed with a *thud*. Jesus, she weighed more than his father's working dog, Rocky.

"There you go, Princess," she said, barely disguising her glee. "You'll be much happier with more space to run around." She petted the animal perfunctorily on the head before wiping her hands on her apron, as if her work here was done.

"Space?" Austin said absently as he glanced down at what was possibly the ugliest cat he'd ever seen.

She was big rather than fat, a Maine coon, he guessed, and her fur, which was wild and thick in some areas and patchy in others, was a dirty kind of orange with streaks of cream. Hair sprouted from her enormous ears—wispy white tufts of it sticking out worse than any old man. She was missing an eye, the lid all wrinkled in its socket, and one tooth stuck out over the lower lip.

The cat squinted up at Austin—not a good look on a one-eyed cat—then glared like he was beneath her contempt and meowed like a fish wife. Princess, his ass. Whoever thought up that name had either a keen sense of irony or had been shit-faced.

"At your ranch," Mrs. Jennings prompted.

Austin frowned. Say *what*, now? "The ranch?"

She smiled at Austin indulgently. "You're a good boy for taking care of this for me."

The cat meowed loudly again, as if she vehemently disagreed with Mrs. Jennings's assessment, then gave Austin a stone-cold glare. He'd never seen a cat with resting bitch face, but he was pretty sure Princess had perfected it. "I'm sorry, Mrs. Jennings. Can we back it up a little? Chief Pike said this was about a missing tiara?"

"Goodness, no." The older woman laughed. "I said she *misses* her tiara."

"The *cat* has a tiara?"

More laughter. "Princess had this cushion with a tiara printed on it, but I had to wash it, because no way was I having that mangy old thing inside my house. But it fell apart in the wash, and things have not been good between us ever since, I'm afraid, and I can't keep dealing with a passive-aggressive animal like this. I went over this twice with Arlo. I'm sure he understood."

Yeah...Austin was also sure Arlo had understood *perfectly*. He was no doubt laughing his ass off back at the station right now.

"He thought you might be able to use a cat on the ranch? Like a barn cat, you know? For the rats."

Princess, who, despite having a forest of hair growing from her ears, appeared to have perfect hearing, meowed most indignantly at that suggestion. Austin stared down at the ugly-ass cat that had the most robust ego he'd ever come across, sitting like a fucking *queen* on his lap. He wasn't sure if it was the word "barn" or "rats" that had caused her reaction.

Whichever one it was, he was pretty sure *Princess* of the Tiara Cushion wasn't going to accept such a lowly station in life.

"You don't need a barn cat?" More indignant mewling from Princess as Mrs. Jennings tutted and worried her bottom lip. "I've asked all around the neighborhood with no luck. Poor Cecil, he's probably rolling in his grave. I'd hate to have her"—Mrs. Jennings mouthed the next two words—"put down."

Austin sighed as the old lady turned the screw. But then an idea hit him. "It's okay, Mrs. Jennings. I know someone who'll take Princess."

A big smile beamed back at him. "Oh, really?"

"Yeah." Beatrice was in the market for a cat, and one had

literally fallen into his lap. And if that wasn't a sign, then he didn't know what was.

He'd just have to convince *her* she needed this ugly, one-eyed, marmalade cat whose ego was writing checks its body could definitely not cash, instead of the cute, fluffy, low-maintenance one she'd imagined.

"What do you say, Princess, want to meet a friend of mine?"

The cat's tail twitched with interest even if her face was the picture of disdain, which was good enough for Austin. Because Mrs. Jennings was obviously not keeping her here one minute longer, and now he had a *legitimate* reason to visit Bea.

Win/win. Whether Princess thought so or not.

CHAPTER THIRTEEN

Bea heard the bootsteps coming up the stairs to her apartment, and her heart began to thump in sync. She'd had two visitors this week already—Mia and Winona—but she'd know these footsteps anywhere. It felt like ages since she'd seen Austin, and she couldn't deny the tiny little trill in her pulse when the knock came, knowing he was standing just outside her door.

She paused *The Walking Dead*—hello, Team Daryl—and slipped out of bed, where she'd been propped against the wall with multiple pillows, balancing the laptop on her knees. There was a TV she could probably use if she took a couple of minutes to work out the remote and find some local channels, but there was something decadent and…subversive about lying in bed all day and watching episode after episode after episode of whatever the hell she wanted.

Also, it kept her mind off going back to the lake.

It was ridiculous to be so breathless when she opened the door, considering she hadn't walked more than a dozen steps to get there, but that was what even the thought of seeing Austin did to her. It was utterly pathetic, like a teenager waiting for her first date, but she couldn't stop the giddiness bubbling like champagne through her blood.

She'd decided she wouldn't actively seek him out, not even for friendship—she could ring any of her new gal pals for that—but if he came to her, then what was a girl to do?

Bea took a steadying breath, then opened the door.

"Hey," he said, standing there all tall and broad and sexy in his police-issue cowboy hat and uniform—who knew beige could be so damn *hot*—with a huge marmalade cat cradled in his arms.

Her breath rushed out on a rough exhale. "Hey."

And neither of them said anything more or even moved, they just devoured the sight of each other, an electrical charge holding them both captive in the moment. It felt like she hadn't seen Austin in a year, and her eyes licked him up like he was a piece of Annie's pie. Despite her usual, unglamorous attire of sweats and a tee, no bra, his gaze ate her up, too, and her body ran riot beneath his intensity. Her nipples hardened, her belly heated, and a hot kind of throb took up residence between her legs.

Until the cat made an indignant *meow*, killing the current between them more effectively than the flick of a switch, and the mutual eye-fucking came to an abrupt end.

"I...ah"—he cleared his throat—"brought you something."

Bea swallowed. The man could have arrived with nothing and would still be everything she wanted. "You'd better come in, then."

She stepped to the side, maybe not far enough to allow him to pass by her without the slightest of brushes, and if he heard the hitch in her breath when his biceps made light contact with the tips of her breasts, he didn't acknowledge it. As he walked to the center of the room, she noticed he was wearing a backpack she'd never seen on him before.

He glanced at the trash basket half-full of beer cans but didn't ask. Which saved Bea from explaining she'd decided to start practicing her three-pointer skills. So far, her proficiency at landing cans from her bed to the basket wasn't great, but she *was* improving, and she was at least picking them up afterward and not leaving them scattered on the floor.

He turned to face her. "Bea*triss*—"

She made a kind of desperate noise at the back of her throat that cut Austin off and made his gaze drop to her mouth. It had been four days since he'd said her name like that, and her ovaries, which had clearly been in deprivation mode, were suddenly hemorrhaging estrogen and controlling her vocal cords.

When she didn't say anything more, he dragged his eyes off her mouth and continued. "Meet your new cat, Princess."

Bea forced herself to look at the animal properly for the first time, which was what any normal person would have done after opening the door instead of ogling a guy she'd already decided should be firmly in the friend zone. Although, given the...unfortunate looks of the creature in question, perhaps it hadn't been a bad thing.

Between the gnarly eye, the snaggletooth, the irregular-fur situation, and the old-man ear hair, the cat wasn't ever going to win best in show. "Wow. Princess, huh? That's..."

"Unexpected?"

Bea laughed. She was going to say *aspirational*. "I think something like Lucifer or Beelzebub would have been more fitting."

As if she knew they were talking about her in not a very flattering light, Princess meowed and twisted in Austin's arms, and he put her down on the linoleum. The cat was clearly in her later years, but she shook herself with all the agility of a kitten as soon as all four paws were grounded and then, pointing her nose in the air, swaggered to Bea's bed like she owned the place, her tail flicking from side to side.

With one graceful leap, she was on the end of the mattress, turning around three times before sitting regally, her head up, her legs out in front like she was a cat goddess guarding the tomb of an Egyptian queen instead of Bea's rumpled bed. Anybody would think she was on an ancient plinth or an antique Queen Anne four-poster instead of a bed that lived in the cupboard.

Not that Bea had bothered to return the bed to its away position since she'd arrived.

Princess regarded them—her *subjects*—with her one good eye, assessing her new surroundings and none too taken with them, apparently. The creature had clearly declared herself the boss.

Bea glanced at Austin. "What's Princess's story, then?"

"Her elderly owner who had doted on her died recently, and she's been staying with the neighbor, but she hasn't taken the adjustment well, and when her most prized possession—a tiara cushion, in case you're wondering"—he shook his head like he couldn't believe he was saying any of the words out loud—"fell apart in the wash, never to be seen again, it was the last straw. And she's been wandering around all cranky and pissed ever since."

Bea regarded the cat with sudden solidarity. She knew exactly what it was like to have the carpet pulled right out from under you and be *mad as hell*. She may not be the cute kitty she had envisioned, but Bea felt a connection to Princess. She was ruffled and pissy and had clearly seen better days.

The cat reminded Bea of herself the day she'd met Austin…

"I know you were after some cute little fluff ball, but you wanted a cat and"—he gestured at Princess—"the universe delivered. And I know you'll make one old man very happy in his grave knowing his Princess is being well taken care of."

Bea didn't have to think twice about it. "Yeah," she said with a nod. "She can stay."

"Really?"

His smile lit his whole face, and Bea's attention was dragged from Princess to Austin, oozing vitality and confidence and wearing the hell out of his uniform. She felt like she hadn't taken the time to fully appreciate that last week. Her gaze drifted to the way his shirt fit a little too snugly across his shoulders and perfectly snug against his abs, and things got very warm inside her sweats.

Absently, she wondered if he worked out and if he had that *V* thing going on between those narrow hips. Wasn't it called an Adonis belt? Or something? When she realized she was staring, Bea dragged her head out from behind Austin's belt, Adonis or otherwise.

"Of course," she said. "She's got spunk."

She almost said *young and perky is overrated*, but Austin was here in her apartment in his uniform, rapidly disproving that theory.

"Awesome." He shrugged his backpack off and lowered it to the floor. "I have supplies in here for you. Food and some kitty litter. Mrs. Jennings assured me she was fully house trained." He unzipped the bag and started pulling things out. "Where should I set up the litter box?"

Even talking about *cat toileting* didn't quell the lick of heat keeping Bea's hormones on a low boil. "Umm...the bathroom, I guess."

Nodding, Austin grabbed what he needed, tossed his hat on the coffee table, rounded the bed, and disappeared into the bathroom. Bea was left in the middle of the room, staring after him. Princess also deigned to look over her shoulder to see where Austin had gone. Bea was pretty sure the cat's gaze also lingered on what was an incredible ass.

Yeah...they were going to get along just fine.

Some noises came from the bathroom, then suddenly Austin reappeared. "C'mon, Princess," he said, picking the cat up off the bed. "You need to see this."

Aware suddenly she was still standing in the same spot as when Austin had disappeared with a less-than-impressed Princess, Bea forced herself into action.

Get a grip, Beatrice.

It was four steps to the kitchen bench and the half-full bottle of wine from last night. It was past five o'clock, right?

She reached for the glass she'd used last night and poured a generous splash, then took a hearty sip. The peppery flavors of the merlot flowed across her tongue, and Bea shut her eyes, relishing the taste as the low murmur of Austin's voice talking to Princess did funny things to her pulse.

"I think she's got it now," he announced.

Bea turned, resting her ass against the counter as Austin placed Princess back on the end of the bed. He petted the cat's head for a moment or two, crooning, "Good girl," to her, like dealing with creatures was second nature to him. Princess certainly seemed to enjoy the attention, tilting her head a little to give Austin better access.

He chuckled and petted her a bit more, and hell if it didn't take Austin's masculinity up about a hundred more notches, standing there in his uniform, showing some love to a one-eyed marmalade cat.

He dished out one last stroke, then dropped his hand and headed in her direction. Bea tried really hard not to check out the long, confident length of his stride and the way his dark pants pulled across his quads, but she failed miserably. By the time he'd stopped beside her at the sink, her pulse was tripping madly.

She swallowed as he flicked on the faucet. "Would you like a drink?" she asked as he washed up, using the pump soap on the windowsill. "There's wine." She held up her glass, like he needed an explanation as to what wine was, but hell if she could think straight with him so damn near. "Or beer in the fridge," she added.

Or maybe just take off your clothes to confirm the presence of an Adonis belt? Please and thank you.

Eep! Heat flooded Bea's face. She was going to hell. This was what happened when a person went too long without sexual release.

Shockingly graphic and utterly scandalous thoughts about

inappropriate men.

He turned his head to look at her and grinned. If he noticed her blush, he didn't say. "Beer would be great." He flicked off the faucet and, when he couldn't find a hand towel, ripped a couple of sheets off the nearby kitchen roll and dried his hands. "I'll get it."

Bea took a breath, and relief, cool as a mountain stream, flooded her veins as he walked three paces away to the fridge and grabbed a beer. Then he cracked the can open and turned, leaning against the fridge door as it snicked shut behind him.

He took a couple of deep swallows. "Ah." He let out a long sigh, then wiped the back of his hand across his mouth, which was hella distracting. "That's good."

"Crappy day?"

"*Long* day," he corrected as their eyes met. "Better now for seeing you."

Bea's breath caught in her throat. Officer Silver Tongue had a way with words. He smiled then but broke their gaze quickly, like he was purposefully taking a step back from the connection she knew he felt, too. Had he decided to keep things in the friend zone as well?

And was she relieved or…disappointed?

He wandered over to the messy coffee table groaning as per usual in assorted *stuff,* now including his hat as he put it down next to the sketch pad still open from the other day. Bea had been ignoring it, but Austin didn't. He picked it up, studying the charcoal drawing.

"This is the lake," he murmured. "Did you do this?"

Bea swallowed, an itch growing under her skin as she suppressed the urge to whip the pad out of his hands and tear that page from the book. "Yes."

"I didn't know you were an artist?"

"Oh, no." She gave a dismissive shake of her head, stalking over to him, then taking the pad from his hand. After flipping it shut, she tossed it back on the table. "I'm not. It's just some doodling."

He quirked one disbelieving eyebrow. "Have you always *doodled*?"

"I dabbled a bit…as a kid. Not for a long time."

"Well, it's good," he said, putting his beer down and picking the pad up again, turning to the sketch.

Her belly looped into one giant knot. "It's okay."

"It's way more than okay," he insisted. "It's remarkable."

Bea blushed at the compliment, somehow both flattered and discomfited. His compliment was like rain on parched earth, but the urge to go out to the lake again had ridden her hard these past couple of days, and his praise only amplified her conflict. "Says the prominent art critic," she said derisively but keeping it light.

He grinned. "Hey, I know what I like." Then he waggled his brows at her.

"Well…anyway." Bea bugged her eyes at him playfully as she once again took the pad from him, tossing it farther away on the couch this time.

"How do you feel about maybe coming out to the ranch and sketching the house? Mom's been talking about getting someone to do it for years now, and it's her birthday soon. I could get it framed, and it'd be the perfect present. I'll pay you whatever the going rate is."

Bea blinked. *Pay her the going rate?* Crap. This was getting out of hand. "No. I'm not…" She shook her head, her chest tightening. "I couldn't do that."

"Why not? You're looking for something different to do, right?"

Well, yes…but. He was looking at her like one and one made two, except it didn't—not in this situation.

"And you're good at it," he continued.

Just like that? She was free, she was good at it, so…why not? God, she suddenly felt ancient in the face of all his fresh-faced optimism.

"Did you enjoy it? Out at the lake."

The pressure to say *no*, to deny the buzz that had consumed her at the lake, drummed in her brain and pushed against her vocal cords, but that wasn't what came out. "Yes."

Her decision to pick up the pad had been intense, and afterward she'd been conflicted, but while she was sketching? She'd freaking loved it. And she couldn't deny it. Didn't want to, either, even if it was just to this guy who looked at her through giant rose-colored glasses.

"Well." He smiled. "Do you need another reason?"

Oh God. She crossed to the sink, then leaned against it as she took a sip of wine, regarding him over the rim of the glass. If only it were that simple. Except, looking at him in this moment, it did seem simple. Or at least *possible,* anyway. Anything seemed possible with Austin. Including crossing that line she told herself she wouldn't cross.

Sure, he was younger, but...sleeping with him wasn't *running away* with him, was it? More than that, *she* was at least free to sleep with him—she wasn't married and she didn't have a kid or family responsibilities. And, as Austin had said, she *was* looking for something different to do.

Her situation was not the same as her mother's situation had been, not at all. So why keep conflating it in her mind?

Bea's gaze drifted to the way he held his body, the way he stood with his feet evenly spaced apart, the way his clothes fit, both hiding and sculpting the musculature beneath. The way his bulky utility belt sat low on his hips, emphasizing their narrowness and drawing attention to the flatness of his belly above...reigniting the question of that V below.

Frankly, it was a much better way to occupy her thoughts than anything to do with art.

"Bea*triss*?"

She blinked at the silkiness of his voice, dragging her eyes to meet his, gratified to find them glowing with the kind of heat that quickened in her veins. It was like being plunged into a thermal pool—heat and steam and the warm caress of water on her bare, aroused flesh. Flowing over her aching nipples, soothing and taunting between her legs. Also running down *his* chest and his abs and funneling lower to his groin, lapping that *V* she couldn't stop fixating on.

"What on earth are you thinking?" he asked, his voice dark and low, vibrating between them.

It was plain, from his husky rumble, he knew her thoughts were carnal in nature, but saying them out loud was another thing entirely. "I…" She swallowed, caught between throwing out an easy lie and the temptation of the truth.

"Tell me."

She cringed. "It's…embarrassing."

A small smile played on his mouth as he hooked both his thumbs in his belt. "C'mon, Bea*triss*. Deep breath. I thought you'd turned over a new leaf and were going to say whatever crossed your mind."

Maybe it was the challenge he laid down—a clarion call to the new Beatrice. Maybe it was the wine, or bringing Princess to her, or the way he'd admired her sketch and simply said *why not* about her art when she'd told herself she *can't* for as long as she could remember. Maybe it was those thumbs hooked low in exactly the spot she couldn't stop thinking about. But the thoughts in her head suddenly became words and the pressure to utter them became too much.

"I was wondering if you had that *V* thing going on between your hips, you know…" She dropped her gaze to the area of his anatomy under discussion. "With the muscles there."

Austin didn't say a word as the smile hovering on his mouth faded. He didn't do anything for a beat or two, either, just drew in a couple of deep, ragged breaths.

Then reached for his belt buckle.

CHAPTER FOURTEEN

Bea's heart thumped like a gong as his utility belt hit the floor with a *thud*. Their gazes locked and her throat went as dry as the Santa Anas in September. He reached for the top button of his shirt and flicked it open before descending to the next and the next.

Oh God, oh God, oh God.

How could she be standing so still and yet her body be in such an uproar? Everything heating and blooming and freaking *melting*. Bea was so damn hot, she wanted to tear her own clothes off.

Inch by glorious inch, Austin's chest was revealed. Smooth for the most part, except for a sprinkling of light-brown hair over his pecs and around his nipples. A smattering headed southward, too—down, down, down—to his belly button and down again, arrowing into a single trail until the low-slung band of his pants cut off her view. He tugged his shirttails out, then shrugged out of the garment and tossed it on the floor next to his utility belt.

And now that she could see the whole, her throat went as dry as the freaking *Mojave*.

A shirtless Austin was something to behold. Acres of smooth golden skin, broad shoulders, and well-defined pecs. Prominent collarbones and that shallow little hollow where the two met. Easily traceable ribs and the dips in between. A ladder of slightly puckered abs bisected by just the right amount of hair.

And yep, there it was. Holy Adonis, Batman. *V* for victory. *V* for vice.

V for *va-va-voom.*

Oh, he wasn't *cut* like a lot of guys who pranced around certain LA muscle beaches, and while his pants were sitting quite low on his hips, she couldn't see what was below, but what she *could* see showed some muscular delineation going on between the hard ridges of his hips. And it was magnificent.

"So…" She dragged her eyes back to his face to meet his gaze. God, even her *eyes* felt hot, like they were boiling in their sockets. "That's a yes, then." Bea took a giant slug of wine. "You…work out?"

He teamed a slow, lazy smile with a slow, lazy shake of his head. "Ranch work is all."

"Well…whatever you're doing…" She flicked her gaze down again for another slow tour of his chest and abs. "It's working."

"Thank you."

He slid his hand to his belly and drummed his fingers on his abs and, God help her, Bea's gaze honed in on the movement, following it like he was tapping out some kind of code and the fate of the world depended on her cracking it.

"I've been told they feel pretty good, too." His smile grew bigger as he lifted his hand from his abs and crooked a finger at her. "Why don't you come over here and see for yourself?"

Bea would've liked to have been able to say in years to come that she regained her senses at that moment and politely declined his invitation. Alas, she was not that strong. It was like he'd opened the doors to Disneyland for a private tour, and Bea was a sucker for a theme park.

As if pulled by an invisible string, she gulped down the last of her wine and walked on unsteady legs to where he stood. The closer she got, the hotter things got, as if he was holding her in the beam of a laser. His smile faded as heat smoldered in his eyes and his gaze held and locked on hers. Bea's heartbeat crashed in her ears and her breathing rasped in her lungs and rattled in her throat.

A small part of her couldn't believe she was doing this— that she was daring. The rest of her surrendered to the burn.

She stopped in front of Austin, close but not touching. Heat radiated off his skin in waves, blasting over her like thermal steam from a geyser, tugging at her like the tide. A faint trace of his cologne tickled her nostrils as the earthier aroma of hot male flesh prickled awareness in that part of her brain that was all primal. All, *You Tarzan, me Jane.*

She wanted this man, damn it. And he wanted her.

With her head thumping to the pound of her pulse, she dragged her gaze from his, zeroing in on the warm bulk of his biceps at her eye level and, tentatively, she touched him there. It was only light, but the shudder of his breath was heavy, and her toes curled as her body swayed toward his. She traced her finger around his biceps, then kept going, moving around him as she trailed across his back.

Goose bumps stippled his flesh, and the honed muscles beneath her gossamer touch rippled in response. The pad of her finger found his opposite biceps, and she kept going, slowly circling his body till she was back at his front. Her finger trekked across his chest from one nipple to the other, more goose bumps following in its wake as her hand slid away and fell to her side.

They were close—*so* close—she could hear his heavy breathing, could see the sprout of his scruff along the hard ridge of his windpipe and the bob of his throat as he swallowed.

"Can I go lower?" she asked, her husky voice loaning a kind of desperation to the bold request. She didn't look at him, her gaze transfixed by the thick *thud* of the pulse in his throat.

He made a low kind of noise in the back of his throat, somewhere between a growl and a groan. "Be my guest," he said, his voice full of gravel, laced with the kind of desperation she recognized in herself.

Permission granted, she placed her shaking hands on his pecs and rested them there for a beat or two, liking the way her fingers looked curling into the cushion of muscle. She molded them, reveling in the soft prickle of hair and the brush of his nipples on her palms as the dizzying whisper of *mine* shot through her system like an illicit drug.

Slowly, she moved them down, watching her hands iron flat over his ribs, then her fingers tent and drift down his abs before just her index fingers brushed along his waistband, outward to the subtle furrow defining the inside edges of his hip bones.

She stroked her nails lightly along the grooves, feeling the muscles contract, the deep suck of his breathing the backing track to her little exploration. She glanced up, and his hot blue eyes blazed like twin lasers down into hers. "You're beautiful," she whispered, because he was pure male perfection, and even if she never did more with him than this, she'd die a happy woman.

"No." He shook his head, his hands sweeping up, furrowing into her hair at the back of her head, cupping it. "You're beautiful."

He lowered his head then, and nothing on earth could have stopped Bea from rising onto her tiptoes to meet his lips as they crashed onto hers, hard and probing and demanding, speaking of a hunger that had been building from the moment he'd *ma'am*ed her and bloomed with every smile, every piece of pie, every Bea*triss*.

And in that instant, she knew that just touching him was never going to be enough. That if she died right now, she'd become a vengeful ghost roaming the earth, pissed that she didn't get to know Austin Cooper in the most intimate way possible.

"Jesus," he said, pulling away, his eyes glinting with a wild kind of fever, his mouth wet, his lungs working hard, and she took a mental picture because *she* had done this to him. Beatrice Archer—mild-mannered, play-it-by-the-book, ex–corporate sheep—had made this sexy man pant and yearn and lust. "I think my heart is about to burst out of my chest."

Bea smiled, slipping her hand over his pectoral muscle again, feeling the brisk, hard bang beneath her palm. She grabbed one of his hands that was still cradling her head and pulled it down, placing it over the frantic beat of her own heart, his big hand cupping her breast over the fabric of her shirt. Her left nipple went rigid beneath his palm, and his thumb stroked over it, causing her to shudder.

"You like that?" he asked, his voice low and husky as his thumb continued its maddening tease.

She nodded. "I do."

"And this?" His hand slid away, only to find the hem of her T-shirt and push under, sliding up the bare skin of her belly and her ribs to claim her equally bare breast, his thumb returning to taunt the nipple some more.

Bea's throat constricted, and she had to lock her knees tight as a surge of lust turned everything liquid. "Yes," she gasped.

His other hand pushed under her T-shirt, sliding onto the other breast, his thumb working that nipple, and Bea thanked all the sweet angels and evolution, she supposed, for opposable thumbs. She actually whimpered this time as a hot pulse shot like a flaming arrow from her nipples straight down her belly, hitting a target directly between her legs.

"What do you want, Bea*triss*?" he asked, his blue gaze boring into hers as he continued to wreak havoc on her body. "Tell me what you want."

Bea had never been asked what she wanted. Normally, at this stage of the sexy times, it was fairly obvious, and one thing led to another and the *P* in *V* thing happened. It was usually accomplished in the standard missionary position, because frankly, it had been too damn infrequent to get particular.

But hell, if she didn't know *exactly* how she wanted this to go down.

"I want to—" Bea stopped abruptly and swallowed, hesitant again as her gaze dropped to his throat. Could she actually *go* there? Sure, she'd declared she was going to say whatever crossed her mind, but could she say *that*?

"Tell me," he murmured. Then he squeezed her nipples, and Bea's eyes fluttered closed on a hot wave of ecstasy, her hand sliding to his hips for purchase as more flaming arrows found their mark. "Tell me how you like to be fucked."

Bea opened her eyes, meeting his with frankness and purpose. That was the thing—she didn't want to just lay there and be *serviced* by him. She'd been too damn passive in the bedroom. Letting men lead. Letting men *do* stuff *to* her, often to the detriment of her own pleasure. And enough was enough.

"*I* want to fuck *you*." Yes. That's what she wanted, damn it. *She* wanted to fuck *him*. Not the other way around. She was so freaking *mad* at herself for her passivity—she wanted to *screw* Austin very, very badly.

Clearly unperturbed by the idea, he grinned and said, "If you insist."

Bea took a step back, and his hand slid from her breasts. He didn't object, but her nipples certainly did. She quashed their rebellion ruthlessly with promises of an imminent orgasm. Planting a hand in the middle of his chest, she shoved him lightly, and he took a step backward.

"I want you to take off your pants and your shoes." Bea gave him another light shove, and he retreated again. "I want you to lie naked in the center of my bed." Another shove, another step backward. "And I want to climb on top of you and ride you until we both come."

Her eyes fell on his hat on the coffee table, and she picked it up. Who needed to ride a horse when she could ride a cowboy? Or the closest thing to one she'd ever met. "That okay by you?" she asked as she plonked the hat on her head, still advancing.

He didn't bother answering, nor did he stop retreating as he reached for the stud on his pants and yanked his zipper down. The metallic tearing was like a gunshot in the quiet of the room, racing down her spine and tightening everything from her belly to her vocal cords.

His boots came next, toeing them off and kicking them aside, yanking off his socks, without falling over or even halting his inexorable walk backward. The only thing that did was the mattress hitting the backs of his knees. He stopped then and so did Bea, probably about six feet separating them.

But then his hands got busy, his blue gaze holding hers as he reached into his back pocket, grabbed his wallet, and pulled out a condom. Bea swallowed at the sight of it.

Things were getting real.

He tossed his wallet on the ground and the foil packet on the bed, then slid his fingers inside the waistband of his pants at his hips and eased both them *and* his black boxer briefs down together. He broke eye contact to bend at the waist and push his pants all the way down his legs and step out of them, but then they were gone and he was straightening, standing buck naked in front of her, his gaze once again seeking hers.

Bea, however, was *not* returning his gaze. Her breath cut off with a strangled kind of gurgle in her throat as her eyes dropped to inspect Austin's body in *all* its glory. Hell...the man was the *full* package—tall and broad and solid. Chest. Shoulders. Arms. Abs. Quads. The perfect symmetry of bone and muscle, of flesh and blood that ancient artists had captured so faithfully in paint and marble.

And that aptly named Adonis belt slung between hip bones

and funneling down to a thatch of darker hair from which rose a magnificently solid penis, standing thick and proud and hard, taut and flushed, ready for action.

If Bea had been a virgin, she might just have been intimidated by the size of him. She *was not*, but it still didn't stop her from swooning a little, and she had to curl her fingers into her palms to keep from reaching for it. She didn't want to get distracted, and Austin's cock looked like it was the ultimate weapon of mass distraction.

As per his instructions and without needing to be reminded, Austin sunk onto the mattress, disturbing an indignant Princess, who meowed loudly, jumped from the bed, and made a beeline for the kitchen. Austin, clearly not put off by the cat's presence, shimmied backward on the mattress—a truly fabulous sight to behold. Bea, however, wasn't sure what the rules were in exposing a pet to what she hoped was going to be explicit pornographic content, so she pulled the cheap plastic concertinaed divider across to keep Princess out.

"Here okay?" Austin asked as she returned her attention to the bed.

Bea blinked. She couldn't be certain without getting out some kind of measuring device, but she was pretty sure Austin was lying dead center of the bed. Maybe it was the cop in him, but Austin was clearly a man who knew how to follow instructions.

And damn if that didn't make her that much hotter for him.

She nodded. "There is just fine." She took a moment to ogle his body again. How could a man in a reclined position look so damn *ready*? Like his muscles were primed to spring, like he was pumped for action. His dick, now resting on that swath of muscle between his hips, was fully cocked. And his balls, pulled in tight, looked locked and loaded.

The very sight of him lying there in such readiness made her sigh. "*You're* just fine."

He shot her a lazy grin—hell, even *it* managed to look eager—as he reached for the foil packet. "Want me to put this on?"

Bea nodded. Hell yes she did. "Please."

He chuckled as if her manners had amused him, but Bea promptly forgot about that as he grabbed his shaft with one hand and lifted the packet to his mouth with the other, tearing the corner open with his teeth. She wanted to lecture him about the dangers of puncturing the condom using that technique, but watching him manhandle himself sucked every atom of oxygen from Bea's lungs *and her brain*, plucking every thought out of her head. Seeing his big hand in such a private place was twisting her belly into knots.

"Wait," she said as Austin went to apply the condom to the taut, flushed dome of his cock.

He stopped, his gaze flicking to hers. "Everything okay?"

Bea nodded. "Could you…" She stopped, swallowed. Her pulse fluttered madly. Dare she ask him that?

"Could I what, honey?" he asked, his voice gravelly, his eyes hot as blue flame as they captured hers in their heat, his chest rising and falling a little unevenly.

"Could you…touch yourself for me?"

"Christ, Beatrice." He huffed out a kind of half laugh, half groan. "I'll do anything for you."

He dropped his hand with the condom to the bed and the other, the one that was already where she wanted it, changed purpose. It went from an impersonal, functional grip to a looser hold, his fingers curling all the way around his shaft, then sliding lazily from root to tip and back again. His eyes closed as his breath hissed out, and Bea had to lock her knees again to keep from melting into a puddle. Her nipples were two hard points against her tee, scraping erotically, causing the ache between her legs to become a throb.

"Like this?" he asked, his eyes flicking open, spearing her

with a look so full of desire, Bea felt as if she could drown in it.

She nodded. Her throat too dry to form words. *Exactly like that.*

"How long?"

She swallowed, wet her lips. "How long can you last?"

"As long as you need me to."

But the strain in his voice, the taut bow of his back, the bulge of the veins in his neck were telling. His hand was still a dirty, *dirty* spectacle, moving lazily up and down his shaft, but he was clearly fighting hard to keep his arousal in check. Bea was flattered by his need to give her what she wanted, and she admired his resolve, his stamina. For damn sure she was going to test it at some stage. But for now, she really just needed to be *on* him.

"It's okay, cowboy, easy there," she relented, still torn between the show and some action. "You can suit up now." Then she removed his hat, whipped her T-shirt over her head, and crammed the hat back on again.

Austin neither removed his hand nor put the condom on as he ogled her breasts. "Holy shit," he muttered, staring as hard at her as she had stared at him. "Beatrice...you are fucking sensational."

Beatrice knew her boobs were a bit on the small side and were disproportional to her wider hips, butt, and thighs, but in this moment, she believed Austin 100 percent. In this moment, she felt like a freaking supermodel. It gave her the courage to push down her sweats and her panties, too, and kick out of them, just as Austin had done, and then to stand there in front of him and let him look his fill.

Until she remembered she hadn't gotten around to doing anything about the state of her hoo-ha. *Crap.* A surge of heat flushed her cheeks, and it took all her willpower not to shove her hands in front of her bikini area and stammer out an apology.

Maybe he hadn't noticed?

Jesus, *don't be an idiot, Beatrice*. Of course he'd noticed. It could probably be *noticed* from *space*. He was staring right at her, and she had the Amazon forest growing between her legs.

She knew from her headful of useless advertising stats that there was an entire generation of men out there who didn't realize women came with pubic hair, thanks to porn and the pressure from advertising, and Austin probably fell smack in that demographic.

Shooting her an impatient look as he quickly donned the condom, he said, "Saddle up, cowgirl. This stallion is champing at the bit."

God yes, *a stallion*. Bea couldn't have described him better had she tried. All fit and honed and lean, solid muscles rippling beneath taut flesh, nostrils flaring.

The hard length of his arousal proud and potent even confined in a thin layer of latex.

"Bea*triss*, honey," he said on a low kind of growl, "you're killing me."

And he was looking at her—*every single inch* of her—from his hat to her knees and lingering at *all the things* in between, and he clearly liked what he saw, and it was just the liberation Bea needed. Suddenly, she didn't give a rat's ass about her lack of grooming. In fact, *fuck* grooming. Fuck…waxing and plucking and lasering and all the other painful, expensive hair-removal crap women felt pressured to do so their bodies were more *palatable* for men.

Yep—from now on, she was going the full bush, and men could take it or leave it.

With that decided, Bea put a knee on the bed and crawled, in what she hoped was a sophisticated, feline kind of way, toward Austin's reclined form. She didn't know if she pulled it off, but the way his eyes roved all over as she advanced led her to believe he appreciated it anyway, which, in turn, did funny things to her breathing. When her knee nudged his hip, she halted, sat back on her haunches, and barely stopped herself from undulating in a lazy feline stretch, pushing her chest out as his gaze settled on her breasts, her nipples reacting shamelessly to his ogling.

The air between them churned with the ragged noise of their breathing. Leaning forward a little, Bea raised her hand, bringing her index finger to his mouth. His lips parted, and she traced them, remembering how he'd tasted. Her finger trailed down his chin to his throat, his windpipe undulating beneath the caress as he swallowed.

Trekking lower still, she swirled the tip of her finger around the hollow at the base of his throat before tracing lower. She paused at the midpoint between his nipples, deciding which way to go, aware of his gaze on her, of the husky timbre of his breath—and hers—of the tension in his body as if he, too, was on a knife's edge over her next move.

That kind of power was heady, and it flushed through her system, supercharging her arousal. Decision made, her index finger trailed left and turned lazy circles around and around and around the nipple.

He muttered a word that would have shocked her grandmother all the way to the roots of her hair as his eyes fluttered shut, his teeth sinking into his bottom lip, his hands fisting the sheet. A low hum of satisfaction joined the buzz of anticipation coursing through her system. It felt good to be able to touch his body like this. To be free to do as she pleased. To be unconstrained.

A few weeks ago, her life had been constrained in ways she hadn't even realized, and now here she was, in the middle of the goddamn country—naked—with a guy—*also naked*—she'd known for a week, touching him freely. Causing him to mutter filthy-sexy words and his body to draw tight as a bow.

Her hand slid away, and she watched his stubbly face as

his eyes drifted open. "You just going to play with me, honey?"

A smile hovered on his mouth, so Bea didn't think he was objecting, but it did raise the question. "Could I?" Because seriously, while every nerve in her body was stretched taut in anticipation of the first orgasm she'd have with another human being in a very long time, this—just *touching* this man—was a climax of a different sort.

The tactile kind that was stimulating on a whole other level.

"Absolutely." He swallowed, his gaze locking with hers. "I am at your disposal."

His words, loaded with innuendo, slid in between the muscle fibers buried deep inside her pelvis and licked, long and slow.

"And as far as I know," he added with a wry smile, "no dude's dick has ever actually dropped off from a prolonged boner."

Bea glanced at the dick in question, looking flushed and potent and all dressed up, waiting for *her*, and a hot wave of arousal surged through her system. Urgent SOS signals from her clitoris demanded she quit screwing around with the foreplay and just *get on top already*.

"Maybe not," Bea said, returning her attention to his face. "But we probably shouldn't press our luck. You know"—she smiled—"just in case."

"Right." He grinned. "'Cause that would be—"

"A tragedy."

"Of epic proportions."

Bea smiled. "You ready for this?"

"Honey," he said, his gaze locking on hers, "I've been ready since the day I saw you eating ice cream outside Annie's."

And damn if her heart didn't do a funny little triple tap in her chest. No twenty-five-year-old should have such a way with words.

With their gazes still locked, Beatrice rose from her

haunches and slid her leg over him. His breath hissed out and his hands went to her rounded hips as the length of him slid between her slippery folds. His groan, deep and low, was followed swiftly by her own gasp as tissues screamingly sensitized by their foreplay reacted to the thick nudge of his head, and it took all her willpower not to rub it over her clit for a few moments as she lifted and notched him at her entrance.

With his fingers biting into her hips and his blue gaze boring a hole into hers, Bea sank slowly down, taking him inside her bit by bit. Her heartbeat roared through her ears and she panted hard, her mouth parted as his length disappeared, inch after delicious inch, watching his face intently as she swallowed him up. He slid in easily, and Bea took a moment to savor the stretch as he bottomed out.

She pulsed around him, adjusting to his girth, her entire body one giant throb as nerve endings flicked on like switches, sizzling and ready, humming in anticipation. When her eyes finally drifted open, Bea found him watching her, his blue gaze heated but lazy, like he'd been enjoying the show.

"Bea*triss*…" His fingers tightened on her hips again as his eyes took in his hat and her mouth and her breasts and her belly button and continued all the way down to where they were joined. It was a slow and thorough perusal, and Bea felt it all the way to the bottom of her heart. "You belong on top of me."

It wasn't said with brashness or bravado. There was no possession implied. It was just a quiet statement of the moment, and it turned Bea to mush.

Gah! This man and his words.

"Now what?" he asked.

Bea dragged herself back from the place where all his lovely words were being stored, because it was rodeo time. Using an index finger, she pushed the brim of his hat back a little and tossed her head. She smiled then, leaning in a little as she planted her left hand on his right shoulder. "Now I'm going to ride you long and slow."

"Because you haven't tortured me enough already?"

She smiled. "Lay back and enjoy."

He gave an exaggerated, resigned sigh, but there was a wicked kind of glint in his eyes as he said, "Yes, ma'am."

She almost laughed at his choice of phrase—like she needed to be any more turned on. Steadying herself for a beat, Bea rocked on top of him, her breathing sucking away at the potent stimulation.

"Oh, *fuuuck*," he muttered, and Bea couldn't have put it any better herself.

Gripping his shoulder harder, she rocked some more. Then, leaning into her hand for leverage, she lifted off him halfway, feeling every damn inch of it. "Oh *God*," she gasped, staring at him incredulously as the tight, slick glove of her squeezed the hard jut of him before she lowered again, taking him all the way to the hilt.

Surely sex had never been this good?

"Yeah." He grunted as she rocked on him a little to ease the delicious burn. "I know."

It had been Bea's plan to wring this out for as long as she could. To undulate like a belly dancer on top of him, like a snake charmer weaving a spell for a cobra, until Austin was begging her to come. But hell if she could do that now. Her months of abstinence had caught up with her in an instant, and the urge to come was a wild beat in her pulse, overriding all her fancy plans.

All she wanted was the shortcut to *O* town. Screw the scenic route.

"I hope you don't mind, but I don't think long and slow is an option for me right now," she admitted.

He gritted his teeth. "Thank Christ for that."

Bea laughed. "Hold on to me tight—I don't want to fall off."

"Yes, ma'am," he said, and his fingers splayed wide on her hips, caging her securely.

And then there was nothing else but to do as she promised and *fuck* him. No slow and long. No teasing. No belly dancing or snake charming. Just leaning into both her hands gripping his shoulders, rising up on her knees and flexing her pelvis, pumping her hips up and down his shaft, performing hasty withdrawals until he was all but out, then seating herself again, taking all of him in one smooth snap of her hips, sending a shudder through her pelvis and a fork of lightning up her spine.

He took it all—everything. Laying there with his body sprung tight as a drum, his jaw tense, denying his pleasure with a grunt at every snap of her hips, his breath quickening, his fingers rhythmically squeezing the flesh of her hips but holding her fast, his gaze fixed hungrily on the rock of her breasts and the wide gash of her mouth as she moaned and gasped. But still letting her call the shots, letting her use his body for her own gratification and hanging on for the ride.

Christ, who knew taking charge in bed could be *this* good? This…heady. No wonder men thought they ruled the freaking earth.

The hum in her pelvis built to a buzz, then to a sizzle as everything that had coiled and tightened started to melt and swirl. Darts of sensation fired like shooting stars from her clitoris, spreading through her pelvis and ass, furrowing under her skin to her inner thighs and her spine and her nipples. *"Austin."* She clawed at his shoulders as the ground below her started to dissolve.

"It's okay," he panted, his hands sliding to palm her ass now. "I got you."

He did, but it didn't help, because the floor was shifting, and she could see a rainbow in a waterfall in her mind's eye— hell, she could feel the mist from it on her face—and it was glowing bright, pulsing with promise, but she couldn't quite reach… It was like there was a barrier between her and it and she couldn't quite get her fingers there.

Rocking her hips faster, Bea chased the sensation, dragging a groan from Austin's lips. But the ground just kept on shifting like quicksand beneath her feet and the waterfall shimmered like a mirage beyond her grasp and she cried out in frustration.

"Beatrice?"

His blue eyes blazed with fever, a dull flush to his cheeks betraying the degree of his arousal as their gazes locked. "I can't…" she panted.

And then, as if he knew exactly what she needed, he lifted his head, his lips seeking and finding a nipple and sucking it into his hot, hot mouth. His fingers, just as deft, slid into the slickness between her legs, straight to the engorged bud of her clitoris.

"God, Beatrice," he muttered around her nipple, "you're so wet."

She moaned at the dual stimuli. "I've been wet since I met you."

But they were all the words she was capable of as his finger stroked in just the right place and his teeth pressed into the puckered ripeness of her nipple and the ground firmed up and she rushed headlong into the throbbing rainbow of light, her hips snapping to a halt as the colors burst into a kaleidoscope of hues, bathing her body in fat droplets of pleasure as she clenched hard around him, pulsing and shuddering through her orgasm.

He took up the slack then, taking over where she left off, one arm banded around her back, gathering her close as he relinquished his mouthful of nipple to bury his face in her throat and thrust. Bea gasped as he plowed through the undulating walls of her sex, stoking her excitement *and* her orgasm higher.

"Austin!"

She clung to his shoulders as he did it again and again, prolonging her pleasure and clearly stoking his own, his big frame starting to tremble as his pants grew rougher, hot puffs of air licking like tongues on her throat.

"Oh, *Jesus*," he muttered, his thrusts losing rhythm for a few moments before halting abruptly, the arm around her banding like a vise. "I'm coming."

"Yes." A bloom of triumph joined her dizzying heights of pleasure. *"Yes, yes, yes."*

And her hips took over again, riding him through his orgasm and the last vestiges of hers, until they were both spent and gasping in each other's arms, and Austin fell backward onto the mattress, taking her with him, knocking his hat off her head in the process.

"I hope you've got more than one condom," Bea said, her breathing erratic, "because I'm going to want to do that again to make sure it wasn't some kind of freak one-off."

He chuckled, also breathing heavily. "There was nothing freak about that, Bea*triss*. That was *divine*. But never fear, I have two more to prove it to you."

Bea, sprawled on top of him with her hair fanned out over his chest, smiled. He was still inside her and his hands were a solid warmth on the small of her back. Her nose was pressed into the hollow at his throat and her heart pounded over the exact same spot his was pounding. It felt good—right—here like this, but she wondered if she should get off him.

"Am I too heavy?" she asked.

One time, a guy—a one-night stand—had responded to that question with *a bit* before he'd moved in a way that tipped her unceremoniously off him, so she should know better than to ask such a leading question. But his arms tightened around her and his, "You're perfect," had Bea's heart skipping a beat.

She smiled, pressing her lips into that delicious little hollow, her eyes shutting as his hand trekked from the small of her back to her hair, running his fingers through it, a wave of goose bumps prickling along her scalp and down her neck. She opened her eyes to a loose lock of her feathery hair falling lightly against his chest, and she felt a thrill all over again at her bold new color.

"You want to eat, drink, sleep, watch zombies with me, or…" She undulated her internal muscles against him. "Go again?"

He gave a half chuckle, half groan as his hand clamped down tight on the small of her back. "Definitely yes to the last one. I might just need a few more minutes' recovery time."

Bea made a *pfft* kind of noise. "I thought you young guys had all the stamina."

Laughing, he said, "I generally need more than two minutes. In the meantime, I like all the other options. Although I had planned on asking you to go with me to line dancing at Jack's tonight."

Bea lifted her head with difficulty, given it felt as leaden with sexual satisfaction as the rest of her. Not trusting it to stay upright, she propped her chin on her curled fist so she could keep it in place as she regarded him. "That would require putting on clothes, right?"

He nodded, a smile on his lips. "Yes."

She scrunched up her face. "Seems a shame?"

"Yes." He leaned in and kissed her nose. "I couldn't agree more."

"So…how about…" She shifted, easing off him, shuddering a little as he slid free of her before settling on her side on the mattress facing him. "You go ditch that condom, I go pop some popcorn, and we watch TV and pet the cat for a while?"

"Mmm." He inhaled deeply, the kind of inhalation that spoke of bone-deep content. "You had me at popcorn."

Bea smiled and scrambled off the bed and to her feet. She went to reach for her clothes, as was her custom in front of a man she'd been intimate with only once, but then stopped herself. Nope. *Screw it.* He hadn't seemed put off by her body prior to having sex with her, so she was damned if she was going to cover it up now.

Pie calories and all, *this* was her body. It carried her where she wanted to go, it performed complex tasks every day, it was strong and healthy. And she was done with wishing it was different.

"Meet you back here," she said, looking over her shoulder.

"Uh-huh," he agreed but didn't move, obviously checking out her ass as she pulled aside the plastic concertinaed curtain and walked away. Bea made sure to put a little extra swing in her step.

"Tease," he called after her.

"Pervert," she replied, so freaking happy, she practically skipped.

...

Austin's watch told him it was just after five the following morning as he woke in the best way it was possible for him to wake—wrapped around a soft, warm, naked woman. His nose was buried in the fluffy lightness of her hair, his arm was tucked around her waist, and his regular five a.m. boner was pressed into the soft cushion of her ass. Gentle light pushed in through the window over the sink as he lay cocooned in the smell of popcorn, clean hair, and dirty sex.

They'd done the wild thing twice more last night, burning up the sheets and scandalizing Princess, who looked at them like *they* were the animals. And he'd like nothing more than to go again—clearly, he was up for it—but he had to be at work in an hour, and he had to head out to the ranch for a clean uniform first.

After contemplating just slipping out and leaving Beatrice

a note, Austin decided to wake her instead. He wasn't sure how she was going to feel about this in the cold light of day—she seemed like the kind of woman who analyzed everything to within an inch of its life despite her protestations of turning over a new leaf—and he didn't want her to think he'd freaked out and left.

"Bea*triss*, honey," he murmured, nuzzling her neck, dropping a string of kisses down her nape, inhaling deeply, determined to take the scent of her neck with him wherever he went today.

"Mmm," she murmured all low and sleepy, shifting against him, which caused a delicious jolt to his groin as her ass slid against his erection.

"I have to go," he whispered as he continued to nuzzle the point where her neck sloped to her shoulder.

"No," she muttered sleepily, her hand sliding up and anchoring around his neck, her fingers laced into the hair at his nape. "Don't want you to go."

Austin chuckled, more than happy with the possessive feel of her arm. He didn't want to go, either. He *never* wanted to leave this bed. "I start work in an hour and I need to go home for a clean uniform first."

"Stay for a bit longer," she cajoled, snuggling back into him, rubbing her ass against his morning glory. "I have somewhere you can put that."

His eyes fluttered closed, inhaling sharply at the delicious kind of torture. "There are no condoms left," he said and smiled at her low, disapproving growl.

She rubbed against him some more. "That is a shame. I am exceptionally horny right now."

Austin almost groaned out loud at her sleepy pronounce-ment. His dick surged. He could certainly relate. Glancing at his watch again, he did a quick calculation. There wasn't time for the full smorgasbord his body craved, but maybe there was a way he could help her out. "Oh yeah?"

"Uh-huh," she said on a sigh.

"How horny?" he asked, his lips trekking up the side of her neck as the hand on her belly moved south.

"Let's just say I have a new appreciation for rabbits." And then she murmured, "Mmm," and arched her back as his hand crept lower and breathed, *"Oh god,"* as his fingers slid between her legs.

"How fast can you come, Beatrice?" Austin whispered in her ear.

Her hand tightened around his neck and she whimpered. "Austin…you don't have to… It's fine."

He grinned. "I *want* to."

"In that case—" She gasped and arched her back as Austin found the hard nub of her clitoris. "I doubt it'll take long at all."

"Then relax." He swiped his tongue against the bony prominence behind her ear. "And allow me."

She made an indistinct kind of noise before going boneless in his arms except for her top leg, which she abducted, resting it against his top thigh, opening herself wide for him. Austin took complete advantage of the invitation, sliding two fingers inside her tight, slick heat as his thumb worked her clit.

Her long, low moan was all the encouragement he needed, and soon, true to her word, she was panting and squirming and riding his hand, her ass against his rock-hard dick the sweetest kind of torture as his fingers rubbed and plundered. There was a drumbeat in his chest and a cyclonic roar inside his head and a furnace between their slicked-up bodies, and Austin felt like the Lord of Orgasms as she flew apart in his arms.

He reveled in the cries of ecstasy torn from her throat and the way she shuddered and the sharp sting of his scalp as she twisted her fingers into the hair at his nape. He felt fucking invincible as he stroked her until her leg flopped down and she begged him to stop.

Austin smiled, his lips nuzzling between her shoulder and neck. "And my work here is done." He pressed a kiss to the spot as he eased his arms from around her and rolled onto his back. "I gotta go," he told the ceiling.

He was going to be late. Arlo would be pissed. But with the long stretch of her naked back open to his view, Austin's give-a-damn was temporarily busted. This sight was worth an ass-chewing from his boss any day.

"If I could move even one muscle, I'd try and stop you again."

He chuckled, sliding his hand onto her shoulder and squeezing it one last time before kicking back the covers and swinging his legs over the side of the bed, because if he didn't make a move, he'd be here all day, and he couldn't leave all the bad-guy catching up to Arlo. "I'll see you this afternoon after work."

"Mmm," she said sleepily as she snuggled on her side. Austin pulled the covers up over her, wishing like hell he could climb back in there with her. "Sweet dreams," he whispered.

"Are made of cheese," she replied in a drowsy voice, and he chuckled as he reached for the plastic curtain and dragged it open to locate his clothes, which still lay strewn on the floor.

Princess, who had decided his shirt was a good spot to curl up, meowed at him indignantly as he shooed her off it and grabbed it up. It was wrinkled and covered in cat hair, as were his pants, but they would have to do for now. He dressed quickly before locating his wallet, keys, phone, and hat—which would forever remind him of Beatrice going all cowgirl—all while the cat meowed and wound itself around Austin's legs.

"Fine." He shook his head at the insistent animal as he grabbed a can of what he knew to be a very expensive brand of cat food from the stash Mrs. Jennings had given him. "But if I get fired, I'm blaming you."

He quickly dumped the fishy-smelling contents onto a

saucer he found in the sink, leaving the open can by the saucer so Beatrice would know the cat had been fed. Austin crouched down and stroked along the cat's back while she ate. "You might be the Princess around here, but she's the mistress, you hear? You look after her, okay? Or I'm only going to buy you the cheap stuff when this runs out."

Princess stopped eating and glanced up at him, regarding him with her one good eye before she meowed what Austin was fairly sure was her consent and went back to her breakfast.

With one more pat, Austin stood, casting a last look at a sleeping Beatrice, suddenly insanely jealous of a cat who would get to spend all day with her...

CHAPTER FIFTEEN

Bea woke to a hot, sweaty scalp and the rumble of what sounded like a 747 engine but could possibly be her stomach. Or a cat, as it turned out, from the irate *meow* Princess bestowed on her when she sat up abruptly. The cat sent her a reproachful one-eyed glare from her position on Bea's pillow, where she must have been curled around Bea's head like one of those Russian fur hats.

"Oh, sorry, Your Highness," Bea crooned with a smile, petting the sparse, tufty fur before picking Princess up, then lying back down with her, the mammoth animal sprawling on her chest as she stroked the cat some more. The rumbling resumed, the loud purr vibrating through her hand and the thick duvet right through to the wall of her chest.

Bea sighed. What a simply wonderful noise. She could get used to this.

Waking late to the purring of a cat—*her* cat—snuggling in bed for as long as she wanted. No breakfast meetings. No deadlines to make. No agenda, full stop.

And Austin all night.

Bea's cheeks heated as she remembered last night in all its Technicolor glory. Austin kissing her and touching her, Austin hard and good inside her, making her pant and gasp and see freaking rainbows as she came. The perfection of Austin's body and the deep vibration of his groan as he shuddered his release. The way he'd gathered her close as they'd fallen asleep—all three times.

But more than that. How they'd laughed and eaten popcorn and drank beer and watched zombies being killed as well as sitcom blooper reels on YouTube and clips of animals behaving badly. She'd never spent a night like that with a guy before. Not their first night together, anyway. In fact, she didn't know if she'd ever achieved such a level of easy intimacy with any guy. And work had always been the oil that lubricated her relationships with men.

Hugging Princess, Bea rolled on her side and smiled. Maybe from now on she should make all her life decisions based on the throw of a dart, because this one, so far, was working out freaking great.

Princess protested the tight hold, and Bea loosened her grasp a little. "Sorry, kitty," she murmured, kissing the patchy fur at her neck, shutting her eyes in sheer delight.

Too soon, though, nature called, and she stumbled out of bed, shoving her feet in her bunny slippers. Entering the bathroom, she did her business, then stared at herself in the vanity as she washed up. Bea liked what she saw very much. A copper-haired vixen who looked as if she'd been thoroughly ravaged, with a slight hickey just near one of her nipples and some stubble rash on her neck.

She was such a badass.

Bea smiled at herself, loving how her eyes seemed to sparkle more and how the fine lines on her brow seemed to have disappeared and how her boobs seemed perkier. She thrust her chest out and shimmied a little. Yep, definitely perkier.

Who needed implants when there was rebellion? And Austin.

She left the bathroom and crossed to the end of the bed

where she'd stripped her shirt off last night, then picked it up and threw it over her head before hunting through her drawers for her Thursday panties. Not because it just happened to be Thursday, but because she loved them best.

When she crossed to the sink for a glass of water, Bea noticed that Austin must have fed Princess before he'd left. She leaned her elbows on the edge of the sink and filled her glass under the faucet, watching the slow pace of Credence tick by down on the street. A big clunker of a car that looked *decades* old pulled up against the curb opposite her building, followed closely by a police cruiser pulling up in front. *Ooh.* Bea perked up. Was that Austin's car?

An elderly man got out and stood by the vehicle, waiting for the police officer to join him, and—bingo—it *was* Austin, striding in that long, lazy way of his, touching the brim of his hat as he greeted the man. Bea grinned, thinking about wearing that hat as she'd ridden him like a cowgirl last night.

The old guy beamed at Austin, giving him a friendly kind of pat on the forearm, and Bea watched with fascination as the two chatted all friendly and cordial. Austin's body language was one of deference as they spoke, but there was obviously a problem with the man's tires, since Austin pointed several times to the left front one. He smiled and nodded a lot but also kept pointing like he had all the time in the world to explain the problem and was perfectly happy to do so.

Suddenly, mid-conversation, his gaze flicked up directly to her window, and although it took him about a second, he smiled as he realized she was standing there. The grin was slow but got bigger and bigger and, even from across the street, her girlie bits hummed in response to the obvious message.

I know what you look like naked.

The older man, who was talking now, cut off mid-sentence, frowning as he looked in the direction of Austin's gaze, obviously realizing he didn't have the police officer's full attention. He squinted as he looked up, which drew his impressive eyebrows together. They were more unruly than even Bea's had been—they had to be if she could see them from across the street—and she wondered if he knew about Mirror Mirror.

She didn't know what the old man said next, but there was a big smile on his face now as well, and he turned to Austin, giving him one of those elbow nudges. Austin laughed, totally unabashed as his gaze stayed fixed on hers, and Bea swore she could read his mind. And it was very, very *dirty*.

The old man, however, was clearly intent on continuing the conversation as he pointed at the tire again and made his case. Or whatever the hell he was doing. Bea didn't know and for damn sure she didn't care as Austin's eyes stayed on her, and a naughty spark of inspiration struck.

Her conversation with him at Annie's the other day came back to her, and before she could second-guess herself, Bea straightened and whipped her T-shirt off over her head. The old guy was oblivious as he continued to talk Austin's ear off, but Austin's face was an absolute picture. It went from shock to disbelief to blatant ogling all within seconds.

From *holy fuck* to *Jesus Christ* to *how you doin'* in the space of a few heartbeats.

She smiled triumphantly, her boobs feeling sixteen again as she wiggled her fingers at him in a cheeky kind of wave, then blew him a kiss. He shook his head and narrowed his eyes, but she'd have felt more chastised had that secretive smile not been tugging at his mouth.

Still grinning, Bea stepped back from the window—just in the nick of time, as the old guy turned his head again, obviously realizing he still didn't have Austin's full attention. She threw her shirt back on as she made her way back to the bed, a glow in her belly and a lift in her step.

Lack of feminine modesty for the win. Sorry, Grandmother.

Except, *not sorry.*

She grabbed her laptop and phone off the floor beside the bed and sat half propped against the wall, her knees bent slightly to accommodate the laptop, the covers pulled up to her waist. Princess joined her, turning around three times before flopping down on top of the duvet beside Bea at about hand level. Princess may have not been favored in the looks department, but she was no dummy, as Bea's hand automatically reached out and started to pat.

Her phone vibrated and she smiled to herself, knowing who it was even before she glanced at the screen. *Austin.* He'd put his number in her phone last night and vice versa.

You're lucky I have serious police business to attend to now or I would have to come and arrest you for violation of bylaw 367 part A schedule 9.

Bea laughed as she read the text. He was so full of shit. She texted back. *But, Officer, I thought public nudity didn't apply in the confines of my home?*

His response was swift. *This is for deliberate distraction of a police officer while on duty.*

Yeah, well, he definitely had her there. But he wasn't going to have this all his own way. **I'd* like to report a peeping Tom spying on me through my window. Tall. Uniform. Hat. Really big dick.* She added an eggplant emoji.

Peeping Tom? In Credence? Impossible. But rest assured we take all complaints seriously. I can take your statement this afternoon. Does 3-ish work?

Three p.m. seemed like a million years away now, but Bea was sure she and Princess would survive until then. She tapped out another text. *3 is fine. I'll be waiting here for you. In my Thursday panties. *Just* my Thursday panties.*

Another fast response. *Tease.*

Bea grinned. *Pervert.*

A licking-lips emoji appeared on her screen. *See you at 3.*

Smiling to herself, Bea dropped the phone as she snuggled down beneath the covers a little lower. "Let's see what's happening in the world, big kitty," she said as she opened her laptop. She'd taken to perusing the headlines for five minutes every morning before switching to whatever show she was binge-watching.

It was almost ten when she logged in to CNN and immediately wished she hadn't. What she saw there sucked away *all* her happy.

"The brilliant and talented young LA advertising executive Kevin Colton, who was recently promoted to the board of Jing-A-Ling, one of the top ad agencies in the country, was arrested this morning for fraud and misappropriating company funds."

Bea sat bolt upright, staring at the screen, a slow mushroom cloud of *what the fuck* rising in her chest as the details of the arrest and the extent of the allegations were revealed.

Kevin Colton? Kevin *freaking* Colton?

The *less talented* and *not at all freaking brilliant* guy who had been promoted over her? The guy who'd been given the much-coveted keys to the kingdom?

The guy who was sitting in *her* corner office?

Rage—the same rage that had burned through her like a California wildfire the day of her dismissal—flared anew. She'd told them Kevin could talk the talk but was *not* capable of walking the walk. Having worked with him for three years, picking up his slack and covering for his lazy ass, she knew that as surely as she knew that putting a Labrador puppy in an ad was the best way to sell...basically anything.

And now, less than two months into the job, she was watching live pictures of him being hauled out of the building she'd practically lived in for fifteen years. Bringing disrepute and God-only-knew-what financial shitstorm down on a company that had been a huge part of her existence. She'd lived and breathed and *bled* for Jing-A-Ling, and Kevin dipshit

Colton had taken a wrecking ball to it in less than two lousy months?

She checked her phone—all her social media notifications were in triple digits. With a very familiar burn in her gut, she opened her Twitter app, determined to figure out what in the hell had gone so wrong so quickly.

• • •

Three hours later, she was about as worked up as she was the day she'd told the CEO to take this job and shove it, and, having lived through that, Bea had thought nothing worse could possibly ever happen to her in a professional capacity, but she'd been wrong. She was so damn stressed and *angry*, every muscle in her body was wound tight. Even Princess had moved away from Bea's increasingly exaggerated patting.

She'd scoured every social media platform, googled everything she thought would unearth information, and spoken to about a dozen people from her old life.

And all the time she was thinking, *why?* If they'd promoted her instead of scumbag Kevin, they could have avoided all of this. That hurt most of all. Knowing they'd thrown her over for an asshole who had robbed them blind.

Her phone rang suddenly, and Bea stared at it for a beat or two as the name *Charlie Hammersmith* flashed on the screen.

What the...? Was he *kidding*? He had brought this on himself through his own bigotry and shortsightedness, and he wanted to call and...what? Make nice with her now? Because he had to be shitting himself big-time, and knowing Charlie as she did, he was probably in the midst of some kind of knee-jerk, super-panicked damage-control exercise.

And she didn't have to answer to know he wanted her back to help fix the mess. Well, screw that and screw him. She wouldn't trade what she had now for that mess in a million years.

Although the temptation to answer and tell him *I told you so* and *suck shit* was strong, her fear that she might actually *cry* again—because goddamn it, she'd cared deeply about Jing-A-Ling and what happened to it—had her throwing the phone on the bed.

She'd left that all behind. It wasn't her concern anymore.

Distracting herself from whatever message her ex-boss was probably leaving on her cell right now and from the urge to scream and/or cry, Bea checked her emails. She hadn't checked them since she'd stopped working, because what would have been the point in leaving if she was still a slave to her inbox?

But maybe there was something in there about what had happened...

There were about a hundred emails waiting for her. It was nothing compared to the normal volume when she'd still been working, which had been more like a hundred a day, but since she wasn't in the Jing-A-Ling address book anymore, that was hardly surprising.

The emails were pretty much the same assortment she usually received, minus work stuff. A bunch of spam trying to sell her everything from solar power to shoes, a couple of invoices, correspondence from her bank and BMW about her next service, and a couple of emails from head hunters who'd heard about her unceremonious parting with Jing-A-Ling and wanted to offer her a job.

During her time at the agency, she'd had frequent offers to leave the firm for more money and better perks, but she'd never been tempted—*idiot* that she was—and had always deleted them. She was even less tempted now that she was done with the corporate rat race.

Could she drink beer for breakfast and go sans bra and elliptical back in LA? No, she could not. So she deleted these emails, too.

Only one of them grabbed her attention. It had been sent two days ago from Kim Howard. Bea and Kim had worked together at Jing-A-Ling for a couple of years, back in those early art-department days. The subject line said "Greet Cute." Bea was tempted to delete it, thinking it was either a sales pitch for a pyramid scheme, a sales pitch for the latest corporate guru workshop, or a sales pitch for some kind of new dating app.

But still, curiosity won out, and Bea opened it instead of hitting the trash icon.

The first couple of paragraphs were general chitchat about what Kim had been up to since she'd left Jing-A-Ling and offering her commiserations on Bea's departure. Apparently, the rumors surrounding the circumstances were rife in LA advertising circles.

Well, not anymore, thanks to Kevin freaking Colton...

Then came the sales pitch. She and two others had started a greeting card company, and Kim remembered how Bea had always done hand-drawn cards for work occasions and how cute and funny they'd been, and had Bea ever considered putting her art skills to use, because they were looking for creatives who might be interested in joining their team.

Creatives? Bea blinked at the screen several times, then read that line again. Okay, sure, Kim was a lovely person and they'd always gotten along, and yes, Bea could draw, but she wasn't a *professional* artist. She wasn't a *creative.* Just because she'd done one lousy sketch, and had been tempted every damn day to do more, didn't mean anything.

Plus, given the Kevin Colton news just now, the last thing she wanted was to be headhunted by corporate-landia. And she sure as shit was not in the mood for the cutesy, schmaltzy, rot-your-teeth sentimentality that had been the catalyst for Bea always making her own cards.

The email ended with, I do hope you'll think about being

part of the Greet Cute team. I know it won't be long before some other agency snaps you up (if they haven't already), but we'd love a fresh new voice, and your particular brand of funny will, I think, work well for us. We'd certainly be keen to see anything you had on offer. Any consideration you could give to us would be much appreciated.

Won't be long before another agency snaps you up?

Bea's blood pressure spiked into the danger zone, the beat of her heart washing loudly through her ears. Did people not think she was capable of doing something else—*anything* else— with her time other than genuflecting to corporate America? Just because her father was an ad man, as his father had been before him, didn't mean she couldn't do something else. Sure, Kim was only being complimentary, but after almost a month dropping out in Credence, it felt like an affront.

Like even the idea that she might choose a different lifestyle was inconceivable.

Super annoyed at these assumptions—yeah, she was in a real *mood* now—Bea clicked on the hyperlink in Kim's signature line, and Greet Cute's website opened in a new window. She clicked on the About Us tab, and three happy faces grinned back at her. Kim, looking regal and kickass with her full Afro and large hoop earrings. Nozo, sporting a nose ring and wearing dramatic sparkly eye shadow and a pair of funky green-framed glasses. And a dude called Mal with a hipster beard and a man bun.

They were relaxed and smiling, arms around one another, standing outside a funky-looking triple-floor warehouse in what Bea was fairly certain was downtown LA. The next picture was their work space, which was massive—the entire top floor, apparently—with four corner offices and a huge glass-walled boardroom on the street-facing wall.

The creative areas were all centralized in an open floorplan—very Google—with color and light dominating the space. There was a lot of beautifully displayed tech as well as all kinds of funky chairs and beanbags, not to mention the giant potted plants and vibrant wall art.

Reading their story, Bea discovered the trio were old college friends who'd started their own home business after they'd all been let go from their jobs a couple of years back. Eighteen months later, the business had grown exponentially and become so successful, they'd hired another five full-time content creators as well as establishing a small production facility with a staff of fifteen that saw to everything from paper production to printing and distribution. The eco-friendly cards were made from recycled materials, and every part of the final product was biodegradable.

Bea did some more googling to see what the Internet said— not just their own PR machine—and she was impressed. It appeared that with their small start-up mentality, they'd been able to stay smart and nimble in the face of fickle market forces, pivoting quickly from things that hadn't worked and using social media to their advantage. They had almost 200,000 Instagram followers and more than 300,000 TikTok followers. Obviously all this had helped them find their niche and was starting to attract the attention of some big market players.

Well done, Kim!

Switching back to their site, she checked out their product on their online shop. And that's where the love affair ended. Greet Cute all right. Bea could feel a toothache coming on just looking at the offerings. There was a large variety of cards, from the more traditional to the sickeningly cutesy, but *nothing* appealed to Bea.

Each to their own but…no.

She wasn't really in the corny greeting card demographic— never had been. But right now, today, the sentimental messages of good wishes and cheer and a perfect world where an expensive piece of folded cardboard was some kind of panacea to the world's ills really grated on her nerves.

Nerves that felt stretched thin and exposed.

Kim thought she'd be into this…this…sappy crap? When, today of all days, she wanted to *burn* everything down?

To be fair to Kim, she had no idea that Bea would open her email right after the Kevin news, but she would like to think that, even on a day when she wasn't contemplating lethal world destruction, she'd never have been a good match for schmaltzy, feel-good fakeness.

And she was pissed enough right now to prove it.

She headed to the couch and snatched up the sketch pad, then yanked her suitcase out from under the bed and grabbed the adult coloring book she'd bought at a rest stop on the way to Credence. It had appealed to her in the moment as something she might fill her time with, but then she'd discovered *Supernatural*. Included in the packaging, however, was a large pack of pencils and a sharpener, and that's what she was hunting.

Returning to bed next to an exceedingly disinterested Princess, Bea's fingers flew over the page, anger peaking and falling and peaking again with every line, every curve she drew, not really even registering that she'd tapped into that same place she'd tapped into at the lake. She hadn't had a clue what she was going to draw when she started, but pictures formed quickly in her brain, and within an hour she'd done three anti-sap sketches that pretty much summed up her *not* Hallmark mood.

All three of them were done mostly in black pencil with occasional color added for emphasis, and they featured *her.* The her she'd been out on the street that day meeting Austin for the first time, still pissed at the world and taking it out on pie and ice cream. Wild, mousy hair in a messy, fall-down knot at the back of her head, baggy sweats, no bra, and floppy-eared bunny slippers. Glaring and clearly cranky.

At her feet was Princess in all her face-for-radio grandeur. Huge body, tufty marmalade fur, shriveled eye socket, exaggerated ear hair, exposed fang, staring straight ahead like she was a freaking *queen*. Bea added the tiara just in case people missed it.

They made a great pair. Ragey, pissed, seen-better-days.

The first one she'd captioned: *Oh, I'm sorry, were you after a Disney princess?* The second: *Look at all the fucks I give.* The third: *They say crazy cat lady like it's a bad thing.*

She stopped and admired them for a moment, feeling a little out of breath at the mental effort they'd taken but weirdly proud of them. They were the antithesis of what was on offer at Greet Cute, which made them just about perfect in her eyes, and before she could think about it twice, she picked up her phone and called the café downstairs.

"Hi, Jenny, it's Bea. Was just wondering if you could tell me where I would go in Credence if I needed something scanned?"

"The library has a scanner," Jenny offered.

Bea smiled. "Excellent! Thank you."

She hurriedly donned some new sweats *and* put on a bra— *that's* how pissed she was. If Princess minded Bea's abrupt departure, she didn't vocalize it or even feign interest in her leaving, and indeed, when Bea returned half an hour later, Princess hadn't moved from her spot on the bed.

After inserting the USB stick with the scanned images into her laptop, Bea made a few clicks and attached the images to the reply email she was sending. It was polite, thanking Kim for thinking of her but explaining that she was more Cranky Bea than Hallmark Bea these days, as she could probably see from the attached images. Then she wished Kim every success. Because she did. Bea *loved* that Kim was kicking corporate ass.

The email had just made that nice little whooshing noise signaling it had been sent when she heard footsteps on the stairs outside her door—Austin's—and Bea realized she'd passed almost an entire day fueled by rage and an all-too-familiar low-level anxiety that had evaporated all her lovely happy feels from last night and her daring little X-rated flash. Not only that, but she was also rethinking everything to do with this new...thing with Austin.

What the hell was she doing? Was this really the way she wanted to start her new life? Getting herself tangled up with a younger man, something that really couldn't go anywhere.

Why *had* she gone there with Austin?

Because he'd felt less reckless than giving in to her artistic tendencies and that slippery slope? *Ugh.* Bea wasn't sure she wanted to explore that too deeply right now. Which only left... because it *felt good*?

Jesus, seriously? She wasn't a child. She couldn't run her life on what *felt good* alone. That was her mother's style—not Bea's. Sure, she could sleep in every day and ditch her bra and her elliptical and watch reruns of *Supernatural* until the cows came home. But Austin was a human being and that wasn't fair to him. He deserved better than being an expression of her...midlife crisis.

Or whatever it was called at thirty-five. He wasn't a shiny sports car. He was a *man*.

The knock at the door felt like the knock of doom, and for a moment, Bea contemplated not opening it. Pretending she was out. But...that was cowardly and she wouldn't be that person. Best to get this over with before it went on and on and *feelings*—Austin's feelings—became involved.

CHAPTER SIXTEEN

Princess accompanied her as Bea opened the door, her warm body pressed against Bea's ankle. Austin was leaning on the wall, one hand on his hip, grinning that grin she loved so much, looking super official in his uniform, which was, sadly for her, superhot. She'd never salivated just at the sight of a man before now.

He gave her the lazy once-over as well. "They're not your Thursday panties."

Bea smiled despite a heavy ache in her chest. "I had to go out."

He gave an exaggerated sigh, sounding thwarted but resigned, his eyes sparkling with mischief. Then he touched the brim of his hat in a formal gesture of hello and said, "Good afternoon, ma'am. I'm here to take your statement."

She wanted to grab him by the lapels of his shirt and kiss him until he was groaning and his hands were siding into her sweats.

"I also"—he pushed off the wall and pulled a brown paper packet out from behind his back, presenting it the way another man might have presented a fancy diamond ring—"bought you some pie. Because pie."

A sudden waft of simple sugars hit Bea's system, and she realized she'd been too damn angry to even eat today. She'd walked to the library and back and hadn't even thought to stop at Annie's.

He waved the package in front of her face. "Lemon meringue made with fresh lemons from Annie's very own tree."

Bea's stomach growled, and she salivated some more. If she wasn't careful, she'd start to drool. "Seeing as how you bought pie, you can come in."

She stood aside, and Austin took the two steps into her apartment, bending over to give Princess some love before entering fully. Bea shut the door, then headed for the sink, moving around the half-full trash basket still in the middle of the floor. She needed to put as much space between them as possible and get as far away from the bed as possible, because all she could think about now was how Austin's abs would taste smeared in meringue, which was *not* helpful.

Why did her brain choose now to combine two of her favorite things?

Bea kept her back to him, looking down at the street as she had earlier today when she'd lifted her shirt. She was hyperaware he was approaching, in the same way she'd been aware of him from the first moment they'd met. He slid in behind her, placing the pie on the cluttered countertop before bracketing her hips with a hand planted on either side of the sink, his front pressing into her back.

Dipping his head, he nuzzled behind her ear and down the side of her neck, the brim of his hat brushing her skin. Every muscle in her body wanted to melt against him, but she held herself erect. "I missed you today," he murmured.

Bea shut her eyes as his husky admission grabbed a hold around her heart. She'd missed him, too, and she wanted nothing more than to relax in his arms. But they needed to talk. So she locked her knees, gripped the edge of the sink harder.

Lifting his face from her neck, he slid his chin on top of her head and didn't say anything for long moments. They both just stood there and stared out the window. Eventually, though, he initiated the conversation she was too chicken to start.

"You're freaking out, aren't you?"

She opened her eyes and gave a half laugh at his typical Austin approach. Casual but direct. Still, his insight was unexpected, and Bea practically folded in on herself in relief. Other men she'd had the it's-not-working-out talk with in the past had always seemed oblivious to the undercurrent.

"A little." Okay…maybe a *lot*.

"All right." He kissed the top of her head and withdrew, and Bea missed him instantly as he stepped away. "You want to talk about it?"

Steeling herself for what was to come, Bea turned. Austin had removed his hat and thrown it on top of her messy coffee table and was ruffling his hair, and, if possible, Bea's knees went a little weaker. Thank God she had the bench to lean into.

"You want to go first?" he asked.

He didn't seem angry or even worried, necessarily, nor did he appear to be humoring her. His body was loose and relaxed, his gaze neutral. His body language was open and inviting. Clearly, he was up for the conversation and wanted to tackle it head-on, which fit Austin's pragmatic personality.

Who knew pragmatism could be so damn sexy?

"I think this"—Bea gestured her index finger back and forth between them—"was a mistake."

One eyebrow winged up. "Really?"

The man had the most expressive damn eyebrows. Just that one eyebrow seemed to say, *Pretty sure you weren't thinking anything of the sort when I was making you see Jesus this morning.* Okay, maybe it wasn't saying that, exactly, and it was just her guilt talking, but the inflection in his voice held a faint note of reproach. And maybe "mistake" *was* the wrong word. But it had definitely been ill-advised. "I mean…we should have stayed friends and not crossed this line."

"Okay." He nodded calmly. So damn calm when Bea's heart was beating like a bongo drum. "Why?"

"Because…" Looking at him now, she couldn't think of one damn reason why she should deny herself the hotness *and* niceness *and* fun—the man was the whole damn package—that was Austin Cooper.

Think, Beatrice, *think!*

"I don't usually do this. Just rush in with a guy. Particularly a random guy I don't really know. Which probably makes me sound like some old-fashioned prude, but it's not that. I've just been busy, focused on my work and my career and I didn't need the distraction. So being with someone I already knew, someone in advertising was just…efficient. And there were commonalities that we could bond over and…"

Bea sighed as her eyes ranged all over the deliciousness that was Austin before returning attention to his ruggedly handsome face.

"We don't have anything in common." Apart from a healthy dose of lust. But that was hardly a foundation for anything. "We've known each other for a week and there's been a lot of changes in my life these past couple of months, and that's probably not the best time for entanglements. You're new to me; everything here is new to me. This life I'm living is new to me, and I don't know where it's going, but I do know I want to start out right."

"I see." He nodded calmly, as if he was a psychologist and she was the patient. "And what brought all this on? You've gone from titty flashing to *I want to start out right.*"

God…even in polite conversation, Austin infused *titty* with just the right kind of dirty. It seemed like such a long time ago now, and Bea marveled at her earlier daring. "Something happened at my old work today that kinda sucked me back into that world again. Also…separate to that and quite randomly, I got offered a job."

"Ah." Austin's voice suddenly went full gravel, and there was a definite tightening of his jaw. "And you...want to take the job?"

"What?" Bea frowned and shook her head vehemently. "No. Absolutely not. But it got me thinking about the reasons I came here and how I might be screwing it all up by...using you as some kind of distraction. Some kind of...treat."

A big, lazy grin spread over Austin's face. "I do remember telling you I was perfectly fine with that."

Why? Why was he grinning? Shouldn't he be more concerned about the outcome of all this? When Bea was twenty-five, she'd carefully thought through every decision she'd ever made, examining it from every angle. A habit she'd fallen into for the rest of her life.

Until recently, apparently.

"I'm trying to be serious here." Bea was aware her eyebrows were almost crossing over each other, her brow was that furrowed. "About whatever this is. I mean...what are we? What are we even doing here, Austin?"

He sighed loudly, full of patience, a sigh she imagined probably got a considerable workout in his job. Cops had to have superhuman reserves of patience.

"Bea*triss*...honey." He took two steps in her direction and stopped. "Why do we have to define what we're doing? Why do we have to *be* anything?" He shrugged. "Why not just be *this*? You and me hanging out. Watching TV, laughing, going to Jack's and the lake. Eating popcorn and drinking beer in bed. Having sex. Or not..." He held up his hands in a surrender motion before dropping them again. "If that's what you really want. But just be *this*, letting things unfold until we decide to either stop doing it or actually give it a name."

It sounded so easy. So simple. And so damn tempting when he said it. None of the angst that she'd attached to it. Just two people living in the moment.

"So just…go with the flow?"

"Uh-huh." He closed the distance between them, sliding his hand into hers and giving it a squeeze. Up close, his presence was almost overwhelming. So big and broad. Solid and dependable. "You came here wanting to break free from the person you were in LA. And you've been doing that, and I've been happy to help. I'm happy to keep helping for as long as you want. So don't worry about me, okay? I'm a big boy. I have a voice and a mouth."

Oh yes he did, and they were both divine. He slid his other hand onto her face, cupping her cheek, and Bea shivered at the touch.

"*And* free will," he continued, the lazy stroke of his thumb causing an outbreak of goose bumps down her throat and onto her décolletage. "I can speak for myself, and if I want to stop, I promise you'll be the first to know."

Bea dragged in a husky breath. The man was persuasive when he put his mind to it, because she *had* come to Credence to break the mold. To be a different kind of Beatrice. To let go of the strictures of her life and just do what she wanted.

And God help her, she wanted to *do* Austin Cooper.

"Okay?" he asked, his voice a soft burr.

Bea swayed toward him, and he stepped in that last little bit to bring their bodies together. He was right, damn it—he was a big boy. He had free will. And she'd given him ample opportunity to turn tail and run. "Uh-huh," she murmured, her tongue swiping out to wet suddenly dry lips as she stared up at him.

"Good."

He smiled, and Bea was utterly fascinated with the curve of his bottom lip. She wanted to bite it, then give it a soothing lick. Her belly was turning loops as everything heated. Her breasts felt heavy, an ache kicked to life between her legs.

"So…what do you want to do now?" His other hand slid

onto her jaw until he was cradling her face, his gaze zeroing in on her mouth like he wanted a piece of hers as well. "Food? Booze? More *Walking Dead*?"

"I want to—" She stopped, swallowed, her throat dry now, too, but absolutely prepared to say what was on her mind. "Take Annie's pie, smear lemon meringue over your chest, and lick it all off."

A slow smile spread over his face. "I do like the way you think." And then his hands slipped away and he took two paces back, reaching for the buttons on his shirt, hastily undoing them, just as he'd done yesterday. "Get the pie," he said as he pulled the shirttails out of his pants and peeled the shirt back.

Bea's legs went weak, incapable of any movement at the sight of all his lovely bare flesh, and her stomach growled in anticipation.

"Bea*triss*," he said with equal amounts affection and exasperation. *"Pie."*

Bea got the pie.

CHAPTER SEVENTEEN

Half an hour later, Austin lay on the bed about as physically sated as he'd ever been, considering Beatrice had made him a bona fide glutton. He never wanted to stop touching her and tasting her and being over her and beside her and inside her, but right now, with the tart aroma of lemons and the sweet smell of sugar mixing with a flood of endorphins, he was pretty damn tapped out.

For the moment, anyway.

She'd scared him when he'd first arrived. He'd known something was up from the moment she opened the door. After her boner-inducing titty flash—not a good thing when trying to tell Bob Downey his tire was illegal and that being the mayor forty years ago didn't give him some special exemption from the road laws—and her promises to be dressed in nothing but her panties, Austin had been busting a gut to get to her place.

Slowest. Day. Of. His. Life.

Of course.

But then she'd been in her sweats and bunny slippers and there'd been a definite coolness to her welcome. Thank God for Annie's pie or she might not have let him in at all.

He hadn't known what happened, but he knew something sure as hell *had*, and a reckless kind of desperation had risen in his chest to find out. Maybe if he knew her better, he'd have known intuitively what was up, but he didn't—yet—and he wasn't too proud to just come out and ask.

Still, to hear her second-guessing what had happened between them and trying to box it into something had made him a little frustrated. If there was one thing he *did* know about Beatrice it was that, for all her bravado, she was skittish— about the age gap, about her uncertain future, about her place in the world. And trying to pin her down or fence her in with all that going on would be dumb with a capital D.

This wasn't a standard relationship where he met someone in May and they fell into a pattern of dating and fucking and hanging out with each other's friends and making plans for Thanksgiving together, only to have it fizzle out in August. It was different. He knew that already. Knew he had to get out of its way and let it become what it was destined to become.

Take it one day at a time.

Thankfully, she'd been prepared to listen to his arguments and be swayed. Because he really was fine with what was happening, and he didn't need her making decisions for him like he was some fresh-off-the-farm hayseed with no agency. Corporate life had obviously made her cautious, and he got that—being a cop was hardly a cakewalk. But he could handle whatever this was.

More than that, he was prepared to be whatever she needed him to be *right here, right now* because she simply didn't know what she wanted yet. And that was okay, too.

Beatrice's hair tickled his nose as he nuzzled the crown of her head. Austin hadn't ever given much thought to the joys of the post-coital state. The part where two people who'd just had orgasms got to bask in the aftermath and enjoy the flood of happy hormones, when every worry was obliterated, every ache was neutralized, every mental mountain was conquered. Even if only for a short while.

Yeah, he liked it and he'd never been the kind of guy who

laid next to a woman plotting how quickly he could leave. But he'd never felt this content, either.

"I figured I'd need a shower after you were done licking that stuff offa me, but I can see"—his hand ran down his belly, surprised to find a distinct lack of stickiness—"you were very thorough."

When she'd slathered that meringue lower and lower, then reached for his belt buckle, Austin's knees had almost given out and, for a moment, he thought it was all going to end there with an embarrassing display of prematurity he hadn't suffered since the night he'd lost his virginity. But he'd rallied, managing to hold on until she'd finished *using him as a plate* and all the pie was gone and she took him all the way to the end with her mouth, and then he'd flipped her onto her back, stripped off her sweats and those Thursday panties, and shown her how much *he* liked to eat.

He felt the upward turn of her lips against his chest as she smiled. "I wouldn't dare disrespect Annie by leaving even the tiniest morsel."

Austin laughed. "I'm impressed. I doubt a forensic crew with a black light could pick up any trace."

It was her turn to laugh, and he snuggled her closer, content to lay quietly with her for several minutes. "So…" he said eventually, his fingers sifting through her hair. "You want to talk about this morning?"

"Nope."

All righty then. "Not even about the job offer?"

Austin didn't want to be the guy who let things slide for fear it would put them in the weeds. He didn't want to be the guy who pushed, either. But it seemed like neglecting his boyfriend/lover/friend/interested-human-being duties to not ask.

Plus, he was curious.

A long sigh escaped her lips, spreading warm air over his

pec. "Somebody I used to work with has started a greeting card company and wanted to know if I was interested in doing some design work for them."

"And are you?" Austin had no idea how that sort of thing worked, but clearly Beatrice did if she'd been headhunted for it, and he couldn't help but think of her magnificent sketch of the lake. "Maybe even a little?"

"Have I ever come across as a Hallmark kinda woman to you?"

Austin chuckled. "No."

"Right."

"So you told them no."

"I explained I don't think I had the temperament for schmaltz. And then I sent them some scanned copies of three quick mock-ups I drew to illustrate the current state of my personality so they had a thorough understanding of my unsuitability. I don't think they'll be knocking down my door anytime soon."

Austin grinned. "Can I see them?"

She didn't say anything for a while, and Austin worried that he had uttered some unforgivable request, given how super squirmy she'd been over the lake sketch. But then she pushed herself up to gaze down at him. "Sure, if you want." She looked over her shoulder. "I think the originals are beside the bed."

She rolled away then, her back to him as half her body disappeared over the side of the bed. Her T-shirt rode up with the movement, and he trailed his fingers down the furrow of her spine from mid-back to ass, because it was impossible not to touch. Rolling back again, she levered into a sitting position, crossing her legs as she gazed at her drawings. Austin also sat up, cross-legged, as Beatrice handed them over.

The drawings were very different from the one of the lake, the caricatures of herself and Princess uncanny in their likeness. They were in mostly black, the addition of color adding flare and detail. He especially liked the tiara for Princess, who was currently lying on his shirt again, glaring at them. She may have only had one eye, but her disgust at their debauchery was coming across loud and clear.

Each drawing was slightly different and so was each caption, which made him laugh. The drawings were funny as hell. "Yeah," he said, glancing at her, "these ought to do it."

She smiled at him. "That's what I thought."

"They're really good, though. You're *really* talented, Beatrice."

If he wasn't very much mistaken, her cheeks pinked up. "They're okay."

She took the sketches off him and swung her legs over the edge of the bed. Clearly, she wasn't comfortable talking about her art, and he couldn't help but feel there was a lot more to that issue than she was letting on.

"You want some water?" she asked as she headed for the kitchen.

"No thanks," Austin murmured, enjoying the view of her half-naked form, the bottom curve of her butt cheeks just peeking out below the hem of her T-shirt. His dick twitched at the sight.

What he wanted didn't involve water.

"You want to come out to the ranch on Sunday?" he asked, watching her fill a glass up at the faucet.

She paused briefly as she reached to turn the faucet off, and Austin watched as she took several long swallows of water before she turned to face him, her ass pressed against the sink. He couldn't see anything—everything was covered—but she might as well have been naked given how thoroughly ravaged she looked. Her expression was cool, but everything else about her was hot.

He doubted anything could counteract her crazy bed/ orgasm hair, the two hard points of her nipples pressed brazenly against the cotton fabric, and the way her T-shirt rode indecently high on the very tops of her thighs.

Thighs he'd been buried between not that long ago, and his dick was doing more than twitching right now. It was expanding. Rapidly.

"Why?"

The question was even cooler than her expression and caught Austin off guard for a moment. It didn't do anything for the state of his erection, but it made him remember her skittishness. Did she think he was inviting her home to meet his family? His *mother*? Or hell, did she think he was pushing for her to do that sketching of the house he'd suggested?

"Nothing to do with my mom's birthday present, I promise. It's just...we have horses," he explained. "If you still want to ride one. And I thought we could sleep out under the stars. Take the pickup and head out to the far corner of the ranch. Throw a mattress in the back."

"You have horses?" Her brow furrowed, but at least her body visibly relaxed at the news he wasn't taking her home to meet *Mommy* or to stick her in front of an easel.

Austin chuckled. "Umm, yeah. I live on a ranch."

"Oh yes." She gave a little laugh as she shook her head. "*D'oh!* Of course."

"What do you say? Let me show you something *I'm* really good at?" Suddenly he wanted her to see where he was from, the place that was stuck deep in his bones. The reason why he'd returned to Credence and the reason he never wanted to leave.

"Riding a horse?"

"Nah." He grinned to hide the fact that his heart was thudding hard in his chest at how important it felt to show her that part of him. "Making you see stars."

She laughed as she set the glass down on the bench top and slinked back in his direction. "You *are* very good at that."

"I am." What was the point of being modest? Austin

had always prided himself on *giving* before *getting*, but with Beatrice, his sexual satisfaction was so closely entwined with hers, it was the most natural thing in the world to reach for the stars.

"Maybe I need a bigger sample size to truly judge, though? One thing I learned in advertising was the efficacy of a decent sample size."

"God, corporate speak." He grinned. "I love it."

Halting at the end of the bed, she asked, "You mean like *effff*icacy?"

Austin swore his dick twitched at her deliberate tease. "Uh-huh."

"And sample size."

"Yup. And for the record, I think you definitely do. Need one. Gotta be sure."

She pulled her T-shirt off over her head, then tossed it on the ground, causing Princess to meow indignantly as the shirt almost landed on her head. But Beatrice wasn't paying any attention to the cat and neither was Austin. His attention was fixed firmly on her breasts and the way her nipples had hardened into two succulent-looking berries just waiting to be sucked.

Putting her knee on the bed, she said, "Prepare to be sampled."

Austin unfurled his legs, straightening them out in front of him, his cock resting hard as an iron bar against his belly. "Be gentle with me."

She wasn't.

• • •

Beatrice woke late and wearing Princess as a hat *again*—she had the whole damn bed for pity's sake!—the next morning after another night of sex, TV, popcorn, and laughter with Austin. And another five a.m. send-off before he crawled out of bed for the ranch, then work, while she went back to sleep, riding a dopamine high.

A high that lasted until she opened her laptop and checked her email, desperately curious about how Kim had reacted to her drawings. She assumed that Kim probably wouldn't answer at all. That she'd either be irritated by Bea's lack of seriousness or annoyed at how Bea had essentially poked fun at something Kim was obviously passionate about.

But Kim was neither of those things. She was…ecstatic?… if the subject line of her email was any indication. It simply said, *Yaaaas! More, please!*

Bea stared at the screen. What the hell? Was Kim on drugs? Had the pressures of a new business and the go-big-or-go-home mentality of LALA land caused her to crack?

Quickly, she scanned the email for the gist, which was that they absolutely loved her Cranky Bea drawings. They loved the irreverence and the complete disregard for the traditional greeting card genre and that they were sure these would appeal to a younger demographic as well as women over thirty-five or for those looking for a card that expressed their feelings of tiredness, dissatisfaction, and exasperation with honesty and humor.

And could they please put them up on their social media platforms to gauge if the public liked them as much as they all did with the view of putting them into their production lineup?

Oh, and they'd pay her for the three drawings. An amount that made Bea blink a little.

If she'd received an email from the king of England asking her to tea at Buckingham Palace, she'd have been less surprised. She glanced at Princess, who was purring loudly beside her, furry chin resting on Bea's leg, the deep rumble of her purrs being felt all the way down to her damn femur.

That snaggletooth was even more off-putting as she looked at Bea through her half-opened good eye. She wasn't sure if the cat was sleeping or if this was just Princess's snooty, regal expression she reserved for commoners. She hadn't yet gotten to know all the cat's faces.

Her initial instinct to reject the request was quickly and surprisingly overridden. She'd done the hard part—she'd drawn the images. What harm could some sampling do? In fact, she was way more comfortable with that side of it than the creative process. It was who she was, after all—an ad executive, not an artist.

She was her father's daughter, not her mother's.

"What do you think, kitty cat?" Bea stroked down the patchy fur of Princess's back. "You ready to have your face plastered all over TikTok and Instagram?"

Princess opened her good eye fully for a beat, then let it fall to half-mast again, obviously not considering Beatrice's question worthy of her brain cells.

"Yeah. My thoughts exactly."

She shot off a quick reply to Kim, basically telling her to go for it, because, hell, why not? She'd wanted a new life, right?

Why not this? Why not now?

CHAPTER EIGHTEEN

Just after three on Sunday, Bea pulled up in front of Austin's cabin. She'd followed his directions from the turnoff and driven past what was obviously the large, rambling main house, to a smaller log-style cabin tucked in about two hundred feet further on. A massive barn was probably another couple of hundred feet behind, along with a series of fenced-off yards.

Beyond that was a whole lot of flat, flat nothing. Fields of pale-green grass as far as the eye could see, the land undulating gently and a line of trees in the distance. The day was absolutely beautiful. A perfect arc of blue sky unspoiled by clouds and gorgeously temperate—not cold, not hot. Just right. The kind of warmth that confirmed the seasons had changed and warmer days were on the way.

Bea was in jeans and a T-shirt, but she'd brought a jacket for later when she figured the temperatures would drop.

Climbing out of the BMW, she was assailed by a sudden wave of bile sloshing around in her stomach. *Nerves.* And not just because she was about to jump on a beast and attempt to ride it with zero skills in that department. But also, because… what if she ran into Austin's mother?

Bea *wasn't* good with mothers. Knowing how to act around one when she'd had very little first-hand experience had left her severely disadvantaged. Which was why she tended to avoid it.

But what if the other woman had put two and two together? The main house wasn't that far away and in full view of Austin's cabin, and Bea imagined his comings and goings could be easily monitored if Austin's mother was the type to do so. Where did she think Austin had been until five in the morning for four mornings straight?

Good lord, why had she let herself be talked into this? Credence was surrounded by ranches. Surrounded by *horses*. Hell, she probably could have stood on the main street and whinnied, and a horse would have appeared. About to chicken out, she saw Austin's cabin door open and there he stood, in jeans and dusty boots and a plaid shirt with the sleeves rolled up to his elbows, showing off golden, ropey forearms.

"Hey," he said as he shoved a hat—not his police-issue one— on his head, a slow smile warming his face and electrifying the air as he crossed the distance between them.

As if he could read her hesitancy, he didn't touch her, didn't lean in for a kiss.

He quirked an eyebrow. "You okay?"

"Sure." She nodded. "Nervous. About the horse," she clarified quickly.

"Don't be nervous." He shoved a hand on his hip and smiled. "You're going to be on my old horse. I've got Buffy all saddled up. She's twenty years old and gentle as a lamb, I promise. I got her when I was thirteen."

Bea blinked. "Buffy?"

"As in the vampire slayer."

She quirked an eyebrow. "Really?"

He shrugged. "Buffy was hot."

"Aww." She laughed, relaxing a little. "You had a crush on Buffy?"

"Honey, *everyone* had a crush on Buffy."

"Hey, no judgment."

"I should think not, *Team Dean*."

Bea returned his grin. *Touché.*

"C'mon." Austin gestured to the barn. "Let's go get you introduced."

They entered the huge old wooden structure, the aroma of hay, gasoline, and engine grease assaulting her as they passed several pieces of machinery and farm vehicles. A veritable wall of hay was stored along the back, the bales stacked one on top of the other like bricks. The loft above also appeared to store hay.

At the far end was a block of six concrete half stalls with wooden gates, their floors covered with hay. They were all empty, but in front of them, head down, munching on even more hay that had been strewn around, stood a light, coppery-colored horse with a blaze of white down its nose and a dirty-blond mane. She was all saddled up, the reins dragging on the ground. Lifting her head as Austin approached, whickered softly in recognition.

"Hey, girl," Austin said quietly, sliding his hand onto her forehead and giving it a scratch.

The horse nosed into Austin's palm before nudging him gently in the belly, encouraging Austin to pat down the long, elegant neck as she turned curious brown eyes on Bea.

She seemed to be an average size—whatever that was. Somewhere between Clydesdale and Shetland pony. And she was very *pretty.* Her face was sweet with long, soft eyelashes no product on the human market could ever hope to achieve, and the blondish mane was thick and luxurious, streaked with rusty-strawberry strands.

Bea could imagine Buffy out prancing in the fields, tossing it around for all to see. She bet that mane brought all the boys to the yard.

"You can pat her if you want," he said.

Tentatively, Bea reached out and lay her palm flat against the horse's neck, instantly aware of the taut pillow of warm muscle beneath, the leashed strength. That glorious mane brushed against Bea's knuckles, and it felt as good as it looked, surprisingly soft and fluffy. "What color is she?" She didn't look brown or red. Maybe auburn?

"It depends who you ask and where you come from," Austin said with a smile. "We call her sorrel, but some would say chestnut."

"Well...either way"—Bea ran her hand down Buffy's neck—"she's quite beautiful."

"You hear that, Buff?" Austin crooned. "You have an admirer."

Bea almost laughed. The horse was lovely, but the way Austin was *with* his horse? His soft tone, his gentle touch, and his obvious affection for the animal in every stroke, every glance?

Holy hot cowboy Batman.

Standing in the barn with him in his plaid shirt and his hat and his boots surrounded by farm machinery and the aromas of horse and hay, Bea had to admit that Austin Cooper looked just as good here as he did in his police uniform. Maybe more. Rancher Austin was a whole other level of sexy.

It really wasn't fair that he kept getting better.

"You love her."

He nodded, glancing at Bea over Buffy's neck. "She was my first love."

"You're lucky. My first love was Tommy butthead Waterson. We were six and going to get married and sail away on a boat to the Galapagos Islands and live with the tortoises."

"That sounds cute."

"It was. Then he callously dumped me for Brandy Baker, whose daddy owned a Corvette."

"What a dick."

They grinned at each other over Buffy's back, and Bea had

never been more pleased to *not* be in LA in her life.

"C'mon," he said. "Let's get you on this horse." Then he made a clicking noise and Buffy, who had resumed eating, raised her head, allowing Austin to grab hold of the reins and lead her out of the barn.

He led them to a very large rectangular yard that smelled faintly of dirt and manure. The fence was made from sturdy wooden posts and wooden crossbars and a wooden top rail that Bea could picture Austin sitting on after a long day on the ranch, his hat pulled low, his boots dusty, a beer in one hand.

Inside was a large oval area that had to be more than a hundred feet across, taking up most of the inside perimeter apart from a small, covered structure with no doors where more hay was stashed along with a bunch of equipment.

"This is where we break in and train horses, and Jill practices her jumps and barrel racing," Austin said as he opened the gate.

"Your sister-in-law competes?" Which explained the equipment.

"Used to when she was younger. She was on the circuit for a while but hurt her back badly during a fall and gave it up. Clay built her this, and now she trains horses for other people."

Shutting the gate behind them, he led Buffy to the center of the arena, and Bea followed. The ground was soft, almost sandy beneath her feet, and churned up from multiple hooves.

"Okay," he said as he bent over a little, holding out his flattened palm low enough for her to step onto. "I'll give you a leg up. Put your foot here and hold on to the saddle."

Bea took a deep, steadying breath, doing as she was instructed, grabbing the saddle as she stepped up and, in one smooth boost from Austin, she was straddling Buffy's back.

The horse moved slightly, causing Bea's pulse to spike, and she clutched at the saddle horn.

"It's okay," Austin assured, making shushing noises and

stroking Buffy's neck. "She's not ridden much these days; she's just getting used to the feel of someone on her back again."

Having just got out from under a bunch of people on her back, figuratively, Bea understood. She eased her grip on the horn, forcing herself to relax, her heart pounding like she'd just mounted a dragon instead of a placid old nag.

"Now what?" she asked.

"I'll lead her around the ring a few times, give you some pointers along the way, then I'll let you take over."

"Okay." Bea wasn't sure she was going to be ready to fly solo after a few turns around the ring, but who knew?

He passed her the reins. "Hold these and put your feet in the stirrups."

Bea took the strips of leather and guided her feet into the stirrups. They were a little low, and Austin adjusted them with quick, efficient ease.

"Right," he said, absently stroking Buffy's rump. "Hold the reins loosely for now and just get a feel for how you're sitting in the saddle. Stay loose and relaxed. Go with the movement of the horse, lean into it."

She nodded. "Okay."

"Good. Let's go." And then he clicked under his tongue and said, "Move on, Buffy."

The horse ambled forward, and Bea's pulse spiked again at the first movement, her torso lurching to compensate for the momentum, her hand gripping the saddle horn. It seemed ridiculous that her heart could be beating as fast as when she'd been executing a burnout in her car, considering there were Galapagos turtles that could walk faster than Buffy at her current speed, but it *was* rattling along in her chest.

Her BMW may have bristled with horsepower, but right now she had the original horsepower between her thighs, and that was thrilling in an elemental way. A way that she wouldn't have thought she was aware of until this moment.

"Relax," Austin said. "Go with the bounce."

"I *am* relaxed," Bea said, instantly stiffening.

"You're going to snap that horn off if you're not careful."

Bea glanced at her white-knuckled grip. Okay, maybe he was right. Forcing herself to ease off, she watched as color flooded back into her knuckles.

"Find the rhythm of the horse."

She rolled her eyes. Clearly Austin's role was to be some kind of Jedi master, spouting horse-riding platitudes that were supposed to build character as well as skill. "Yes, Yoda."

He chuckled. "Lean into the horse, you must."

Ignoring him, Bea forced herself to take some deep breaths and relax into the *rhythm of the horse* as Buffy dutifully plodded around and around the oval.

After a half dozen turns with Austin's occasional pointers, he brought Buffy to a stop with a quiet, "Whoa there, girl."

The horse stopped abruptly and Bea had to grab the horn to prevent herself from pitching forward.

"You could have warned me we were stopping."

"Sorry," he said, looking completely unabashed and hiding his amusement poorly. "It's not usually an issue when the horse is barely moving."

"I think you're enjoying this a little too much."

His face broke into a broad grin. "I am. I'm also a little turned on."

Bea arched an eyebrow. "Because a grown woman requiring training wheels to ride a horse is some kind of kink of yours?"

His hand slid onto her ankle and traveled slowly up her calf…to her knee…to her thigh, a hot tingle crawling the rest of the way up and settling between her legs. "It is when the woman is you."

"You're having Lady Godiva fantasies, aren't you?"

He chuckled. "I am now."

The temptation to get the hell off this horse and go check out Austin's cabin was *strong with this one*, but there was time for that later. "How about I master this clothed first?"

"Spoilsport." He laughed. "Okay, your turn. Take the reins and ride her around a few times like we just did."

Bea blinked. "Ohh-kay."

"You don't have to if you don't want to, but don't worry, until she's instructed otherwise, Buffy'll walk at the same pace and I'll be sitting"—he pointed at the nearest railing—"just there."

"What if she spooks?"

He chuckled as he looked around. "At what?"

Bea shrugged. "A rattlesnake? I've seen that happen."

"What?" He laughed. "In a movie?"

Well...yes. Bea might not have seen much television in the last fifteen years, but she'd been raised on the old black-and-white Westerns favored by her grandmother. "I know you have them out here. I googled it before I moved."

Sue her if she liked to be prepared where deadly creatures were involved.

"Uh-huh, we do. But did you see a rattlesnake the six times we've been around already?"

"Well...no."

"Okay then. So do you want to try going around a few times yourself?"

Bea nodded, remembering she'd worn her Thursday panties today, on a Sunday, for just this reason—to bolster her courage. "Fine."

Austin smiled and stepped a few paces away. "Over to you, then."

CHAPTER NINETEEN

Right. She could do this. Bea glanced down at the horse, waiting for her to move. Buffy did not move. She shot a quizzical look at Austin, who had climbed the fence and was watching her perched on the top rail with the faintest trace of smugness on his features. She should be mad, but all she really wanted to do was kiss that expression right off his face. "So…how do I get her to move? Pull on the reins or…?"

"Give her flanks a gentle dig with your heels."

Bea blinked. *Right.* Just like that…but Austin was looking at her like he was expecting her to fail, and she sat a little straighter in the saddle. She tapped Buffy's right flank with the heel of her boot. Buffy didn't budge. Austin's eyebrow kicked up when she looked to him for guidance, and Bea narrowed her eyes a little before trying with her other heel.

But Buffy, apparently, was disinterested in moving.

"Try both of them together."

"That won't hurt her?"

He shook his head, that damn sexy smile playing with his mouth. "She's as tough as old boots."

Bea tried both heels. Still no luck. It was clear Buffy wasn't just tough, she was freaking immovable. But Bea was not going to be defeated. She made a clicking noise like Austin had done and wriggled in the saddle a little as she said, "Let's go, girl."

It barely caused an ear twitch. She looked at Austin. "I don't think she likes me."

He shrugged. "Nah, she can just be old and crotchety sometimes."

A rather inelegant snort slipped from Bea's lips. "I know how she feels."

Austin laughed, but then he clicked twice under his tongue. "Walk on," he commanded, and Buffy ambled off again.

Her hands tightened on the reins as Bea glared at him. "Could you not just have done that to start with?"

He grinned. "Learn, you must."

Rolling her eyes, Bea held on tight and tried to remember to relax again and get into the rhythm. After two rotations, Austin asked, "You okay if she picks up the pace a little?"

Feeling brave and, hell, even a little daring, Bea nodded. "A fraction, sure." *No need to go wild.*

He nodded and clicked again. "Hey up, Buff," he commanded.

And just like that, the horse picked up speed. It wasn't exactly a trot, more a fast walk, but enough to accelerate Bea's pulse for a short burst until she realized she could handle it, and it settled again. She was definitely bouncing more now as she tried to relax into the rhythm and keep her center, which was a lot harder than she'd have thought.

Despite her concentration on the horse, she was very much aware of Austin's gaze. She couldn't *see* it because she was keeping her eyes firmly fixed on Buffy, but she could *feel* it. And it wasn't one of concern or anxiousness. He was totally checking out her ass as it lifted off the saddle.

And for damn sure he was staring at her bouncing chest.

"Don't think," Bea said as they went around another time, "I don't know you're staring at my boobs."

"Ugh, aren't men the worst?" a warm female voice asked.

Startled, Bea glanced over her shoulder to find an older

woman sitting next to Austin on the railing. "I thought I raised you better, Austin."

God…Austin's mother. Bea was so surprised to see her out here, she almost fell off the horse, but she managed to stay seated as Austin gave the command for Buffy to slow, then return to him. Within a minute, Bea was off Buffy and meeting not only Austin's mother—Margaret—but his sister-in-law, too, who had ridden up during the introduction on a muscular black stallion that looked like he could eat Buffy as a snack.

"You've got a really nice seat about you," Jill said.

Jill was a petite brunette who looked about thirty, with a rangy kind of vitality. "Thank you, but I think you're being too kind."

"Nonsense," she dismissed. "A few more lessons and you'll be riding like a pro. You're a natural. You can come out here anytime if you want to ride some more. I can teach you if Junior here isn't home."

Bea blinked at Austin. "Junior?" Oh, dear God. They called him *Junior*?

Austin rolled his eyes at his sister-in-law before addressing Bea. "The hazards of being the youngest of many," he explained.

"Yep," his mother confirmed with a smile. "By the time Austin came on the scene, there were a *lot* of names to remember."

"I told Margaret they should just have called him six," Jill said cheerily.

"We contemplated it," she confirmed, with a very definite twinkle in her eye. It was clear Margaret Cooper didn't take herself too seriously.

Ignoring his mother, Austin glanced at Jill, who was clearly having a fabulous time at his expense. "Why don't you show Bea*triss* some of your moves?"

Even standing here in front of his family, he added that soft, seductive little accent to the end of her name that was definitely not *junior*. It was like a tray of oysters and a shot of tequila to her libido.

"Oh, yes." Austin's mom clapped her hands. "That's a great idea. Why don't you help Jill set up, while Beatrice and I find a perch."

"Oh, just Bea is fine," Bea assured. Austin had claimed Beatrice for his own, and she liked it that way.

Margaret nodded affably. "C'mon, Bea, this way."

Bea followed Austin's mom with some trepidation. Was this just a friendly overture or an excuse for the third degree?

Margaret climbed the railings like a damn billy goat in three quick, effortless moves before seating herself easily. Bea followed, looking more drunken penguin, but she managed, clutching the top bar tight as she squirmed around a little to find the most comfortable position.

"Austin was telling us this morning that you're from LA."

Okay...Margaret was getting right down to it, then. "Yes," Bea said as she kept her gaze trained on the setup occurring in the arena.

"We've spent some time in LA."

Bea prepared herself for a scathing assessment of her home city. Bea knew it could be brash and pretentious in all its trendy, cilantro-loving, turmeric-smoothie-drinking, freeways-and-Hollywood, faux-glittery facade that often hid deeper vices.

But she'd loved it, too. Sure, she'd turned her back on it, but it was as much a part of her as Credence was of Austin.

"It was fabulous," Margaret said. "We had such a good time. It was so...I don't know. Potential seems to sparkle in the air there. And all those amazing food trucks and *omigod*"—she clutched Bea's arm—"the ramen noodles! I salivate whenever I think about them!"

Bea blinked. She'd expected complaints about the traffic and the smog and the sheer vanity of the place, but Bea got the feeling Austin's mother was a positive person. The kind who always saw the good in things.

She could see why Austin was the person he was, growing up with his mother at the helm. Optimistic, enthusiastic, pragmatic. Like all things were possible. Bea had been raised with the up and downs of her mother's moods and then the shadow of her death and the strictures that had come as a consequence.

"The ramen is excellent," Bea agreed, smiling at the rapture on Margaret's face.

"Unfortunately—" Margaret sighed. "There's not a lot of that around here."

"True." Bea nodded. "But you do have Annie and her pies, which really should be proclaimed as some kind of national treasure. They alone are worth a dozen food trucks and all the ramen in LA."

"Ah…so you've found our very own culinary angel and her heavenly delights?"

"I have. And they have found my ass."

Margaret laughed. "I hope this isn't a weird thing to say considering we've only just met, but I think your ass is just right. And, by the way my son was checking it out as you rode around on Buffy, I'd say Austin does, too."

It *was* weird, and a tide of heat rose in Bea's cheeks, but as their eyes met, Margaret didn't seem too self-conscious about it, and her gaze was open and friendly. Bea wondered if she was about to get *the talk*, but Margaret just gave Bea's arm a little pat before turning her attention to what was happening in the middle of the arena, and Bea felt absurdly like crying.

How she could have done with some of Margaret Cooper's brand of mothering when she was growing up. Austin was a lucky man.

"Oh, look, Jill's saddling up." She glanced at Bea. "She is utterly thrilling to watch. Just you wait and see."

Bea cleared the thickness from her throat, turning her attention to the ring to discover Margaret was not wrong. The horse, whose name was Kong—*unsurprisingly*—was fast and amazingly agile, turning on a dime, and the control that Jill had over the beast was absolute. The horse may look as if he could stomp an entire city into the ground, but he was totally under Jill's command. And if Bea had batted for the other team, she'd have a huge girl crush right now.

Hell, who was she kidding? She *did* have a huge girl crush...

Jill was very good. Also, clearly passionate about the sport and about horses. Not even Austin, who had joined them, his thigh a hairbreadth from her thigh, was enough to break her attention.

"She's amazing," Bea breathed out in a husky kind of rush as Kong rounded the barrels in a quickstep figure-eight pattern. "How long did it take her to learn to do that?"

"Jill grew up on a ranch on the other side of Credence," Margaret answered. "So she's been riding a long time, but she'll be the first to admit anybody can do it as long as they love horses, have the nerve, and practice."

Bea laughed. She couldn't even get a horse to *move*, and Jill was making her valiant steed turn tight and leap over jumps without putting a single foot wrong. She'd need more than practice. She'd need divine intervention. Maybe wings.

"Can you do that?" she asked Austin.

"No way. I've been thrown from a horse enough to make me far too chickenshit for that kind of stuff."

He grinned at her, completely unconcerned that she might judge him as somehow less of a man for not wanting to try. But she didn't. She actually *liked* that about him. A guy who didn't need to prove himself to anyone, who was comfortable enough in his own skin to say no.

She nudged her thigh against his, and her breath hitched at the contact, which felt both electric *and* soothing at the same time.

After half an hour, Jill called it a day, slowing Kong to a stop and dismounting, sliding off the saddle like she was wearing chiffon instead of denim and landing on her feet light as a freaking fairy. Austin and his mother dismounted the rail, and Bea followed suit, taking care to leave some distance between her and Austin.

"That was amazing," Bea gushed as Jill joined them.

Jill smiled. "Thanks. I get a kick out of it."

"Do you miss being on the circuit?"

"Yes and no. Probably more before I married Clay. Think I'd find the traveling and the long separations from my man too hard."

My man. Jill said those words with gusto. With pride and a certain amount of *je ne sais quoi* that left Bea in no doubt that Jill was utterly into Clay.

"And I love teaching." She shrugged. "I'm good at it. Plus, it gives me an income, independence. I miss that most from being on the circuit, I think."

Bea understood that. She'd been independent since she'd left college and scored her first-ever job straight out of the blocks at Jing-A-Ling after refusing the leg up from her father at the agency he worked for, determined to cut her own path. And the fact that she could quit her job and still support herself was not only enormously freeing but was also a source of pride.

"Finding what you love to do in life is a gift." Bea had felt that about advertising. But since quitting, she'd discovered that sometimes what you loved could be bad for you. *Toxic* even.

"Yeah." Jill nodded. "It is. Finding someone *to* love, even more so."

Jill's gaze met hers, but before Bea could parse if the comment was general or pointed, Austin jumped in.

"I'll give you a hand to put the equipment back," he said, turning away and heading for the arena.

"Nah, leave them," Jill called after him. "I'm doing some training with one of the Watsons' quarter horses tomorrow. No point putting them away just to pull them out again."

"Okay."

He returned to the group, but instead of maintaining the distance Bea had created, he stepped closer, his fingers finding the backs of her thigh, his biceps rubbing against hers.

"Well, I think it's time for afternoon drinks on the porch," his mother announced. "Brian and Clay should be home soon, and I have a hankering for a nice chardonnay." She smiled at Bea. "Would you like a glass?"

Bea was torn. She was curious to meet the man who had Jill utterly smitten and also more than a little curious to meet Austin's father, but Austin's thumb was brushing lazily at the point where her thigh met her ass, and desire to be alone with him drummed an even louder beat.

"Umm." She glanced at Austin. "Do we...have time, or...?"

Their gazes met, and she saw the same desire flaring in Austin's eyes. He draped his arm around the front of her shoulders, his big forearm a solid weight against her chest, his body hot and hard against her back, her Thursday panties well and truly tangled.

"Sorry, Mom, we have plans that don't involve chardonnay."

The smiles on Margaret's and Jill's faces left Bea in little doubt that they knew exactly what Austin's plans were, but it didn't make Bea blush this time. It made her feel...special.

"Okay, okay." Jill grinned as she gave Austin's shoulder a playful pat before turning her attention to Bea. "Have a lovely evening. I hear you're camping out under the stars, and you're going to have a gorgeous night for it."

"Yes," Margaret agreed. "You haven't seen stars until you've seen Credence stars."

"I'm looking forward to it." Bea smiled and hoped neither of the women could see that the only stars she was interested in right now were the kind that came with orgasms. Although she suspected they both could.

Hell, she suspected *Kong*, who was staring straight at her, knew it, too.

"Remember what I said," Jill pressed. "If you ever want to come out and ride Buffy again, just give me a call. Junior"—she stopped as Austin glowered at her—"sorry, *Austin* has my number."

"If you want to come out for any reason," Margaret added, "we'd love to see you again."

"Thanks." Bea nodded. "I might just take you up on that."

Why not? She was making friends. Why not Margaret and Jill, too? There was something appealing about the warmth between these women. It spoke of affection and fondness and *family*, and didn't that open up a thick vein of yearning.

"Okay, bye now," Austin said.

Bea smiled and bid them goodbye one more time before allowing Austin to turn them around and head for the gate. Once they were out and walking back toward his cabin, she said, "Do you think they know we're going to your cabin to fuck?"

He laughed. "Probably. But all that really matters to me is that *you* think we're going to my cabin to fuck, because I swear I'd made a pact with myself to be the perfect gentleman until I got you alone under the stars tonight."

Bea shot him a look full of abject horror. "Austin, I am so horny, I'd drop to the ground and do it right here, right now if we didn't have an audience. I don't want you to be a gentleman. I want you to be a freaking *cave*man."

His hand tightened on her waist as he picked up speed. "Hurry."

CHAPTER TWENTY

Two hours later, Austin threw the air bed and some bedding into the back of the pickup, along with a shopping bag full of camp food and some booze—a six-pack of beer, a bottle of red wine, and another of bourbon. It was always good to have choices.

"So where are you taking me?" Bea asked as he shut the tailgate.

Austin turned to find her coming out of his cabin. Man... the things they had done in his cabin. Beatrice was the first woman he'd slept with who appeared to have zero hang-ups. He hadn't been with that many women, but the ones he had been with were often too worried what they looked like to just enjoy the experience.

Beatrice didn't require reassurance and was very definite about what she wanted and what she didn't. If she needed something different, she just asked for it, and if it wasn't working for her, she changed it up or demanded he did.

Her sexual confidence had him in her thrall.

But what really slugged him in the chest as she wrapped her hand around one of the rough-hewn posts along the front porch wasn't what they'd done inside the cabin but how *good* she looked coming *out* of his cabin. And how much he'd like to see more of it.

"We're going to my favorite place on the ranch," he said. "It's out near the tree line not far from the stream."

"Oh yeah?" She cocked an eyebrow. "That where you took all your girlfriends?"

Austin chuckled. "No. That was the loft in the barn."

"Ooh now. That sounds…"

"Romantic?"

A small smile ghosted her lips. "I was thinking scratchy."

"Yeah, it was that, too." A big laugh hooted from his mouth. "Come on, let's go."

They climbed in the vehicle and Austin set out across the open fields in front of him. He had planned on giving her a bit of a tour, but the last streaks of light from the brilliant blood-orange sunset were just fading and it would be dark soon.

Another time. *Hopefully.*

"So," Austin said as he eased back on the gas to decrease the rock and bounce as he drove across the rough terrain. The shocks on his old pickup had seen better days. "Was riding a horse all that you thought it'd be?"

"Not really. I was thinking it'd be more like me flying bareback across the fields, my hair streaming behind me, wearing a fringed jacket and leather chaps. You know?"

Austin laughed. "Nope. But for what it's worth, I'd have paid good money to see that."

"Me riding across the plains?"

"You in a fringed jacket and chaps."

She rolled her eyes at him. "Austin Cooper. I thought your mama raised you better than that."

He grinned. "Yeah, but my daddy didn't."

She looked like she was going to burst into laughter but stopped, distracted by the scenery as the last light of day softened the landscape to gauzy shadows.

"Wow," she said on a breathy exhale. "It's so beautiful. Does it kick you in the chest every time you come out here like this?"

"It does. I love it." A swell of emotion flooded Austin's chest. The family ranch was part of his heart and soul.

"But..." She frowned. "You didn't want to work it?"

"No." He shook his head. "Not like Clay. Don't get me wrong, I want to always live here and be around to help out, be a part of its prosperity and its growth. But...the ranch is Clay's calling. Me? I always wanted to join the police force." He glanced at Beatrice briefly before returning his attention to the rutted landscape ahead. "I love it. Being a small-town cop. A *Credence* cop. That's *my* calling."

She blinked, clearly surprised at his admission. "Yeah?"

"Yep." Austin smiled. "I'm gunning for Arlo's job. I figure when he's ready to retire in about twenty years or so, I'll have enough experience to just slide on into the role."

"You don't want to hit the city again, become a detective or specialize in another area of policing? SWAT? Vice? Forensics?"

"Nope." He shook his head. "I've done the big-city thing with five years in Denver, and yeah, I could bounce around other PDs for the next decade, trying to find the same kind of feeling that walking into the Credence PD every morning gives me, or I could just cut to the chase."

"Well...go you."

He changed gears as he traversed a gully, glancing over at Beatrice, her profile pensive. "Guess you can take the boy out of the small town but not the small town out of the boy, huh?"

Shrugging, she said, "There are worse things to have in you."

"Brussels sprouts for one."

"Kale." Beatrice laughed. "I know that's not very California of me, but—" She gave a little shudder.

They both laughed then. "Maybe I'm not ambitious enough," Austin said as their laughter settled. "But it's like what you were talking about earlier with Jill. Finding what you love to do in life is a gift. Why waste your life looking for something better or...different when it's right in front of you?"

The heat of her gaze warmed Austin's cheek, but he couldn't look at her right now because he wasn't entirely sure he was just talking about his job, and he didn't want to spook her.

He'd been cognizant of her wariness when his mom and Jill had joined them, so overwhelming her with how he was feeling didn't seem a smart move. Beatrice reminded him of a skittish foal—one wrong step could send her bolting.

"I don't think ambition needs to be lofty or...hard or constantly changing. Ambition can be small."

"But not for you?" Austin sent her a gentle smile. "You were a corner office girl all the way, right?"

She gave a harsh half laugh. "Ambition can also be bad for you."

There was regret and bitterness in her proclamation, which clawed at Austin's gut. Things had suddenly gone dark, and it had nothing to do with the sun finally sliding below the horizon. Time to lighten things up. "You know what else is bad for you?"

"Sunbathing between ten and three, more than five tequila shots in any given night, and googling yourself?"

Austin laughed at her quick-fire response. "Waffle cones full of chocolate and marshmallow wrapped in foil and shoved in the fire."

"Oh my God." She slid her hand over the top of his, where it was resting on the stick shift. "This would be a seriously *bad* thing for you to joke about and then not follow through."

"Honey, I never joke about s'mores in a cone."

She smiled. "If you can produce such decadence, I might even let you put it in unspeakable places."

"Challenge accepted."

...

Ten minutes later, Austin pulled up at the spot he'd prepared earlier in the day. He'd come out and set up the fire, ready to light with a box of extra wood, also ready to go, and two large logs sitting at right angles to each other for their seating. The dark shapes of the trees were about thirty feet away in one direction, the gentle trickle of the stream about thirty in the other.

"Boy Scout, huh?" Bea said as she climbed out of the pickup and ambled over to where things were all prepared.

Grinning, Austin said, "Yes, ma'am."

He lit the fire, the cool of the evening starting to draw in already, and grabbed them both a beer. Then he told her to sit while he pumped up the air mattress with his trusty foot pump in the back of the pickup and got their bedding set up.

"I love a fire," she said absently, and Austin looked up from what he was doing to watch her drinking beer and staring into the flames.

The truth was, the fire loved *her*. Orange firelight flickered through the bright coppery strands of her hair, transforming it to a blazing corona around her head. It shimmered over her body, licking golden light over her denim-clad thighs, over her breasts, dancing all the way up her neck. She literally glowed with the fire like some ancient volcano goddess, and Austin's heart just about stopped in his chest. It felt like everything that was important in life was right there and he was king of the fucking world.

Jumping down from the tray, Austin picked up the beer he'd set on the log next to hers and took several long swallows. She smiled at him and said, "Cheers."

"Cheers," he returned as he touched the neck of his bottle to the neck of hers, the *clink* loud in the utter silence of an Eastern Colorado evening.

And for the next couple of hours, they drank beer and then wine straight from the bottle, because he hadn't thought to bring glasses, and chatted and laughed. Austin told her some stories about growing up on the ranch, which she seemed to enjoy even if she deflected whenever he tried to get her to share some of her stories.

But conscious as always of his *gently, gently* approach with her, he didn't push. She was all mellow and Austin was nicely buzzed as he let the fire burn down enough to put the griddle on and cook their gourmet s'mores.

The night had cooled considerably, but the heat from the fire reached out and wrapped him up in a warm hug that seeped into his bones as deftly as Beatrice's laughter and *company* had seeped into his heart and his freaking soul. But he was *not* going to analyze that—he'd told her they didn't have to put a name on what was happening, and he'd be damned if he wasn't going to follow his own advice.

Austin filled the cones with chocolate chips and mini marshmallows, then wrapped them in the aluminum foil before placing them on top of the griddle resting over the coals.

"You want some of this?" Austin asked as he unscrewed the cap on the bourbon.

She narrowed her eyes playfully at him, the lavalike smolder of the coals turning down the blaze in her hair from flame to glow. "Trying to get me drunk, Officer?"

"I think," Austin said, smiling around the mouth of the bottle, "I've proven I don't have to."

She feigned an outraged expression. "Are you calling me easy?"

"No, ma'am." Austin took a deep swallow of the liquor, feeling and savoring the burn all the way down his esophagus. "I'm calling you insatiable." The firelight might be low, but Austin could still make out the flare of her nostrils, which he felt all the way to his groin.

"I am, it appears, where you're concerned."

"Well," he said, passing the bottle, "that's good news for me."

Five minutes later, he grabbed the wrapped cones off the griddle, and they sat side by side, devouring the treats, nothing but the occasional pop from the fire, the low resonance of appreciative moans, and the licking of fingers to break the cold, clear silence of the night.

When he was done, Austin watched Beatrice make what he was fairly sure was a deliberately pornographic display of licking her fingers clean, and he shook his head. "You missed some."

She held her hands up to the fire, fingers spread, an orange aura outlining their shape. "Where?" she asked, turning her head to face him.

Austin smiled. "Here."

And he closed the distance between their lips and claimed her mouth. She melted like the proverbial marshmallow, leaning into him, her immediate moan like rocket fuel to Austin's bourbon-infused state. His heart raced and his breathing turned thick as soup as he plundered her mouth with his tongue, licking up every last sweet morsel as she was doing to him.

"Mmm," she said when Austin eventually relinquished her mouth, his forehead pressing into hers as they both panted raggedly into the night air. "I think it's time we made use of all that pumping you did." And she squeezed his leg.

"My thoughts exactly." Austin stood, grabbing her hand and tugging her up, taking two steps toward the pickup, when he felt the resistance. He turned. "Problem?"

"Yeah…I'm going to need to empty my bladder first." She looked out into the darkness beyond the fire. "I don't suppose you stashed a port-o-potty out here somewhere?"

Austin laughed. "I'm afraid not. I'll get the flashlight. Just head to the tree line and go there."

She took a step closer to him. "What? By myself?"

"It's only thirty feet away."

"Sure. But...what about the..." She glanced out again. "Animals?"

He quirked an eyebrow. "Like rattlesnakes?"

"Yes." She turned reproachful eyes on him. "Like rattlesnakes. And...wolves and coyotes. And...do you get bears out here?"

A big belly laugh escaped Austin's mouth. "I think you'll be safe from wolves, coyotes, and bears."

"But not rattlesnakes."

"You know they're more afraid of you than you are of them."

She shoved her hands on her hips. "You wanna bet?" Then she looked out into the night one more time, chewing on her bottom lip.

"I can come with you." God knew he could certainly do with a little bladder relief, too.

Her shoulders sagged a little. "Thank you."

Austin smiled as he trudged to the cab of the pickup for the flashlight. Returning with the light, he clicked it on and held out his hand. "Come on."

She slid her hand in his, and they followed the powerful beam to the first row of trees. "Here should do," he said, handing the light over and stepping away a bit.

"Where are you going?" she asked, a slight edge of panic in her tone.

"Just giving you a little space to do your business."

"It's fine. Stay close, okay? Just...turn your back."

Austin pressed his lips into a line so he wouldn't laugh and turned dutifully around. He heard the noise of a zipper coming down and then rustling as the beam of the flashlight danced. He heard a *thud* and the beam went low, and she cursed, but within seconds the light bounced around again as she picked it up off the ground.

All was quiet for a beat or two, and then he heard, "Can you whistle, please?"

"Whistle?" Austin frowned.

A loud, exasperated sigh hit him square between the shoulder blades. "Yes. The thought of you hearing me tinkle is putting me off, okay?"

He laughed this time. "Do you have any requests?"

"Very funny, Austin."

He suppressed another laugh. He thought it was *hilarious*. Definitely a story he hoped to tell one day about the night they'd first camped out under the stars. But, with her wish being his command, Austin whistled "Home on the Range," which wasn't easy when he was trying to also pee *and* fight the bubble of laughter in his chest.

"Okay, okay," she muttered after he got to the end of the chorus. "Enough already."

Austin grinned as he zipped up.

"Remind me in the future not to get so boozy where there's no restroom in sight," she said from behind him as her hand slipped between his body and his arm, curling around his elbow.

He looked down at her, and she smiled at him big and happy, like he was her knight in shining armor who'd just slayed a dragon for her instead of sticking close and whistling while she'd whizzed. Austin had been in his share of situations at work where people had been grateful to him, had looked at him as some kind of hero. But he'd never felt quite as special as he did right now being *Beatrice's* hero.

They headed back to his pickup, kicking out of their shoes on the tailgate before getting under the covers and shedding their clothes, pushing them to the bottom of the bedding so they wouldn't be freezing to get back into in the morning.

"Wow," Beatrice said, her voice full of wonder as she gazed up at the sky above. "It's magnificent."

"Yeah."

The moon hadn't yet risen, there wasn't a cloud in the sky, and the glow from the coals was too low to interfere with their night vision. A chandelier of stars hung overhead, puncturing the cool, crisp veil of night. A shooting star streaked across the sky, and Beatrice pointed and exclaimed in pleasure.

"You know any constellations?" she asked.

Austin didn't. His brother knew all of them. Hell, Clay could probably pass as some kind of amateur astronomer, but Austin had preferred the mystical to the facts as far as the stars were concerned. That being said, he was totally up for faking it.

"Absolutely. They call me Galileo around these parts." Pointing just above them, he drew a half-ass *S* shape between a band of stars. "That there is Rolly, the rattlesnake. See how there's that little kick at the end? That's it's rattler."

She laughed. "Okay. Sure."

"And over there." He pointed to the left. "That's Beatrice the Beautiful."

"Really?"

"Uh-huh. See, you can just make out the curve of her waist." He drew a line with his fingers between completely unrelated stars. "And there and there"—he dotted the air twice—"are her nipples."

Her hair brushed against his neck as she turned her face into his chest, smothering her laughter as she gently bit just above *his* nipple. His body hummed with heat and anticipation. "You are full of shit, Austin Cooper."

Austin grinned. "What gave me away?"

She rose up onto her elbow, her hair falling forward. "I think I'm going to have to punish you for impersonating an ancient astronomer of good standing. What town ordinance governs that, Officer?"

"Ah, that would be five six nine four subsection B three. Any particular punishment you have in mind?"

"I think it definitely requires a damn good boinking."

Austin pressed his lips into a line to stop from laughing. Or begging. "Well…if you insist."

She grinned, then reached under his pillow where Austin had stashed their condom supply earlier. Grabbing one, she ripped it open as her leg slid over his belly. In the blink of an eye she'd straddled him, the blankets falling down around her ass, leaving them both exposed, the cold air skimming an erotic brand against his heated flesh, her cool fingers utter torture on the taut, feverishly hot flesh of his cock as she applied the condom with ruthless efficiency.

His breath hissed out, fogging into the air. How was it possible to be so cold and so damn hot at the same time? Austin's hands moved to her hips, his gaze lapping up the line of her neck and the curve of her breasts as she reached between them, guiding his dick in line with her center.

Slowly, slowly, her head thrown back, she slid onto him, and Austin groaned as she sank down, down, down, enveloping him in her slick, satiny heat until he was seated so high and tight in her, he didn't know where she ended and he began. His heart was a slow, heavy thump in his chest. "You *are* a witch," he murmured as she sat atop him, gloriously naked, her nipples hard points, her hair crowned with a galaxy of stars like some goddess of the night.

She held out her hands. "Shall I put a spell on you?"

Austin slid his hands from her hips to capture her fingers, interlinking his with hers, their palms pressed together. "You already have."

She smiled and started to undulate her hips, and Austin moved in sync, and there were no spells, but there were moans and sighs and gasps of pleasure until the stars blurred and the earth shook and the heavens came tumbling down.

CHAPTER TWENTY-ONE

Monday morning, just after six, Bea let herself into her apartment, stopping only to shuck her smoky clothes and to feed a royally pissed Princess before tumbling into bed, wearing a T-shirt, panties, and an unholy smile on her face. It had been a magical night under the stars with Austin, an orgy of sexual exploration that seemed to intensify the later into the night it became.

But there hadn't been a lot of sleep, so, ignoring Princess's not-so-subtle display of neglected feline animosity, Bea slept the sleep of a woman who had been absolutely, positively, *thoroughly* fucked.

It was almost one in the afternoon when she woke. Princess was in her usual spot on Bea's pillow, purring up a storm, and Bea stretched up, scooping the cat down as she rolled on her side and hugged Princess in tight to her chest. She didn't object.

If anything, she purred louder.

"I'm sorry I left you all alone last night, kitty cat," Bea apologized in a whisper. Even though she knew from their short time together that Princess had taken to Bea's hermit lifestyle like a duck to water.

"You ever been with a boy cat who just…blew your ever-loving mind?" Bea asked.

Princess let out a very smug-sounding meow. "Yeah." Bea

smiled. "I bet you have, you foxy feline, you." Princess had probably cut quite the figure before she'd lost her eye and most of her fur and her tooth had gone rogue.

Of course, it hadn't just been the sex. It had been the way Austin had *looked* at her every time he'd been buried deep, like he was rummaging around in her soul.

Like she was the only woman in the world.

It was the intensity of his stare, his singular focus on *her* and what he *saw* in her and what he was *offering* her that had elevated the entire night beyond the physical.

Sighing, Bea kissed Princess's neck before climbing out of bed and heading for her shower. Her hair smelled like woodsmoke and her skin smelled like marshmallows and the bourbon Austin had licked off certain parts of her body.

And sex. Good God, she smelled utterly *debauched*.

Princess was still on the bed when Bea stepped out of the bathroom fifteen minutes later, totally naked, her fine, damp hair all fluffy from being towel dried. She stepped into her Monday panties and sweats and a tee and padded back to bed, sitting cross-legged on top of the duvet as she opened up her laptop. Her Winchester brothers screen saver stared back at her, and Bea almost laughed.

Prior to this, her screen savers had always been the latest ad campaign she'd worked on, and Bea marveled at how dramatically her life had changed in such a short period of time.

Clicking to her email, she downloaded the dozen that had come in since Friday, including one from Kim with the subject line: *You've gone viral baby!!* Blinking at that rather startling claim, Bea opened the email, which had so many exclamation points, she wondered if Kim needed some kind of intervention.

Oh Em Geee!!! BEA!!!!!!!

Cranky Bea cards are a hit!!!! Our socials have gone off!! over the weekend. Like, ballistic!!!!!! Everyone wants to know when they can buy them!!!!! We need more, Bea!!! More! So we can go into production immediately!! Immediately!!!! We want a range of at least two dozen and aiming to double!! that for next month and keep that level of production going to the end of the year at least!!!!!

Congrats, you're a social media phenomenon and I'm begging you to come work for us!!!! Please call me ASAP!!!! As soon as you get this email so we can discuss in more detail!!

And then Kim left a list of six different numbers she could be reached at. *Just in case!!!!*

With her advertising background, Bea knew that *going viral* was the kind of advertising money just couldn't buy. Not even the most outstandingly beautiful or searing insightful, multimillion-dollar ad campaign could beat a lol Cats or Baby Shark for exposure and potential riches.

But she doubted her quick, sarcastic sketches were in the mega-influencer realm.

Grabbing her cell phone, Bea checked out Greet Cute's socials and almost fell out of bed. No, it wasn't Kardashian-esque, but it was still impressive. They'd posted the three images as separate posts on their Insta and TikTok accounts, and each one had been liked several hundred thousand times, with the comments over the three posts running into the thousands, not to mention the reposts and the myriad story shares.

She blinked. *Holy cow.* Her head started to buzz, her veins started to prickle, her chest started to tighten as Kim's *we need more* caused a creative rush of potential images she could draw. Not that *they* were causing the buzz. No, it was the success of the sampling exercise. She always felt this way when one of her campaigns took off.

Picking up her phone, she tapped in Kim's cell number with shaky hands.

• • •

Bea was still finding it hard to wrap her head around it all several hours later, when Austin clomped up her stairs. Kim's offer had been a lot to take in, and she wasn't sure if she wanted to go there. Well, part of her—LA Beatrice—was excited at the possibilities of contributing to an ad campaign again because she was still, at heart, an ad woman. But the other part—Credence Beatrice of the sweats and beer for breakfast and flaming red hair—wasn't so sure.

Spending the afternoon in bed with Princess, Daryl Dixon, and a bunch of zombies for company while absently doodling on the sketch pad hadn't really helped clarify her position, either.

Austin's footfalls and his key—she'd given him the spare one this morning so she didn't have to get her ass out of bed— in the lock were a welcome distraction, and she paused the screen mid–zombie bite as the door opened and shut and Austin suddenly appeared in her line of sight, coming to rest a few feet from the end of the bed. He looked hotter than an LA summer in his police uniform and hat, his hands behind his back as he looked down at her like she was the next thing on his to-do list.

Like he hadn't *to-done* her thoroughly all night long.

"Hey," he said.

Bea smiled. "How was your day, dear?"

He laughed, a low, sexy sound that slid onto the mattress, slithered up her foot and her calves and her thighs, and settled between her legs. "All the better for seeing you. How was yours?"

"Interesting," she said. "Very interesting."

"Good interesting or bad interesting?" He cocked an eyebrow.

"I...don't know?" Because she really didn't.

"Would pie give you more clarity?" He pulled out his left hand from behind his back to reveal a brown paper bag.

Bea's visceral reaction to its appearance was almost as potent as her visceral reaction to his low, sexy laugh. "It might."

He grinned as he took two paces toward her, placing the bag on the end of the bed with all the due care and attention a piece of culinary joy should be afforded before undoing the buckle on his utility belt. Their eyes met and that smile played on his lips as he slid it off and placed it on the couch. His hat followed as he kicked off his shoes, then undid the buttons of his shirt, pulling the tails out of his pants as he went. He didn't remove it altogether, but there was enough flap of material going on to reveal flashes of his truly spectacular abs and chest.

"I think things are already getting clearer," she teased.

He laughed again as he picked up the pie and prowled up the mattress on his hands and knees, pushing aside the multiple discarded sketch pages strewn across the bed. When he got to Bea, she quickly moved her laptop aside as his body claimed the space between her legs, and he leaned in to kiss her hard on the mouth.

Pie was temporarily forgotten as Bea opened to him—her legs and her mouth—welcoming the taste and the smell of him as his tongue stroked against hers, welcoming the feel of his body, hard and perfect, cradled between her legs. Welcoming the harsh suck of his breath and the deep, guttural resonance of his groan that ruffled over her like a hot breeze and was satisfying in ways she didn't fully understand.

Every breath she took was full of Austin, and Bea slid her arms around his neck, sinking lower in the bed, taking him with her.

Princess and her very loud, very disapproving mewl dragged them out of their spiraling passion. The look of utter disgust from that one gnarly eye spoke volumes.

"Like you've never driven the boy cats wild," Austin called after her as she jumped off the bed, and they watched her amble away, her tail twitching indignantly. He glanced back at Bea. "Well, at least she saved the pie from being squashed," he said as he shifted a hand precariously close to the brown paper bag.

Levering himself into a sitting position, he pulled the cover back and settled beside her. Bea also sat higher in the bed, her back to the wall, her shoulder rubbing against his. "You want cherry or pecan?" he asked, peering into the bag.

"I don't mind." It was fair to say that the quality of Annie's offering had made her a pie agnostic.

He reached into the bag and pulled out the slice of cherry, then held it close to her mouth. "Open," he said softly, and Bea, whose pulse had barely settled from their mini make out, felt it kick up again.

She opened obediently, their hot gazes meshing as she bit into the divine combination of tart and sweet. He fed himself then, and his low, appreciative noise of satisfaction also had an effect on Bea's pulse. He offered her another, but she shook her head, reaching in for the slice of pecan and making a start on that.

After he was done, Austin picked up the sketches still scattered on the mattress.

"You've been busy." He picked up a few more that had fallen to the floor on his side of the bed and perused them like he was some kind of art collector.

"Just messing around, really." She'd forgotten how much she'd doodled as a kid. When she'd been anxious from her parents fighting or her father fretting about her mom's whereabouts, it had helped calm her. During college, it had helped her clarify her thinking about an assignment or memorize something for an exam.

"Are you craving honey?"

Bea frowned. "What?"

He shuffled through the sketches. "All of these are bees."

"Oh...yes." She hadn't really been conscious of what she'd

been doodling, but now that Austin had mentioned it, she'd clearly been *obsessively* drawing bees all with different body quirks and expressions on their little bee faces.

"Has this got something to do with your interesting day?"

"Yeah." She supposed it had, and she filled Austin in on everything from the email to the phone call.

"And?" he prompted as she got to the end of her tale. "What did you tell her?"

"I told her I…didn't know. I wasn't sure."

He shuffled through the sketches one more time as if looking for one in particular and, when he found it, he placed it on her lap. This bee had its brows beetled together in an irritated little frown, its mouth a foreboding slash, and the buzz coming out from a word bubble near its head was written expletive style—buz@z$zz#zzz!!!

"I think you are." Tapping the drawing, Austin said, "Looks like a logo to me."

Bea stared at the cranky little bee. Just like her—Cranky Bea. She smiled, marveling at her subconscious and the power of doodling. "What do you think I should do?"

"It's not up to me."

"I know, but…I'd appreciate your take." Maybe she was wrong, but she didn't think Austin would be too excited about anything that might shift her focus from Credence, and it would be good to have that perspective strongly represented.

"I…" He shrugged, seemingly reluctant to venture it even if he did have one. "Think you're an artist, Beatrice. I think maybe you always have been?"

"No." She shook her head vehemently; he was dead *wrong* about that. She had an appreciation for art and an eye for design because so much about advertising revolved around that process, but an *artist* she was not. "This"—she picked up the logo from her lap—"isn't art."

"Okay. If you say so." Clearly, he didn't believe her

declaration. "Whatever it is," he said, then lifted a shoulder in a half shrug, "I think maybe you're liking it, so...why not keep doing it? For as long as you're enjoying it? You didn't know what you wanted to do when you came here, and yeah, this has kinda fallen into your lap, but maybe that was for a reason? Especially if, as you say, Kim is happy for you to work freelance. Then you get the best of both worlds. Advertising *and* art while working to your own timetable and staying away from corporate life."

Bea nodded absently. Austin was, as always, separating things down to their most simple parts. But her deepest worry bubbled to the surface, and she expressed it before she even knew what she was saying. "What if it's a slippery slope?"

"You mean, what if you start wanting more? If advertising starts to suck you back in?"

She blinked, suddenly not entirely sure that *was* what she'd meant and she hadn't just channeled her grandmother's fears about the perils of surrendering to an artistic temperament, which she knew all too intimately. Bea was an *ad* woman, not an artist. Art was a part of the process—a means to an end. Not the whole.

That had never been in doubt. Until recently. Until the lake.

"Yeah," she said huskily, because the other stuff was too big to contemplate.

His hand nudged hers, and he entwined their fingers. "I say, take it one day at a time. If you start feeling like it's getting to be too much and you don't want to do it anymore or you want to ease back, then ease back. You left for a reason, Bea, so go back for a reason. Like believing in Kim and Greet Cute. But with your eyes open. And maybe give yourself an out?"

Her heart skipped a beat. This twenty-five-going-on-one-hundred guy was more than she'd ever hoped for, and this thing between them was madness. Sudden, intense, and inexplicable—but also very real.

Bea rubbed her cheek against his shoulder. She had no clue what to say, but she was inordinately pleased that Austin was here with her in this moment.

"Of course," he said, a smile in his voice, "when all else fails, you can always ask, WWDD?"

And just like that, the intensity of their conversation lifted. Bea laughed. "He *wouldn't* laze around in his bed all day, sketching."

Fucking, maybe, but not something so damn passive.

"True," Austin agreed. "But he never backs away from a challenge. Or an opportunity. And isn't that exactly what Greet Cute is?"

Bea nodded. She couldn't dispute that.

"Look, Bea*triss*, honey." He looked down at her the same time she looked up, and their gazes met. There was humor lurking there but also a streak of seriousness. "Whatever you decide to do, just know I'll keep you supplied with pie and orgasms, okay?"

Bea's breath got stuck somewhere between her lungs and her throat. How could she resist that offer? "Okay," she agreed, her voice breathy.

"Good." He grinned at her wolfishly as he tossed the sketches over the side of the bed and reached for her, dragging her up and over his lap until she was straddling him, the hard ridge in his pants causing that breath she'd only just caught to get stuck again. "So…I've taken care of the pie…" And he leaned in and kissed her.

CHAPTER TWENTY-TWO

When Sunday rocked around again, Bea found herself back at the ranch, taking more riding lessons with Austin on a short trail where Buffy ambled along companionably beside Austin's horse, Star. He pointed out aspects of the ranch as they worked to a bit of a trot and the sun warmed her through. After they returned, she and Austin sat on the rail again and observed Jill working a horse from a nearby ranch.

She was so absorbed that she didn't even hear Austin's mom approach until she was hauling herself up the fence and swinging her leg over the top rail. "I could watch her all day," Margaret said.

"Me too," Bea agreed.

Which was exactly what they did, at least until Jill finished her set and Margaret invited them up to the big house for some afternoon drinks.

"Thanks for the offer, Mom," Austin said, "but—"

"Actually." Bea gave Austin's thigh a squeeze. "We'd love to, Margaret."

Sure, she wanted to get him back to his cabin and have him follow through on his offer to massage liniment into her thigh and ass muscles to counteract the soreness he promised her she'd feel tomorrow. But she was curious now to meet the rest of Austin's family.

His mother beamed at her, and Austin returned her thigh squeeze with one of his own. He smiled at his mom. "We'd love to."

Margaret grinned at her son. "Good answer." Then she performed a nimble half turn, swinging her legs to the other side of the rail. "Come on up when you're done here," she said, then scrambled down, landing with a little jump.

"You don't have to," Austin murmured as his mom made a beeline for the house.

Bea rubbed her cheek against his shoulder, the fabric of his shirt warmed from the sun. "It's okay. I want to."

"More than you want me to *rub you down*?"

She grinned at the dirty, *dirty* emphasis he'd used. "You can do that later."

"You'll be sorer later."

"Well, you'll have to be gentle with me, then, won't you?"

He waggled his eyebrows. "I can give it to you however you like."

Oh yes. Yes, he could. "We'll make it a quick drink."

· · ·

There was a magnificent view from the back porch and, despite herself, Bea felt the tug—the *urge*—to recreate it *and* the magnificent simplicity of the stone-and-wood house. To immortalize it in pastels as the sun sunk low in the sky and cast long shadows over the land. She ignored it, throwing herself into the lively ebb and flow of Cooper family conversation, instead, and the enjoyment of Margaret's spiked iced tea.

There were the inevitable questions directed her way, but, as if they knew to take a light hand, they didn't probe too deeply, which left ample opportunity for her to ask a zillion questions about the ranch and the Cooper family and Credence.

"So...you create greeting cards?" Brian Cooper clarified

eventually as the conversation turned back to her.

He was a handsome man in that weather-beaten-rancher kind of way. The kind who sold tractors and Levi's. With his quick, easy smile and his low, rumbly laugh, Bea could see exactly what Austin would look like as he aged.

Which was *not* a bad thing.

Bea nodded. "That's right."

After toying with the decision for a few days, she'd spoken to Kim on Wednesday and accepted her offer. Her brain had been exploding with ideas for Greet Cute and, like that dart in the board, she'd taken it as a sign.

"I didn't even know that was a job. I assumed that sort of stuff was all done on computer these days."

"It is," she confirmed. "But it still requires design people. Some do it from scratch on a computer, using a bunch of different design tools and software packages. More bespoke companies like Greet Cute tend to use original artwork and convert that into a graphic."

"I see." He nodded.

"And can you do that from home?" Margaret asked.

"Yes. They've hired me as a freelance designer. All I need is a laptop and access to the internet."

"And do you have some kind of brief as to what they're after?" Brian asked.

"Beatrice created her own line, Dad," Austin said. "It's called Cranky Bea." Glancing at her, Austin said, "Show them the logo."

Bea dutifully found the logo on her phone and handed it over. Kim had been super thrilled with the image of the irate little bee and had suggested they call their new line of sarcastic cards Cranky Bea—with an *a* not two *e's*—and that it be placed on the back, underneath the Greet Cute logo. She and Kim had gone back and forth on the font and placement of the two words until they'd come up with the design currently being passed around the Cooper family.

"Looks like that'll cause quite a buzz," Brian said with a grin.

Bea laughed, remembering Austin's grumblings about his father's penchant for puns. But many years in advertising had made her queen *bee* of wordplay and puns. "It'll keep me buzzy."

He nodded gravely. "And on your best bee-havior."

"I'll have to take my vitamin bee, for sure."

"I can loan you my Bee Gees albums if you need some creative stimulus?"

Bea pretended to consider the offer while her brain scrambled for a snappy rejoinder. "I'm more a Bee-yoncé kinda gal."

Brian shook his head in faux disappointment. "Now you're just pollen my leg."

Clay, who, along with the others, had been following their rapid-fire banter as if watching a grand slam tennis final, groaned out loud. He fixed Austin with a what-the-fuck look. "There are *two* of them?"

Austin chuckled, clearly unperturbed. "That's my honey," he confirmed.

Jill slid her palm onto Clay's knee. "I think your brother has been bee-witched."

Clay gaped. "You too?"

"Nah, son, that's not the question." Brain paused for dramatic effect. "To bee, or not to bee, that's the question."

He really cracked up then, and Bea joined him because it was a truly magnificent addition to the pun fest. She'd never had *this*. This easy affection, this contentment in company, this feeling of family. And she loved it.

"Oh God." Clay rolled his eyes before appealing to his mother. "Can't you make him stop?"

Margaret shook her head. "You know your father, Clay.

Best to just let it bee." Her straight face lasted for about two seconds before she dissolved into laughter, which caused another round of hilarity. Even Clay, who'd clearly decided if he couldn't beat them, he might as well join them, cracked a wry smile.

And Bea's heart was fuller than it had ever been. She could definitely get used to this.

CHAPTER TWENTY-THREE

Austin smiled as Beatrice's laughter drifted across Jack's to where he was seated at the stools. Since she'd said yes to Kim a month ago, Beatrice spent her days creating magic for Cranky Bea and her nights with him creating a different kind of magic. Except for Sundays. They spent Sundays at the ranch with his family.

And on Wednesdays, she line danced.

He was in the corner closest to the small dance floor, where there were currently about a dozen people following the line-dancing instructor. Pearl was in her sixties with high hair and low expectations.

He hadn't been able to take his eyes off Beatrice since she'd walked into Jack's tonight. He'd had to work back and had arranged to meet her here, and it was just as well, because if she'd been wearing *that* at the apartment, there was no way they'd have made it to Jack's.

It was a dress. A bright yellow dress. *Big Bird yellow.* A stark contrast to the vibrant red of her hair. And it was strapless with two ties that sprouted from the fabric at a point between her breasts, which she'd pulled up and crossed at her nape to anchor around her neck before being brought through to the front and crisscrossing under her breasts, and then winding around and around the bodice several more times, before they'd been tied at her waist at the back, their ends almost trailing to the floor.

It was made from some kind of slippery fabric that draped lovingly against her body and disguised the fullness of the skirt. But when she spun around, the skirt flared out like a spinning top, flashing glimpses of bare thighs and those sexy red cowgirl boots she'd bought online especially for this class.

It was a far cry from sweats and bunny slippers.

But the thing that made the dress shine and made every person in the class with her—all of them at least thirty years her senior—smile indulgently and nod was that *she* knew, maybe for the first time, that she looked hot. It was in the way she swished around and put a little extra roll in her hips, and the way she flicked her hair and exaggerated the snappy little foot movements as she performed each heel dig.

And then there was the way she kept sneaking glances at him as she went through the routines. A side glance over her shoulder, a peek from under the cover of her rich red hair as it swished around her face. The way she smiled all playful and secretive, her lips shining with a clear gloss that he knew tasted like bubble gum. She was bristling with sexual energy, and he felt its force all the way across the bar.

Someone whistled quietly beside him, sitting on the stool next to his. "That's some kind of dress."

Austin glanced to the side—Drew.

"Yup," Tucker agreed, also joining them, leaning his elbows on the bar, watching the dancers as they popped and locked it to *Hoedown Throwdown.* "Should be illegal in all fifty states."

"How'd you get so lucky, Junior?" Arlo added as he, too, joined the fray.

Austin should probably be affronted at the way these guys were *appreciating* Beatrice. But he was just exceedingly fucking pleased that Beatrice had stumbled across *him* first.

"Must be the uniform," Drew offered.

Arlo shot his friend a scowl. "*I* wear a uniform."

Tucker snorted. "Yeah, but you also wear yours to bed. Women *do not* dig that shit. Clearly, given how long it's been since you've seen any action."

Drew nodded. "I bet your underwear even has *police officer* stamped across the ass."

Arlo flipped them both the bird. "Bite me."

"Face it, man." Tucker shook his head, trying to control a smile as he attempted seriousness. "You have no idea how to turn that crap off."

"I know how not to be a cop," he protested. "I can relax and…unwind."

Drew and Tucker laughed like Arlo's statement was the most hysterical thing they'd ever heard. Austin joined them, and Arlo pierced him with a look he'd come to know well. A look that said he'd be doing paperwork tomorrow. "You don't think I can, Junior?"

Well, crap. Austin's smile died. "I think you…" Austin chose his words carefully. "Take your role and responsibility in the community very seriously." He nodded, happy with his response. Then he added, "Chief," for good measure.

Tucker and Drew cracked up a little more. "Man, you are such a suck-up," Drew said when he'd drawn enough breath to form a coherent word.

Which was true, but no way was he going with the real answer. Which was Arlo made RoboCop look like a bumbling British bobby. But Credence need never worry while Arlo was at the helm, which was exactly what the town demanded of him and, when Arlo finally hung up his handcuffs, would hopefully demand of Austin. In the meantime, there was a lot he could learn from his boss about being a small-town cop.

Arlo clapped him on the back and announced, "This kid is going far."

Austin's hackles suddenly rose as he shrugged away Arlo's

hand. He wasn't a goddamn *kid*. He might not be near *forty*
like the other three guys, but he wasn't some wet-behind-the-
ears virgin, either. He'd grown up on a ranch where he'd fenced
what felt like halfway around the planet, had delivered calves
in the dead of night while a blizzard howled around him, and
put down dying animals with a bullet.

He'd trained as a cop, where he'd seen tragedy and miracles
in equal measure. He'd seen the helplessness of poverty and
the excesses of wealth and witnessed the depravity and the
humanity of both. He'd arrested people and he'd dug holes
looking for missing people and he'd held people who had
collapsed during the dreaded death knock.

Hell, he'd delivered a goddamn baby.

"I'm not a kid," he growled, glowering at his boss and the
other two. "I'm not *Junior*. My name is *Austin* or *Deputy*."

The music cut out, and Austin glanced over at the dance
floor to see Beatrice hugging her golden oldies—as she
called them—goodbye. The elderly folks were beaming at
her, obviously still infected by that special kind of energy
she was pumping out.

"Gotta go, bye."

He didn't wait for a response to his previous statement
or his farewell, just ambled across the bar and met Beatrice
halfway. She went straight into his arms and up onto her tippy
toes, winding her arms around his neck and kissing him in
front of everyone.

There was clapping and good-natured whistles and calls
to get a room, but Austin was oblivious. He only had eyes for
Beatrice in her yellow dress, red boots, and her bubblegum lips.

"I hear my apartment calling," she whispered as she finally
broke the kiss.

Austin's whole body thrummed with the desire to get
her out of that dress. But she was *sparkling* tonight, her eyes
dancing, her body brimming with a vibrant sexuality. She was

like a sunbeam, and hiding her away seemed criminal. She deserved to shine in all her glory, and he couldn't help but think she belonged in nature right now.

"I've got a better idea," he murmured. "C'mon." And he took her by the hand and led her outside.

. . .

Twenty minutes later, he was pulling into the parking lot at the lake. At seven thirty, the harsh sunlight of the day was softening into rose golds and would soon be pink and purple.

"It's so pretty out here," Beatrice said on a sigh as she looked out over the lake, which was also changing color from blue to slate.

Soon it would turn silvery, and Austin couldn't wait to see the siren yellow of her dress and the red of her hair streaking along in the twilight. "You want to go for a walk?"

"You trying to get me alone, Officer?"

Austin grinned. He hadn't planned on there being anyone out here at this time on a Wednesday evening, but given that the days had turned suddenly warm and were getting longer and longer, he shouldn't be surprised. There were several groups on the grassy areas leading to the lake. They mostly seemed to be packing up now, but Austin didn't want to wait to be alone.

"Yes, ma'am." He made sure he added a little dirty to the *ma'am* because he knew how much it turned her on.

"Ya know, we could have already been on round two by now."

Maybe, but tonight, the lake seemed like the perfect destination for the force of nature that was Beatrice.

"You ever heard of delayed gratification?"

She shot him an impatient look. "Only a twenty-five-year-old would think that was a good idea."

It was the first time she'd mentioned their age difference in a while, and with his irritation at the guys from the bar still fresh, it picked at the scab a little more.

"Humor me," he said as he reached across her to open the glove box and grab the flashlight for when it got darker.

Hand in hand, they walked along the shoreline, away from the jetty and the few remaining people, following the arc of the narrow, rocky beach. To their right, a wide stretch of long grass delineated the beach from the woods that stood farther back. Tiny purple wildflowers that had sprung among the grass waved in a light breeze as dainty as the trunks of the nearby towering pines were solid.

As they wandered, the grassy area started to narrow until it disappeared altogether, and the tree line thinned out as it merged with the shoreline. The road was visible through the woods in places, and the headlights of cars heading back to town poked through the trunks.

They talked about inane things as they wandered. And all the time, the lake lapped against the shore and the last beams of sunshine faded from the sky and the pinks and purples fused to a dusky kind of mauve, which deepened and darkened, giving way to night and the first pinprick of stars overhead.

It felt as if they were the only people in the world and, as a lone bird cry rang around the lake, Austin flicked on the flashlight.

Suddenly the beach widened and became sandy. Patches like this were few and far between, which made them popular, as evidenced by the well-worn track through the woods to their right.

Austin drew them to a stop, and Beatrice turned. "That is some dress, Bea*triss*."

"What? This old thing?" she demurred, a smile on her mouth as she let go of his hand and performed a little twirl.

"You like?"

"Oh yeah." He shone the flashlight straight at her, pointing it at her feet and slowly raising it, his eyes devouring every inch of her body. "You still a rule breaker, Bea*triss*?"

She raised an eyebrow. "What do you have in mind?"

"Town statute four three eight subsection fifteen," he said, plucking numbers out of thin air.

"Which would be?"

Austin reached for his belt and undid it, pulling it through the loops and tossing it on the ground. "Public nudity." He reached for the button on his pants next and undid it as he kicked out of a boot. "I seem to remember skinny-dipping was something you wanted to try?"

He kicked out of his other boot as the suggestion floated between them. Her rule breaking seemed to have gone by the wayside this past month as she'd settled into her work routine for Greet Cute.

Was she still interested?

For a moment, he thought she might decline and he was going to have to go all WWDD on her ass, but then she smiled. "Is that why you brought me out here, Officer Cooper?"

He smiled back. "Maybe."

She didn't do anything for a beat, then, in the beam of the light, she reached behind to the tie that circled her bodice several times and had trailed enticingly just off the ground. It loosened as she undid the bow, and Beatrice unwound it from her body before pulling it from her neck, the tails pooling against the sand at her feet.

Austin, his pulse thumping, his hands trembling, yanked his shirt off over his head and threw it down on the sand. Beatrice followed by peeling the dress off her body, taking her underwear with it. Stepping out of it, she stood before him in nothing but her red cowgirl boots.

"Jesus," he whispered, his gaze roving over all her lush

curves, the swell of her breasts, the tight scrunch of her nipples reacting to the cooling night air, and the dark patch of her pubic hair.

She nodded at him. "Now you."

Fumbling for a second, Austin managed to step out of his jeans and underwear in a far less elegant fashion than Beatrice. But, when he stood, his boner bobbing out front like a fucking divining rod, her low, appreciative hum made him forget *everything* but her.

Bending over slightly, she slid her legs and feet from her boots and pushed them toward the pile of clothes on the ground. With one last glance at his erection, she said, "Race you to the water," then bolted.

Austin was far less capable of sudden movement, and it took him a beat or two to respond as he watched the red fan of her hair across her back and the flash of her lily-white ass as she legged it into the lake.

Her gasp followed by a "God, it's *freezing*," galvanized him into action.

Despite the chill of the water, she wasn't turning around, and Austin, finally getting signals from his brain to his muscles, tossed the flashlight on the ground, gave a loud *whoop*, and followed her in. The water hitting his testicles was excruciating and should have given him an instant soft-on, but not even a plunge into polar ice was going to kill that fucker.

He sucked in a breath as he immersed his body in the lake and struck out after Beatrice, who was churning the water in a brisk freestyle just ahead of him. He caught her easily, grabbing her by the ankle and pulling her back to him, then kissing the hell out of her as she twined her arms around his neck, their wet lips cool and slippery as they devoured each other.

After long, drugging moments, she pulled away, smiling at him as she swam just out of reach. Austin enjoyed the tease as she cavorted around him, coming close and kissing him, drifting her hands over him, lingering on his ass and his hips, stroking his chest, brushing her lips against his neck and her fingers along his dick, dragging a groan from his throat before sliding away with a grin and a splash of water.

There was something about the gleam in her eyes, about her knowing how close he was to the edge and keeping him there, that cranked up his desire. And he returned the favor. Getting in his own touches, grazing the hard tips of her nipples, feeling the roughness of goose bumps beneath his fingertips as he stroked her belly and squeezed her ass. It might be dark, but he could see the glitter of sexual fever in her eyes. Knew it was the same fever reflected in his.

It appeared delaying gratification was working for both of them.

They chased and splashed and dived around each other for what felt like forever, his balls as tight and heavy as sinkers. It was excruciating and arousing all at once, and Austin knew when the moment finally came—he was going to utterly disgrace himself.

"Well," Beatrice announced casually after they'd frolicked for about half an hour. "It's getting cold—think it's time to leave."

She grinned at him, clearly knowing the kind of torture that announcement was inflicting, then turned away, flashing her ass at him as she swam toward the shore. Austin laughed at her gold-embossed come-get-me invitation. He waited and watched, moving slowly toward the shore, his feet hitting the bottom but staying low, partly to keep out of the cool air, partly to get ready to spring.

Water sluiced off her hair and down her body as she rose from the lake, heading to their pile of discarded clothes. She picked up the flashlight, then turned, finding him and catching him in the beam. "You want some of me, Austin Cooper, you better come and get it."

With a deceptive grin and then a roar, Austin did just that, springing from the water like an alligator lunging at prey in a huge churn of water. Beatrice squealed in surprise, dropping the flashlight as she turned to run, but Austin was bigger and faster and his need had reached a breaking point. He was on her in several strides, wrestling with her slippery, naked body for a moment as she twisted and tried to evade his grip to no avail. Swinging her up in his arms, he laughed as she squealed in protest.

"Let me go!" she yelled at the top of her lungs before laughing some more. "Let me go."

With her hands anchored around his neck, Austin growled, "Not by the hair of my chinny-chin-chin," and strode back into the water, sinking down when they got deep enough.

He hadn't caught his breath and neither had she when he kissed her, but Austin didn't care that his heart was hammering and his lungs were starved of oxygen as she slid her legs around his waist and they kissed like the world was about to end.

Settling her hot, slick core over the top of him, she whispered, "Now."

But, even this far gone, Austin was aware they had no protection. He knew she had a contraceptive implant, but he had to be sure. "No condom," he panted against her mouth.

"I don't care," she also panted. "I'm protected and I need you. I need you more than I've ever needed anything."

Her eyes were huge and earnest, her pupils dilated with lust, and Austin tried not to read any more into her statement other than the same immediate and urgent need for sexual joining that was burning through his system. He plunged inside her then, bare and hot and wet, and she gasped, her nails digging into his shoulder.

Austin groaned, withdrawing quickly and entering again, their gazes locked. And he kept doing it, quickly reaching a crescendo with her as they ground together in the cold waters of the lake. Stars blurred overhead. Black holes formed. Galaxies came to life while others sputtered out their last dying breath. In a matter of seconds, Austin had lived and died and was born again, and it was gratifying to hear the same kind of noises from Beatrice as she pulsed around him.

"Are you okay?" he asked when he could finally speak, holding her close in the water that now felt as warm as a spa.

She half laughed, and it was low and breathy and spoke volumes about her satisfaction, and he loved it. "Uh-huh."

"You want to do that again in your bed?"

"You have no idea how much," she replied.

Except he *did* know. He wanted to get her alone and naked and horizontal so damn badly. "We're going to need to get dressed and walk briskly," he murmured.

"I'm up for that."

He smiled and kissed Beatrice's forehead as he withdrew on a shared moan. They emerged from the water then, slow and stumbling and laughing at their newborn-foal-like progress. The very last thing he expected as he stepped onto the gritty sand was the harsh beam of a flashlight and a voice barking, "Stop right there."

Reacting purely on instinct, Austin shoved Beatrice behind him as he grabbed for his genitals. "What the fuck?" Austin demanded, blinking against the spotlight.

"Ju... *Austin?*"

Austin blinked. "Chief?" Great...this was going to make for awkward conversation at work tomorrow.

"What the hell are you doing?" Arlo demanded as he quickly dropped the beam of light and turned his back.

"Who is it?" a woman's voice somewhere behind Arlo demanded. It was high and no-nonsense. Then there was an "Oh dear," as Winona's face came into view, clocking it was Austin—a naked Austin—with Beatrice sheltering behind him, before turning abruptly around, following Arlo's lead.

"I thought I told you to stay at the house," Arlo grouched.

"Why would I do that?" she demanded.

"Because it's a direct police order."

Winona snorted. "Settle down, RoboCop. In what universe would I obey your orders?"

Austin and Beatrice exchanged a look. On any other day, it'd have been *cute* to witness Arlo being owned by an erotic romance author, but now wasn't the time or the place.

"What are you doing here?" Austin demanded as he picked up Beatrice's dress and handed it to her before reaching for his own clothes.

"Winona reported that there were lights flashing around down here and a woman yelling *let me go*."

Austin and Beatrice exchanged a guilty look. He'd not realized they were so close to Winona's place. *Sorry*, Beatrice mouthed, and Austin almost laughed out loud despite the absurdity of the situation.

"Well, as you can see," Austin said, shoving his legs into his jeans, not bothering with his underwear for efficiency's sake, "there's nothing to see here." Not *now* anyway. "Perhaps we could have some privacy and we'll head back to town. And maybe…we can never speak of this again."

"No arguments from me," Arlo agreed, his voice laced with relief, like seeing his deputy with his balls in his hand had been the epitome of too much information.

"Ah…*not* okay with me," Winona said. "Bea…call me tomorrow."

Austin watched a quick grin curl Beatrice's mouth. "Sure thing," she said.

"Okay," Arlo announced, flicking the flashlight beam at the ground. "Let's go, Winona."

Winona huffed out a breath and mumbled something about Arlo not being the boss of her, but she departed with him without further incident, although she didn't go quietly. Their particular brand of bickering banter gradually faded as they moved farther away.

Austin glanced at Beatrice, who was dressed now, her wet hair slicked back, water droplets from the wet ends dripping onto her shoulders. "That was…unexpected."

She laughed, and he joined her, relieved she was seeing the funny side. "C'mon," she said after their laughter died. "Let's go home."

Home. His breath hitched a little at the word, and Austin suddenly felt warmed all the way through. Did she mean it? Or was it just a generic term for the place she lived? Because Beatrice felt a lot like home to him.

But was it reciprocated? Or was he just a stopgap?

CHAPTER TWENTY-FOUR

Bea was admiring her latest sketch for Greet Cute around lunchtime the next day when her phone rang. The sketch featured Cranky Bea and Princess looking their most bedraggled—Princess's overbite was more pronounced, and Bea's boobs had hit new lows—but they were both sporting globs of glittery blue eye makeup and big rouged cheeks. The caption was going to read: *Too glam to give a damn.*

Just looking at it gave her a little ache in the center of her chest. Of happiness and joy and...accomplishment. Was this how her mom had felt about her creations? Would she—a bona fide artist with regular shows in prestigious LA art galleries—have approved of her daughter's Cranky Bea and Princess cards?

Bea wished she knew. She wished her mom was still around to ask her.

Searching for her phone in the debris of stuff on her cat-hair-strewn duvet—an open, empty pizza box; multiple scrunched-up sheets of paper towel she hadn't yet gotten around to tossing in the wastebasket in the middle of the floor; art supplies she'd acquired online; her yellow dress—she found it under a sleeping Princess. Hardly surprising given the cat was stretched out across half the bed like some kind of furry Slinky.

Princess opened her good eye and let out an irritated meow. The phone stopped ringing just as she hit the Answer button, but, glancing at the screen, Bea noted it was from Kim and hit Redial.

"Hey, you," Kim said as she answered.

"Sorry," Bea apologized. "I couldn't find the phone."

"It's fine, thanks for getting back to me so quickly."

They discussed the dossier of ideas for the next month's designs that Bea had been working on and had sent off last night just prior to leaving for Jack's. Bea's heart fluttered for a moment, thinking about Jack's, about how she'd felt Austin's eyes on her body the entire time she'd danced and how damn *wonderful* it had made her feel.

"I've got another proposal for you."

Kim's words were like a machete severing Bea's wandering thoughts. "Oh?"

"We want to get national exposure across *all* media for Cranky Bea. We think it's smart to capitalize on the free viral media we've got into something more long-term and sustainable. We want to run an ad campaign, and with your advertising background, we want to put you in charge of it; we want you to run the show."

Bea blinked. Now *that* she hadn't been expecting. It was a smart move—viral sensations had a pretty short shelf life—but...Bea had cut that string a few months ago. "When you say *all*, you mean traditional media?"

"Yep. TV. Radio. Newspapers. Billboards. Obviously, our budget is modest, but I think if we're smart and strategic and keep using social media impressions to drive response to the traditional stuff, we can do it. And there's nobody in the business better than you for flair, creativity, and cross-media strategy."

Bea tried not to let Kim's flattery go to her head, but it was true. She had several awards to her name for just those things.

Which was why missing out on that much-coveted promotion this year had been particularly cutting. "Look, Kim...I'm flattered. Truly. But I'm not in the business anymore."

Even as she said it, though, Bea felt that old buzz in her blood, the tingle in her fingertips, the flash of images on her inward eye. The beautiful potential of a new campaign that *she* got to craft and manage from the ground up. She'd worked collaboratively on many projects over the years, creating advertisements to very specific briefs from clients, working within those parameters and with multiple people in multiple departments, and she'd always delivered.

But the thrill of running the show herself was tempting. The awards and accolades she'd earned over the years had always come from campaigns where the client had given her free rein. Which was exactly what Kim was doing.

"It's not about getting back into the business," Kim dismissed. "It's just a one-off campaign that you can do from Credence and fit in around your Cranky Bea designs. We'll support you with everything you'll need on this end, including a team to work with, but it'll be your baby. You'll be in charge. Everything from the copy through to the hiring of the actors for the TV ads—it'll be all yours."

Bea couldn't believe how tempted she was—she'd *loved* doing TV ads the most. Prior to her career coming to a rather ignoble end, she would have said that advertising had given her the best years of her life. But it had also dealt her the biggest blow, and living here, becoming part of Credence—the polar opposite of LA—had made her realize that *best* was subjective.

That there were multiple versions of *best*.

Thoughts churned and clashed inside her head, about a zillion questions swirling in with the mix. *Could* she do this? Did she *want* to? A national campaign under her control, introducing and selling Cranky Bea—essentially *her* product—to the market. It was an advertising wet dream and would get her back into doing what she was good at—*selling* product.

Not creating it.

Because selling was what she knew. Selling was what she'd lived and breathed. It was what she excelled at. These doodlings had given her something to do and had opened up this opportunity, but they weren't who she was. She was an ad woman. Not a…*creative*. And this was a massive chance to prove to the LA advertising scene, to her father, to *herself*, that she was still the same person. She was just doing it in her own way this time. On her own terms.

"What time frame are you thinking?" Bea asked.

"We'd like to have a plan mapped out in, say, about a month?"

A month…that wasn't much time to come up with a national strategy, but Greet Cute was hardly Coca-Cola, and Bea had always done her best work under pressure.

"The aim is to have the campaign up and running by the end of the summer," Kim added.

The end of the summer. Even as part of Bea rejected the idea, the other part of her was already becoming invested. Cranky Bea *was* her. And if anyone could sell the crap out it, she could.

"Look," Kim said, "don't give me your answer now. Let me email you a bunch of information and you can have a think and get back to me in the next couple of days."

Bea shook her head. "I don't need a couple of days. I'll do it."

There was a slight pause on the other end, like Kim had been expecting a no and was trying to regroup. "Really?"

"Really." Bea laughed. "Send me what you've got and let's talk some more."

Suddenly Bea had never been more sure of anything. She hadn't known what she wanted and she'd never pictured this—going back to the industry that had used and discarded her.

But it was a one-off campaign. Which she could orchestrate from her little apartment here in Credence.

Sure, it might take up a bit of her time for a few months, but then it'd be over and things would get back to normal and everything would be rosy.

So, as Austin was fond of saying, why not?

CHAPTER TWENTY-FIVE

The footsteps Bea had come to know so well clomping up her stairs made her smile at just after four o'clock. She'd been on and off the phone with Kim all day and was already underway with some preliminary work for Cranky Bea's advertising strategy, and she couldn't wait to tell Austin.

The key turned in the lock, and Bea glanced up from where she was sitting on the couch, the laptop placed in front of her on the coffee table as Austin pushed the door open and stepped inside. His big grin of greeting died a quick death as he looked around him.

"What the hell happened in here?" he asked, removing his hat, clearly taken aback.

Bea laughed at his shocked expression. "I tidied."

"Tidied?" He glanced around again at the spotless floors and the gleaming, uncluttered surfaces of the kitchen. At the cleared coffee table and couch that had been relieved of layers of junk and the beautifully made bed. Even Princess sitting regally square in the middle looked like she'd been spruced up. "I could have my tonsils out in here."

Smiling, Bea stood and crossed to him—a process much simpler now that she didn't have to dodge the wastebasket in the middle of the floor and the paper that hadn't quite made it or the discarded clothes.

Slipping her arms around his waist, she beamed up at Austin. "I thought it was time."

She kissed him then, and he kissed her back with the kind of hunger that still felt special even as it also somehow felt familiar. She'd been busy today, but not too busy to miss this. To miss Austin and the way he made her feel like the only woman in the world.

His hands slid to her ass, and the kiss broke off abruptly as he pulled away a little and glanced down her body. "You're..." He frowned. "Dressed?"

Bea laughed again. "If you call cargoes and a T-shirt dressed, then yes."

Austin tossed his hat on the gleaming dark wood of the coffee table, then took a step back, shoving his hands on his hips. "Who are you and what have you done with Beatrice?" He softened the question with a slight smile on his mouth, but he was clearly nonplussed as he looked her up and down. His frown deepened. "You're wearing a bra."

She shrugged. "I can't work with boob sweat."

He laughed, and Bea breathed a little easier. All that frowning was concerning. "You seem to have managed pretty well this past month."

Bea dismissed his statement with a casual flick of her hand. "That's creative work."

Being braless and lounging in bed, surrounded by uneaten pizza crusts and a giant, slumberous cat, or sometimes driving out to the lake, was for the fanciful life of an artist. Advertising was business. And for that, Bea needed ruthless order. Everything in its place.

He was frowning again. "Are you doing *other* work?"

Trying not to dance a little jig on the spot, Bea grinned as she bounced on the balls of her feet. "Yes." And she stepped right in and kissed him again. She kissed him hard, moaning as he kissed her back just as hard, his hands sliding back to her ass and pulling her in close, squeezing and kneading.

When he finally pulled away, Bea's pulse was trippy and she was seeing stars as well as a hazy aura around his head. He looked so damn good, and she was so damn content.

She slipped out of his arms and headed for the fridge. "You want a beer?"

"Thanks," Austin said with a nod and caught the can Bea tossed to him, giving it a few beats to settle before popping the tab.

She grabbed one for herself and headed for the couch, sitting side on and crossing her legs. Austin looked down at the couch like he'd never seen it before. "The couch is blue?"

Bea grinned. "Yeah, yeah. Just sit."

He sat in that sprawled, easy kind of way of his, all long-legged and loose-limbed and so damn masculine as she launched into her exciting news, gabbing away about Kim's job offer. Princess deigned to join them at some point, and there they sat on her blue couch, a large purring cat jammed between them as Bea relayed the content of every phone call and email.

Austin, for his part, was encouraging and clearly pleased for her, nodding and smiling and making all the right noises, but when Bea finally ran out of steam, he was a bit too quiet, his gaze speculative.

It was her turn to frown. "What?" She swiped her hand across her face. "Did I have a booger on my nose this entire time?"

He laughed and placed his beer can down on the coaster. He glanced at her in surprise. "You have coasters, too?"

"I found them in one of the kitchen drawers." Was that a problem? "Are you okay?"

"Yeah." He nodded. Then he reached for her beer can and set it down on the other coaster before taking both of her hands. "It's just... Are you sure this is what you want?

I thought you were done with advertising? You were kinda burned *and* burned out by it when you first got here."

Ah. Okay. He was worried about her health, her sanity. God...this man was so freaking thoughtful.

"I thought so, too." She slipped her hands from his, then stood to make her case, maybe as much to herself as to him. "I thought I was done. I thought it was Credence or advertising and there was no in-between. No middle ground. But I think what Kim's offering *is* the middle ground. It's just one campaign—selling *my* product—that's it. One and done. And I can do it all from here. I think this is the best of both worlds. And, *Austin*...the ideas floating around in my head! I'd forgotten what a buzz it could be."

He smiled and reached for her hand, and she let him drag her closer until she was standing between those sprawled thighs—a most delectable view. His hands slid to the backs of her knees. "You're really excited about this."

"Yes. I am." She could feel the heat of the buzz in her cheeks. "I know my current lifestyle will have to change for the next few months. I'll be juggling the Cranky Bea card design stuff with the Cranky Bea advertising stuff, but don't worry, I have no intention of letting it take over my world again." Bea stepped in closer, and he took advantage, dropping a kiss on her belly as she funneled her fingers through his hair. "There'll still be Wednesday night line dancing at Jack's and the ranch on Sundays."

He shook his head and flicked his gaze up. "I'm not worried. It's your life, your career; you gotta follow your heart."

"Mmm." Bea ran her fingers through the scruff at Austin's jaw. "Good answer."

Smiling, he said, "Like I told you already—you do you, and I'll keep bringing the pie and orgasms."

Bea laughed. "Even better answer." Her heart broke open a little at how easy it was to be with Austin. How low drama it felt. How natural it felt. For the first time, she considered that maybe having a relationship and a career didn't have to be mutually exclusive.

"I think we should go to Jack's and celebrate," he murmured, planting his chin just above the waistband of her pants and looking up her body, capturing her gaze. "You should wear that yellow dress again."

She smiled. "Oh, I think we should definitely *celebrate*." And she leered at him in a way that could leave him in no doubt as to her immediate need.

He grinned. "So that's a no to Jack's?"

Bea slid her hand to Austin's chin, taking it in a firm grasp. "That's a no." Then she pushed him until he was sprawled back against the couch, looking as hot as the Mojave in August.

Reaching for his hat, she placed it on her head, smiled, and straddled his lap...

· · ·

Over the next month, Austin got used to seeing Beatrice dressed and at her desk—yes, she'd bought a desk from IKEA and had it shipped to Credence. It was the opposite of how she'd been that first day in her stained sweats with crazy hair and ice cream dripping down her arm, but that was fine. He'd liked all the faces of Beatrice, from the sweats to the day-of-the-week underwear to the yellow dress and now the businesswoman.

Actually, the businesswoman was kinda hot. He knew from that rambling speech her first day that this wasn't the LA version of Beatrice, but all that ruthless efficiency—from the way she kept things on her desk *just so* to how she wrote lists on Post-it notes and got excited when she checked everything off—was a surprising turn-on.

He always brought pie as promised, and she always stopped and shut her laptop down and joined him on the couch or the bed, devouring whatever was in the packet as they chatted about their respective days. He laughed at her latest Cranky Bea designs—although she seemed less invested in them now than the actual campaign itself—and she laughed at whatever tale he had to tell from whatever zany incident he'd had to deal with during his shift.

It was a rare day in Credence when some kind of zany *wasn't* going down.

They went to Jack's for line dancing on Wednesday nights and to the ranch on Sundays. They'd watched all of *The Walking Dead* now and had moved on to watching *Friends*. And he was still supplying her with all the orgasms she wanted.

Ostensibly, nothing really changed. To an outsider, it probably just looked like they were settling into a groove. Which should have made Austin happy. But...things were shifting, he could *feel* it, in the little moments. Like, Beatrice had stopped drinking beer for breakfast. Okay, that was probably wise and advisable, and she was still eating all the pie, but now she brushed off all the crumbs immediately and scooped them into the trash. After sleeping with almost constant crumbs the last couple of months, it had apparently become a problem.

She took a *lot* of phone calls—a lot. Which of course she would now that she was working on a big project. He understood. No biggie. He could adjust. But the entire time they'd been together, Beatrice had been 100 percent focused on whatever *they* were doing, and he couldn't help but wonder if it was a sign of her wavering attention.

And *that* sat like a lump of lard in his belly.

As did her insistence last week, during his stint of three night shifts, that he slept back at his cabin afterward. Because she was worried she'd disturb his sleep with her phone calls and, he supposed, her *key tapping*? He'd seen her for a sum total of about six hours those three days and they'd been intimate only once in that time.

The most telling of all, however, was that Beatrice was now wearing the correct day-of-the-week underwear.

He tried not to let any of it bug him. The last thing she needed was a spoiled, whiny man-baby lamenting her lack of attention. Austin wasn't *that* guy. He didn't want to be the guy standing in front of her opportunities, making everything about him and his needs.

Because that was total bullshit.

He just wished that he and Beatrice had talked about the state of their relationship prior to this, instead of studiously *not* putting a name to it. He'd deliberately never broached it because he hadn't wanted her to bolt. But it did leave him unsure of where he stood now, and damn it, he'd never been *that* guy—the insecure one.

And he didn't like it *at all*.

All those things weighed on his mind as he made his way up the stairs to her apartment on Wednesday. He'd had to work late to finish off a stack of paperwork that had been building, which had made for a very long day, and he was tired. But he knew, the second he saw Beatrice, that would all lift, and it was line dancing night. They could get out and socialize for a while—kick back, have some fun.

But when he opened the door, she was still sitting at her desk, in her shorts and T-shirt, her glorious red hair he'd last seen loose and tangled and spread over his pillow caught up in a neat little knot at the back of her head.

"Hey," she threw over her shoulder as she stabbed at the keys on her laptop.

"Hey," he returned as he dropped a kiss at her nape. "Mmm." He nuzzled her neck. "You smell good." She *always* smelled good.

"So do you," she murmured, and he could hear the smile in her voice.

It was tempting to stay right here, to slide his hands down the front of her shirt, cup her breasts and feel her nipples harden beneath the brush of his thumb. But if they didn't shake a tail feather, Beatrice would miss the start of her class. "You wearing that to Jack's?" he asked as he reluctantly straightened.

"Oh." Her fingers stopped tapping on the keys, and she looked up at him over her shoulder. "Do you mind if I take a rain check tonight? This has got to be done by Sunday night, and I'm really down to the wire now."

Austin forced himself to casually shake his head. "Of course not." Then he forced himself to drop a casual kiss on her head. "Don't worry about it."

"Thank you." She smiled at him and slid a hand over his where it rested on his shoulder. "But you should still go and catch up with the regular crowd."

Austin opened his mouth to decline, then shut it again. Actually, getting out would be a distraction from the bubbles of anxiety that simmered in his gut and demonstrate he had interests outside of…whatever this was. Plus, he didn't want Beatrice thinking he was looming over her shoulder, impatiently waiting for her to finish so he could have some *him* time.

"Yeah. Think I will." He squeezed her shoulder. "I'll just get dressed."

"Uh-huh," she said, but she was already turning back to the keyboard. And when Austin dropped another kiss on her neck and said goodbye fifteen minutes later, she didn't even look up. She just murmured, "Bye," and kept typing.

. . .

When he got back from Jack's at just after nine, Beatrice was still at her desk, on the phone. She smiled at him and mouthed, "I'm sorry," as he entered the apartment.

Austin returned her smile as he crossed to her and kissed her on the head. "It's fine," he whispered. "I'm going to bed; I'm beat." Which was the truth. He really was tired.

She nodded and mouthed, "Okay," then replied to something somebody—Kim, he assumed—had said on the other end.

By the time he'd shucked his clothes and shooed Princess off his pillow, Beatrice was saying her goodbyes. She hung up just as he flipped off the bedside lamp and slipped between the sheets. "I'm sorry," she apologized as she strode toward the bed, putting one knee and then the other on the mattress and crawling up it. Austin spread his legs to make room for her, and within seconds she was settling herself against him. Suddenly parts of him weren't feeling so tired anymore.

"I thought I'd be done by now."

Her lips landed on his, and Austin slipped his hands onto her ass and held her close. "Mmm, beer," she murmured against his mouth before she continued the kiss. The sweet intoxication of her scent filled his senses. His breathing roughened and his heart slugged against his rib cage as the kiss deepened.

Christ—he could do this all damn night.

Too soon, though, she broke off the kiss with a sigh, and he knew she was going back to her desk. "I'm sorry," she apologized, "I've got to get back to it. I'm nearly done."

Austin ran his fingers down her forearm. "It's fine," he assured. It *was* fine, damn it. This was what happened in relationships—even if they weren't calling it that—after the initial heady stuff.

She glanced down at the bulge under the sheet. "I could"— she waggled her eyebrows—"help you with that real quick if you want?"

Austin wasn't opposed to the idea of a quickie hand or blow job as a general rule, but *Jesus*, what sort of an asshole would he be to agree to that when she was clearly trying to get this done?

He didn't need a pity orgasm no matter how much his cock disagreed.

"Thanks." He grinned. "It'll survive. Wake me when you're done and you can have at it."

She grinned. "Deal." Then she wriggled off the bed.

Austin chuckled as he pulled up the sheet, and she made her way back to the desk. God, he'd missed her at Jack's. He'd quickly grown used to having her at his side, and when she wasn't, it felt like he was missing his other half. And what that meant, he didn't want to think about, because if he slipped and voiced *any* of this stuff around Beatrice, this *thing* they were doing, might all come toppling down...

· · ·

When Sunday came around, Austin went to the ranch by himself. Beatrice's proposal was finished and she'd been looking forward to getting on Buffy but then the phone had rung. *Kim.* Something had come up to do with Monday's presentation requiring a major rework and Beatrice had begged off accompanying him.

Which was fine. Of course she had to deal with whatever crisis had arisen. Couples just didn't spend every waking and sleeping hour in each other's pockets. But he got the feeling she was pulling away—if only subconsciously—and a trickle of unease had run down his spine.

None of his family thought anything of it when he arrived without Beatrice, and Austin did his level best to be chipper all afternoon. He even stayed for dinner to give her more time to work things out.

Still, he was relieved when dinner was over and it was time to leave.

"Everything okay with you?" his mother asked as she walked him out to his pickup.

He nodded. "Yep."

"You seem a little...distracted today."

Austin wasn't surprised his mother had sensed his unease. She'd always had a strong *mom* radar. "I'm sure."

She nodded, but she didn't look convinced. "Everything okay with Bea?"

"Yeah...she's just busy with the campaign.."

"Okay," she said with a smile, then fell silent for a beat or two. "You're in love with her, aren't you?"

He glanced at his mother swiftly, shocked at the suggestion, rejecting it immediately. "Mom...no. That's ridiculous. It's only been a few months."

She gave him one of her wise old smiles. "Some people know within a few hours, Austin."

He snorted. "That's *lust*, not love."

She held up her hands in surrender. "Oh, to be young and know so much," she teased.

Austin gritted his teeth at the reference to his age. A month ago, it hadn't been an issue for him—it had *never* been an issue. But a lot had changed recently, and he'd be lying if he didn't admit to being anxious that Beatrice's issue with their age difference could, once again, become a *thing*.

Bugging his eyes at her, he said, "*Good night*, Mom." Then he leaned in and pecked her on the cheek.

"Night, son," she called after him.

Austin departed, glad to be away from the shrewdness of Margaret Cooper's wildly pinging *radar*. Still, her question turned over and over in his brain as he drove into Credence. He *liked* Beatrice—very much. He liked her more than any other woman he'd been with. He'd never laughed so hard or enjoyed himself so much. Did he lust after her? Hell *fucking* yes.

But *love…?*

He shied away from it. From its enormity. From the sure and certain knowledge that Beatrice would reject it *and* him, outright, if it was even uttered. They needed more time before declarations were made. Time to become so much a part of the fabric of each other's lives that *not* being together was simply unbearable.

And that's where he needed to keep his focus.

Austin felt much better about their direction as he climbed the stairs to Beatrice's apartment twenty minutes later. She was here with him in Credence and that was all that mattered. Okay, she was no longer a woman of leisure and her new job was demanding a lot of her time, but his job was demanding, too.

The first thing he noticed when he stepped inside the apartment was that Beatrice wasn't at her desk. The second was the small suitcase sitting ominously on the couch. And all his bravado and mental pep talks crashed to the ground into a fiery death spiral.

"Hey," she called from behind him.

Austin turned to find Beatrice sitting up in bed, her red hair a vibrant splash against the dull gray of the wall. With one hand, she was petting Princess, who was sprawled across her thighs, and with the other, she was holding a sheaf of papers.

"Did you get things sorted?" Austin asked, trying to sound normal while all the time the suitcase loomed in his peripheral vision like a loaded shotgun.

She grinned and held up the papers in her hand. "Finally, yes."

Austin nodded, his gaze wandering to her suitcase. He swallowed against a mouth that was suddenly dry as Eastern

Colorado dust. "Are you..." He returned his attention to Beatrice. "Going somewhere?"

"Yes. To LA. In the morning. Gotta leave at five to make my flight in time."

There was no hesitation, no tentativeness, no apology in her voice. No, *hope you don't mind.* Of course, she didn't need his *permission.* But it did put his position in her life squarely in place. This, he realized suddenly, was the downside to avoiding any relationship tags.

If nothing was official, there wasn't any need to consider the other person's thoughts/feelings/opinions about decisions that, while up to the individual, could impact the other person.

"Oh...when did that happen?"

"Kim and I were talking on the phone and we decided it's so much better to pitch these things face-to-face. Teleconferencing is fine for a lot of things, but for something like this, being in the same room is so much more advantageous."

"Right."

She gave a half laugh. "You're looking a little weird. It's just for Monday. I'll be back Tuesday."

Austin's relief was like a cool breeze blowing through his system as he forced the muscles in his face to smooth out and smiled. He sighed with faux-dramatic intensity. "Except if you're dazzled by all those big city lights and we'll never see you again." He kept his voice light and teasing, but that right there was his absolute worst fear.

"Not freaking likely," she said with vehemence. "I'm a country girl now."

Her words were comforting, and the tension across Austin's shoulders eased.

"I don't know," he continued to tease, because he *would* act like this was no big deal if it killed him, "all those guys in suits."

She smiled and shook her head, her gaze taking a very thorough wander over his body. "Give me a guy in jeans and a hat who knows how to do a burnout any day."

"Oh yeah? I know somebody just like that." Austin threw his hat on the bed as he toed off his shoes.

Her gaze dropped to his crotch. "Lucky *me*."

Princess, who by now had some uncanny feline intuition when it came to their sexual signals, sat herself up with an irritated meow. Rising to her feet, she walked off the bed, leaving them to it, her paws hitting the floor about the same time as Austin's belt.

He pulled his shirttails out and started on the buttons. "You sure you want to do this? You have an early start." And right now, he just wanted to be with Beatrice, even if it was just curled around her while they slept.

In the blink of an eye, she'd whipped off her T-shirt. Her bare breasts, the nipples hardening before his eyes, were as tempting as ever. "What do you think?"

Think? The rush of blood to his dick from his brain left Austin incapable of thinking anything other than *boobs*. He closed the distance between them with more speed than grace, settling his body on top of hers. Their mouths fused, her arms wound around his neck, her legs wound around his waist as she kissed him deep and hard, and he almost lost his mind. It felt good. It felt perfect. Like everything he'd ever wanted was right here in his arms.

So why did it also feel like goodbye?

CHAPTER TWENTY-SIX

Bea's pitch to the team at Greet Cute went better than she'd expected. She'd been anxious to start with, but the nerves soon fell away and she was back in the groove. Like she'd never left. She knew the product inside and out, she'd studied the demographic data Kim had sent, she knew her knock-it-out-of-the-park proposal by heart.

It was like the good old days, except she finally felt like the people around the boardroom table, dressed casually in jeans and T-shirts, were interested in what she had to say. She didn't have to prove herself to them, like she always felt she was doing at Jing-A-Ling—they just accepted that she knew her stuff and were ready *and* eager to take it on board.

And they all adored the *creative*. Cranky Bea and Princess were a huge hit, which was, surprisingly for her, the biggest buzz of all.

The Greet Cute team were dynamic and egalitarian. There was no head honcho who everyone deferred to, and it was no *executives-only* meeting. Everyone was at the table, and they all just jumped in and asked questions and sought clarification without fear of looking foolish or being rebuked. It felt collaborative and wonderful.

The kind of agency she never knew existed. An advertising utopia.

And then, after a day of hashing out and workshopping and looking at the campaign from every angle and tweaking and massaging, everything was approved and given the green light. Which meant there was a ton of other stuff to do now—people to hire and plans to put in place—and doing that all while she was in LA seemed the most logical thing to do.

Sure, she could get it all done over multiple emails and phone calls and Zoom meetings over multiple weeks. Or she could spend a few days here setting it up, then return to Credence with everything ready to go.

After a celebratory dinner with Kim, Nozo—apparently short for Nozomi—and Mal, Bea was back at the hotel the company was paying for by ten and picking up the phone to call Austin to tell him about her change in plans. She was happy. And possibly a little tipsy. Very definitely horny. She wondered how Austin felt about phone sex?

He picked up on the first ring. "Bea*triss.*"

"Well, hello there," she said, the smile in her voice morphing into a kind of a purr at the way his voice husked up the end of her name. "You must have been sitting on the phone." Bea pictured him on his bed in his cabin, buck naked, in front of the big floor-to-ceiling window that overlooked the vastness of the ranch.

"I was. I've missed you."

She smiled again. "I missed you, too."

"How'd the pitch go?"

"Oh, Austin…it was *so* good. I kicked ass." Bea laughed then and spent the next ten minutes filling Austin in on all the ins and outs of the day.

When she ran out of steam, Austin said, "Looks like I'm going to have to get you a whole pie as your welcome-back gift tomorrow."

Bea pressed a hand to her chest—this guy was just too good to be true. But then she remembered she wasn't going to be home tomorrow. "You're going to have to hold that pie. I won't be back in Credence till Thursday now."

There was a pause on the line. "Oh. Okay."

The pause and his subdued reply pinged her radar. There was disappointment in his voice and something else she couldn't place. Her smile fizzled. "It's just a few more days."

"Yeah, I know."

She frowned, hoisting herself into a sitting position as the buzz from the booze evaporated into thin air. "Is everything okay?"

"Of course. I…"

Bea waited for him to elaborate. And waited. "You what?" she prompted.

"Nothing. Everything's fine. I'll just…miss you, is all."

And Bea would miss him. But it felt like there was more to it than that. "It's going to be so much easier to manage the campaign if I stay on these few days and get things in place."

"Of course."

The fact that his *of course* lacked enthusiasm suddenly grated. "It's my *job*, Austin."

"I know," he said. "It's fine for you to stay."

Bea blinked. What the *what* now? So much for phone sex. "I don't need your permission."

Had she been so swept up in this thing between them that she'd failed to realize that Austin was the kind of guy who thought women needed permission from their *man* to do stuff? Surely not?

There was a long sigh from his end. "Of course not. I didn't mean… I just… Look, I'm sorry, okay? Of course it's your job and you need to stay in LA to get it done. That's great. I'll be here waiting for you when you get back home."

Home. Bea turned it over and over in her head. Credence, her little apartment above Déjà Brew, *Austin*…she hadn't set out to make them her home, but they were nonetheless.

Wow—that had happened fast.

Mollified, she said, "Okay then." Which was followed by an awkward kind of silence, and she hated that there was this weirdness between them now when all she wanted was to talk with this guy who'd become a scarily big part of her life. Just... listen to his voice. "How's Princess?" she asked.

He started to talk then, his voice softening again, and Bea fell back against the mattress and got lost in the low rumble.

• • •

By Wednesday morning, it was evident that Bea was going to need to extend her trip by another day to get a bunch of interviews done on Thursday, and she rebooked her ticket yet again for midday Friday out of LAX. With everything running to plan, she should be driving into Credence around six o'clock. It would be a long day, but Austin would be at the end of it and she couldn't wait.

It felt like forever since she'd seen him, and she'd missed him. After that awkward conversation on Monday night, things had gone back to normal—including a very sexy session on FaceTime—and when she'd called to tell him she was extending her trip by another day, he'd taken it in stride and simply asked her if she preferred to have peach cobbler or cherry pie smeared all over her body.

Her relief at his reply had been palpable. Keeping their physical attraction front and center, she could deal with— weirdness over a change of plans due to her job, she could not. All that did was shine a huge spotlight on the reasons she'd been reluctant to get involved with Austin in the first place...

• • •

Kim poked her head in the office at the end of Thursday. "You must be exhausted," she said.

Bea nodded. "Yep." But it was a good exhausted. The kind of weariness that came with accomplishment at having achieved all the things she'd set out to achieve. She'd spend a few hours tomorrow morning at the office, checking off some minor, last-minute things before she had to get to the airport, but otherwise she was done.

"You were a machine today," Kim teased as she entered and sat on the chair on the other side of Bea's desk.

Well, it wasn't her desk—it had been loaned to her for the week—but *wow*, what a desk. They'd given her the empty corner office with its third-story view over tree-lined boulevards and the vibrant street art of downtown LA. Sure, it wasn't the kind of corner office she'd once craved in the glass high-rise belonging to Jing-A-Ling, but it was spacious and airy, with huge windows and modern art and a pervasive feeling of potential.

Jing-A-Ling's offices were claustrophobic by comparison, and the only things that pervaded the air there were tradition and patriarchy.

"That's why you pay me the big bucks," Bea quipped as she shut down all three screens of her state-of-the-art computer console.

"And that," Kim said as she crossed her legs, "is what I wanted to talk to you about."

"Oh?" Bea quirked an eyebrow. "This would be a bad time to tell me you can't afford to pay me," she joked.

"On the contrary. I'm here to offer you more money."

Bea laughed. "Really?"

"Yep. We want to expand and build our name for all our products, and for that we need major advertising. Rather than outsource it, we want to do it all in-house. We want to give it to you. We want you to take on advertising for the entire company." Kim paused. Bea wasn't sure if it was for dramatic effect, but she needn't have bothered—her mind was already kinda blown. "Come back to LA, Bea. Join us on the board. Executive in charge of advertising. Let's make this office"—Kim glanced around the high walls and the large windows—"yours. Permanently."

To say Bea was speechless was an understatement. She'd just been offered an executive position and a corner office—something she hadn't been able to achieve at Jing-A-Ling in fifteen years—within a couple of months of being involved with Greet Cute.

She was *stunned*.

"I..." Bea's heart hammered so loudly through her ears, she could barely hear herself talk. "I don't know what to say."

Kim grinned. "*Yes* would be nice."

A few months ago, this would have been everything Bea had ever wanted. Back before she knew better, before she knew there was a life outside advertising. Sure, she'd had a great time dabbling this past month, but running *one* ad campaign for *one* product was one thing—being solely responsible for multiple campaigns was another entirely.

Was she up to it? Could she do it? And where did that leave her art?

Wait...Bea blinked. Her *what* now? Where the hell had *that* come from? She was being offered something far more concrete and tangible, far more *her*, and she was worrying about something completely *in*tangible. Something *not* her.

Cranky Bea had been an enjoyable distraction when she'd made her giant leap into the unknown. Fun and frivolous. Like a holiday fling. But vacation time was over.

Shaking off the anxiety those two words—*her art*—had caused, Bea forced herself to get back on track. "And the others? Nozo and Mal, they're on board with this, too?"

Kim nodded enthusiastically. "Mal said if I didn't persuade

you to join us, he was going to go into a year of mourning."

"Oh, Kim." This was just too damn big. "I'm not sure—"

Kim raised her hands in a placatory manner, cutting Bea off. "I know this isn't the kind of corner office you craved. I know we're not Jing-A-Ling. But think about it, Bea. You'll be getting in on the ground floor with us, we're on the cusp, and we want you to come with us. We want Greet Cute to be up there challenging Hallmark's supremacy, and we want you to help us build that. You'd be part of creating something, not just helping maintain the status quo."

Kim's enthusiasm and belief in her company were not only palpable but justified as she went into detail about what exactly they were offering. Bea didn't think for a moment that Greet Cute wouldn't be the powerhouse Kim was portraying. And she couldn't deny that was exciting.

Except...there was Credence. And Austin.

She opened her mouth to decline, but, as if she could sense the answer, Kim jumped in first. "Look, don't give me an answer yet, okay? Take the night, think about it. The money's good, the team's great, the challenge is exciting. And we want the best damn ad executive in LA to be part of it all."

Bea gave a half laugh. Kim sure knew how to both turn a screw and flatter at the same time. But the thing was, she wasn't *in* LA anymore. "I don't need the night," Bea said. "I'm sorry, Kim, but the answer is no."

"Oh, Bea, really?"

She nodded. "Really. I'm sorry. And I'm very flattered. I can't thank you enough for the offer, but I like my life right now."

"Come on, Bea," Kim cajoled. "I know you. You must miss the energy of a new ad campaign. I've been watching you this week and, pardon the pun, but you've been buzzing."

Bea laughed. "Yes. I've enjoyed it very much." It would be so easy to step back into her corporate shoes. "And I am tempted. But…I line dance now. And I'm learning how to ride a horse."

And Austin…

But *no*. She couldn't let him be a reason. She couldn't let a man be a reason to not take a job. Or to take a job, either, for that matter. This had to be about *her*. She and Austin were not officially anything. He was ten years younger than her, for crying out loud. Sooner or later, some pretty young thing was going to come along and turn his head and she was going to be toast.

Old toast.

Her decision to decline this offer had to be based on how much she liked the new life she'd carved for herself. And she liked it very, very much.

"Well." Kim laughed. "I guess line dancing and horses are hard to compete with."

Bea knew Kim didn't understand. She wouldn't have understood a few months ago, either. But Credence was… home now.

It was where she wanted to be. Right?

• • •

Bea didn't bother to tell Austin on the phone that night about the job offer. What was the point when she hadn't taken it? She'd tell him tomorrow when she got home and she was wrapped around his body and he could *see* she'd chosen Credence.

Then they could laugh about the crazy turns of her life.

Still, as she walked through the deserted open space of Greet Cute early on Friday morning to get a head start on the things she needed to do before she caught her plane, there was an undeniable kernel of temptation. Maybe there always would be any time she was sucked into the orbit of LA, because LA *was* advertising for her and she'd loved her job.

But there was something about *here*, about Greet Cute's office, that was extra tempting. The kind of place she'd never imagined existed when she'd been cloistered behind the high-rise steel-and-glass of her old-school ad agency. The kind of place that reeked of inclusion and collaboration and diversity. It was evident in the people from all walks of life who worked here. And in every potted plant, every piece of funky art and stick of modern furniture.

Yep, if she ever were to get back into this world again, it would be somewhere like this. Where everyone worked together and every contribution was valued. And she didn't have to wear high heels and tight skirts.

But for now, she was finishing up a few things and heading home.

• • •

By nine, Bea was all done. She'd sent her last email and shut down the desktop and was heading out of her office—*the* office, not *her* office—to say goodbye to everyone when her cell rang. The name flashing on the screen was Charlie Hammersmith.

She frowned. What the hell? Why was her old boss calling? And why the hell hadn't she deleted him from her contacts?

Bea's finger hovered over the button to decline the call and she *almost* tapped it. Had she been pressed to afterward, she couldn't have said why she *did* answer.

"Charlie?"

"Bea. A little birdie tells me you're in LA."

Typical of Charlie not to bother with preliminaries or niceties. "You have me LoJacked now?"

He chuckled heartily like he had a mouth full of marbles. "You know what LA's like—word gets around."

Unfortunately, Bea did. Word of her departure had spread like wildfire. "Is there something I can do for you?"

"I'd like to take you to lunch."

Bea blinked. She'd rather dine with a rattlesnake. "No thank you."

"You're not available? I can fit in with your schedule."

Well, that was a first. But it didn't change her mind. "I'm available. I just don't want to." Her voice was perfectly polite, but if Charlie thought she'd be gracious and forgiving, he was sorely mistaken. There was no need to play nice anymore.

"Okay," he said, his voice irritatingly reasonable, "you're still upset."

Bea stiffened, the vertebrae in her spine snapping together like LEGO. She gripped the phone, her cheeks warm. "I've moved on."

"That's a shame. I wanted to offer you the executive position. The one you wanted. The one with the corner office."

Bea breathed out a slow breath as all she'd ever once wanted was offered to her on a platter. A few months ago, she'd have grasped it with both hands. Now, standing in this beautiful, innovative work space, she wouldn't touch it with a ten-foot pole.

"The one you gave to Kevin instead of me?" Her voice shook more than she'd have liked, and she knew she'd kick herself for that later.

"Clearly that was an...error of judgment."

Bea laughed out loud. "I'd say that's an understatement." She could almost hear him squirming, but there was no way she was going to let him off the hook.

"Irregardless—"

"Regardless," she interrupted. Normally, Bea ground her teeth at Charlie's incorrect usage of that word, but today, she was done wrecking three years and ten thousand dollars of her father's hard-earned money in corrective braces. "Irregardless

is *not* a word."

She was pretty sure she could now hear Charlie grinding *his* teeth. "Quite," he said, obviously determined to continue as he plunged on. "The board would like to offer you the job. You are clearly the best person for the role. You have an exemplary work ethic. You had a long list of clients who valued your expertise. And a unique insight into marketing to millennials. We both welcome and value the experience and the diversity you would bring to the agency."

Right. So…interpretation. The scandal with Kevin was costing them financially. Clients were obviously walking. They needed a quick diversity hire with a good track record and a high profile who could steady the ship and help prove they weren't the cast of *Mad Men*.

She gave a half laugh at the audacity of Charlie to even offer her the job. "Ahh, that would be a no." A big, fat no.

"It's a lot of money, a lot of prestige," he pressed, as if he'd known she'd be resistant and already had his counterarguments lined up. "There's partner's dividends and bonuses, and you can call your own shots. Hire your own staff." He paused and took a breath, injecting a faint note of reproach. "It's what you *wanted*, Bea."

Yeah, she had. It was like that damn high-rise had been misting the air with company happy juice and providing company Kool-Aid in the drinking fountain.

But she was out now and her perspective was twenty/twenty.

A part of her wanted to yell at him for being a sexist, old dinosaur, but she had to accept that she'd *let* this happen to herself. Sure, the power dynamic had not slid in her favor, but she was mad as hell at herself for putting up with the crap. For not speaking up or getting out earlier. Charlie may have ruled over the culture, but she had been silent in its presence, and that was on her.

"I don't want it anymore. Not with you."

Bea was proud of the steady finality in her voice. She didn't. She really didn't.

He didn't say anything for long seconds, and then he laughed. "Oh, I see. You think someone else will employ you?"

Bea's hackles rose. "I think any company would be falling over themselves to hire me, as well you know."

Okay, she didn't *want* another job in LA, but hell if she was going to let Charlie know that. She was confident enough in her cachet—despite her recent absence from the scene—to know that she could go to half a dozen ad agencies right now and be employed on the spot.

So *screw* him.

"Oh, Bea. Have you forgotten how much sway I have? And how incestuous advertising is? Come on…you haven't been away that long."

A prickle shot up Bea's spine. Unfortunately, Charlie was right. He was a *big deal* in advertising circles. He could tank her career before breakfast if he wanted.

"A word here, a word there," he continued, his voice almost musical as he spilled his ugly threats. "Calling in a favor here. A favor there. Letting a rumor or two slip about why you were *let go* from Jing-A-Ling in the first place. A gambling habit, maybe, or a fondness for pills."

Bea shook her head at his bullying, her heart suddenly banging hard against her ribs. She wished she didn't believe he was capable of the litany of horrors he was trying to intimidate her with, but she didn't doubt it for a second.

"Bea," he said, all low and fake reasonable again. "You'll *never* work, let alone make it, in LA without me. And if you think my reach doesn't extend to the East Coast, then think again."

"Are you…*threatening* me, Charlie?" Bea kept her voice neutral, unwilling to betray how his treachery was affecting her as she eased her trembling body against the desk for support.

He laughed, and there was an undertone to it that made her shiver. "I always knew you couldn't hack it at the big end of town. Too squeamish for the ad game. Too girlie. Good luck, Bea. You're going to need it."

The phone cut off in her ear, and Bea stared at it blankly. She couldn't figure out what she felt more—shocked or enraged. How *dare* he? How freaking *dare* Charlie Hammersmith threaten her with career ruination?

The man was really showing his true colors today. How could she ever have looked up to this utterly *deplorable* piece of work? Jesus...he was so getting the Cranky Bea treatment next time she sat down to sketch.

"Bea?" Kim came to the door, looking at her watch. "Shouldn't you have left by now?"

Bea looked up from her phone, barely making Kim out through the red mist clouding her vision. "No," she said, a decision crystalizing, snap-freezing in her brain and coming right out her mouth. "Does your job offer still stand?"

Kim seemed confused for a beat before a slow smile tugged at her mouth. "Yes."

"And this will really be my office?"

"Yes."

A corner office was a corner office. It didn't matter how high it was off the ground—it was all about the statement. "When can I start?"

"Whenever you want." Kim clasped her hands together, as if she was having a hard time containing her excitement. "As soon as possible?"

"Is today okay?"

The smile morphed into a grin that practically split Kim's face in two. "Today is perfect."

"All right, then." Bea also grinned, some of the rage and mist dissipating at Kim's delighted reaction. "I'll get back to work."

Kim nodded sedately, even though she looked like she was about to levitate in excitement. "I'll leave you to it."

Then she practically skipped out of the room.

Bea walked around to the other side of her desk, her legs still shaking. Sitting slowly, as the enormity of her sudden snap decision sunk in, she took some deep breaths and reached out to push the start button on her computer, staring at it absently as it booted up.

She'd show Charlie dipshit Hammersmith *and* his ilk that she'd not only make it in LA but she'd fucking *thrive*. His influence might extend into all kinds of advertising circles and that could well have thrown some wrenches in some plans, had she wanted to keep working the old-school way—except she didn't.

These days, there was more than one way to *make it*— dinosaurs like Charlie just hadn't realized it yet. And she looked forward to being a thorn in his side.

But...there was no getting away from the fact that she'd just put a nail into the coffin of any kind of continuing future in Credence. Or with Austin. Who thought she was coming home in a handful of hours.

And she needed to tell him she wasn't...

CHAPTER TWENTY-SEVEN

Of course, the right thing to do would be to catch the flight, take the weekend, and tell Austin about her new plan face-to-face. But Bea both shied away from and rebelled against the idea at the same time. She and Austin had had a lot of fun together but, ultimately, they were just *sleeping* together, right?

There wasn't a ring on her finger. There'd been no conversations, no discussion about their future or their *present*, for that matter, since the original one in her apartment.

They'd just been living in the moment.

Also...if she did go back, they'd end up in bed together. Bea knew that as clearly as she knew the sun would rise tomorrow, and that would only muddy the waters. What she needed—what they both needed—was a clean break. She'd loved her time in Credence. It had welcomed her with open arms and given her a place to hide and lick her wounds, but right now, she needed to do *this*.

So, best to make the cut quick and clean.

Bea ignored the ache around her heart as she tapped Austin's contact in her phone and waited for him to pick up. He was at work, so he might not be able to answer, in which case she'd leave him a message to call her back. But Bea really hoped he would pick up.

Now that her mind was made up, she just wanted it done.

"Hey." Austin answered on the third ring, his voice quiet as if he was answering it at work when he probably shouldn't be.

The low burr to his voice was sexy and intimate. It slid into all her *good* places as well as wrapping fingers around her heart and squeezing.

"You on your way to the airport?"

Bea shut her eyes as a wave of something hot and charged filled her chest. Something a lot like guilt. She gripped the phone harder.

"Bea*triss*?"

Oh no. *No, no, no.* Why did he have to do *that* now?

She gave herself a shake. *Stop this, Bea. You've known him for three months!* Why on earth would she blow this amazing career opportunity over him? Putting her career on hold and breaking all the rules with a guy—a much younger guy—a few months ago had been just what she'd needed, but it was time to be sensible again.

"Sorry." She cleared her throat. "There's been a change of plans."

There was the slightest of pauses. "Oh?"

Bea heard the pause loud as a jumbo jet. "I'm…not coming ho…" She stumbled over the *H* word. "Back."

"You need to delay another day?" His voice was brisk and efficient now, no signs of hesitation.

"No. I'm not coming back. At all. Period." There was more than a pause now. Silence stretched taut—fraught—between them.

"I…don't understand," he said finally. It was quiet and calm, but there was a very definite edge.

Bea could hear shuffling as if Austin was walking, then the opening and closing of a door, then the sound of a nearby car passing by. He must have walked outside.

"Kim's offered me an executive role in charge of advertising for Greet Cute and I've taken it." Bea breathed out shakily.

"Oh...kay."

"They're offering me executive privileges, carte blanche with their advertising budget, an opportunity to build the department from the ground up. *And* a corner office. They're giving me everything I ever wanted."

"I thought you didn't want it anymore?"

The question was direct as an arrow strike and just as deadly. He was still calm, but his words cut into her logic, making her defensive. Which made her annoyed. And she was already pissed enough at Charlie Hammersmith to burn down the whole damn town.

But that was a good thing. Anger was better than the sick feeling in the pit of her stomach, the ache around her heart.

"Neither did I," Bea admitted, fighting to also stay calm. An emotional response was too risky. She straightened her spine. "But this is the best of both worlds. I get to do something I know and love, something I'm really *freaking* good at, but in the best environment possible. I get to call the shots. To be the boss. But a good one. A better one. The kind who influences workplace culture for the better. And works collaboratively with a broad range of diverse interests. I get to bring people along with me instead of setting them against each other."

All those hundreds of little irritations that had crawled like ants under her skin when she'd worked at Jing-A-Ling she could make better.

And maybe she wanted that most of all.

"I get to stick it to Charlie Hammersmith for once and for all."

"Wait, what?" There was a long pause. "This is about your asshole ex-boss?"

"Of course not." No. *Nope.* "But he rang me earlier and offered me my old job back and when I declined, he threatened me. He actually *threatened* me." Her hand trembled a little, thinking about it once more. "He implied that I'd never work in advertising ever again if he had anything to say about it. And then he told me I was too girlie to make it in the big end of town, so *screw* him."

"He's an asshole, Beatrice. You know that. You shouldn't let him get under your skin like that."

"He didn't."

"Oh come on." He gave an incredulous laugh. "He pissed you off and now instead of coming back to Credence, which is what I thought you wanted, you're staying in LA."

No. Charlie was just the catalyst not the reason. And besides, it went deeper than that. "Austin, he didn't just piss me off. He *humiliated* me."

Her voice wobbled just thinking about. She didn't blame Austin for not understanding the depth of her feelings over this because apart from her initial ranting about what an asshole Charlie was, she hadn't really opened up to him about that day she walked out on the job she'd given her all.

"I'd worked my *ass* off for that company. For that executive office. Twice as hard as anyone else. I brought in a shit ton of money for them and won more awards for my campaigns than all of them put together. I stayed late and I worked weekends and I picked up whenever he called no matter the time or day or whether I was on *vacation*. Not that I had many of those."

Everyone else had gone to Cabo or the Caribbean for their summer breaks and skiing in the winter. But no, not her. Bea had rarely taken any time away.

"And when head hunters knocked on my door, I sent them all packing because Charlie valued loyalty above all else. Except when it came to me, apparently. Giving the corner office that I'd earned ten times over to this *guy* who was utterly incompetent and, in doing so, said to the entire advertising community, my *peers,* that I wasn't good enough. I wasn't executive material. That I was *sub-par*."

Her voice cracked on the last word. Losing out on that job had made her feel so damn powerless, just like when she'd been a kid and hadn't been able to control the circumstances of her home life.

"Beat*riss*, honey…I'm sorry that happened to you. You are amazing and he's a fool."

The softness in his voice heightened her state of emotion. Here she was breaking up with him, but he was showing her nothing but kindness and compassion.

"So why give him any more control over your life?"

Bea shut her eyes. It was a fair question she realized as she loosened her death grip on the phone and tried to quell the tightness in her lungs. But he just didn't understand. He was too young and had grown up in a family where everyone was normal and life had been peachy. She knew it wasn't fair to ask what she asked next. She knew it was wrong to play on that honorable streak, but she did anyway. "I *need* to do this, Austin. For me. Not Charlie. It's important. Please understand."

Another long, *long* pause followed. "Then that's what you should do," he said eventually.

A hot lump lodged in Bea's throat at the heaviness of his voice, and she shut her eyes as tears threatened to spill. "Thank you."

"Of course."

His response was stiff, but that was to be expected. "I'll… send for my stuff when I get sorted here."

"I'll take Princess out to the ranch with me."

Gah! Princess…another connection she'd made in Credence. She wanted to tell him she'd send for the cat to come live with her in LA, but Princess was as much a part of Credence as Austin. She swallowed. "Thank you."

"Yeah." More silence that stretched to the point of discomfort. "Well…anyway, go kick some corporate ass, Beatrice."

The phone went dead in her ear, and Bea stared at it for the longest time, a tear trekking down her face. She *would* kick ass. This *was* what she wanted.

So why did she feel so horribly wretched?

CHAPTER TWENTY-EIGHT

Austin had been too stunned, two weeks ago on the phone, to put up much resistance to Beatrice's *so-long, goodbye* call. It had been a terrible moment to realize he'd fallen in love with her.

Terrible and ironic.

There she'd been, breaking up with him, and there was his heart realizing what, deep down, he'd always known and been too chickenshit to acknowledge—he was in love with Beatrice Archer. How was he supposed to compute the wellspring of love rising in his chest at the same time he was losing her?

How could he be elated and crushed in the same breath?

From the moment he'd confronted her outside Annie's, eating ice cream in her bunny slippers, he'd been absolutely sunk. He'd dismissed it as attraction, a sexual thing, but even then, Beatrice's funny, irreverent, pissed-at-the-world routine that day had opened a portal into his heart.

They're giving me everything I ever wanted. Man, that had stung. He'd obviously been kidding himself that he might be everything she'd ever wanted.

What about me, Beatrice?

Those words had sloshed through the quagmire of his brain as she had broken up with him. Along with *I love you.* And then she'd shared how deeply it had cut being forced out of Jing-A-Ling, something she'd never talked about before. He'd thought she'd just been angry. She'd certainly arrived in Credence with a head of steam. But that had been hiding something much deeper—humiliation. And the way her voice had cracked...Then she'd asked him to let her go. Not exactly in those words, but it's what she'd meant.

I need to do this. For me. Please understand.

What else *could* he have done? He hadn't been able to deny her anything from the second he'd laid eyes on her. He'd put her in the *pokey*, for God's sake, because she'd demanded it. And then he'd remembered that saying about setting something you love free and he'd done it—he'd let her go.

It had been hard—crushing, actually—but he'd done it. And he refused to mope around about a woman who had ended things so cleanly. *Over the phone.*

There was no point in acting like a grouch and taking it out on the people of Credence. It wasn't their fault he'd been a dumbass and fallen for a woman who'd been wary of commitment from the get-go. So what if he'd written up an extraordinary amount of parking and speeding tickets, including one for Clay, who was still pissed? He'd even given out his first-ever jaywalking ticket to a disbelieving, generally otherwise upstanding member of the Credence community. And he was all over the noise complaints about the teenagers fooling around down at the lake now that school was out for the summer.

But other than that, he was dandy.

He'd moved through the five stages of *grieving* in lightning speed. He'd been disbelieving that first day, then kinda pissed for a couple of days, and had moved on to several days of thinking about ways he could have done things differently with Beatrice. That had morphed into a period where he was just so damn *sad* about the loss of what could have been.

Princess had ridden shotgun during that ride.

But now, two weeks after that phone call, he was out the other end. He was fine. *Just fine.* A shining example of how-to-survive-a-breakup-and-get-on-with-your-life.

Gold star for him.

It wasn't his fault there was a sudden rash of lawlessness in Credence. He was a cop, for God's sake. It was his *duty*. And he was feeling pretty damn accomplished about it, too, when he plonked his ass down on a stool in an almost deserted Jack's and asked Tucker for a Bud Lite. He'd have a couple of those and some of that cheesy garlic bread he liked so much, then get back to the ranch so Princess wouldn't start to fret, which she did if he came home late.

Poor kitty had lost two owners in only a few months. No wonder she was clingy.

"Cooper!"

His name cracked across the bar just as Austin was taking a sip. He looked over his shoulder to find Arlo striding toward him. "Boss?"

He flung himself down on the stool next to Austin. "Why in the hell do I have Bob Downey on my ass about police harassment?"

Austin sighed. "He has a bald tire. Left front."

"So...give him a warning." Arlo indicated to Tucker he'd have what Austin was having.

"I gave him a damn warning three months ago and it's still bald."

That was the day Beatrice had flashed him from her apartment window. One day, he hoped that memory would make him smile, but right now it was like a knife jabbing under his ribs.

"So. Take his keys and drive him down to the auto shop and make him buy one. Or go and get one yourself and bring it back and put it on for him. The man's like one of those sticky little flies buzzing around a bad smell when he's riled up."

Two weeks' worth of suppressed emotion gushed up inside Austin like a geyser. "He's eighty years old," he snapped. "He was the goddamn *mayor* back in the day. He knows this town's bylaws better than I do, and he doesn't need his hand held like some little kid."

"Yes, he does. It's called being a small-town cop. And this is what *you*"—he poked Austin in the chest—"wanted to be. When I interviewed you, you said you wanted to police in a small community. Well, this is what we do." Clearly exasperated, Arlo took a long drag of his beer, then pointed at a booth. "Over there," he said, his voice brooking no argument as he slid off his stool. "Now."

Sighing, Austin drained the remainder of his beer, gesturing to Tucker for another one, who said, "I'll bring it over."

"Could I get some cheesy garlic bread, too?"

Tucker laughed. "I love that you think you're going to have an appetite after Arlo's done with you."

Ignoring Tucker, Austin reluctantly left his stool and headed to the booth where Arlo was making himself at home. He slid in opposite, and before he even got a chance to say anything, Clay and Winona both appeared. Winona slipped in beside him, and his brother sat next to Arlo. He looked at both newcomers. "What's this?"

"It's an intervention," Tucker announced as he also joined them, handing over Austin's beer, then sliding in beside Winona.

"An intervention?"

"Yeah," Clay said, glaring at his brother. "An asshole intervention."

"About Bea," Winona said in a much gentler tone.

"Oh, hell no." Austin shook his head. He'd rather change all four of Bob Downey's tires. "No way."

"Yes way," Clay insisted. "You're pissing everybody off

and you're freaking Mom out."

"I'm fine." Austin barely resisted slamming his bottle down on the table.

Four sets of eyes brimming with exasperation and pity pinned him into the corner of the booth. "You want to go first?" Arlo said, flicking his gaze at Winona.

"Why?" She shot Arlo an irritated frown. "Because I'm the *girl*?"

"No." Arlo's sigh spoke volumes about his level of frustration. Credence's chief of police had never been known for touchy-feely stuff, so Austin figured this had to be just as excruciating for Arlo as it was for him. "Because you're supposed to be the *love* expert, remember?"

"Oh, Jesus," Austin muttered, guzzling his beer.

"Bartenders make pretty good love experts," Tucker, who seemed to be enjoying this agonizing spectacle a little too much, threw into the mix.

"Thanks," Arlo replied grimly, "but we need someone whose expertise didn't evolve from reading smutty graffiti in the john."

Ignoring them, Winona, who looked right at home despite her earlier protest, nudged him with her shoulder. "What happened? With Bea?"

"Nothing. It's fine. I'm *fine*."

Arlo muttered something before drawing in the kind of deep breath usually reserved for weary mothers about to chastise misbehaving children. "Well, nobody," he proclaimed in his annoyingly superior cop voice, "including *you*, is leaving until this gets sorted, so you might as well cut to the chase."

Austin looked at the faces of the people around him. Most of them he'd known a long time and he'd trust with his life. Even Winona had become a friend. He glanced at Clay, who was watching him closely. "C'mon, Junior—"

"Goddamn it, Clay," Austin yelled, not resisting the urge

m his bottle down this time as he glared at his brother.
ame is *Austin*." He hadn't been able to shake the feeling
his age had been a major factor in Beatrice cutting him
se, so he was done with the *Junior*.

There was a moment of silence around the table as everyone
aped at the usually affable Austin. Clay raised both his hands
n a display of surrender, his face creased in brotherly concern.
"Sorry, man." He left it a beat or two before continuing. "Look,
Austin...it's obvious you're head over heels for her."

"It doesn't matter." Austin stared at the label on his bottle.
"She doesn't live here anymore."

"Gee, if only there was a machine with, oh, I don't know,
wings that could get you to LA in a couple of hours," Clay
said, clearly over his brotherly concern.

Ignoring them again, Winona probed gently, "You love
her?"

Glancing around the circle at the faces again, at the people
who only wanted the best for him, Austin sighed and nodded.
"Yes." It was the only way he was getting out of here tonight
anyway. Right now, he'd admit to every unsolved crime in the
county just to make it stop. "But it doesn't matter; she doesn't
love me." That's what it boiled down to, after all. Just a case
of long-distance, unrequited love.

"Is that what she said when you confessed your feelings to
her?" Winona probed.

Austin shook his head. "I didn't tell her."

Winona blinked. In fact, everyone at the table blinked.
"Why the hell not?" Clay demanded.

"Jesus, dude," Tucker *tsk*ed. "Rookie error."

Winona just rolled her eyes and shook her head. "What is
wrong with all of you?" she demanded, stabbing a glance at
every guy at the table. "No wonder you needed a Facebook
campaign to attract women here."

"Hey, I'm taken," Tucker protested.

"Me too," Clay said.

Everybody looked at Arlo. "How did this get to be my fault?" he asked before glaring at Austin. "First Bob and now them. Time to get your shit together."

"And do what?" Austin demanded. "She wants what's in LA. She has something to prove. She asked me to understand."

"Christ on a cracker." Arlo shook his head in utter disbelief.

"What a dumbass," Clay agreed.

"What?" Austin snapped. "She's a grown woman. She's allowed to do what she wants and go where she wants. I was *trying* to be *understanding*. Setting her free to do what she needs to do and all that crap."

Arlo turned his gaze to Winona. "I got nothing."

She sighed and glanced sideways at Austin. "What Arlo *means* is...of course Bea is entitled to leave and live her own life far away from here, and you supporting her in that move is admirable and honorable, especially when you sacrificed your feelings. But she made that decision without all the information. Would she still have made it if she'd known that you love her?" Winona shrugged. "Maybe? I don't know. But you gotta give her that choice, Austin. If you tell her and she doesn't feel the same, then you're no worse off than you are now."

Austin doubted that. If he told her and she rejected him again, he was pretty sure he'd feel *twice* as shitty.

"But if she does feel the same?" Winona said, and the potential of that glimmered on the air between them.

What if Bea loved him, too?

"Yeah." Arlo nodded. "What she said."

Crap. His emotions seesawed between hope and despair. He knew there was something between them, something deeper than sex and the thrill of breaking some rules. He felt it every time they were together. And he'd thought she had, too... But was that love?

Did she love him? Or was that wishful thinking?

"Yeah, man," Tucker said. "You gotta leave it all out on the field."

"Right," Clay enthused. "Go to LA, doofus. Tell her you love her. Go big or go home."

A trickle of excitement seeped into Austin's veins. He'd felt impotent for two weeks, torn between trying not to love her anymore and loving her too much to rock any boats. But, like Winona said, didn't he owe it to himself and to his happiness to at least let her know how he felt? So she could have all the facts before deciding her future?

"If it works out, it'll mean moving to LA," Austin said, eyeing his brother. If Beatrice loved him, he'd move to the fucking North Pole if she wanted.

Clay shrugged. "So move."

"I have contacts in the LAPD," Arlo offered. "I could put in a good word."

All his life, Austin had wanted to be chief of police in Credence, so following Bea would mean giving up on that dream. That was just the facts. Which made this decision a very big deal. Probably not one he should be making on a whim. But...ultimately, he wanted to be with Beatrice and that was that. Was he disappointed? Yes. Did he wish it was different? Yes. But life didn't always work out the way you wanted, and who knew what opportunities might arise for him within the LAPD?

It wasn't all SWAT and Vice.

It would be very different from being a small-town cop. There was no denying that it would be a huge change. But he wasn't a stranger to city policing. He'd worked in Denver and yeah, LA was bigger with a much bigger crime problem, but he was *good* at his job and he *would* adjust.

"Mom will be disappointed."

"Again, the machines with the wings," Clay said.

Austin glanced around at his merry band of interventionists. God…was he *really* going to do this? Just turn up in LA and tell Beatrice he loved her and hope to God that made some kind of a difference?

The cast-iron steadiness of his gut told him he was. And there was no time like the present. "I'm going to need a few days off," he said to Arlo.

"You got them."

"Okay, then." Austin nodded and smiled, and suddenly everyone was smiling, and it felt like the best kind of omen. He turned to Winona and Tucker. "You guys are going to have to get out of my way. I have things to organize."

Tucker practically leaped out of the booth, and Winona wasn't far behind. "Good luck," she said as Austin slid out and got to his feet.

"Thanks." Hopefully he wasn't going to need it, but he'd sure as hell take it.

...

Two days later, Austin was striding into the funky converted warehouse building belonging to Greet Cute while a herd of elephantine butterflies stomped around inside his belly. He'd rehearsed his speech over and over in his head during the flight from Denver, and he was as ready to make his case as he'd ever be. He'd had no idea where Beatrice was staying now, but he knew with a high degree of certainty, she'd be at work at one thirty on a Thursday and, thanks to Facebook, he knew the corporate address.

Riding the elevator to the third floor, he stepped out and asked a woman in jeans and a Greet Cute T-shirt streaking past where he could find Beatrice. She did a bit of a double-take before pointing to the far corner, to a big glassed-in office.

"Thanks," he said and headed in that direction.

The fact people stopped and stared at him as Austin made his way across the large, airy space barely registered. He supposed in his jeans, boots, and Stetson, he didn't exactly look LA chic, but he only had eyes for the redhead who was staring intently at the monitor in front of her.

By the time he was a few feet from her door, Austin's pulse was beating thick and slow through his temples and his neck and his groin. This was it.

This was the time to *leave it all on the field.*

Her door was open and Austin slowed, stopping under the frame and leaning his shoulder into the jamb, just watching her for a beat or two, engrossed in her work. She looked *good.* Her red hair was still as vibrant as he remembered, and it was loose around her shoulders. She was wearing the same kind of T-shirt the woman near the elevator had been wearing.

And if there was any doubt he loved her, that it had been merely fondness or pining or missing their sexy times instead of love, that was all put to instant rest. He knew without a doubt he would go to the ends of the earth for this woman. If she'd have him. Hell, even if she wouldn't.

She'd only ever have to call and he'd be here.

"Did you get those figures, Jaz?" she asked, not looking up from her screen, a little *V* of concentration pulling her brows together.

"It's not Jaz."

Her head snapped up and she pierced him with those green eyes. *"Austin?"* she said, her voice disbelieving as she pushed to her feet.

He didn't know if it was a good thing or a bad thing that she was suddenly standing, but her eyes were roaming all over his body and not in a sexual way, in a just-making-sure-it's-really-you way. It didn't seem hostile, and it set his pulse pounding through every inch of his body.

"Surprise," he said, shoving his hands in his pockets in case he did something ill-advised, like opening them, inviting her in, only to have her stay behind her desk. He didn't want to come closer until he was asked.

"I..." She tucked a strand of hair behind her ear. "What are you doing here?"

"I came to see you. To...talk to you."

"Oh. Right." Her voice was still faint, and she looked like a deer caught in headlights.

Oh crap...a spike of unease lanced right through his middle. He shouldn't have come. He should have done this over the phone. Like she'd done. Part of him wanted to turn around and keep on going, taking her stricken look as a statement about her feelings. But he didn't. He hardened his resolve. He was here now.

It was showtime.

"Well...come in," she said, awkwardly gesturing him to the chair on the opposite side of her desk. Like she was a doctor and he was the patient she'd been dreading seeing all day because she had bad news to impart.

Crap, crap, crap.

"Shut the door."

Austin shut the door, noticing the keen interest outside as everyone, it seemed, eyed Beatrice's office. He ambled toward the desk, but he didn't sit. And neither did she. They just stared at each other, him with his hands in his pockets, her hands hanging loose, her fingertips absently touching the desk. She was wearing jeans, he noted, and to her right there were three Cranky Bea prints that had been framed and hung on the only non-glass section of wall.

"How are you? How's Princess?"

Oh God...they'd been reduced to awkward chitchat when once they hadn't been able to stop talking. "I'm fine. She's fine. She misses you." He clenched his jaw, biting down on the urge to say *I've missed you*, but damn it, it was a good lead-in to the conversation he was here to have. Why beat around the bush? "As have I."

He watched the slow bob of her throat as she swallowed. "Austin."

There was a quiet warning in her voice, like she'd read in his eyes why he was here and she didn't want to go there. But that was too bad, because he did. Okay, maybe her work wasn't the best place, but it wouldn't take long. And if she rejected him, he'd turn around and walk away and never come back. That would be the end. But he had to say it.

"I'm moving to LA."

"*What?*" Beatrice blinked. Yeah...*that* she hadn't been expecting. "Austin? *No.*" She leaned forward a little. "You *love* Credence. You *love* working in the police department there."

"Yeah, I do. But...I love you more."

A giddy rush to his head almost took Austin out at the knees. There, he'd said it. It was done. Now it was in the lap of the gods or fate or the fucking alignment of the planets.

Or *whatever.*

"And if you want, if you *need* to be here," he continued, "and you happen to love me back, which I'm hoping you do, then LA is where I want to be, too."

"Austin...I..." She shook her head.

Clearly, he'd floored her, and Austin didn't know whether that was a good thing or a bad thing. Had she not ever even thought about the possibility?

"This is..." She seemed to be searching for a word to fully encapsulate her disbelief. "Unexpected."

"Really, Beatrice? *Really?* We've been living together for a couple of months. Is it really that hard to fathom?"

She recoiled a little, then covered with a quick, dismissive half laugh. "We weren't living together."

Austin frowned. *Was she being serious?* "I slept in your

bed every night. My clothes are in your closet. My toothbrush is at your sink. I got you a *cat*. You gave me a key. What the hell did you think we were doing?"

"That was just..." She swatted at the air like she was swinging at a fly. "Convenience."

Convenience? Okay, they might have studiously avoided talking about their relationship status when they'd been together—clearly a big mistake, he was realizing now—but he'd thought it was pretty obvious they were *living* together.

"Oh my God." Austin pressed his fingers into his temples. Was this really happening?

"Austin..." She looked helpless for a beat or two. "You're *ten* years younger than me. I don't shack up with twenty-five-year-olds."

The incredulity in her voice struck him hard, and he realized suddenly she'd never been on the same page as him. "God." He shoved a hand through his hair. He'd been a fool. "You never even considered us as a couple, did you? You never even *entertained* the idea?"

"Austin..." She spread her hands in appeal. "You're... *twenty-five*."

Of course. It was the age thing again. She'd labeled him *fun*. Play. A distraction. Not a person she could have something real with. He was *Junior*.

"You don't want to give everything up for me," she continued. "Someone who's ten years older than you."

He gritted his teeth. "Yeah, Beatrice. I do."

"No, you don't." She shook her head. "Go back to Credence. To your job. Go fu..." She stumbled over the word for a moment but plowed on. "Fuck other twenty-five-year-olds. Shack up with one of them. *Marry* her if you want. Have babies with her. Don't you want babies?"

Austin's head spun. This had jumped ahead *fast*. "I don't know. Yeah, I guess." He'd always assumed he would have children. "If I could have them with you."

"Oh, no." She groaned. "No, no. no. Not me. I have *old* ovaries, Austin. *Bad* eggs. *Overcooked* eggs. I'm running out of time, and I don't even know if I want babies."

"So we won't have babies."

"Austin." She came out from behind her desk, her gaze imploring as she stopped in front of him, leaving about a foot between them as she reached out and touched his forearm. It was bittersweet, and he closed his eyes briefly.

Her touch was all he wanted in his life, but he knew this was goodbye.

"I'm sorry," she whispered, and he opened his eyes to find her looking at him, clearly unhappy. "But I *don't* love you. Please just go back to Credence."

Her quiet words cut like an axe through his heart, splicing it in two, but the certainty in her gaze was even more damaging. That gouged at his soul. He'd told his truth and spilled his heart and now he had his answer.

I don't love you.

Too numb to think or feel, he nodded slowly, stepping back, her hand sliding away. "Goodbye, Beatrice."

And this time he knew it was for real.

CHAPTER TWENTY-NINE

A week later, Bea was sitting under leaden skies at an alfresco café for a breakfast meeting three blocks from Greet Cute HQ with Kim and Nozo. Mal was attending a dental appointment with his daughter, which Bea loved. She could only imagine how Charlie Hammersmith would have reacted to a man wanting to accompany his daughter to a dental appointment.

There'd have been much talk about lack of balls being tossed around in the boardroom.

They were meeting with Leilani Leota, a young Instagram influencer who had been born in Hawaii but was now living in LA. Bea had been watching her—she was smart, innovative, and from an advertising background, and Bea wanted to work with her *really* badly. She thought Leilani could bring something unique to the online space for Cranky Bea, but also several of the other lines in Greet Cute's portfolio.

The menus arrived and they decided to go ahead and order, as Leilani had just messaged to say she was stuck in traffic— *of course!*—and might be twenty minutes late. Kim ordered an egg white omelet. Nozo ordered a chia bowl. Bea found nothing on the menu appealing. In fact, all she could think about was a piece of Annie's key lime pie and a beer.

Sadly, there was no breakfast pie or breakfast beer on

the menu.

And, had there been, she couldn't even begin to imagine the shock on Kim's and Nozo's faces if she ordered something so *carb-laden*. And alcoholic. For breakfast. A Bloody Mary was acceptable, but a turmeric chai latte was more in vogue.

Sighing, Bea ordered what was expected of her—an egg white omelet—and hated herself for it, but mostly she was just too distracted by the silky underwear currently moving steadily north up her ass crack. All her LA underwear had been waiting for her when she got back to her apartment, and while she may have ditched the corporate power suits from her wardrobe and corporate America from her résumé, she hadn't yet gotten around to purging it from her lingerie drawer.

Day-of-the-week underwear might not be sexy, but it sure knew how to cling to hips and ass cheeks. God, how she missed her Thursday panties…

Along with a million other things from Credence. Like Princess. And the lake. And *dear lord*, Annie's pies. Also binge-watching TV shows on her laptop, her bunny slippers, and the golden oldie line dancers at Jack's.

But most especially Sundays at the ranch. And Austin… Austin, who had walked into her office last week and turned *everything* upside down.

It had been so easy to keep him and their time together in a neat little box when she'd ended it over the phone. Much harder to ignore it when he'd been standing at her door, looking all freaking Wild West and causing a hundred different micro-memories to bombard her all at once.

I love you. That's what he'd said. *I've fallen in love with you.* And she'd absolutely panicked. Because it was ridiculous— they'd known each other for *three* months, and worst of all, she'd realized in that moment, she'd become her mother.

The thing her grandmother had most *feared* and her father had most *dreaded* and she'd always told herself she *couldn't* become. Because look at what had happened. Disaster. Tragedy. Grief. A household defined by a ghost. Her grandmother trying to erase the influence and a father trying to ignore it.

Austin had been right—she hadn't ever considered them a couple. In fact, she'd deliberately avoided thinking of them as *anything* because of the age difference and how close that cut to the bone. He'd obviously been getting emotionally invested, though, spinning castles in the air about them *living together*, and she'd hit the retreat button as soon as it had fallen from his mouth.

No matter how much she'd ached for him since.

But that wasn't *love*. That was lust and…nostalgia. She *missed* him. Of course she did. But she missed Princess, too. And Molly and Marley and Winona. She missed all of them.

She missed *Credence*.

Especially sitting here listening to Kim and Nozo chatter about the latest colonics on the market and the salon that had opened its doors nearby, offering all kinds of scrubs, a vast array of hair removal options, and the latest in *injectables*. Nozo was talking about getting fillers in her lips because she thought her perfectly nice mouth was a little on the thin side, and Kim was seriously considering getting some Botox in her perfectly smooth forehead.

They were both in their late twenties, for crying out loud. But despite their very nontraditional corporate life, they were LA natives through and through. Having work done was just what one did when young and upwardly mobile in LA.

Which made her miss Credence even more. Credence, where the content of a person's character was more important than how they pouted or how many lines they had on their forehead. And people were always so genuinely pleased to see each other. And no one was twenty minutes late because of *traffic*.

And where it was perfectly okay to wear day-of-the week

panties. And the sound of Austin's boots on the stairs outside her door could make her pulse beat a little faster.

Goddamn it, *Austin*. Why'd she have to miss Austin most of all?

Hot tears pricked at her eyes, and she was glad for her sunglasses to cover it up, but they didn't help with the tightness in her chest or the ominous internal cracking as small chinks became deep fissures in the wall around her heart. The one she'd built to block thoughts and feelings of Austin *out*. His appearance had been the first chink, and with every memory of Austin this past week, more had appeared. And now they were deepening into ravines.

How much longer until it disintegrated entirely?

. . .

Fifteen minutes, it turned out.

When their meals arrived and she looked down at her plate, at the healthy lump of plain, congealed egg white with three drops of truffle oil and a sprig of alfalfa. All the things that she disliked about her life in LA—which had only been amplified by Austin's visit—were suddenly represented on this plate that would have had any LA food critic in absolute rhapsodies.

Tears more than pricked her eyes this time—they spilled out as, in one pure moment of clarity, she realized she'd made a huge mistake. She'd made the *wrong choice*. Because the omelet wasn't a piece of pie, and her fancy decaf soy latte—the foam made into a freaking *swan*—wasn't a beer.

And because…she loved Austin Cooper, too.

She'd let her humiliation and rage at Charlie Hammersmith and her *pride* override everything else. She'd let that prick of a man goad her into something she'd given up months ago because her need to prove to him that she could *make it* had superseded everything else.

Why in God's name was she proving anything to *that* man?

She must have sniffled a little then, because Kim and Nozo stopped talking and stared at her. "Bea?" Kim frowned. "Are you...crying? Are you okay?"

Hastily wiping at a tear that had slid beyond the rim of her sunglasses, Bea gave a half laugh, half sob. "No."

"Oh my God," Kim said as both women reached their hands across the table and placed them on Bea's forearms. "What's the matter?"

"I want pie." And she did sob then as her composure really started to slide.

The women looked at each other. "Okay?" Nozo said gently. "I'm sure the kitchen could rustle you up a piece."

Yeah, but it wouldn't be Annie's, would it? "I'm sorry, but... do you think you guys could handle this meeting without me? I need to... I need to think awhile."

Bea felt guilty because they were taking this meeting at *her* insistence. But both the competent women opposite had been part of her strategy to bring Leilani into the fold and were completely on board. They could easily handle it without her.

"Of course," Kim said, patting her arm. "Go and think."

• • •

Bea had no plan or clue, really, where she was going after she left the restaurant on foot. She just walked. Aimlessly. The pavements beneath her feet unfamiliar and yet an intricate part of her DNA. Thoughts churned around in her head. About Austin. And love. And Credence. And how badly she'd screwed up. About Greet Cute and her future.

About her mom and her dad.

Shards of memories from her childhood—good and bad— flitted through her head like sunbeams she couldn't quite catch.

At one point, it started to rain, and Bea ducked into the

nearest store for shelter, one of those places crammed full of knickknacks and trinkets from a mishmash of art to furniture and ornaments. Wicker baskets, linen, pretty glass, and old china shared shelves and wall space with fake moose heads and gawdy, waving cats. She wandered aimlessly here, too, waiting out the storm, her brain deciding its best way to cope with this morning's whammy was just to check out for a while.

Which was how she found herself standing in front of a large, gilt-framed painting of wildflowers, the style as distinct and individual as a fingerprint.

A style she knew as intimately as she knew her own heartbeat.

Bea's breath stopped in her throat. Her pulse throbbed through her ears. A hot rush of moisture pricked at her tear ducts and overflowed, spilling down her face. She hadn't seen this piece for almost thirty years, but she remembered it as if it was yesterday. Sitting with her mother as she'd put the finishing touches on it. *Feeling* the sheer breathtaking beauty of the bloom as viscerally as if she had been there.

Just as she was right now.

It had lost none of its vibrancy, the kaleidoscope of color as vivid as it had been back when it was first painted. It had obviously been well cared for.

A guy wearing a name badge pulled up beside her. "Art can get you like that sometimes, can't it?" he said gently, like he was used to random customers crying in front of paintings.

Bea nodded, not bothering to wipe away the tears. "Uh-huh."

"It's called *Wildflower Blooms on Carrizo*."

Yeah. Bea remembered. She didn't look at him—she couldn't move—she just asked, "How much?" her voice raspy and foreign to her ears.

"For you, seven hundred dollars."

Without thinking twice, Bea dug in her handbag for her

credit card. "I'll buy it," she said, passing it over.

She'd have bought it no matter the cost.

Thanks to her grandmother's purge and her father's passivity—or maybe complicity—in the less-than-flattering narrative that had been constructed around her mother's life, Bea had *none* of her mom's art. She hadn't even gone online as an adult and tried to track some of it down, because her gut too often churned with her own conflicted feelings, and it had felt disloyal to the people who had raised her as best they knew how.

Her father and grandmother had tried to shield her from the worst of the mood swings that marred her mom's mental health, to give her stability and structure both before and after her mom's death. As an adult, Bea could see that. She didn't *blame* them. But in doing so, Bea had lost that thing vital to every human being—connection.

To the person who had known and loved her *first*. And she still felt that loss today. Despite her determined denials otherwise.

It flared inside her now, standing in front of her mother's painting, as bright and as strong as ever. *Connection*. To her mother. But more than that, to this thing that had nagged and nagged at her over the years no matter how hard she'd tried to suppress it.

Her muse.

The guy whistled as he took the card. "You have a very good eye, and lucky, too. It's just come in this morning from a deceased estate and won't last long. It's from an LA artist called Phoebe Archer who was highly acclaimed back in the eighties. Super collectable," he added as he walked away to ring up the sale.

"I know," Bea said. "She was my mother."

. . .

Twenty minutes later, she was back on the street, with the wrapped painting at her feet, waiting for an Uber, which was six minutes away. Without giving it much thought, she called her father. He picked up on the second ring.

"Hey, Dad."

"Hey, Bea, how's that corner office going?"

He and her grandmother had been thrilled that she'd *come to her senses* and was back working in LA. Even more so that she'd started out with an executive position and that much-coveted corner office. She drew in a shaky breath, knowing he wouldn't like what she was about to say. "I think I'm about to quit."

"Beatrice." He sighed a sigh leaden with disappointment and exasperation. "Why?"

"Because"—she sniffled as more tears threatened—"I'm standing here on the sidewalk outside a curio store in downtown LA, and one of Mom's paintings was on the wall and I bought it and it just...*speaks* to me." She took a breath. "I'm an artist, Dad. I've denied it all my life because I didn't want to hurt you or Granny and make you worry, but...I just can't anymore."

He didn't say anything for the longest time, and Bea waited for him to lecture her about getting a reputation as being unreliable and *flaky*, but when he eventually spoke, he simply asked, "What painting?"

"*Carrizo*."

She didn't have to explain which one it was; she could tell from his silence that he remembered the circumstances and upheaval around its creation as vividly as she did. "Yeah... that one's really pretty."

Bea swallowed the sob that rose in her throat. "I wish Granny hadn't gotten rid of her paintings."

"Me too," he said softly. "I'm sorry. It just...felt like the best thing at the time."

Bea shut her eyes to stop the tears from falling. "Did you love her?"

She'd never asked her father that question. And he'd never volunteered the information. The topic of her mother was one that had been rarely ever directly broached. But Bea needed to know. She *wanted* to talk about her mom.

And maybe her father did, too.

"I loved her more than was good for me or her." So often, he'd been brusque in any reference about her mother. Not today. His voice was wistful and tinged with sadness. "But it's hard to love someone like your mom. She was such a free spirit, and trying to hold on to her was like trying to hold on to a moonbeam. But I did try, and when it worked, it was... *wonderful.*"

Bea remembered those times. Probably more vividly than the *other* times. Her father laughing. Her mother *sparkling.*

"And even when it wasn't, even with everything that happened, I still loved her, Bea. I still do."

It couldn't have been easy for her father. To have been the straight man, the steady hand in a roller-coaster relationship, always trying to hold on when the other person was always trying to pull away. Loving someone whose capacity for love was so big and all-encompassing, it could never be contained to just one person.

"I'm not her, Dad."

"I know, love."

"But I *need* to know her, to connect. Which kinda sucks considering she's dead." Bea gave a brittle half laugh. "Until this morning, I had nothing of hers, but now I have this painting, and when I look at it, I *feel* her and I feel *me* in her, and I know how to connect to her now. Through my art."

There was another pause that went on for so long, Bea almost asked if he was all right, but she didn't. This was a conversation they should have had a long time ago; it was okay that he didn't know what to say.

"Then that's what you should do," he murmured, when he finally spoke.

Bea shut her eyes. She didn't need his permission or his approval, but she did need him to understand. "Thank you," she said, then hung up the phone.

CHAPTER THIRTY

Three days later, Bea pulled her rental car up outside of Austin's cabin, trying to quell the nervousness that had been ramping up since she'd landed in Denver a few hours ago. She'd called Austin's mother to let her know she was about to do some major groveling to her son and ask if it was okay to do it at the ranch.

Margaret had been delighted. Over the groveling and the fact that Bea would soon be in town. "You're here to stay, then?" she'd asked.

"Yes," Bea had confirmed. "Whether Austin wants me or not, I'm here to stay."

"Good. Credence needs people like you," she'd said with a smile in her voice.

Margaret had instructed her to go straight to the cabin and let herself in, overriding Bea's reluctance to take such liberties with assurances that Austin wouldn't mind. The first thing Bea saw when she opened the door was *not* the magnificent vista through those huge windows but Princess curled up in the middle of Austin's bed looking as regal and shabby chic as ever.

If she hadn't known it before this minute, Bea knew it now—she loved Austin Cooper.

"Princess," Bea murmured, crossing to the bed and crawling onto it, scooping the un-protesting kitty against her chest and hugging her tight. "I missed you," she whispered into the patchy fur. "Thank you for looking after Austin."

Although Bea would be lying if she didn't admit to being a teeny bit jealous that Princess had been sleeping with her man.

Bea blinked—*her man*. She'd remembered Jill saying *my man* about Clay, and now she knew exactly how the other woman felt.

"Should we call Austin?" she asked the cat.

Ignoring Princess's apparent disinterest in the question, Bea scrolled to his number on her cell. Her fingers trembled slightly as she tapped the screen.

He picked up on the third ring. "Beatrice?"

She sucked in a breath. His voice sounded guarded but so damn good. Her pulse fluttered, and Bea took a moment to gather herself, to make sure her voice was flirty rather than shaky.

"Yes..." She cleared her throat. "Officer. I'm just calling to report a crime in progress at the Cooper ranch."

Bea didn't miss the quick intake of his breath. "You're... in Credence?"

Her belly tightened at the strained caution crackling over the airwaves, her anxiety cranking up a notch. She'd hoped that Austin would welcome her back with open arms—it hadn't even been two weeks, after all. He couldn't have fallen out of love with her in that time, surely?

But she didn't blame him for being wary—she'd rejected him. And if the distance in his tone was like an icepick to her chest, then she only had herself to blame.

"Yes, I'm back."

"Okay." He paused. "For how long?"

"For good." Bea hated that her voice trembled but she was almost sick with nerves.

There was silence at the other end, which turned the screw on the tension building between her shoulder blades. "Why are you at the ranch?"

She swallowed. "Because I thought it might be a private space for me to do some groveling."

"There's going to be groveling?"

Bea thought she detected a slight lightening of his tone and her pulse fluttered madly at her temple as she gave a nervous kind of half laugh. "There is."

After a beat or two, he cleared his throat. "A crime in progress, you say?"

Bea smiled a wobbly smile as a cool flood of relief washed through her system. It wasn't a green light but it was a start. "Yes. An abuse of the Gregorian calendar is currently taking place in the cabin between the main house and the barn."

"Gregorian calendar, huh? Would you care to elaborate?"

She couldn't tell if he was smiling or frowning on the other end; all Bea really knew was how good it was to hear his voice again. "Of course," she said, keeping in character. "I have it on good authority that there's a woman inside currently wearing Thursday panties."

"I'm not sure that's a problem, ma'am?" he said, then added, "I'm kinda partial to Thursday panties myself."

Tears pricked the backs of Bea's eyes at the warmth creeping into Austin's voice and she pressed her lips together, daring to hope. "But it's *Wednesday*. Which is in direct violation of the calendar."

"I see... Pretty sure it's also in direct contravention of Credence county bylaw four seven three subsection eight."

"That's what I thought, Officer. Maybe you should come and check it out? Before it descends into any further anarchy?"

"Yeah, Arlo does not approve of anarchy."

Bea heard someone in the background—Arlo, she thought—querying what was happening. "Noise complaint," he lied. "Out at the lake."

The reply was distant but clear. "Give it to Reynolds. I

need you here."

Austin didn't hesitate in changing his story. "Beatrice is at the ranch."

There wasn't any sound then. Even the muffled background office noises she hadn't realized were audible suddenly stopped.

"Oh, for the love of... Go. Fix it. We're sick of your sorry ass around here."

Amid general laughter, Austin was back in her ear. "I'm on my way."

Stupid tears blurred Bea's vision as he hung up and she whispered, "Hurry."

. . .

Bea heard the sound of a vehicle slowly approaching twenty minutes later. Her pulse leaped and she performed an instantaneous sit-up from her position curled around Princess on the bed. God...this was *it*.

Austin had thawed over the phone conversation, but she still had ground to make up.

She stood. Then she sat. Then she stood again, nerves making her indecisive as she moved to the kitchen, leaning her elbow casually on the bench. Quickly dismissing that as ridiculous, she stalked to the mantelpiece, resting her hand on that. *Ugh*—no. Too staged.

What about the couch?

She crossed to it, sitting on the arm, facing the door, crossing her legs. Then uncrossing them again. Then crossing them once more. A car door slammed, ricocheting along her nerve endings as she leaped up, standing undecidedly like a pimple on a pumpkin in the middle of the open floor plan, the beat of her heart a low echo in her ears.

Footsteps came next, and she couldn't move at all. Then the sound of feet scraping on the mat. Then the door opened abruptly, and he was there, right there, filling up the doorway, his hat pulled low, scruff on his face, hands on his hips, his feet spaced evenly apart like he was the sheriff staring down the gunslinger.

He was breathtakingly male standing there like that and she *could not* take her eyes off him. Nor, apparently, could he take his eyes off her as his gaze ate her up. A surge of estrogen mixed with the adrenaline already flooding her system.

God, he looked *good*, this man she loved.

"Ma'am," he said, his eyes burning into hers, his voice low and gravelly. "I understand there's an issue with some panties?"

Oh, *dear lord*. Bea swallowed. Would she ever get used to the way he said *panties*. "Hey, Austin."

He nodded. "Beatrice." Then he stared a bit longer before saying, "So...you're really back?"

"Yes."

"Why?"

She blinked at his rapid-fire reply. It wasn't harsh, but it was direct, which was fair enough. And it deserved a direct answer. "Because I don't want to be anywhere else."

He nodded slowly. "That's...good then."

She smiled. "I brought you something."

It took her another beat or two before she finally coaxed her legs into moving to the couch, where she'd placed the object in question earlier while waiting for him to arrive. She was relieved to see him enter and close the door after him. He ambled closer and was probably about halfway to her position when she reached over the back of the couch and grabbed the rectangular-framed three-by-three sketch, propping it along the top for him to see.

He halted abruptly, and she watched his face as his eyes roamed over the charcoal lines of the ranch house and the pastel shades of the landscape as the sun set.

"Beatrice," he murmured eventually, his tone hushed as

his gaze met hers. "It's…"

Goose bumps prickled along her arms. "If you don't like the frame, I can get it changed." She'd chosen a rustic, wooden style to suit the internal decor of the ranch. "Or it can come out of the frame altogether."

"No." He stalked forward until he was a foot away from both it and her, taking his time to admire it again. "It's perfect. It's"—his eyes flicked to hers and locked—"exactly what I wanted. Mom will absolutely *love* it. Thank you."

Bea smiled, almost giddy with relief. She knew it didn't make up for the way she'd behaved, the way she'd ended things, but once she'd decided she was coming back to Credence, the urge to sketch the ranch as Austin had asked her to do all those weeks ago became an imperative.

And it had felt *wonderful*—not fighting her instincts, not pretending it was just doodling or unimportant. *Embracing it*. The lines of the ranch had flowed from her in less than an hour, sketching them from memory and the rose-gold hues of nostalgia for those Sunday afternoons drinking spiked iced tea with Austin's family.

He stepped in, taking the frame from her and sliding it down to lean against the cushioned back of the couch. Turning to face her, he was close now, his hip pressed into the couch. She turned, too, mirroring his pose, her blood pumping thick and slow through her system as she realized she could just reach out and touch him. If he let her.

"So. You…*are* an artist?"

Bea's smile faded. "Yes. You were right. I am and I always have been." It felt good to say it again. To declare it to the other man she loved. "Just like my mother."

"Your mother's an artist?"

"She was."

He raised an eyebrow. "She's retired, or…"

"She died," Bea supplied, filling in his blank. "When I

was ten."

"Oh, Beatrice." His brow creased. "I'm so sorry." His gaze was soft with empathy which soothed the rawness of her emotion.

Bea shook her head. "It was a long time ago," she said quietly.

"Did she..." He stalled. "Was she...?"

"She died in a car accident."

Grimacing, he shook his head. "God...that's awful."

"There was a man in the car with her, who was also killed. A much younger man. They'd run away together a couple of weeks prior."

"Ah." He nodded slowly. "That's why you were skittish about being with me?"

"Yes. And why I've spent a lot of my life denying and suppressing that part of me that was clearly artistic. My dad had been through a lot with my mom, so creativity wasn't... encouraged. Between him and my grandmother, who moved in with us after my mom died, there were a lot of rules. A lot of...redirection. I understand why; I was always drawing and I was *good* at it, but they loved me and were terrified that I'd be a chip off the old block. God...*I* was terrified I'd be a chip off the old block."

"And then I came along and..."

"Uh-huh." Bea smiled. "I was breaking all those rules, but you were like ground zero. The ultimate don't-go-there. Until I couldn't stay away any longer, and then I justified it as being okay, because I wasn't *running away* with you. We *weren't* in a relationship. Which, of course, we were."

He reached for her hands and lifted them to his mouth, dropping a kiss on her knuckles and Bea's heart skipped a beat. "Fucking-A we were."

Austin tucked their hands against his chest and Bea reveled in their nearness. "But actually. You *weren't* my ground zero at all. It was this." Bea tipped her head sideways at the framed sketch. "I was terrified of this. Surrendering to this *pull* inside me that's always been there. Surrendering to *art*. Because my experience of art as a kid was quite fraught, and there was so much emotional baggage attached to it. Which was why advertising was such a great fit." She gave a wry laugh. "There's no crying in advertising."

He chuckled but sobered quickly. "I'm so sorry, Beatrice. About everything you've been through. And especially because I never asked you about this stuff. It always seemed like you could bolt at any minute, and I didn't want to scare you by pushing too hard too fast. But I knew there was deeper stuff. And I should have been ballsier."

"No." Bea shook her head. "You gave me openings and I didn't take them, and for that *I'm* sorry." She took a steadying breath as her gaze locked on his. "I'm sorry I was too busy *not* falling in love with a twenty-five-year-old guy I'd just met that I actually missed the moment it happened."

A deliciously slow smile morphed into a very sexy grin, the last remnants of wariness in his gaze evaporating. "You love me?"

Bea laughed. "I do." She slid her hand onto his cheek. "I wasn't looking for you, Austin. I came here to get away from things, start over, figure some things out, but here you were, and now I can't imagine my life without you."

"Yeah." He nodded. "I know exactly how you feel."

He closed the miniscule distance between them, their bodies pressed tight as he lowered his mouth to hers, soft and slow. A kiss that explored, that savored. That said, *Hello again.* And, *Remember me?* And, *I love you.* A kiss that whispered about forever and happily ever after. Bea sighed into it, her hands sliding to his shoulders as she lost her breath to its sweetness and her heart to its fullness.

When they parted, they were both breathing a little harder.

"What now?" he asked, his forehead pressed to hers. "Are you sure about Credence? My offer to move to LA stands. As long as I'm with you, I can live anywhere."

Hell, he was just too much. The perfect guy who she'd put through the wringer. His consideration, his willingness to sacrifice what *he* wanted for *her*, spoke volumes about his love. Just as she hoped her moving back to Credence *permanently* would be a signal to him about the depth of *her* love.

She shook her head. "Trust me, three weeks in LA was enough." She eased back a little. "I was back to ordering *egg white omelets*, Austin."

He chuckled. "That sounds awful."

She shuddered. "It was."

"What about your corner office?"

"Yeah, that was kinda neat. But then I got it and I realized I didn't want it more than I wanted *you*. More than I wanted an office looking out over that." She turned her head to gaze out the floor-to-ceiling window overlooking fields where horses and cows grazed in the distance. "If that's okay by you." She turned her attention back to him. "I understand if you want to take a step back and take things slower, given how I flaked out on you and—"

She didn't get a chance to finish the sentence. Austin swooped in, silencing her with his mouth, dropping a string of kisses against her lips that left Bea dizzy. "I love you, Bea*triss*," he whispered, his warm breath caressing the parted line of her mouth. "Nothing would make me happier than you living here with me." He pulled back a little and smiled. "I'm pretty sure my mother will throw you a parade."

Bea laughed. Prior to meeting Austin, she would have thought it weird to have family living on top of one another, but the Coopers made it work, and she couldn't wait to be part of their village.

"So you're going to work for Greet Cute from here?"

"Only on Cranky Bea creative."

Bea loved how that word—creative—no longer made her want to go and hide under the covers. It still felt new and shiny, but she *was* a *creative* and she was done pretending otherwise. "They've contracted me for a dozen new designs every month, but that's it. And in between doing that, I'm going to see what else my muse throws at me."

He shook his head, lifting his hand to caress her cheek. "I can't believe you're here. That you're staying." His eyes roamed over her face like he wanted to memorize every detail. "I missed you every damn day, Bea*triss*."

Bea smiled. "I missed you, too."

He pressed his forehead to hers again, the breath shuddering out of him in a big, deep sigh, and Bea held on to him tight, realizing how close they'd come to missing out on *this*.

They stayed like that for a long time until Austin eventually stirred. "Now"—he unglued his forehead from hers—"about those panties... I believe, to conduct a thorough investigation, I'll need to see the offending item."

Bea laughed as things inside her Thursday panties got very excited at the prospect of being *investigated*. "You don't need to get back to work?" She knew what a stickler Arlo was, and she'd probably kept Austin long enough. "It's okay." She ran her finger down the side of his face. "We've got the rest of our lives."

He smiled, grabbing the finger and kissing it. "It is *incumbent* upon me, the first officer on scene, to gather evidence. I wouldn't want to besmirch the good name of the Credence Police Department by shirking my responsibilities."

Bea sighed, spying the handcuffs hanging from his utility belt, and her heart beat a little faster. "I'd hate to be arrested for hindering an investigation, Officer."

Then she yanked down the zipper of her fly and kicked out

of her jeans, smiling as Austin muttered, *"Holy fuck,"* under his breath, his eyes zeroing in on her Thursday panties.

Recovering quickly, he looked at her and said, "Turn around and spread 'em, ma'am."

Ma'am. Gah! For that, she was going to do him twice.

EPILOGUE

The main street of Credence buzzed as elegantly dressed city folk rubbed shoulders with elegantly dressed town folk at the newly opened art gallery. The first ever exhibition of Phoebe Archer's paintings since her untimely death twenty-five years prior had drawn quite the crowd. From critics to journalists to collectors, they'd come from all over the country, to this tiny speck on the map in far Eastern Colorado.

And Beatrice was at the center of it all.

As well as making her Cranky Bea cards an outstanding success, she'd spent the last year scouring the internet and buying every single one of her mother's paintings she could get her hands on. Her father—he and Bea's grandmother were both here—had also helped and between the two of them, they'd managed to recover over fifty of her paintings.

It had started out as a curiosity and fast become an obsession that had led Bea down all kinds of rabbit holes and taken her to obscure galleries, junk stores, yard sales, and inside people's houses. And when it had got to the point that the space in their log cabin on the ranch had run out of room to store them all, she and Suzanne, who Bea had met that day out by the lake, had come up with leasing neighboring shops in town as an art gallery space.

But the exhibition had been Austin's idea.

"Happy?"

Bea smiled as the man in question sidled up behind her, sliding his arm around her shoulders and dropping a kiss just behind her ear. His cologne mixed with his body heat to form a heady cocktail, and she inhaled deeply, letting the breath out on a sigh. "I never knew it was possible to be this happy."

Which was a startling admission but true nonetheless.

She'd spent so much of her life trying to make her father and her grandmother and her colleagues happy, she'd thought external validation was the only way to achieve that state. It wasn't until Credence and Austin she realized that true happiness came from within, from the people and passions that lit a person up from the inside.

"It looks great on you," he murmured, his lips nuzzling at her temple now.

Bea smiled. Austin had been the best part of this last year. Being with him—living, laughing, loving—had been a revelation and the depth of her feelings for him had grown so big and so wide she honestly didn't know how she managed to contain them inside her body.

Knowing he felt the same way was both humbling and thrilling.

"My dear." Jasper Remington, a dapper elderly gent with gray hair and a curly, waxed moustache, approached from the left. "Are you sure I can't tempt you to sell me *Carrizo*?"

None of the paintings were for sale tonight, and Jasper knew it, but as a renowned private collector he wasn't known for taking no for an answer. Bea shook her head as she stared at it now, taking pride of place in the gallery, the connection with her mom flaring bright.

He had a great eye, but *Carrizo* would never be for sale. "Sorry, Jasper. That one's coming home with me."

Austin had hung it in their main living area in the cabin where Bea could look at it every day and remember her mom, young and passionate, utterly lost in the bloom of the wildflowers.

"You know where I am if you change your mind."

Bea smiled. "I do."

Austin's low chuckle tickled her temple as Jasper departed. "Is it wrong to be turned on now?"

"Is that ever wrong?" she replied with a laugh.

"Good answer."

Tucker, who had volunteered as waiter tonight, passed by with a drinks tray, and Bea swiped two glasses of champagne, handing one to Austin. "This place looks amazing, Bea," Tucker said. "Any thoughts about what else you're going to use the space for?"

"Suzanne's going to have an exhibition next."

"And then *you* are," Austin said, repeating one of his favorite talking points.

"Maybe." Bea had been painting for a while now, mostly landscapes, and she was gathering quite a collection thanks to the studio Austin had built her on the side of the cabin.

"I think Winona's trying to set up a bit of an artist enclave out by the lake," she continued, "so the gallery space might come in handy for any of her friends."

Tucker raised an eyebrow at Austin. "Let's not tell Arlo about that just yet."

Austin chuckled. "I'm happy for him to discover that in his own time."

Someone called to Tucker from across the room and he excused himself. "You should, you know," Austin said, his voice low. "You're an incredible artist."

Bea knew her art was good in that way she assumed all true artists knew. She just wasn't sure she was ready to share it yet. "And you're not biased at all of course."

He chuckled. "Not even remotely." He held his glass up in front of her. "A toast," he said. "To you."

"No." Bea shook her head and held her glass up to *Carrizo*. "To my mom."

"To Phoebe," Austin agreed. And they clinked.

ACKNOWLEDGMENTS

This book has been on a bit of a wild ride these past couple of years with world events conspiring to keep it off shelves for what felt like forever. So it is, indeed, a joy to be writing these acknowledgments knowing that it's finally going to happen. And a real joy to be bringing another Credence story to bookshelves.

As always, birthing a book is a team effort, and I am indebted to the many fine people at Entangled Publishing that make it all happen. To Liz Pelletier, brainstormer extraordinaire, and Lydia Sharp and Stacy Abrams for their editing insights. To Elizabeth Stokes and all in the art department for the *ah-mazing* cover. The book went through several different design concepts, and I seriously may have cried when I opened the email with *final cover* in the subject line to discover the feast of absolute gorgeousness. And to Curtis Svehlak for all his fabulous behind-the-scenes wizardry that makes everything flow smoothly and in a timely fashion. Thanks also to the team at Macmillan.

Personally, like many others on the planet, it's been a challenging couple of years for me, and I'd like to thank dear writing friends that helped me through with sprints or advice or just general hand-holding. Clare Connelly, Ally Blake, Michelle Douglas, Tawna Fenske, Regina Kyle, Stefanie

London, Jane Porter, Ainslie Paton. And extra big thanks to Joanne Grant who helped me immeasurably at the end of 2021.

Love and thanks always, of course, to my life champions. My husband Mark, my sister Ros, and my bestie Leah who are staunchly Team Amy, for which I am grateful every day.

And to my readers. To those who are new to Credence or have been along for the ride from the beginning. Thank you so much for your reviews and your messages and emails—they seriously make my day. Knowing how much you love my quirky little town and its even quirkier inhabitants means so very much to me. Big love to you all.

Fans of *People We Meet on Vacation* and *The Unhoneymooners* won't be able to resist this witty and heart-stealing road trip tale about taking the (incredibly) long way round...

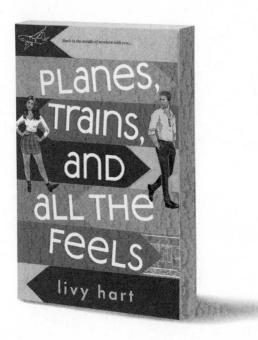

Turn the page to start reading for FREE...

CASSIDY

I jolt upright and whip my head left and right. Recognition of my surroundings dawns as my sleepy brain flickers to life. *Airport.* The lights are dim but not out, like a theater just before a show.

And here I was hoping the diversion was a dream.

My attention falls to a foreign bundle of gray fabric in my lap. A tired squeak leaves my mouth as I shove it off my legs. *The heck?*

With a pincer grip, I pluck it off the ground. It has a hood, but no drawstring. The cotton is threadbare and faded. A quick peek inside reveals the tag is missing.

This is the baby blanket of sweatshirts, worn to death.

I lift my chin and search the area.

Of the hundred or so people camping in this gate, there's only one I could pick out of a lineup. And the last thing Mr. *Is This Your First Time Being Right?* would do is offer me a sweatshirt. His dislike of me is so intense he chose to argue with me instead of conceding that I was right about the hotel situation, even after we'd achieved a mutual understanding and respect as our plane landed.

Or so I thought.

That's what I get for attempting to turn over a friendlier leaf: Luke sass. A glimpse at his ego. I bet if I told him the airport was on fire he'd have to google it to be abundantly sure rather than trust my assessment.

So what if he doesn't like me? I didn't like *him* first. I've got squatter's rights on this grudge.

And yet, I have a sweatshirt in my clammy hands.

I spot Luke and his tousled shock of hair across the walkway. It appears he's ransacked it with his hand a time too many. Even the WASPyish among us are susceptible to the harrowing realities of an all-nighter, I guess. He's putting the *lap* in *laptop* as he pecks away at the machine perched on his thighs. His glasses reflect the glow of the screen.

I could ask him. But if it isn't his and belongs to a random good Samaritan who saw I was uncovered—or a random person who intended to smother me in my sleep and failed—I'd be mortified.

Playing *The Sims* until the airline provides an update is safer.

My phone lights up at my touch. *Five twenty a.m.* The drained battery icon winks at me.

I scan for an open outlet. Too many people have fallen asleep body-blocking their charging phones. All plugs are taken except for the top half of one.

The bottom half has been claimed by Luke.

This ought to be fun.

I gather my stuff, cross the crowded space, and approach with my chin lifted and the sweatshirt tucked under my arm. "Can I use the top half of that outlet?"

He looks at me for approximately half a second before returning his gaze to the keyboard. "Sure."

I'm reveling in the ease of this interaction when he adds, "I mean, I don't own it."

"Could've just left it at yes," I mumble as I dig my charger out of the front pocket of my suitcase and plug myself in.

Muscles tight from the plane and sleeping upright, I extend

my legs. I've got enough room for a full straddle, but I don't push it far. Just a half. My hamstrings hum in objection, which means it's all the more important I do this to avoid injuries. Even a small one could put me out of work.

"What are you doing?"

I glance to the right as I stretch further. Luke's face is aghast.

I keep my voice low to match his. "I'm stretching my legs."

"*Here*?"

With the scandalized tone of his voice, you'd think I stripped naked and bent over. "Sure. Why not?"

He slides his glasses off his face and buffs them on his shirt. "I've never seen anyone do a *split* in the middle of an airport."

"This isn't a full split, nor am I in the middle of anything. We're on the side of a room where barely anyone is awake. It's not like I dropped down while in line for security." I lean against my elbows, and my muscles sing. "Does this bother you?"

"No."

"Then why do you sound bent out of shape?"

"I'm not." He returns to his computer, peck-peck-pecking.

"Great." I shift even further until my legs are almost a perfect 180, which I had no intention of doing until he questioned me. There's something about his tone—that there are right and wrong ways to do things, and his ways are right—that makes me want to poke him until he snaps. "It's part of my job to be flexible. I'm working, too. Just like you are with your type-type-typing."

The typing ceases. "Your job?"

"Choreographer. Dancer. Professional stretcher, as it were."

He swivels his head roughly ten degrees, runs his gaze up my body, and returns to working. He could weaponize that sharp jawline. "Fascinating."

Heat creeps up my neck. "Astounded by my talent?"

"Moved to tears."

"I'll get out of your way soon enough."

He lets out a strained sigh and scrubs his hand over his mouth. His hoarse voice suggests a lack of sleep. "I didn't say you had to move. Forgive me for asking a simple question."

"Speaking of simple questions." I cross my legs and hold up his sweatshirt. "Any idea where this came from?"

He freezes for a good four seconds. The volume at which his silence yells rails against my eardrums.

I purse my lips and lift it to my nose. The scent is vibrant and refreshing, evocative of California with a hint of citrus, like cold lemonade sipped on a beach. I'd know it anywhere thanks to a summer in high school working at JC Penney and huffing enough cologne to jump-start puberty: Ralph Lauren. "Smells good."

While he continues to ignore me, I lean sideways into his bubble and sniff the air around him.

His gaze remains firmly on his computer. "Did you just smell me, Cassidy?"

"Absolutely not." The delicious scent lingers in my nose as I breathe deeply. "Gosh, it's just the strangest thing. I woke up and it was *on* me. I guess I'll have to go ask every single person in this terminal individually so I can thank—"

"You were freezing." His brow furrows. "Your arms were going to fall off."

I grin, pleased that he admitted it. "So it *is* yours."

He shrugs a shoulder. "It's not a big deal."

I scoot a little closer. At this angle, I get a peek of a color-coded spreadsheet filled with numbers on his monitor. Gag me with a calculator. "That was very nice of you."

The words leave my mouth and heat trickles across my cheeks.

It *was* nice—unexpectedly so.

"Can I do something in return?" I scan the darkened room.

"I don't know, buy you a snack from the vending machine or something? You a Doritos guy? Wait—blue bag or red? This is a crucial distinction."

"Not necessary."

"Okay, no Doritos. Soda? Chocolate?"

He pushes his glasses a fraction of an inch up his nose. "You were in danger of frostbite, and I'm not even sure this town has a hospital. Consider it a public service."

"That's actually a perfect comparison. I put out a huge basket of Snickers and Cheez-Its for overworked delivery drivers every December. To thank them for their service. I wish you'd tell me what zero-nutrient crap you like so I could thank *you*."

He eyes me warily. "Not a big fan of snacks. Can we drop this, please?"

"Who isn't a fan of *snacks*?"

His laugh is incredulous. "Have you ever had a conversation that doesn't end in frustration?"

"Actually, my conversations usually reach a satisfying conclusion." My lips arrange themselves in a smile. "Except with you, apparently."

He presses his eyes shut. "And to think, I could've been sleeping this whole time and missed out on all this fun."

I swivel toward him and push up on my knees. He tenses and rears back, hitting his head on the wall.

"I'm not going to smother you with it, Luke." I reach for the suitcase standing upright near his feet, loop the sleeves through his handle, and tie it in a knot. "There. Tiny soldier has returned home."

I catch his eye, and my stomach twists. My neck heats as he studies me.

"You're something else," he says quietly.

I've been on the receiving end of that tilted-head, appraising look before. Like I've rattled off a complex riddle and forced him to solve it against his will.

It's fine being something else—until someone goes out of their way to point it out. It then becomes a judgment. A branding.

I drop back into my seat and angle my body away.

We co-exist in silence long enough that an inkling of color threatens the cloudy horizon. It is the La Croix flavor of sunrise, an almost imperceptible taste. In the interest of letting my battery fully charge, I forgo *The Sims* and dig a notebook out of my purse. I'm halfway done filling the page with pointless doodles when my and Luke's phones light up in unison on the ground between us.

Atlas Airlines JLN to LAX. Canceled. Stand by for updates.

"No." I topple back into my stretch of carpet and snatch the phone off the ground. "No, no, *no.* This can't be happening. How can they just *cancel*? Oh my god, how long are they going to leave us here?"

"That's the airlines for you." His voice has precisely one degree of heat. No urgency.

"This is a nightmare! I can't just wait around here forever."

"Exactly why I'm not counting on a plane." He nods toward a hallway. "The car rental place opens at nine if you're looking for an alternate way out. The desk is near baggage claim."

A few people have stirred in the area, all glaring daggers at their phones.

Our eyes lock.

In unison, we scramble to gather our stuff.

If this entire terminal is trying to escape, I need to be *first* in line.

. . .

We blaze into the quiet baggage claim area, collecting a few looks as we skid to a stop at the back of the rental line.

Luke beats me by a hair.

"I would've been here even faster if you didn't kick my suitcase over," he grumbles.

"You must have me confused me with someone else. I'd never disrespect Samsonite luggage that way."

"Must've been another pint-size redhead with an agenda."

There are eight people ahead of him, and we've still got an unholy amount of time before it opens. My breathing calms as we file in, with two people already queuing up behind me.

Luke's neck hovers just above my eye-line, his perfectly precise hairline hitting like visual ASMR. Smooth and weirdly satisfying. This one doesn't skip his monthly stint in the barber's chair. The strip of tan skin above his travel-rumpled collar brings dull friction to the tip of my finger, like I accidentally traced it.

His physical presence is overwhelming up close. Long legs that perfectly fill a pair of dress pants. A lean but strong back that tests the seams of his shirt. Broad shoulders, perfect for throwing a girl over. For swing dancing purposes, of course—

My phone stirs to life, sending a pulse through my hip. A peek at the caller sounds my internal alarm.

Isabelle, calling at six a.m. her time.

Admittedly my nervous system is hair-trigger sensitive this morning, but this doesn't bode well. "Hey. You okay?"

"Cursdy," she slurs. "You were supposed to call me back!"

I inhale a sharp breath. "Are you drunk?" At six in the freaking *morning*?

"Nope! I slept for two hours. That cancels the drunk."

"Yeah, not how it works. What's going on?"

"This wedding is a *disaster*. I should cancel the whole stupid thing."

My stomach plummets. "Slow down, Bells. Did something happen? Did you and Mikael have a fight?"

"The caterer can't get salmon because of some kind of boat problem, the florist's cooler broke and all my flowers died—*died*!—and I have to go find more and make my own bouquets I guess? Wait, what about the table flowers?" She groans straight into my eardrum. "Mikael's been mostly MIA working on a big, dumb lawsuit. It's like he doesn't even care we're getting married."

"You know that's not true. He's obsessed with you."

"We haven't had sex in three days. *Three.* And two of those were weekend days!" She sucks in a fast gulp of air, a pseudo-hiccup. "Guess he's not attracted to me anymore. I stayed up all night waiting for him to get home from work, and he just passed right out! I had wine and everything. *Gah*, fucking florist, stupid caterer—"

"—Isabelle—"

"—I'm in way over my head with this stuff. And my PTO is *not* time off because my boss is a fuckwad. Mom is useless because she's being so *Mom*, worrying about random stuff I don't care about." She sighs, regaining composure before adding, "I need you."

I saw my lips together. I *knew* I should've come home a week sooner. I could've been attacking the smaller to-do list items, leaving this week free for the more important stuff. But Isabelle is always so meticulous and competent I hardly thought we'd find ourselves in meltdown territory. I never expected we'd be on doubting-our-fiancé's-attraction terrain.

She's losing it. My mother, as a result, is going to lose it. It'll be fire and fury when I get home. The makings of a panic attack simmer at the base of my brain, threatening to alert the rest of my body.

This is my fault. Not much I can do about her tragic three-day sex drought, but the rest of those problems I *must* fix. Somehow.

"Bells, you still got your drink? I want you to put it down."

"But—"

"Down, girl."

I wait until I hear the faint *thud* of a glass. I don't often get to be the boss—little sister problems—but Isabelle needs a firm hand.

"You're going to be okay. We're going to get through this. The wedding is not a disaster. I'll call the caterer and florist today. You need to go back to sleep."

A beat of silence passes. "One more thing. Dad's not coming. Called him last night, which—you know I don't *ever* call him. And...no-sir-ee. No answer. Just a text back. 'Can't make it, Isabelle. It'll be all the better for it.' What does that even mean?"

My heart pangs. "You called him, though. That's the important thing. I'm happy you tried."

"What's it matter if he's not even bothering to come?"

"If you want a relationship with him moving forward, it matters. He's just being stubborn because he's terrified of Mom's wrath, and he doesn't want to upstage you on your big day."

"He's punishing me for Mom being Mom."

I let my head fall back. It's not the time to have this discussion yet again about our biological father. That's a conversation best left for when she's stone-cold sober and we can give it the unpacking it deserves. "I'll call Dad."

"I mean, I don't want you to *drag* him to the wedding."

"It's clearly important to you. You only get one wedding, and he should be there. Let me handle this, okay? Sleep. We'll talk soon."

"What time is your new plane coming?"

Like the time I borrowed and promptly lost the Ariat boots she bought for Coachella, I have to pick the perfect words to soften the blow. "About that. I'm going to be a bit longer getting there. Having a slight transportation issue. It's looking like tomorrow at the latest. I'm going to get a car and drive straight through."

"*What?*"

"I know it's not ideal—"

"*Not ideal?* Sixty percent humidity is not ideal. You not being here right now is a crisis! I swear, if *one more thing* goes wrong, I'm calling off—"

"Whoa." I jolt at the mere mention of calling anything off, even if it is just tipsy threats. "Don't even say those words, Bells. Everything is always more okay after a good sleep, I promise. I'll make calls to vendors as I drive. I'll even call your boss if he doesn't back off the bride."

"Jack Astaire would drop all the way died"—hiccup—"*dead* if someone talked to him about anything other than profits and numbers."

"Then I'll speak to Jack *Ass*-taire in binary code. Jack Ass Tear. Wow, what an unfortunate name."

"Promise me you'll be here soon, please? I can't do this without you, Cass."

Determination snakes its way through me until I'm nodding. It's more important than ever that I show up for her. Even if it's just for this week, to check off all one hundred to-dos. To talk her off ledges. To keep my stepfather's side of the family distracted so they don't accidentally perceive Mom's blood relatives and how poor they are, the shame of Mom's existence.

Isabelle, pillar of human perfection, needs *me*. Trusts me to be there for her.

"I'll be there," I say firmly. "I promise."

And when I get there, I'll be the best fucking maid of honor that has ever maided or honored. I may have chosen the wrong flight, but I will do what it takes to get this job done. I want to show Isabelle, Mom, *everyone* that I can be good at this.

Because if I'm not good at the role I've trained for my whole life—standing by while Isabelle shines, helping her look good, and building her up—then maybe I deserve Mom's constant criticism.

We say our goodbyes, and I perch on my suitcase, studying Google Maps for what feels like an eternity, until the desk opens.

When the clerk materializes, she scans the now *long* line of waiting patrons and anxiously fluffs her short salt-and-pepper hair. She receives a lot of intense stare-downs from people awaiting their turn as she works with the first two customers, the kind of impatient scrutiny that would turn me into a blubbering mess. After observing her pace as she hands out the seven rentals in front of Luke, I almost want to climb over the counter and help the poor thing.

She raises her voice to a solid 30 percent intensity when it's Luke's turn. "Next."

Luke lopes to the counter and draws his wallet like a sword. I'm close enough to hear his measured tone. "I'd like a vehicle, please. Something bigger, if you've got it."

She clacks chipped mauve nails against a keyboard.

"Oof." *Clack clack clack.* "This is, um…"

Luke, already gripping the speckled countertop, slides his hands farther apart, bracing himself. "Really, anything will work. Size isn't important."

Her thin, pursed lips and wide eyes suggest she's on the verge of a meltdown. She glances past Luke at the line, catches my eye, and quickly drops her gaze to the computer. "We've only got one vehicle left."

To read more, visit EntangledPublishing.com

Breaking All the Rules is a fearless and humorous romance about a woman who's determined to take her life back and have the most fun possible while doing it. However, the story includes elements that might not be suitable for some readers. Death of a parent in a character's backstory; mental illness themes; alcohol consumption; misogyny; and profanity appear in the novel. Sexual intimacy is also shown on the page. Readers who may be sensitive to these elements, please take note.

AMARA
an imprint of Entangled Publishing LLC